IKON

Born in Edinburgh, Graham Masterton trained as a newspaper reporter and later edited *Mayfair* and *Penthouse* magazines. In 1974 he took up writing full time, and his first occult novel, *The Manitou,* was made into a film starring Tony Curtis and Susan Strasberg. His novels are marked by their intensive research and their devotion to political and historical detail. For *Ikon,* he travelled to Washington, Los Angeles and the Arizona desert, and met many people concerned with the politics of the 1960s.

Graham Masterton is married to his literary agent, Wiescka Masterton, and they live in Epsom, England, with their three sons. His interests include painting, music, politics, and law.

D0582988

IKON

Graham Masterton

A STAR BOOK
published by
the Paperback Division of
W. H. ALLEN & Co. PLC

A Star Book
Published in 1984
by the Paperback Division of
W. H. Allen & Co. PLC
44 Hill Strret, London W1X 8LB

First published in Great Britain by
W.H. Allen & Co., 1983

Printed and bound in Great Britain by
Anchor Brendon Ltd, Tiptree, Essex

ISBN 0 352 315326

'RINC (usually pronounced "rink") is the acronym coined by the Joint Chiefs of Staff for the current talks between the United States and the Union of Soviet Socialist Republics aimed at an eventual mutual Reduction in Nuclear Capability.'

— Joint Services Review, No. XVII, 1981.

'We instructed our officers to dismantle (the weapons) and return them to the Soviet Union.'

— Nikita Khruschev, October, 1962.

'Others were as physically beautiful as she was, but there was obviously something more in her – a combination of wistfulness, radiance, yearning – that set her apart.'

— Lee Strasberg, 1962.

One

He had been searching for her for so long, twenty empty and irritating years, that when at last he caught sight of her sitting in the darkness of the cocktail lounge of the Arizona Biltmore Hotel, her freckled hands cupped around a large mimosa, he regurgitated some of his lunch into his mouth, and had to walk quickly across to the Men's Room to spit it out and stand there staring at himself in the mirror over the washbasin in both triumph and jangling alarm.

Jesus, I've found her. After all these years, I've actually found her. Jesus. But, looking down at his hands on the rim of the washbasin, hands that were twenty years older than the day he had first started trying to find her, he suddenly thought to himself: I hope it isn't her. I hope I'm hallucinating. If it's her, I'm going to have to kill her. They want me, quite literally, to bring back her head.

And apart from that, what am I going to do now, for the rest of my life? Who's going to employ a man who has done nothing for twenty years but cross and re-cross America; from rainy days in Philadelphia to snow-bound Januaries in Oregon; looking for one woman?

He came out of the Men's Room and the door squeaked loudly behind him. She was still sitting there, alone, in one of the bulky 1920s sofas, under the tinkling art-deco chandeliers. The Arizona Biltmore had been designed in the mid-1920s by Frank Lloyd Wright, outrageously modern, a Jazz-Age resort for America's rich and notorious, with pre-cast concrete bungalows in floral gardens, dining-rooms with deco fountains and combed-plaster

7

ceilings, hand-made carpets in geometric motifs. And here she was, amidst all this decadent splendour – fat, as he had imagined she must be, at least 185 pounds, in a pleated lilac tent-dress, with skin as pale as milk. Her hair was gingery-brown, with streaks of grey, and drawn back tightly away from her face and fastened with combs. It would have been a better disguise if she had stayed platinum-blonde, he thought, or dyed her hair henna-red. But he had always believed that she would be brunette when he found her, and so she was.

There were no obvious signs of plastic surgery. To anyone except a man who had spent twenty years of his life studying photographs and sketches and clay simulations of her face and head from every possible angle, in every kind of light, the fat would have made surgery unnecessary. Her eyes were puffed into Mongoloid slits, and she had developed a deep double chin. She had probably believed that as soon as she reverted to her plain unglamorous self, the self she had been born with, she would be safe. Unknown, unwanted – an ugly-duckling orphan whom nobody wanted to adopt. Her lack of deviousness had betrayed her all her life. Now it had betrayed her again.

He sat down opposite her, quite close, crossing one Evvaprest leg over the other; and lit a cigarette; and watched her. If she was conscious of being watched, she didn't show it. She sipped her mimosa, and fiddled with the single gold band on her wedding-finger, and occasionally glanced towards the sliding doors which led out to the lawns and the bungalows and the brilliant afternoon sunshine; and once she smiled at a three-year-old blond-haired English boy who ran past her calling for his mummy. The sad, indulgent smile that any 56-year-old woman would have given, childless after three marriages, and precluded from marrying again because she was a fugitive from vengeances far more terrible than justice.

The cocktail waitress had just come on duty. She came over and asked him what he wanted. He thought about it, and then said, 'A Bud, and some nuts,' mainly because it seemed appropriate to order beer on an occasion like this, kind of dated, a baseball-park drink. Maybe it was a nod to Joe DiMaggio. He wondered how she had coped with that; knowing that Joe DiMaggio had so regularly laid roses on that grave in Westwood. He rubbed his eyes, and smoked, and the past twenty years came silently crowding into the cocktail lounge like a coach party of unwelcome ghosts.

His name was Henry Friend, and he had started to look for her two weeks and two days after his 38th birthday. He was now 58, two years older than she was, a tall, crumpled, offhand man with eyes that were screwed up in what looked like a permanent headache. He had a bulbous nose, loose wrists, and a funny-dry way of talking that always reminded the people he met of Walter Matthau. His friends had no opinion on the matter because he had no friends. He had an older brother in Bend, Oregon, and that was his only family. He spent his life in hotels, motels, boarding-houses, trailer-parks, and hostels – and (occasionally) in the arms of widows, or whores, or lonely wives, behind the dim net curtains of mid-Western bedrooms. He smoked Winston, read *Playboy* and *Guns & Ammo*, and drove, as an affectation, a 1969 Ford Thunderbird Landau. He washed his shorts in hotel washbasins, with those little sachets of powder they give you, and he talked to himself in hotel mirrors.

He had been a mechanic once, which is the polite word for killer. He had probably been the best of his entire generation. But he often wondered after twenty years if he still had it in him. Jack Ruby had once told him, 'You can think you're the greatest. But your talent can disappear down the goddamned toilet while you're still washing your goddamned hands.'

Jack Ruby. Walter still smiled to himself when he thought what a transparent *non-de-guerre* that had been. Jack Ruby, Ruby Red, Red Jack. After all these years, nobody had twigged. It made you wonder what the FBI were doing for a living, apart from filing their nails and

9

going to Senate cocktail parties and jousting each other for offices with more than one widow. Jack fucking Ruby.

She had finished her mimosa too quickly, like a woman who needed to drink. In a moment or two, she would be trying to catch the cocktail waitress's attention for another one. Henry didn't know it, but she always came in here at five o'clock in the afternoon and drank three of them, sometimes four, always alone. Alone, after everything that had happened; after all the crowds. But she was fat now, a middle-aged Sun-Belt matron, living a life of loneliness, and beauty parlours, and failed diets, and *The Price Is Right*.

He said to her, quite loudly, 'Pardon me, I couldn't help noticing. You remind me of someone.'

She looked towards him and blinked. Her mind had been exclusively fixed on beckoning the cocktail waitress. She said, 'What? Are you talking to me?'

'I'm sorry,' he smiled. 'I didn't mean to surprise you. But you remind me of someone. I can't believe the resemblance.'

She stared back at him with those slitty little eyes. The cocktail waitress came up to her, and said, 'How're you doing, Mrs Schneider? Can I bring you another mimosa?'

Henry offered, 'Will you have one on me?'

Mrs Schneider said nothing, but looked from Henry to the cocktail waitress and back again, as if she were suspicious that something was going on between them which she couldn't quite understand. Some secret joke.

Henry said, 'Go ahead. Another mimosa. And I'll have another Bud.'

When the waitress had gone back to the bar, Henry picked up his beer and came over to sit right beside Mrs Schneider, not uncomfortably close, but close enough. He offered her a Winston, but she shook her head. 'I gave up. My doctor insisted.'

'You look well enough to me. Can I say blooming?'

She placed a hand on her chest. 'I have to watch my heart, that's all. It's nothing serious. But it's better not to smoke.'

'Do you mind if I do?'

'I'd rather you didn't.'

He tucked the cigarette back in the pack. 'In that case, okay, I won't.'

There was a difficult pause. Mrs Schneider glanced towards the sliding door. Outside, in the heat, baize tables and bright-yellow parasols were being set up for the weekend's Easter Fair. A hotel handyman walked past with three large wooden rabbits under his arm, green and white and red.

'Are you staying through Easter?' she asked Henry.

'I don't know. It depends. I'd like to.'

'You're here on business, right?'

He nodded. 'That's right, Motorola.'

'I guessed as much,' she smiled. 'If it's not Mafia, it's Motorola. The two big Ms in Phoenix. Well, I hope you're having a successful trip.'

'I am now,' said Henry.

Another pause. She looked across at him. 'You said I reminded you of someone. Who was that?'

'I don't know. It was a long time ago now. Nineteen or twenty years, at least. None of us are getting any younger.'

'But who? You really can't remember?'

'A girlfriend, maybe,' said Henry. 'I never married. I guess I wasn't cut out to be a husband. So, I've had girlfriends. All pretty, mind you.'

'I'm a widow, myself,' said Mrs Schneider. The cocktail waitress brought them their drinks, and set them down.

'I'm paying,' Henry reminded her, and laid a ten dollar bill on her tray. 'Keep the change.'

Mrs Schneider took a large mouthful of champagne and orange-juice. She closed her eyes as it fizzed down her throat. Then she said, 'My husband used to fly from Luke Air Force Base, you know out near Litchfield Park? A major, flying F-16s. A handsome man; and a good one, too. Do you know what they paid him? One thousand seven hundred dollars a month. A major, with twelve years' service. And one day he flew straight into the side

11

of the White Tank Mountains, and so that was the end of that. I was left with a house, an Air Force pension, and a small collection of dirty magazines which I found in his sock drawer.'

Henry finished his first beer and picked up his second. He gave Mrs Schneider an understanding but rather refractive nod, as if he were listening to the story of her life for the third or even the fourth time. As a matter of fact, all this business about an Air Force major flying straight into the side of the White Tank Mountains was quite new to him, but then whatever biographical details she gave him, they were all bound to be fabricated, carefully rehearsed during twenty years of hiding. To Henry, they were irrelevant, the sound of a moth beating against a blind, and that was why he scarcely listened to what she was saying. She would never deflect him from the serious task he had in hand.

In truth, he quite liked the bit about the dirty magazines in the sock drawer. That gave 'Major Schneider' some imaginary depth, some touch of reality. Whoever had invented *that* little detail for her had been a genuine professional.

She said, 'I never drink anything else, only mimosas. Sometimes just orange juice. If I drink too much, I can't take my sleeping-pills, and if I can't take my sleeping-pills, I start to panic. Do you know what it's like when you can't get to sleep? When your mind races over and over until it feels like it's going to burn itself out? That's what it's like for me, every night – or would be, if I didn't take my sleeping-pills. Over and over, like a wheel.'

Henry smoked, and watched her. 'You've lived here long, in Phoenix?'

'Ten years. They were going to post us to Wheeler, in Hawaii, that was before Martin had his accident. I was looking forward to that. I don't know if Martin was. Before that, we were at Myrtle Beach, that's in South Carolina. I didn't like it there too much, at Myrtle Beach. The wives were all too upwardly mobile. Rank was everything. A major's wife was never expected to speak to a colonel's wife unless she was spoken to; and nobody spoke to warrant officers' wives at all.'

'But Luke is friendlier?'

She patted one plump white hand agitatedly on top of the other. 'It *was*. I guess it still is. I don't see too much of my Air Force friends any more. You know how it is. Now that Martin's gone, there really doesn't seem to be too much point in it. What do I care if Colonel Bickerstaff thinks that Captain Willis is a cretin; or if Major Hodges is screwing Mrs Bickerstaff every Wednesday at the Mesa Motel on Indian School Road?'

Henry made a face. 'Sure, what do you care?'

There was a silence between them; but she was not at ease. She seemed so anxious and agitated that he almost expected her to change her mind and ask him for a cigarette.

'Do you have the time?' she suddenly wanted to know.

'Ten after.'

'Well, still early,' she said, although she didn't say still early in relation to what. To dinner-time? To bedtime? To dusk? To the end of the world? 'You shouldn't let me keep you,' she said. 'You must be a very busy man.'

'You're not keeping me,' he said placidly. 'I don't have any more appointments until tomorrow.'

'Oh? Well, there isn't too much to do here in Phoenix. We're still Westerners, you know. Eat early, go to bed early. Healthy, wealthy, and wise as all hell.'

'That sounds like a good idea. Early to bed, I mean.'

She frowned at him. She sipped at her mimosa again, quick sips like somebody who is thinking more than drinking. Henry's calmness obviously made her unsettled; yet he hadn't said anything or done anything that could give her an excuse to tell him to go. She said, after a while, 'What the hell are you *doing* here?'

It was then that he was completely convinced that he had found the right woman. Nobody else would have said that; no genuine Western widow would have challenged him with such arrogance, and yet expected him not to be offended. She turned to look at him, and it was clear from the expression on her face that she didn't dislike him, not particularly, and that she hadn't intended to upset him. She was simply speaking the half-forgotten lines from some half-forgotten movie.

He said, 'I'm working. I'm a salesman. I sell semiconductors.'

'I don't mean that,' she said impatiently. 'I don't mean that at *all*. What I mean is, what are you doing *here*, talking to me?'

'I like you,' said Henry, in a flat voice. Flat, but still strangely provocative.

'You *like* me?'

'I like the look of you. Do you think we could go someplace else?'

She peered at him closely. 'What do you mean by someplace else?'

'It's kind of formal here. Don't you think so?'

Abruptly, she laughed out loud. 'You're making a *pass* at me. Isn't that it?'

Henry pretended to be embarrassed. He lowered his eyes, and gave an offhand, goofy, High-School kind of shrug.

'Well, you *are!*' she smiled. Then she laughed again. 'I don't believe it. You're actually making a pass!'

'I didn't mean to be fresh,' said Henry. 'It was just that you remind me strongly of – I don't know. I can't think who it is. But you look like a movie star. You have that charisma, you know? You have that kind of magnetism.'

Mrs Schneider patted her hair. 'They always said that I did. No matter what.'

'Who did?' asked Henry.

'Everybody. Martin. My friends. Just about everybody.'

Henry nodded. 'Sure,' he said.

After ten minutes or so, they left the Biltmore and walked out into the sunshine. The temperature at Sky Harbor was 97 degrees, according to the radio. There was a smell of heat and dust and blue paloverde. Henry unfolded his orange-lensed Ray-Bans and carefully put

14

them on to his bulbous nose; Mrs Schneider kept her face shielded from the sun with her wide-brimmed white hat.

'Why don't we take my car?' Henry suggested. It was a dark blue Oldsmobile from Avis, parked under the shade of the trees on the far side of the parking lot. Anybody who saw the two of them climbing into it, smiling and nodding to each other, and backing slowly out of the parking lot, sedate and careful, would have assumed them to be a newly retired couple, members of the Biltmore's golf-club perhaps, going home for a snooze after nine holes in the hot morning sun and a Mexican lunch at the Adobe clubhouse. They did good empanadas at the clubhouse, and good ribs, too.

She said, 'Make a right at 24th Street, and then another right at Lincoln.' Henry smiled, and drove with exaggerated smoothness and courtesy. The very last thing he wanted now was to be noticed; or, worse still, to be involved in a traffic accident. Tomorrow afternoon he would deliver the car in person to the Avis desk at Los Angeles International Airport, and his alibi would be simply that it would have been impossible for him to drive all the way from Arizona to Los Angeles if he had been here, in Phoenix, with Mrs Schneider.

Mrs Schneider said, 'You live in Los Angeles?'

'That's right. A little bachelor bungalow on Sixth Street.'

'I used to live in Brentwood.'

'Really? That used to be movie star country, twenty or thirty years ago, didn't it, Brentwood? Was your husband posted there?'

Mrs Schneider didn't answer. She looked out of the car window at the dusty roadsides, at the dry and distant view of Camelback Mountain. Henry touched her hand, and said, 'You mustn't take too much mind of me. I'm an old Hollywood fan from way back. Greta Garbo, Bette Davis, Marilyn Monroe, Jayne Mansfield. I loved them all. Loved them.'

They had reached the crest of 24th Street, where it met up with Lincoln Drive. Henry said, 'You still haven't told me your name. If we're going to be friends – '

She smiled, although not at him, 'Margot', she said. 'Margot Schneider. Née Petty.'

'Ah, *Margot*,' said Henry. He waited for a Trailways bus to toil its way past him; then made a right on Lincoln towards Paradise Valley. The road curved upwards, glaring and hot and dusty. Far away to their right, the tall buildings of downtown Phoenix wavered in the late-afternoon heat, the Convention Center, the Compensation Fund Building, KOOL Radio. Henry felt as parched as a Gila lizard in a vivarium, trapped under the sun. He took out a cigarette, and pushed in the electric cigar-lighter on the Oldsmobile's dash, but when Margot Schneider gave him a reproachful sideways look, he let the lighter pop out, untouched, and patiently put the cigarette away.

She lived in a one-storey ranch-style house on Oasis Drive, a select suburb in the eastern wrinkles of the Phoenix Mountains. Below the veranda, sprinklers sparkled on a vividly-green rhomboid of lawn. Wind-chimes hung along the eaves, tinkling in plaintive celebration of the first breath of wind that Oasis Drive had felt all day. Margot Schneider led Henry up to the front door, fluted glass backed by gilt- and wrought-iron roses. The street number was 62, which Henry thought was morbidly appropriate.

'Nice place,' he remarked, as she opened the door. 'How are your neighbours?'

'Quiet. The Millers next door are really sweet. He runs a bathroom boutique in Scottsdale, Tub Time. Across the road, the Kargs, they're okay. He works for Mountain Bell.'

'What do their wives do?'

'Oh,' she shrugged. 'They raise the kids, and watch *As The World Turns*.'

'I'm a *Guiding Light* fan myself,' smiled Henry.

She led him into the house. There was a large white-painted living-room, with an angled ceiling, and an oak fireplace. On the walls were luridly-coloured Red Indian prints by Barrie Tinkler. The rug was off-white, shaggy, and needed a clean. The few pieces of furniture were

16

reproduction antiques, a mock-Louis XIV console, a pair of mock-Chippendale chairs. But it was the little spindly-legged table in the smallest corner of the room which interested Henry the most. There was a cluster of black-and-white photographs there, framed in silver. Mrs Schneider at the age of twelve. Major and Mrs Schneider on their third anniversary. The family dog, Natasha. Major and Mrs Schneider at a barbecue at Myrtle Beach. Henry picked up a photograph of Major Schneider standing confident and clean-profiled beside the nose-needle of an F–16, and marvelled at the care and attention which had gone into creating Mrs Schneider's new life.

'Your husband was a good-looking man. When did you say you met him?'

'I didn't. But, December, 1950.'

'Ah, December, 1950. That was when they were shooting *As Young As You Feel.*'

She was unwrapping her purple silk scarf. She stopped suddenly, and said, 'What?'

'I told you,' Henry grinned. 'I was always a movie fan. Movies, and soap operas. Did you ever see *River Of No Return*?'

She squinted at him, her eyes deep in her fat-pillowed cheeks. 'No,' she said. 'I can't say that I ever did. Was it on *Midnight Movie*?'

'Maybe. Yes, maybe it was.'

There was another pause. In the far distance, they could hear the warbling of a siren. Then Margot Schneider said, 'Would you care for a drink? I don't have any beer.'

'Anything will do. Whiskey, wine, you name it.'

'I have some Stag's Leap riesling, from Napa Valley.'

'Okay. Stag's Leap riesling would be fine.'

They sat on the terrace overlooking the Phoenix Mountains and drank wine which, for Henry, was too cold and too sweet. It was very late afternoon now, and as the sun sank over Yuma County, to the west, the mountains were filled with crumpled shadows. Their faces, like Margot Schneider's face, were revealed by the light to be suddenly old.

Margot said, 'I never liked the movies much myself.'

'You didn't like the glamour?'

She made a *moue*. 'They were never glamorous. Not really. They *looked* that way, but a human being is only a human being, after all. You don't think when you see one of those movie stars on the screen that they ever get *sick*, or have *headaches*, or painful periods, or get frightened to death because they don't believe they're going to be able to act a part well enough. You don't think that, do you? But, it must be true.'

Henry watched her closely. 'Sure,' he said, after a while. 'I guess it must be.'

'It's like my husband,' Margot went on. 'He never understood that anyone else could be weaker than him; that anyone else could find it impossible to cope. He *said* he understood, oh sure, but deep down he couldn't, because *he* was equipped to cope with the world and I wasn't. But, well, I *have* to cope now. I have to. Though it's lonely, for most of the time.' She brushed her dress straight, and then looked up at Henry and gave him an embarrassed, apologetic smile. 'You don't want to hear about me, though. You didn't come all the way out here to be burdened with somebody else's troubles.'

'On the contrary,' said Henry. 'I think you're one of the most interesting women I've ever met. I've been looking for a woman like you for a very, very long time.'

'Would you care for something to eat?' she asked him, abruptly. 'I have pepperoni pizzas in the freezer.'

'I don't think I'm hungry,' Henry told her. 'All these business lunches, they build up on you. Clog your system after a while. I'll stick with the wine.'

'Well, then, would you mind if I changed into something more comfortable?'

'Go ahead. I'll help myself to another drink, if that's okay.'

She went inside through the patio door, turning for a moment to give him a look that she must have thought was coquettish. Henry sat by himself, carefully sipping his wine, and watched a distant Air Force jet sparkle like a needle in the dark lilac-coloured sky. Then he reached into his pocket and brought out a black vinyl wallet, which he laid on the table; and a pair of surgeon's disposable plastic gloves. He whistled between his teeth, *Some Day I'll Find You*.

From inside the house, he heard the sudden blurt of the television, turned to KPHO ' – *a dust storm alert between Gila Bend and Yuma on Highway 8 . . . if you observe dense dust blowing or approaching the highway, do not enter the area . . . pull off the pavement as far as possible and stop, extinguishing your lights . . .*'

He unfastened the flap of the black vinyl wallet, and drew out a portable saw, two feet of shark-toothed blue-steel wire, with black wooden handles at each end. It was like a garrotte, with a serrated edge. He flexed it, and it made a slight metallic musical twang. He had bought it in a hardware store in Rumney Depot, Vermont; one of those old-fashioned stores with a black pot-bellied stove and Red Man Tobacco and glass jars crowded with candy sticks. The proprietor had assured him that it would cut through a six-inch hickory branch like a wire through cheese.

He finished his glass of wine, and made a face of absent-minded distaste. Then he carefully stretched his fingers into his plastic gloves, and tugged them until they were tight. He could feel his pulse beating at that regular, almost-forgotten pace, the pace it always used to beat when he was preparing himself for a kill. It had been twenty years, but it still felt the same. A sense of calm, controlled elation. A tremendous sense of power. In the old days they had called him Gentleman Henry, because of his self-control, few of them ever understanding what a pitiless nature it actually took to kill a human being to order. He had specialized in revenge killings – jobs in which the client required the victim to suffer in agonizing and appropriate ways. After his work had been completed, he would matter-of-factly report back on what he had done, how the victim had mutely appealed to him for mercy, in spite of the fact that he had left most of his intestines in the next room. How the victim had screamed and sobbed. And the client's eyes would never rise to meet his. The money would be passed across the desk without a single look being exchanged. Henry had concluded that hardly anyone has a stomach for killing, not even by proxy, and he had put up his prices, twenty years ago, to $5,000 a job. The next week he had killed a man in Pittsburgh with a Bosch electric drill, boring five holes into his skull before he finally died. He had never heard anybody scream so much, not before, nor since. But he never had nightmares about it.

He wiped his wine-glass clean with his soft white linen handkerchief. He also polished the arms of the chair, and every other surface he might have touched. There was no point in washing his glass up completely, no point in trying to make it look as if Margot had died accidentally, or as if she had committed suicide. Nobody could do by accident what Henry was about to do to Margot; and nobody could ever do it to themselves.

He got up, and crossed to the patio doors, still flexing the saw, and stood listening for a moment. Then he stepped inside.

She had taken a quick shower, and now she was sitting in her bedroom brushing her hair and warbling happily to herself. Henry didn't find it more difficult to kill happy people than he did to kill angry or frightened or miserable people. In fact, it was more satisfying if they died happy. He had an old-fashioned sense of what was right.

He walked into the bedroom without knocking. The off-white carpet was soft and quiet, and so she didn't hear him. The television was showing a news report of angry parents who were picketing a newly-destreamed public school in Flagstaff. There was a queen-size bed with a white quilted satin bedspread, and white drapes; a white bedside telephone; a bottle of Nembutal. The door to the bathroom was still ajar, and inside, Henry could see Margot's clothes strewn on the floor, her purple tent-dress, her slip, and one discarded sandal. Margot herself was sitting in front of her white rococo dressing-table, wearing a white satin bathrobe with a large silver satin star sewn on to the back of it. She was pouting at herself as she lined her lips with Vivid Pink.

He thought: that's a hangover from a long, long time ago. A pink like that, only a blonde would wear.

He came right up behind her, only a few inches away, and it was only then that she focused on his reflection in the mirror, and realized that he was there.

'Well,' she said, without turning around. She replaced the cap on her lip-liner, and reached for her blusher. 'If I'd known you were the kind of guy who likes sneaking into a girl's bedroom . . .'

'What would you have done?' he asked her. His pulse was still beating with that even, purposeful rhythm, but his voice sounded light and amused. On the television, an angry parent was saying, 'I won't have my child educated side by side with hoodlums and trouble-makers and ignorant Indians, that's all. My child has a right to lead the life that *I* had.'

'I don't know,' she said. 'Maybe I wouldn't have asked you home.'

'I knew you were going to ask me home the moment I set eyes on you,' he said.

'Oh, yes?' Her voice was a little sharper.

'No slight intended,' said Henry. 'I didn't think you looked cheap, or easy, or even particularly lonely. But I could see what qualities you possessed, straight away. Star qualities, you know? You're a star, in your own way.'

'I wish I was.'

'Oh, believe me,' said Henry. He raised the flexible saw behind her back, his hands firmly grasping the two wooden handles, stretching the blade out until it was taut.

Margot Schneider touched up her cheeks with blusher, then pressed her lips tight together and stared at herself closely in the mirror, as if she wasn't at all pleased with the way her face looked.

'I should lose some weight, you know? But it's so difficult when you don't have anybody to lose weight *for*.'

'Why don't you lose it for me? I'm as good as anyone.'

'I don't suppose I shall ever *see* you again, shall I, after today? That's the way they all are. Horny, tired, sick of business. All they need is one evening of comfort. Then they go back to their wives.'

While she rummaged in her dressing-table drawer, Henry raised the saw higher, until it was only a few inches above her head. 'I'm so *untidy*,' she said. 'They used to tell me that when I was a little girl, you know? I can never find *anything*.'

Henry said, 'Look up. Look at yourself in the mirror. Now, what can you say about a woman who looks like that, at fifty-six?'

Margot Schneider kept on rummaging for a moment, and then froze. Henry could see the muscles in her back tighten up. It seemed like a whole minute before she spoke, and when she did, she sounded like someone else altogether, someone frightened and small.

'You know who I am, don't you?' she whispered.

'What do you mean? You're Margot Schneider, that's what you told me.'

'You said fifty-six. How do you know I'm fifty-six?'

'You told me.'

'I never told you any such thing. I always tell people I'm fifty-one.'

'Well, I don't know,' said Henry. He was trying hard to make his voice sound normal, praying even harder that she wouldn't turn around and see him standing right behind her with that thin whippy steel saw held upraised in both tense fists.

She said, in a haunted gush, 'Haven't I given *enough*? I never had anything to start with. Haven't I given *enough*? For the love of God, all of you, you've taken everything!'

'Listen, Margot – ' he told her.

'Don't lie to me,' she whispered. 'You've been taunting me all afternoon with it, haven't you? Hollywood, the movies, the *River Of No Return*? and I was dumb enough not to understand what you were doing to me.'

He said, in a tone that was almost shocking because it

sounded so sincere, 'Margot, believe me, I don't think you're anyone but Margot Schneider. Why should I?'

Seconds went past. One of the parents on the television snapped, 'If they want guinea-pigs then let them use guinea-pigs. They're not using *my* kids.'

Then, almost as if she knew what was going to happen, and had decided to accept it with the dignity of Joan of Arc, or Lady Jane Grey, Margot raised her head and stared at herself full-face in the mirror. In that instant, and in that last instant only, she looked just the way she had always looked in all her photographs, wide-eyed, surprised, frightened by everything she knew but even more frightened by everything she didn't.

In that same instant, Henry Friend snapped the saw down past her face and pulled it tight against the flesh of her bare neck. He was so fast, he had trained for this single act of killing for so long, that she didn't even have time to take in enough air to scream. All she made was a high inward gasp, and then Henry had ripped the saw hard to the right and hard to the left, tearing through soft white skin, through the strong sternocleidomastoid muscle at each side of the neck, through the fibrous sheath which contained the carotid artery, the jugular vein, and the vagus nerve.

He let out a loud, desperate, '*Ah!*' of effort and horror, and then he gave one last rip to the right, and the wire-bladed saw pulled clear through the cartilage between her cervical vertebrae, and her head rolled off her shoulders and dropped with a hideous drumming noise on to her dressing-table, amongst her combs and her make-up.

Blood fountained spectacularly out of her gaping neck, gouting and splashing all over her mirror and halfway up the wall. Her body tilted off the stool and fell heavily to the floor still pumping pints of sticky red all over the white carpet, all over the bedspread, like some ghastly and unstoppable action-painting, Jackson Pollock in gore. One foot twitched and shuddered, and actually kicked off its fur-trimmed satin slipper.

It took Henry a long time to recover himself. He stared

down at the floor because he couldn't face the severed head which was lying on the dressing-table. The head was splattered with blood, but it still looked unnervingly alive, as if Margot's eyes would suddenly roll and stare at him, as if Margot's voice would whisper from its lips.

'Jesus,' he said to himself. He was shaking all over. He must be losing his nerve.

After two or three minutes, he turned away from the chaos of blood and went to the bathroom. It was still steamy and fragrant from Margot's shower. He washed the saw under the basin faucets. The mirror was too cloudy for him to be able to see himself: all he could make out was a foggy pink face, an indeterminate monster from a past that was probably better forgotten, the ectoplasm of other people's nightmares. Blood circled the basin and whorled around the drain.

He packed away the saw with the neatness of a professional workman. Then he left the bathroom, closing the door behind him, and walked straight across the bedroom, deliberately diverting his eyes from the dressing-table. He went into the kitchen and found a large green plastic trash bag under the sink. He peeled off his bloody surgeon's gloves, rolled them up, and dropped them into the bag. For a moment, he closed his eyes, like a man with a migraine. But it had to be done. He returned to the bedroom, carrying the bag, and forced himself to step right up to the dressing-table and look down at Margot's head.

It wasn't the blood that disturbed him. He had seen plenty of blood before. Once, in Oklahoma City, he had crushed a young Italian up against a parking-lot wall in his car, and severed both of the boy's legs, femoral arteries spouting blood like hoses. And aferwards, as he drove away on Kelley Avenue under a blue Oklahoma sky, he had lit a cigarette with a hand as steady as Black Mesa on a clear night. Blood was no problem. Blood was part of the job.

Yet, Margot's head unsettled him badly. He wasn't sure why. Maybe it was because, historically, she was already

24

dead, twenty years buried; and while he might have succeeded in murdering her body, her personality had somehow survived this execution unscathed; as if Henry had
done nothing more than lop the head off a waxwork
dummy. Her life-force, her legend, remained intact. That
inexplicable radiance that had always made her appear to
be far greater and far more glamorous than she actually
was – that radiance still shone. He had killed her, but she
was still alive. For Henry, this wasn't like the old days at
all. It was too much like Hollywood voodoo, Sharon Tate
and Jayne Mansfield and Anton LeVey. It was too much
like Helter-Skelter. Henry looked down at her head, at
the way she stared so intently and yet so blindly at her
pots of cosmetics, at the garish blue tongue which was
beginning to slide out from between her parted lips, at
the congealing blood which had stuck up her hair like a
coronet, or a coxcomb; and he knew that *he* was fated too.
Twenty years of his life, for this. Twenty years to discover
what doom really was.

He gingerly picked up the head by its sticky, blood-
soaked scalp, and tumbled it into the green plastic bag.
His stomach turned over, but he managed to keep the
rest of his lunch down. He took one last look around the
bedroom, deliberate and slow, making absolutely sure
that he had left nothing behind which could identify him.
In the living-room, he carefully collected up all the family
portraits, and systematically went through every drawer
and cupboard, searching for photographs and letters. It
took him over an hour.

It was almost dark when he closed the door of Margot
Schneider's house behind him, and crossed the driveway
to his car. He unlocked the trunk, and stowed the head
carefully on top of the spare wheel, so that it wouldn't
roll around when he turned corners. He spread a plaid
blanket over it, just in case. Then he climbed quickly into
the car, started it up, and drove back down Oasis Drive
without lights. In a few moments, he was speeding along
Lincoln Drive, back towards 24th Street, where he would
turn left for Sky Harbor airport.

The getaway contingency was simple. It had been devised years ago, when Henry had first started looking further afield than California. Henry would park the Oldsmobile at Sky Harbor's long-term parking-lot, unscrew the licence-plates and peel off any special decals. Then, from the terminal, he would telephone his people in Los Angeles and tell them what had happened. While he boarded his flight at Phoenix, an exactly similar vehicle would be rented from the Avis desk at LAX, and by the time Henry arrived in Los Angeles, this new vehicle would be waiting for him, minus its licence-plates, in the LAX parking-lot. Henry would attach to it the plates from the car he had rented in Phoenix, and check it in to the Avis desk, making a point of telling the girls there how arduous the drive had been from Arizona. 'And those dust storms, phew. . .!'

The accomplice who had rented the car from Los Angeles would fly to Phoenix with *his* licence-plates, screw them on to Henry's old car, and then drive immediately to Las Vegas, and check it in there, pretending he had driven up from Los Angeles.

The switch would remain undiscovered until one or other of the cars was serviced; and even then the mechanics probably wouldn't bother to check the vehicle numbers.

Henry turned on the radio as he drove south on 24th Street towards the airport. The yuccas on either side of the road were silhouetted against the evening sky like black-paper cutouts on a Carmen Miranda stage set. KTAR radio was playing *Hotel California*: 'You can check out any time you like, but you can never leave. . . .' He lit a cigarette and his hands were trembling. Twenty years between killings was far too long. Twenty years between anything was far too long. He felt like a medieval mariner, hoary, bearded, hopeless, who had suddenly reached the brink of the world.

Two

Daniel was woken up by a loud, insistent purring, like a cat eating its breakfast. He opened his eyes and blinked at the sunlit adobe ceiling above him, and wondered for nearly a minute where he was, and what century he was in. He thought: Buck Rogers must have felt like this, when he woke up from that gas-filled mine in Pittsburgh and discovered that he was in the twenty-fifth century. Where am I, and who is this woman lying next to me, and why is she snoring so loudly?

She was a coppery redhead, although her hair was all that Daniel could see of her. He seemed to remember that her name was Cara. At least, that was what she had said it was. Hitch-hikers rarely told the truth, and it was a kind of unwritten law of the highway that they didn't need to. It was enough that they were entertaining, or sexy, or both. Cara from South Dakota, making her way to the Coast. Daniel had been to South Dakota himself, playing the Treble Clef Club in Rapid City, and he didn't find her story at all incredible. All that South Dakota was good for, as far as he could tell, was escaping from.

'Hey,' he said, gently shaking her shoulder.

'Hmmph?' she said, stretching herself out.

'You're snoring.'

She wrestled the sheet around herself. 'I am not, either,' she told him, without opening her eyes. 'Ladies never snore.'

'Oh no? Well, what's that purring noise you're making?'

'Emphatic breathing,' she said. 'Now, let me get some sleep, will you? It isn't even dawn, for God's sake.'

Daniel leaned over and looked at her in close-up. 'It's six-fifteen,' he announced. 'I have to be open at seven.' He decided that he still had pretty good taste in women after all, as long as she didn't have herpes. She was sharp-faced, white-skinned, and big-breasted, with those wide flaring hips that always reminded him of milkmaids.

27

It was amazing the women you could encounter on the highway between Superior and Phoenix on a hot Thursday evening, or any evening, come to that. Vassar graduates, lady truck drivers, hookers, viola players, feminist activists, gambling shills; and now Cara.

She kept on snoring, deep and low, but Daniel couldn't really complain about it. Last night, after the last of his customers had gone home, she had helped him to stack the dishes and clean up; and then, sweet and high on good red wine and Bruce Springsteen records, she had tumbled among the sheets with him with such fun and energy and unembarrassed lust that it had taken all his self-control not to let out his famous window-vibrating rebel yell, just for the sheer joy of it. This morning, his back and thighs were scratched like Brer Rabbit in the brambles, and his lips felt as if they had been caught up in a catering-sized garlic press.

He climbed stiffly out of bed, and the springs squeaked. His jeans and his T-shirt were crumpled up on the bare-boarded floor in the most peculiar heap, as if he had leaped out of them last night without even undoing them. The large Mickey Mouse alarm clock on the bureau said 6:20. He yawned so hard that he almost dislocated his jaw, and sniffed.

Susie was standing just outside the door, in her long pink Mary Poppins nightdress. She watched him silently as he took out a clean shirt and dressed, and then followed him along the corridor as he went to pee and to throw cold water in his face. It was only when he had risen from the depths of his towel to stare at himself in the cracked bathroom mirror that she said anything.

'Who's that?' she asked. She was seven, with blonde braids, and a pretty little perky face, and china-blue eyes. Just like her mother. Mega-cute.

'That's, er, Cara. Cara from South Dakota.'

'Is she staying for breakfast?'

'I guess so.'

'Do you like her?'

Daniel stared down at Susie for a long time. In the end,

he said, 'I don't know yet. We haven't really done a whole lot of talking.'

'But she's staying for breakfast?'

'Sure. We didn't argue or anything.'

'And you don't hate yourself? And she doesn't hate *her*self?'

'I don't know. She's still asleep. It's kind of hard to assess how much you like or dislike yourself when you're still asleep.'

'I can *sing* when I'm asleep.'

Daniel shuffled down the narrow wooden stairs to the old-fashioned Mexican-style kitchen. Susie followed him, with all the intentness of a concerned wife. Daniel opened up the huge Amana icebox and began to take out bacon strips and eggs and hamburger patties and sausage links in preparation for the morning stampede. In addition, there would be two gallons of coffee to perk, three dozen oranges to press, twenty-five buns to be sliced and nine tables to be laid. He drank a large gulp of grapefruit juice straight from the carton, and helped himself to a handful of stale Cheetos.

Susie said, 'It's time you settled down, you know.'

'Settled down?' Daniel demanded. 'I *am* settled down. What could be more settled down than living here with you, doing what I'm doing?'

'I mean you could marry.'

Daniel shook his head. 'I tried it. You know that. I'm not the right type for marriage. I don't have the right amino-acid chains for marriage. Besides, I'm allergic to fidelity. It brings me out in hives.'

'You've been faithful to me.'

'You're my daughter. Being faithful to your children is different.'

Susie toyed with the magnetic clips stuck to the front of the icebox. 'Don't you ever think about mommy, ever?'

'You know I do. Your mommy was the prettiest lady who ever lived. And to prove it, you're the prettiest daughter who ever lived. But she wanted something else, somebody else. Not here, and not me. I couldn't do anything about it.'

Susie said, 'Would you take her back, if she came?'

Daniel had an armful of fresh eggs. But he stopped where he was, and looked at Susie seriously, and then set the eggs down one by one on the counter so that he could take her into his arms and hold her very, very close. She had that warm-bready smell of a young child who has just been sleeping, a hostage freshly released by the sandman.

'Susie,' he said, in a hoarse, affectionate whisper, 'I have all I need in you.'

'You won't take her back then?'

'No,' he said. 'It wouldn't be fair.'

She looked closely at him, and there were tears in her eyes. 'Who wouldn't it be fair to?' she asked.

'It wouldn't be fair to your mommy, nor to me, nor to you. We'd argue all the time, you know that. We'd shout. We'd wind up hating each other when we should always love each other.'

Susie pressed her forehead against his, and then said, in the smallest voice, 'I miss her.'

'I know,' said Daniel. 'So do I.'

A cat-curious voice interrupted, 'I hope I'm not breaking up anything meaningful here.' Daniel looked up. It was Cara, sleepy-eyed but awake, with her red hair brushed into chrysanthemum curls. She was wearing one of Daniel's blue denim workshirts, unbuttoned, so that she was revealing her deep alabaster-white cleavage, her flat white stomach, and the rusty tangle of red pubic hair between her long white thighs. She was unashamed, provocative, and highway-stylish – possessed of that same vagrant elegance that had attracted him to Candii, his first-ever wife and Susie's mother. Susie recognized the breed, and kissed her father on the nose with childish promptness, and left.

'Did I drive her away?' asked Cara, not altogether without satisfaction.

Daniel stood up, and rubbed the back of his neck. 'She's

30

used to it. She's only trying to make me feel guilty. She misses her mommy.'

'Understandable,' said Cara. She came up close and kissed his cheek, then his mouth. 'Do you want me to fix us some coffee?'

'Don't worry. I have to fix enough for the whole of Apache Junction in any case. Would you pass me that skillet?'

Cara stood beside him as he melted lard in the skillet for the hash browns. She touched his shoulder sensitively, as if she couldn't quite believe that he was real. The sun crept in between the slats of the venetian blind and suddenly illuminated the white china bowl of Spanish onions, so that they took on the charmed radiance of a detail by Vermeer. And as he stood over the hot kitchen range in his jeans and his white short-sleeved shirt, slightly-built, dark-haired, a little used-looking but still attractive, Daniel appeared to Cara to become irradiated with some of the same domestic magic. Portrait of the chef as a tired but friendly angel.

'You were strange last night,' she told him. 'Strange and wonderful. Too gentle for a short-order cook.'

'Restaurant proprietor,' he corrected her. He scraped frozen onion slices into the skillet and they began to sizzle.

'Restaurant proprietor, whatever,' she smiled.

'You think I'm *strange*?' he asked.

She nodded happily. He frowned at her for a moment and then shrugged. As a matter of fact, he had often thought himself that he must have been born into some kind of backward-facing looking-glass land. His life and his career always seemed to turn out the polar opposite of what he really wanted, and of what he was really capable of achieving. The only points he ever managed to score in the 36 years he had been alive were into his own goal. Even his face, when he saw it in photographs, looked as if it were the wrong way around; as if the man he glimpsed in mirrors and store windows was the way he actually should have been, and the face with which he

31

walked around all day was his awkward other-self, his klutzy doppelganger.

He should have been a famous TV entertainer, a kind of alternative Johnny Carson, a poor man's Dan Rather. Instead, he ran Daniel's Downhome Diner, in Apache Junction, Arizona, beside the heat-wavering horizon of the Superstition Mountains, near the famous Lost Dutchman Mine. Daniel's Downhome Diner was popular enough, if popularity meant anything at all in a town of 2,391 and falling. There was an intermittent passing-through trade, truckers and tourists and windpump salesmen, as well as hitch-hikers and assorted mysteriosos. Sometimes the customers were friendly; sometimes offensive. Sometimes they cried into their coffee, or threw chairs through the window. There were nine gingham-covered tables, red gingham, with plastic tomatoes full of ketchup, and a 1967 jukebox with *Happy Together* by the Turtles and *Penny Lane* by the Beatles, not because Daniel held any special memories of 1967, but simply because the lock was broken and nobody could get into the jukebox to change the records. On the wall there was a smeary blackboard menu, Franks & Beans, Minute Steaks & Beans, Tamales, Empanadas, Cheeseburgers. All good downhome stuff, although Daniel was actually capable of tossing together *oysters Bienville*, or *pompano en papillote*, or even *pigeonneaux royaux au sauce paradis*, with equal equanimity. His father had been a chef at Alciatore's in San Francisco in the 1950s, and had taught him to cook with all the care and patience and calculated disgust of a real professional. Daniel rarely prepared such exotica these days, mainly because he was more than seriously tired of cooking by the end of the day, and because nobody else in Apache Junction would have wanted to eat anything like that anyway. Apache Junctioneers ate a lot of steak and a lot of beans and that was just about it. He could just imagine the reaction he would get from Indian Bill Hargraves if he served him up tender fragments of crab and mushrooms and fish in a paper poke. 'What the hell's this, a Western Airlines sickbag?'

He had never meant to run a restaurant, especially not here in Pinal County, Arizona. He had tried singing, and selling, and sucking out sewers, and collecting tolls on the Indian National Turnpike in Oklahoma. He had even worked as a stand-up comedian in a quasi-Victorian top-less nightspot in Nevada called the Gaslight. 'And Moses is standing on top of the mountain, right, and he says to Jehovah, listen, let me get this straight, you want us to cut the end of our *dicks* off?' That was where he had met and married Candii, Susie's mother, blonde curls and snub nose and Little Annie Fanny eyes, giggly and small and sexy, with breasts so big that when she jiggled down the street men used to stop and stare with their mouths wide open, a tabletop dancer supreme, a burlesque artiste out of her time, the rage and the love of his life, gone now, of course, like a sad hoarse-throated song by Dr Hook ('To think I was the kind of guy who could have kept her . . . would be taking too much credit on myself'). Candii had sworn filthy curses at him in the obstetric clinic in Reno, while a red neon light across the street had flashed the word DIVORCE on and off all night, and the doctor had warned vaguely that Susie would probably die. Susie hadn't died, thank God, but Candii had left them after eight months, taking her tight silk dresses and her seamed stockings and her giant-sized pink vibrator, which he had never seen her use. He missed her badly, even now, six years later, because she was an unassailable sexual fantasy and because she always used to laugh at his jokes and because he loved her. What was more, her name was actually Candii, on her birth certificate.

He had arrived in Apache Junction by accident. He had been heading towards Santa Fé, New Mexico, to show off Susie to Candii's mother (only 42 herself, by God, and just as busty as her daughter) and to panhandle a few hundred dollars from Candii's father to pay off some of his arrears in rent. A few miles outside of Phoenix, his old green Mercury had finally collapsed on its worn-out suspension and died by the glaring roadside. When he had looked around, the signs had said *Apache Junction*.

They had also said *Thriving Diner for Sale*. The Navajo mechanic from the nearby Exxon garage had stared Indian-wrinkly-mouthed at the Mercury's rusty green carcass, his waist girdled with shiny wrenches, and then at last pronounced, 'No point in fixing *that*, my friend. Transmission's shot.' The moon-faced man who was selling the diner had peered out suspiciously from his darkened porch and said, 'You're not wasting my time, are you? I get more time-wasters, I can tell you.'

There wasn't much in Apache Junction. A couple of gas stations, a few peeling houses, an Indian jewellery store. But it was as good or as bad as living anyplace else. The weather was warm and dry and helpful to Daniel's sinus condition. The crime rate was low. The only habitual offender was a halfbreed Navajo called Ronald Reagan Kinishba, and he and Daniel were good friends. They played cards together occasionally, and got themselves drunk on Löwenbrau, and sometimes Ronald took Daniel out on the pillion seat of his Honda 749cc Nighthawk, blaring through the night at 110 mph, oblivious to anything but speed and grit and hot wind, and lights that flashed past them like space missiles out of *Star Trek II*. Afterwards, they would sit astride the bike at some unmapped desert intersection, trembling and saying, 'Shit, wow, phew,' over and over.

It was a silent life, sometimes; a life in which a man could turn in on himself. At night, in high summer, with the sky as clear as a black lawn sprinkled with silver daisies, with Susie sleeping in her rumpled cot, and the odd aromatic smell of the desert on the breeze, Daniel would sit out on the balcony at the back of the diner listening to the small voice of KSTM inside the kitchen, and wonder if he was real or not. He would cheer himself up by remembering one of Woody Allen's characters, who hated reality but realized it was the only place to get a good steak. He often felt like a Woody Allen character himself these days: anxious, and just about able to cope. And the longer he lived in Apache Junction, the greater his uncertainty about coping became.

Cara said, 'You don't feel like a vacation, maybe?'

He looked up from the onions. 'A vacation? What do you mean?'

'Well, getting away from it all.'

'You don't think *this* is getting away from it all? Apache Junction?'

She kissed him, and then reached forward a little nearer and kissed him again. 'This is *work*,' she said. 'I'm talking about swimming, or surfing, or climbing up mountains and making love on the snowline.'

'Oh, yes? And who's going to take care of Susie?'

'Don't you have a friendly old couple who could take her in for a week or two?'

Daniel stirred onions, and then reached for the seasoning. 'I'd miss her,' he said.

There was a long pause. Then Cara said, 'Would you mind if I stuck around for a little while? Maybe a day or two?'

Daniel glanced at her, and smiled. 'You're welcome, if that's what you want.'

Cara took his wrist, and nudged back the shirt she was wearing, and held his hand firmly over her bare left breast. She stared at him challengingly, and he felt her nipple crinkle and rise against the palm of his hand. 'Destiny,' she said.

'What is?' he asked her.

'You and me, meeting. Destiny. Not *great* destiny. Not thunder and lightning and whole continents catching fire. But good sweet destiny; something we can both remember for ever, when the mood comes over us.'

He kept staring into those pale blue eyes of hers, and gently rotating the palm of his hand around her breast. 'Cara,' he said. 'Cara from South Dakota. I don't even know your surname.'

'Does it matter?'

Just then, there was a rattling knock at the kitchen window; and through the frosted glass, Daniel could see the blurry outline of a man's face. 'Daniel! You there? Daniel!'

'Willy?' called Daniel. 'Hold on a second, I'll let you in.'
He turned to Cara, and said, 'It's a friend of mine. Do you
want to go get dressed?'

Cara looked down at herself. 'Oh, sure,' she said. She
blew him a kiss, and then, with a sassy twirl, turned
around and pranced back upstairs.

'Holy shit,' came Susie's voice from the diner next door,
although Daniel had paddled her twice in the past week
for talking like a trucker. But sometimes women knew
when they could get away with it, and Susie was no
exception.

Three

Daniel lowered the gas under the onions and went to
open the back door. Willy Monahan came tumbling in
with his usual awkwardness, brushing dust off his Air
Force uniform. 'Whose damn chickens are those? Are they
your damn chickens? Damn things almost pecked the
laces straight out of my damn shoes!'

'They're Bill's,' said Daniel, mildly. 'Pima Indian who
lives out back there, he's peaceful enough and gives me
plenty of eggs, too. Do you want some coffee? You're
early.'

'I'm not early, I'm damn late,' Willy retorted. He hung
up his major's cap next to a huge Hungarian salami. 'I've
been working all night in the armoury.' He sniffed, and
then he said, 'What's that smell?'

'Onions.'

'No, the other smell. The subtle, sensual, underlying
smell. Do I detect woman with a capital W?'

Susie came into the kitchen, carrying a stack of clean
red gingham napkins. 'Hi, Uncle Willy.'

'Hi yourself. Don't tell me the old man has company again.'

Susie nodded. 'Redhead. From South Dakota.'

Daniel took down another skillet, and scraped some more lard into it. 'I'm outnumbered, you know that? My daughter, my best friend, who's it going to be next? Just because a pretty young lady from Woonsocket decides to spend a little time here, helping me out – '

'Woonsocket? You're serious?' asked Willy.

'Of course I'm serious. Woonsocket is in Sanborn County, a couple of hundred miles south of Huron.'

'Oh, *that* Woonsocket,' teased Willy. 'Well, my friend, if it's *that* Woonsocket, you don't have much to worry about. They're known for their obliging redheads. In fact eight Woonsocket women out of ten are redheads. They're also known for the Woonsocket Jew's Harp Orchestra, and Woonsocket Pie, which is a whole gopher in a flaky pastry crust.'

Susie giggled, but Daniel closed his eyes and raised his head as if he were appealing to the Lord to save him from smartass Air Force majors. 'To think, Willy, that we depend on you to protect this great nation of ours in time of war.'

Willy noisily pulled across one of the red-and-gold Mexican kitchen chairs, and sat down on it, propping one angular leg across the other. 'You don't know how damn lucky you are,' he said. 'The reason I spent all night in the armoury was because single-handedly and unaided I have discovered a flaw in our air-to-air radar systems. Now, what do you think about that?'

'What should I think?' asked Daniel.

'What *should* you think? You should only think that you have sitting in your humble little kitchen the greatest genius in ordnance and navigation systems in the entire United States Air Force. And that's just for beginners.'

'Have some coffee,' Daniel enjoined him.

Willy was unusually disconnected and disarrayed-looking for an Air Force major, particularly an Air Force major who flew regular tactical training missions in a jet airplane which could fly at 920 mph and had cost the American taxpayer something over $18 million. He was thin, Willy, with a large hatchet nose, and bright dark eyes. He had been married once, years ago, but his wife Nora had left him during Viet Nam, and he had sworn to himself that he would never try marriage again. Instead, he had devoted his on-duty hours to familiarizing himself almost fanatically with the Air Force's new and sophisticated weapons systems, becoming an amateur expert in radar and guided missiles; and his off-duty hours to Chivas Regal, poker, and scandalous womanizing. He was the only officer in the Air Force who had completely overhauled a Boeing 8–1 defensive radar system singlehanded, and the only officer in the Air Force who had actually succeeded in tugging the white nylon pants off Corporal Sherry P. Kearns, the Junoesque but notoriously inflexible secretary of General 'Tailpipe' Truscott, at Nellis Air Force Base.

Willy was Nebraskan by birth; rangy, funny, but also very good at what he did, an Air Force man through and through. If his wife hadn't left him, and if he had behaved himself, he could have been a major-general by now, on $38,000 a year. But he had remained a major for six years, while younger and correcter men were promoted over his head, and his latest posting to Williams AFB to train inexperienced young pilots on F–15 Eagles had been an unmistakable message from Tactical Air Command that he could expect to rise no further. He called Williams 'the Graveyard of Dreams'.

He hadn't quit the Air Force. There was nothing else he could do, not happily, at least. But now and then, when he was drunk, his chagrin rose to the surface like the boiling bubbles from a sunken submarine, and he foully cursed all wives, and all superior officers, and most of all he foully cursed himself.

He sipped his coffee noisily, and helped himself to a handful of chocolate-chip cookies. 'I can't wait to lay all this stuff on Colonel Kawalek's desk. I can picture his face already. "Well, Willy, what's all this, Willy? What do you mean our radar's up shit-creek? Apart from being *distasteful*, Willy, it's politically impossible." ' Willy did a particularly cruel impersonation of the blustery Kawalek.

Daniel peeled strips of bacon out of a greasy plastic pack, and laid them in the skillet. 'Is it serious, this flaw you've found?'

'Is it serious? Was Hiroshima serious? Of course it's serious.'

Willy munched cookies and swallowed coffee as if he were trying to win himself a place in the Guinness Book of Records as the man who gave himself indigestion the fastest.

'Well, are you going to tell me?' asked Daniel.

'It's very technical,' said Willy. 'I'm not sure I could explain it to a short-order cook.'

'Restaurant proprietor, if you don't mind.'

'Whatever. It isn't easy to understand, not unless you have a moderate grasp of the principles of X-band pulse-doppler radar.'

'Are you kidding?' said Daniel, flipping the bacon over. 'My mother used to tell me bedtime stories about X-band pulse-doppler radar. Didn't you ever hear the one about X-band pulse-doppler radar and the seven dwarfs?'

'Seriously,' said Willy, 'this is one of those high-tech discoveries a man makes just once in a lifetime.'

'Will you pass me the pepper? No, that one. Thanks. Go on, then, tell me what you've found out.'

'Ah, shit,' Willy despaired. 'How do you explain anomalies in APG–63 multi-mode radar to a guy who's frying onions?'

'Try, will you? I'm listening.'

Willy dragged his chair across to the table without even taking his backside off it. He laid a wooden spoon on one side of the table, and a blue-and-white china butter-dish on the other. 'This radar is highly sophisticated, very advanced. It fits into the nose of a fighter-plane, and it controls every move that the fighter-pilot is going to make in any kind of combat situation. It can track one enemy airplane, and at the same time it can carry on looking for others. It can lock from one target to another instantly. Up until now, I thought it was the best air-to-air radar in the entire world.'

'In that case, I'm glad that it belongs to us, and not to the Russians'.

Willy blinked at him.

'That's all I could think of to say,' Daniel apologized.

Willy took the pewter flour-shaker, and carefully sprinkled a fine coating of white self-raising flour all over the surface of the table. Susie watched him with grave interest; Daniel thought, God in Heaven, here we go again, another Willy Monahan hobby-horse. He remembered the time that Willy had got a bee in his bonnet about missiles with non-imaging infra-red seekers, and how he had single-handedly persuaded his bemused commanding officer to lobby the Pentagon for all TAC airplanes to be re-equipped. Unsuccessfully, of course.

'This table is our attack scenario, right?' said Willy.

'I thought you were making shortcrust pastry,' Daniel retorted.

Willy raised a hand to silence him. 'Don't make fun. This is serious. This wooden spoon is an enemy intruder, right? And this butter-dish is me, okay, in my F–15. I'm protecting the homeland in the late stages of a protracted nuclear confrontation. Enemy wooden spoons are coming in from all sides.'

'What do you do, Uncle Willy?' asked Susie, frowning.

'Do? I'll tell you what I do. I get up there in my F–15, fully armed with a 20mm M–61 multi-barrel gun with 960 rounds of ammunition, plus four AIM–7 Sparrow air-to-air missiles and four AIM-9 Sidewinder air-to-air missiles, and I track those wooden spoons on my radar until I've locked right on to one, and I'm ready to blow it right out of the sky, and then I fire one of my Sparrow missiles, and then what happens?'

'You're telling us,' Daniel reminded him. He sneezed, twice.

'I'm glad that's not *my* breakfast,' said Willy, caustically.

'Just tell us what happens,' Daniel told him.

'Okay – I've fired the missile. It's really hot stuff, this missile. Radar-guided, with a PD capability and lock-in up to 10 db clutter in the look-down mode.'

Daniel turned over the strips of bacon one by one, setting up a tremendous sizzling chorus. Lannie Watts from the Globe Trucking Corporation would be pressing his nose to the diner's window in five or ten minutes from now, demanding his breakfast. Lannie always ate seven strips of bacon, three eggs, toast, and a heap of hash browns, but he insisted on drinking grapefruit juice with it to keep his weight down.

'Are you listening to me?' Willy demanded.

'Sure I'm listening,' said Daniel. 'Listen, I'm *listening*. But I'm not at all sure what the hell you're talking about. What's this "clutter"?'

'Just shut up,' insisted Willy. 'I fire the missile, the missile locks on to the woden spoon, here it comes – ' he traced an unerring missile-track through the dusted flour ' – it's two hundred yards away, one hundred, fifty, and then what happens? ' – his finger sharply veered away – 'it misses. Just like that.'

'It misses? You mean, every time? You're trying to tell me the US Air Force is equipped with missiles that *miss*?'

'It's a one-in-a-million flaw,' said Willy, with satisfaction. 'If it hadn't have been for the tests I was running on X-band radar, I doubt if anyone would have discovered it.'

'But surely they've *tested* these missiles?' Daniel told him. 'They worked during their tests, didn't they?'

'Oh, sure,' Willy agreed. 'And they still work now, when they're tested on the Air Force ranges. But what you have to realize is that we never test them against real Soviet airplanes. We usually use a PQM-102 RPV, which is a pilotless Delta Dagger. Now, each airplane has a different and distinct radar signature, do you understand me? and although our radar is obviously happy to lock-on to the signature of a Delta Dagger, or any other US target plane, it seems to have a widespread aversion to Soviet signatures.'

Daniel forked out Lannie's bacon. 'This is really true?

This isn't just some one-off error in one particular piece of equipment?'

Willy shook his head. 'I've run diagnostic programmes through the armoury computer on three different radar systems. Each system failed in exactly the same way, at exactly the same moment. But, of course, if a pilot didn't realize that his radar was snafu, he'd simply believe that he'd missed. Mind you, if he was in a real damn combat situation, he wouldn't have too long to worry about it, since I doubt if the Soviet air-to-air missiles have a similar aversion to hitting *our* planes.'

'But it's *insane*,' said Daniel. 'How can a whole Air Force be equipped with missiles that don't work?'

'What can I say?' asked Willy, blowing flour off the table. 'It's the greatest damn scandal in the history of the Air Force. And I mean the greatest. Heads will start rolling, believe me.'

'Jesus,' said Daniel.

'I have more tests to make,' Willy added. 'I want to take a look at the IR seeker nose on the Falcon; and maybe check the laser-beam proximity fuse, too.'

'Don't befuddle me with technicality,' said Daniel.

'I'm simply telling you that I want to check the guidance and detonation systems on other missiles, too. Every missile has its own fancy new system, and some of them are so far out you'd hardly believe them. Some of the latest ground-to-air missiles have phased-arrayed radar that's capable of surveillance, acquisition, track/engage and guidance. They can do everything except serve up lunch.'

'None of which is any use if they don't hit the airplanes they're supposed to hit,' said Daniel.

'Precisely,' Willy agreed.

Susie sneezed, because of the flour.

'Leave it,' Daniel told Willy. 'Cara will clean it up.'

'Oh, Cara, that's her name? Nice name, considering she comes from South Dakota. Usually, they're called Waynette or Laurene or Trixie.'

'Or Candii?' said Daniel, purposely trying to embarrass him.

Willy made a face. 'Sure. Or Candii.'

There was a shuddering knock at the front door of the diner. That must be Lannie Watts, wanting his breakfast. Daniel said to Susie. 'Go let Lannie in, will you? Tell him I'm just cracking his eggs.'

When Susie had gone through the plastic-strip curtain to the diner, Daniel said seriously to Willy, 'This thing you've found out. It's pretty serious, isn't it? I mean, it could be trouble.'

'Just like I said, Daniel, heads will roll.'

'You're sure it won't be *your* head? You know what Kawalek's like, all jokes apart. And Kawalek's only a co-lonel. There have to be plenty of generals and top brass at the Pentagon who won't particularly feel like being embarrassed by a know-it-all major from Williams training base.'

Willy said, 'I have to do what's right, Daniel.'

'Of course you do. But you also have to protect yourself. Whoever designed those missiles, whoever ordered them, whoever passed them as okay for active duty, all those people are going to want you out of the way. You just think to yourself how much money changes hands in a successful missile contract. Billions. Well, people get killed in the streets for pennies. So, be warned.'

'Daniel,' insisted Willy, 'it's all a question of *fact*, that's all. The missiles don't work against Soviet radar signa-tures and that's it.'

Daniel wiped his hands on his jeans. 'You want some breakfast?'

'You don't want to talk about it?'

'Get yourself some more information, that's all,' Daniel told him. 'Don't go breezing into Kawalek's office with something you can't totally substantiate. And before you go, leave a copy of whatever it is you've been working on here with me. Or somebody else you trust.'

Willy pushed back his chair, and stood up. Susie came into the kitchen and announced, 'Lannie says please move your hindquarters with his breakfast.' Daniel smiled, and nodded. 'Okay.'

Willy said, 'I guess I'll go home and catch myself a couple of hours' shuteye. Then I'll go back to the armoury and run the last of those programmes. I'll meet you at ten for a drink at Hank's. Is that okay?'

'That's okay. But you'll leave your findings with me before you go talk to Kawalek?'

'So that you can sell them to the Russians, and make yourself rich?' joked Willy.

'Willy,' Daniel cautioned him.

Willy came over and flung an awkward arm around his shoulders. 'I know, Daniel. I know, Discretion is the better part of valour. Don't fire until you see the whites of their eyes.'

Daniel, one-handed, cracked two eggs. They had played racketball together, he and Willy. They had talked for hours, all night sometimes, until they knew each other like brothers, or maybe closer. Daniel had never been to Omaha, but he could have found his way to the hollow tree in Fontenelle Park where Willy used to hide his catapult and his Tom Mix plastic 'look-in' TV set as if he had played there himself.

They were buddies, in the curiously old-fashioned sense of the word. Astrologically, psychologically, and physically. But now Daniel had the unsettling feeling that the responsibilities of the real world were about to come between them; and although he tried to smile, he couldn't. His face was fixed like rapidly-cooling glass.

Four

Titus had seen Joe Jasper's Cadillac approach through the willows, its amber marking-lights dipping and bouncing through Beahms Grove; and so by the time Joe had awkwardly parked by the bank of the river, and picked his way in his highly-polished Bejan shoes through the rough muddy grass that sloped down to the water's edge, Titus had been able to wade twenty or thirty yards further into midstream, still near enough to hear what Joe might shout out, in case it was anything interesting, but far enough to pretend that he was out of earshot, in case it wasn't.

It was a silent foggy afternoon in the Shenandoah Valley, a few miles upstream from Front Royal, overlooked to the east by the Blue Ridge mountains, and to the west by the Massanuttens; old Civil War country. Titus was taking his first fishing vacation in three years, and whatever Joe Jasper had to say, it couldn't be half as absorbing to Titus as the deep swirl of the Shenandoah River, or the distinct dripping of condensation from the overhanging trees, or the call of vireos and thrushes. Titus, after three-and-a-half years as Secretary of State, and five-and-a-half years of marriage to Nadine, was awarding himself three days and three nights of complete peace; peace that was punctuated only by the stitching-up sound of a fishing-reel, or the whirr of nylon line.

'Titus!' called Joe. He was teetering on a boggy clump of grass, desperately trying to keep his $200 shoes out of the mud. But Titus kept his back to the bank, and puffed at his corncob pipe, even though it had died on him almost twenty minutes ago, and generally tried to look occupied with the current, and the weather, and the fish. He'd often heard that the greatest actors could communicate volumes of Shakespeare through their turned backs, although he wasn't quite sure how. What he was trying to communicate now was: get the hell out of here, Joe, unless it's something really good.

'Titus!' Joe called again. He had a thin voice, like a whippet. 'Titus, can you hear me?'

Titus took two or three steps further into the stream. The water-level was uncomfortably close to the top of his waders, but he stayed where he was, deaf as a rock, occasionally turning his head upstream to make it look as if his pose were natural, whistling too for a moment but then forgetting to keep it up.

'Mr Secretary, this is absolutely vital!' Joe yelled. 'It's too sensitive to shout out to you; you'll have to come in to the riverbank and listen close!'

There was a long pause. The river gurgled and flowed. Titus stayed where he was, his fishing-pole held up numbly, his eyes closed. Of all the instincts that Joe could have appealed to, his curiosity was the most easily aroused. He could stay here, pretending to be inextricably absorbed in the Shenandoah and her fish, chilled to the thighs; or he could admit that he had heard Joe calling, and wade back, and listen to what this sensitive news might be. It was too damned exasperating for words, especially since Joe would say nothing at all about his apparent deafness, but gloat silently, and make him feel angrier than ever.

He was still trying to make up his mind when he heard water splashing close by. He turned around, and to his complete astonishment, Joe was wading right up to him in his $750 Christian Dior suit, his thin triangular face fixed in the kind of expression you might expect to see on a man who has had an entire bowl of lime Jell-O emptied slowly into his jockey shorts.

'Mr Secretary!' he gasped.

Titus was so surprised that he forgot to pretend that he hadn't heard Joe calling before. 'Why the hell didn't you stay on the bank? You gone crazy or something?'

'Titus, Mr Secretary, this is urgent.'

They stood facing each other, nearly waist-deep in the river. Titus took the corncob pipe out of his mouth, then stuck it back in again, and started to wind in his line.

'I wouldn't have disturbed you for anything, Titus,' said Joe. 'But I think we've come up with the answer to the RINC problem, accidentally, fortuitously, and I knew you'd want to be the very first to know.'

'How can I be the first to know when *you* already know?' growled Titus, reeling in his line as if it were his vacation, prematurely over, wrapped up and wound up like everything else he tried to do that wasn't connected with the State Department, or Nadine, or Nadine's nauseating children.

'What I mean is, you're the first VIP to know,' Joe corrected himself. 'And, well, what we decide to *do* about it depends entirely on you.'

'Do you realize you're soaking?' Titus asked Joe. 'I mean, do you realize that you're absolutely fucking soaking wet?'

'Yes, sir,' said Joe. Then, more lamely, 'I have another suit in the car.'

Titus fastened his hook and then began to make his way slowly back to the bank of the river in deep, rhythmical strides. 'That's typical of you, Joe. Do you know that? Heroism without inconvenience. You're always prepared to get your hands dirty, provided there's a handy pack of Wet Ones around.'

Joe sloshed after him. He reached the edge of the river and stood in the mud with water running out of his suit in a noisy cascade. Titus opened up his fishing bag to put away his diptera fly and his hook, and dismantle his expensive carbon-fibre pole. Nadine had given him the pole as a present when they were married. This was the first time he had taken it out. The walls of his library were crowded with trophies from his younger days, stuffed and mounted river fish from Virginia to Colorado, badges and medals and certificates; but he hadn't added a single decent fish to his collection since he had left the Army and sought greater glory in politics.

Joe said, 'It was one of those real breaks. One of those real one-in-a-million breaks.'

'Why don't you change your suit before you tell me?' Titus snarled at him. 'You might as well be comfortable.'

'Well,' said Joe, trying to be self-deprecating.

Titus walked across to the Cadillac and climbed into the passenger-seat unbidden, tossing his fishing-bag on to the back seat. The leather upholstery was virgin white, and his waders were very muddy, thick with that black silty Shenandoah bottom-mud; but he figured it would do Joe good, to have to sit there and watch his pristine custom-upholstered car being gratuitously besmirched, without being able to do anything about it. Good for his soul.

Joe changed into his fresh suit behind the upraised trunk. Titus put down his window and called, 'Don't be too long about it. Any man without pants is considered fair game in West Virginia.' Joe reappeared in less than a minute, tucking in his shirt-tails, tightening his tie, sweating and discomfited.

'I was only joking,' said Titus, as Joe climbed in behind the wheel.

'Well, it's not a thing to joke about,' said Joe. His sub-stitute suit was considerably less ritzy than his first suit, a rather nasty number in light blue locknit, but Titus felt that it probably suited the occasion better. 'Do you have any of those rotten cheap cigars you smoke?' he asked.

Joe opened the glove box and passed over a white hide cigar-case containing four first-quality Havana coronas. Titus took one, crackled it next to his ear, and said, 'Noise, as well as smoke. You got a cutter? I don't know why you take so much trouble to prize off those white plastic tips.'

Joe took the cigar from Titus in long, well-manicured fingers, and clipped a neat V-shape out of the end. Then he passed it back, and took out a box of British Swan Vestas matches, which were his ultimate snobbery. Titus could tell that he felt very uncomfortable in his blue lock-nit suit, and made a point of rubbing the fabric of his lapel between finger and thumb as Joe lit his cigar for him. 'Nice stuff,' he said, as he puffed.'You ought to have it remodelled into a Batman suit.'

Joe, his face lit by the flickering match, said calmly, 'We've found a hooker who spent the night with Roberts during the 1979 primaries. She's prepared to say publicly that he asked her to perform some very unnatural acts. She has a friend who may be prepared to be a witness. All her facts and dates and times add up. And, most stunning of all, she has some Polaroids.'

Titus examined the tip of his cigar to make sure that it

was burning evenly. 'You've seen the Polaroids for yourself?'

'I've got copies of them here.' Joe reached under the driver's seat and produced a small buff envelope. He handed it to Titus and watched him closely for his reaction. Titus didn't open the envelope at first, but tapped it against Joe's sleeve.

'You've tape-recorded the girl's evidence?'

'Better. Video-recorded it. *And* the evidence given by her friend.'

'Her friend's a hooker too?'

'No. A chambermaid at the Las Vegas Futura.'

Titus opened the envelope and took out the Polaroids. 'Anything known?'

'On the chambermaid, no. Clean as a whistle. First-class witness.'

'Better and better,' said Titus. He held the Polaroids up to the Cadillac's dome light, and squinted at them narrowly.

'You want your eyeglasses?' asked Joe Jasper.

Titus shook his head. 'I see what's going on. A big fat guy in a toupee is lying on a hotel bed while a naked girl with very big gazongas is pissing straight into his mouth. Or am I mistaken? Maybe I've got it upside-down.'

'It's the correct way up,' said Joe, tightly.

'Well,' said Titus, rubbing his eyes. 'This is pretty bad news for our glorious President, wouldn't you say so? I mean, it's obviously him.'

Joe nodded.

Titus examined another Polaroid, then another. 'I don't know what the hell turns anybody on about doing that,' he remarked, turning one of the pictures around to show it to Joe. Joe shrugged, non-committal. Titus demanded: '*You* don't get turned on by doing that, do you?'

'No, sir.'

'Good,' said Titus, shuffling the pictures and then tucking them back in their envelope. 'Good.' Then, after a long silence. 'Wouldn't want anybody on my staff capable of enjoying something that I don't.'

'Right,' said Joe.

Titus wiped the side of his filthy wader on Joe's off-white rugs. Joe watched him in a kind of martyred fascination, while the names of several brand-names of auto upholstery cleaners went through his mind. Delco did quite a good one of their own, he remembered.

'Question is,' said Titus, 'what are we going to do about this lady? What's the best way to handle her?'

Joe tried a smile, but then he realized that Titus hadn't meant any double entendre, and quickly looked grave instead. 'First off, we have to protect her,' he said. 'The minute the media get a sniff of what's going on, they're going to be after her like hounds. And if I know anything at all about Uncle Roberts, the Unfortunate Accident Squad isn't going to be close behind.'

Titus nodded, and pursed his lips in serious acknowledgement. 'You're right, Joe. See to it. Fix her up in some dinky suburban house just outside of Washington. Rockville, some place like that. Keep her guarded, and make sure that she's available when we want her. Keep her happy. Give her good food, and lots of booze. Give her a couple of well-hung guys if that's what she wants. Dope, anything. But keep her secret and keep her ready. Better still, I might persuade Nadine to take care of her.'

'Yes, sir,' said Joe.

'Where is she now?' asked Titus.

'Fort Worth, seeing her mother. But Nielsen's with her.'

Titus was about to say something lashing, but held his tongue. Just because he personally hated the sight of his own mother, that didn't mean that other people shouldn't go to visit theirs. It was one of those human aberrations that couldn't be avoided, like excessive religiosity, or homosexuality, or reproduction furniture.

'We'd better get back to the hotel,' said Titus. 'I want to talk to Senator Rodney.'

'There's a phone right here,' offered Joe, picking up the car telephone, and switching it on.

'You think I want to talk to Senator Rodney in my waders?' demanded Titus.

'No, well, I guess not,' said Joe.

'Right then,' said Titus, folding his arms. 'Let's go.'

It took them only ten minutes to get back to the Elkswood Hotel, a white timber-lapped building overlooking the trees and the foggy curve of the Shenandoah River. Joe carried Titus' fishing-tackle for him as Titus walked with loudly-wobbling waders through the lobby, and up to the two-bedroomed suite where he was staying. A Secret Service agent was sitting outside on a folding chair, deep in The Playboy Advisor. He got up and stood uncomfortably to attention when Titus came past, but Titus absent-mindedly squeezed his shoulder, and said, 'Don't worry about it. Thanks for letting me get away for a couple of hours.'

Joe raised an interrogative eyebrow at the agent as he followed Titus into the room, and it was clear from the agent's slight inclination of his head that Titus had never been really alone. Another Secret Service agent would have been waiting patiently in the woods by the river, with a pair of binoculars and a high-powered rifle. Titus was too unpopular with too many nuts and oddballs to let him go off on his own, unprotected. Somebody had already taken two shots at him in Cleveland; and he had been hit on the side of the head in Fort Worth with a can of chick peas. His office received at least a dozen threatening letters a day, including a recurring promise of 'fiery execution' from somebody who called himself 'the Great Blast'.

'Fix me a drink, will you?' Titus told Joe, as he struggled the shoulder straps off his waders, and unbuttoned his shirt. 'No, it's over there, inside that thing that looks like a writing-desk.'

Joe opened the front of the desk, and found a bottle of Johnnie Walker Black Label, and lead crystal glasses. He poured out a large splash of whiskey, and carried the glass to where Titus was now wrapping a royal-blue towelling bathrobe tight around his hard, grey-pelted body.

Titus took his cigar out of his mouth just long enough to swallow a mouthful, and then coughed, 'Get me Rodney on the phone.'

Joe opened the black security briefcase which Titus carried with him wherever he went. It contained anti-bugging alarms, infra-red detection equipment, and a scrambler telephone which could be plugged straight into the wall socket like a normal telephone. He punched out the 414 number and waited for the call tone to disturb Senator Rodney in his large split-level house in Kenosha, Wisconsin. Senator Rodney was a keen fisherman, too, and most of the time he was able to spend back in his home state he devoted to the lake, and his 23-foot boat *Spirit of Southport*.

Titus stood by the window looking out across the hotel driveway. It had been foggy all day, and now that evening was drawing in, it was almost impossible to see down as far as the river. A time of ghosts, he thought to himself. A time for cold visitations, and prophesies to come true. He believed in destiny, particularly the kind of destiny which stalked through castle bedchambers carrying a bloody knife.

Titus had been a three-star general, Korea and Viet Nam. He had been the last general to leave Saigon; and he had always privately sworn to himself that he would be the first general back in again. At 52, he was fit, muscular, and handsome as an uncarved slab of Mount Rushmore. He exercised every morning, one hundred pressups, fifty burpees, twenty back stretches. He could punch a hole through an average modern plywood door with his fist, and he had once laid a nuclear disarmament demonstrator out cold. He wasn't rich. His father had owned a body shop in Peoria, Illinois. But he had been a tough and uncompromising soldier, and he made his way in politics with the help of powerful friends in the Pentagon, and campaign contributions from defence-related industries who were anxious that the tone of America's foreign policy should remain hotly belligerent.

Titus had once said, 'I would rather see America *melt*

than fall into Soviet hands.' *Newsweek* had dryly remarked that when Israel Zangwill had referred to America as 'the Great Melting-Pot', that wasn't exactly what he had had in mind.

Joe suddenly said, 'Senator Rodney? Good evening. Yes, sir. I'm sorry to disturb you at home. It's Joe Jasper. I have Mr Alexander for you. No, from the Shenandoah Valley.'

Titus took the phone, wiping it first on his towelling robe as if Joe Jasper might have left some slime on it. 'Ken? It's Titus. How are you doing? Yes. Sure. Did you hear the latest on RINC?'

Senator Rodney was suffering from a summer cold, and he wheezed a little. 'I heard that Marshall is already talking about standing down a third of our cruise missiles. Provided, of course, he gets some reasonable guarantees from Moscow on Afghanistan.'

'Yes, well, that's partly correct,' said Titus. He snapped his fingers at Joe to bring him over his drink. 'He's expecting some wider Soviet cutbacks in Europe as well; but still nothing that could possibly justify reducing our cruise missile complement by one-third.'

Senator Rodney sniffed, and coughed. 'There was an NBC editorial last night saying that he was going soft on the Soviets for no particular reason at all. Compromise without credit they called it. And considering the way he *used* to talk, before he was inaugurated . . . He used to make the hair stand up on the back of *my* neck, and you know what *I* feel about arms limitation.'

Titus swallowed more whiskey, and then said, 'We may have a way of stiffening him up again.'

'Is this why you're calling?' asked Senator Rodney, cautiously.

'That's right. Joe Jasper has just stumbled across some very interesting visual and recorded material which shows President Marshall Roberts in a position which you might euphemistically call compromising.'

'Witnesses?'

'The very best. The lady herself, and also another lady

of spotless character who happened to see them go to his suite together, and who had the unenviable task of cleaning up when they'd finished.'

'Cleaning up? What kind of cleaning up?'

'I always said you were prurient, Ken. Let's just say that our beloved President asked the lady to give him a little shower.'

There was a digestive silence. On the other side of the room, Joe Jasper thrust his hands into his pockets and gave a funny little shiver of pleasure. Then Senator Rodney said, 'What are you going to do? This is pretty hot stuff.'

'What I'm *not* going to do is rush around to the Oval Office waving a fistful of Polaroids and tell Marshall that he's got to call off the talks on Reduction In Nuclear Capability right away, or else.'

'But you don't want RINC to go very much further, do you? Nor do any of us. The further we go, the more promises Marshall makes, the more difficult it's going to be to extract ourselves with any kind of credibility. The worst thing you can do in politics is look as if you're always changing your mind. It's worse than being wrong.'

Titus said, 'I'm not going to put any kind of a squeeze on Marshall until I'm sure of my strategy. Let's be realistic. There's always the possibility that next week's RINC talks may break down of their own accord. Jesus, Ken, it took them three months to decide how long each delegate could spend in the men's room. And the point is that I don't want to waste the nastiest, smelliest piece of information I've ever had against Marshall, not if it isn't really necessary. This stuff could be even *more* useful at election time.'

'Still got your eye on the Lincoln Sitting Room?' asked Senator Rodney, with noticeable sharpness. Titus had often visited President Nixon in the Lincoln Sitting Room when the President was working there after dinner, and he had always made it obvious that he coveted it.

'When destiny calls, destiny calls,' said Titus, unmoved. 'Meanwhile, I'm going to install our principal witness in a house just outside of Washington, where we can get to her easily in case we need to produce her out of a hat; and I'm going to make sure that she's guarded day and night. Joe tells me the other lady is probably safer where she is, at home in Las Vegas. If we start putting pressure on Marshall because of what he did at the Las Vegas Futura, and one of their chambermaids goes mysteriously missing, then Marshall's men are going to know who to look for. The woman has a husband and children, and the last thing we want is to have her chickening out because Marshall has threatened to incinerate the family home.'

Senator Rodney said, 'This is going to be dangerous, you know. Marshall isn't going to like it one little bit.'

'I'm not frightened of Marshall.'

'Well, maybe not. But he won't take it lying down.'

'These days, I'm not so sure,' said Titus. 'All the guts seem to have dropped out of him. Don't you remember that speech he made at the San Francisco Cow Palace, during the primaries? All that talk about 'the light of liberty'? All that rhetoric about 'containing Communism'? Well, what happened to *that* when he promised the Soviets that America would keep hunter-killer satellites out of space? What happened to *that* when he pardoned that Soviet spy, what was his name, Nevsky? The light of liberty? You'd better believe it. Let me tell you, Ken – Marshall used to be the backbone of American political conservatism. Now he's the goddamned jellyfish.'

'I agree with you, Titus, you know that,' said Senator Rodney. 'The only problem is, he's strong. Marshall's very, very strong. Not just strong but paranoid. He's got a water-tight security set-up, and the best intelligence network since Eisenhower. It's going to be hard to get to him, I warn you, and even when you do, you won't be safe.'

'Safety,' Titus retorted, 'is not my primary consideration. I was at Changjin Reservoir, remember? I was at Khe Sanh. I didn't care about my safety then, and I don't care about it now. All I care about is putting a stop to these goddamned disastrous RINC agreements.'

'Well, I hope you won't be sorry,' said Senator Rodney. 'Keep me in touch, will you? When are you going back to Washington?'

'I'm going to drive back now. I have a few traps to set.'

'How was the fishing?'

'Good enough. A fair catch of trout. Not what it used to be, though. Maybe I've lost my touch.'

'There are bigger fish in Washington, Titus. Whales, and swordfish, and sharks, too. Plenty of sharks.'

Titus grunted in amusement, and then put the phone down. Joe Jasper said, 'You don't have to go back straight away, Mr Secretary. The girl won't be arriving in Washington until the day after tomorrow. You could have yourself one more day's fishing, if you wanted to.'

Titus finished his drink, and held out his glass for another one. 'Joe,' he said, 'fishing requires calm, and concentration. Right now, I'm not in the mood for it. I smell blood, thanks to you, Joe. I smell blood!'

'You're flattering me, Mr Secretary.'

Titus stared at him. Joe Jasper was such a weasel, such a sharp, nibbling, chiselling kind of a creature, that Titus found him compelling company. Joe would accept any insult, and perform any task, no matter how menial or degrading. He had first come to Washington with Nixon's West Coast *cosa nostra*, John Ehrlichman and Hank Haldeman and John Dean; but he had survived Watergate by attaching himself ('like a leech,' Titus often thought) to the caretaker administration which followed. Joe Jasper, despite his pale, unappealing face, despite his fastidious clothing, his Bijan shoes and his ostentatious gold rings, could worm his way in anywhere in Washington and get the goods on anyone. Anna Wuschinski, of the *Washington Post*, always called him Smeagol, after the snivelling, whining Gollum in *Lord of the Rings*. She was more accurate than she knew: Joe Jasper had a bite just as sharp as Smeagol, and just as much bony strength.

'Pay the check,' said Titus. 'I want to leave for Washington right away.'

'What about your luggage?'

'Send Wilkins down to collect it in the morning.'

Joe closed the communications briefcase, and gathered up the papers and notebooks which Titus had left around his suite. A thorough search would be made of the entire room tomorrow, to make sure that not even the slightest scrap of classified documentation had been left behind. Other, personal objects would be removed, too. It wouldn't do for the left-wing media to discover that the Secretary of State regularly ate Ex-Lax chocolate, nor that he used Chestnut-7 hair colorant.

Titus showered, and dressed in a grey slubbed mohair business suit, with a 2nd Infantry Division necktie, and a pocket handkerchief of exact isoceles sharpness. Meanwhile, Joe told the Secret Service man outside to arrange for Titus' official black Cadillac to be driven around to the front of the hotel, ready for the drive back to the capital. It was almost 6:30 p.m., a grainy Shenandoah evening, and because of the fog it was practically dark.

'We're all set to go, Mr Secretary,' said Joe, as Titus came out of the bedroom smelling of Jules aftershave, the last of his cigar still clenched between his teeth.

'Did you put in that call to my wife?'

'Yes, sir. She's decided to stay in Philadelphia one more night, but she's expected back by Thursday afternoon. Your stepchildren are both at home.'

'Shit,' said Titus, tautly tugging at his left cuff, and giving himself a last inspection in the mirror. 'That's all I need. Carl and Samantha, unlovability incarnate.'

Joe picked a wiry grey hair from Titus' shoulder. 'There was a call from Mr Nott, in Britain, but apparently it wasn't urgent. And Mr Yusef called, about the pipeline arrangement.'

'Any word from Schmidt?'

Joe shook his head. 'None. He seems to be playing this one really close to the chest.'

'Hm,' said Titus. Then, 'Let's go. We got everything?'

They left the suite and walked down the overheated, red-carpeted corridor. From inside one of the rooms they passed, there was the buzzing of somebody shaving, and from inside the next room, the muted burble of the *Mary Tyler Moore Show*. The Secret Service agent walked a pace or two behind them, whistling between his teeth. His colleague was waiting in the lobby, bulky, nondescript, with brush-cut hair and the kind of belted weekend suit they advertise in the Saturday newspapers.

'Mr Secretary,' nodded the second agent, as Titus came down the staircase to the lobby. 'Everything's ready. I'm real sorry you had to cut short your fishing.'

'Well, can't be helped,' smiled Titus, wryly. Over the hotel's reception desk there was a large stuffed pike, illuminated with a spotlight. The Front Royal Towers had always advertised itself as 'The Compleat Resort for Anglers'.

They descended the wet stone steps outside. Titus' official black limousine was parked just outside the wall that surrounded the sun patio. This evening, the sun patio was barely visible, puddled and mossy, with a solitary sundial dripping in the twilight like a forgotten tombstone.

'I think I'll travel with Joe,' Titus told his Secret Servicemen. 'Joe? I want to go over some of this RINC business with you. Maybe we can work out some angles.'

'Mr Jasper's car isn't bulletproofed, sir,' one of the agents pointed out. 'If there should be any kind of irregularity. . .'

'Don't you love it?' said Titus, cracking into a grin. 'They call an assassination attempt an "irregularity". Well, I can tell you son, the only irregularity that's going on around here concerns my bowels, and that's only because of those damned stepchildren of mine occupying both damned bathrooms for hours on end, making-up and shaving and popping their zits while I have to get myself off to the State Department. And let me tell you this is the first time in my life. I was so damned regular in Viet Nam that the USS *New Jersey* used to fire off its morning salvo as soon as their lookouts saw my toilet door open. Better than a goddamn naval chronometer.'

The Secret Servicemen shrugged, and walked across to the official limousine with that arms-swinging round-shouldered gait exclusive to bodyguards. Titus climbed into Joe Jasper's car, and said, 'How about another one of those cheap cigars of yours, Joe?' The car's windshield was beaded with moisture, so Joe switched on the wipers, and cleared it away.

'I've got to tell you, this is the first time I've gladly cut a fishing-trip short,' said Titus. 'You've got to tell me how you managed to lay your hands on that stuff. That was a stroke of genius. You hear that? I'm paying you a compliment.'

Joe started the engine. 'The whole thing came to light when I was talking to a man called Iacono in Atlantic City. He simply said that he'd met a girl who was boasting that she'd once –'

With a shattering crash, like the bow of an icebreaker cleaving its way into a glacier, the car's windshield imploded, and dumped a slushy pile of sparkling broken glass into their laps. A nano-second later, the car rose and bucked and dipped on its suspension.

Then they heard the explosion, so loud that it deafened them, and their ears sang as they saw Titus' huge black polished limousine rise into the air, its doors flapping open as if it were desperately trying to fly, turning over on its back twenty feet above them, tumbling, swallow-diving, and then rolling over and over on to the sun patio, crushed, smashed, and still rolling as it hit the sundial and broke through the stone balustrade which overlooked the garden.

There was a second explosion, and Titus said tightly, 'Gas tank.' A ball of flame licked up into the fog, and then the Cadillac was blazing fiercely from end to end, with a soft and a hungry roar which Titus hadn't heard since Nam.

He climbed out of the car, brushing showers of glass

off his suit. Joe said, 'Titus – Mr Secretary – we ought to get the hell out of here. They may have marksmen.'

But Titus ignored him, and walked across to the ten-foot wide hole in the brick-paved driveway where the explosives had gone off. The device had probably been slipped under the Cadillac while it was parked there a few minutes ago, and been detonated by remote control. Titus looked narrowly up at the hotel windows, checking one after the other, but they were all blank and blind and gave nothing away.

He climbed the low stone wall on to the sun patio and walked across the scoured, battered flagstones. The car was still burning, although its bodywork was already blackened and blistered, and there was more smoke now than flame. Hanging from the passenger window, he saw a human hand, charred, shrivelled-up, bare to the bone, but with the tips of its fingers still spouting little flames like a menorah. There was something ominous and super-natural about it, and Titus bit his lip and turned away, disturbed.

Joe came hurrying over with his gun held high in his left hand. It was a gigantic .357 revolver, and if he had ever fired it, the recoil would probably have knocked him flat. But he had only bought it to impress Dan Duggan of the National Rifle Association that he was doing his bit to uphold the spirit of the Second Amendment. He said, 'Holy Christ,' when he saw the burning car, and stopped where he was.

People were running down the steps of the hotel, and opening up their windows. Lights were being switched on everywhere. Somebody said, 'Call an ambulance. There's been an accident.'

An accident? thought Titus. He started to walk back to the car, and he was trembling like an old man of 80. No, not an accident. An *irregularity* that's what it was. And he dearly and deeply wanted to know who was responsible.

Joe said, 'Holy Christ,' again, and then suddenly began to walk after him.

Five

Chief of Police Walter Ruse considered himself to be a true Westerner, in the sense that he believed in justice being fair, prompt, and memorable. He would not uncommonly deal with traffic offenders by giving them a swift hard kick in the pants, rather than write them a ticket; and all of Phoenix remembered the time when he had caught the Yapton boys for drunk driving on Van Buren Street, and knocked their heads together so hard that their lawyer had successfully pleaded in court that they had already been punished to the limits of the law.

He was a big man, huge-bellied, with a fat, tanned face, and two little near-together eyes the colour of cold steel. Kathy Forbes always said that his eyes reminded her of two nails sticking in a pig's behind. Chief Ruse always said that Kathy Forbes reminded *him* of a medium-class madame. There was little love lost between the Press and the Police department in Phoenix; particularly that summer.

Because of his direct attitude to justice, Chief Ruse was not at all happy with the obvious complexities of the homicide on Oasis Drive. Here was a woman found with her head sawn off, one of the most brutal attacks he'd ever seen. Yet there was no apparent motive, no robbery, no rape, no vandalism, not even 'Death to Pigs' scrawled in blood on the wall. Just her head sawn off; and, worse, her head was missing. Police dogs had searched the area all morning and all they had come up with so far was an unpleasantly dead coyote. Chief Ruse hoped very much that this wasn't going to be the beginning of one of those inexplicable new fashions in homicide. He had enough to contend with right now, keeping the husbands and wives of Phoenix from blowing themselves away with their own handguns. It always happened in the summer, when the temperature hit the high 80s. Chief Ruse took off his large

61

Western hat and wiped the inside of the brim with his handkerchief, and sniffed.

The headless body had just been taken away. Chief Ruse heard the ambulance siren warbling away down 36th Street. He stood with his hands on the bulges of fat which overhung his hips, and contemplated with absent-minded seriousness the hysterical splashes of blood on the walls and bedspread, and the dark tide of coagulated gore which spread out over the white carpet beneath his feet like a monstrous scab. He heard the front door of the house close behind him, but he didn't turn around. He knew who it was. Lieutenant Berridge, humming to himself. Berridge was arguably the best homicide detective that Phoenix had seen in fifteen years – young, fit, intelligent, well-trained and well-experienced. Chief Ruse found him unbearable, not only because he was so damned *good*, but because he looked like one of those toothy California tennis-players, all flashing incisors and tanned knees, and because he was only 31 years old, and because he had thick sun-blond hair and sharp blue eyes, and because his wife Stella was exactly the same, a twin almost-blonde, athletic and wholesome; and because he was such a conceited paralysing pain in the ass. *And* because he would never keep still, but was always hopping or jumping or shuffling around as if he were warming up for a basketball contest.

'You want to tell me *your* opinion, chief?' asked Berridge, lacing his fingers together and popping all his knuckles, one after the other, in a controlled salvo. Chief Ruse closed his eyes. He hated people who made gratuitous noises with their body. He said, without opening his eyes, 'Whatever opinion *I* happen to have, I know that *you've* got yourself an opinion which is a hundred times more dynamic, so why don't you tell me what it is now and get it over with?'

'Right, okay,' said Berridge, raising his finger instantaneously to make point one. 'There isn't any question that we have some unusual difficulties here, particularly as far as identification is concerned. But I *do* think that we can safely assume that the dead woman is in fact Mrs Margot Schneider, widow of the late Major Rudolph Schneider, of the United States Air Force. Everything we have here supports that assumption. We have no ID. No Social Security card. In fact, we have nothing with a picture. But we do have her pension papers, and when I checked with Luke Air Force Base, they confirmed her age and her general appearance – and they tally. Her doctor confirmed her blood group, which is another plus. What's more, there are letters in her writing-table from old girlfriends in the service, going right back to 1951.'

Chief Ruse opened his eyes, and turned around with fat Michelin chins to stare at Berridge as if the young lieutenant were babbling complete nonsense. But Berridge, though hyper-active, was too arrogant to allow Ruse's famous death-ray stare to put him off. He raised a second finger, and said, 'As far as I'm concerned, the most important question is not *who* she is, or *why* she was murdered, but *why would anybody want to take her head*? Don't you agree? And, personally, I think there are three possible answers to that. One, her killers may have wanted to remove all traces of some unusual and incriminating head-wound. Perhaps she was killed with something incredibly specialized, like a glazier's hammer, or a carpet-fitter's tool – which is possible, but not particularly likely. Second, they may have taken it for kicks.'

'You mean they wanted to play soccer with it?'

This time, Berridge was genuinely startled. But he managed to say, in words that fell out like a shower of loose teeth, 'They may have taken it for some kind of *ritual*, that's what I mean. Sexual, or magical. *Those* sort of kicks.'

'And the third possibility?'

'The third possibility is that they may have taken her head as proof to some third party that they'd actually killed her.'

'In other words, our poor Air Force widow was killed by contract? *Bring Me The Head Of Alfredo Garcia*, that kind of stuff?'

'That's the inference, yes.'

Chief Ruse slowly scratched the capacious seat of his pants. 'Well, now,' he said, 'those are all possibilities. But they still don't get us any nearer to finding out who killed her, and why.'

'On the contrary, chief,' argued Berridge. 'The first thing we should do is run a computer make on any violent crimes which have involved blows to the head with unusual weapons. Then run a second make on any sex or black magic cults which hold the human head or skull to be particularly significant. And finally a make on any contract killings in which the head or other parts of the body were taken as proof of death.'

There was a chime at the front door. Berridge said, 'I'll get it. It's probably the food I ordered.'

'You ordered *food*?'

Berridge looked surprised. 'I shall probably be working on this thing for the rest of the night. Besides, it's only a diet burger.'

'God help us,' breathed Chief Ruse, hitching up his pants. 'A diet burger.'

There was talking by the front door. After a while, Chief Ruse went out into the corridor, and said, 'Berridge? What's going on?'

'Ah, chief, there you are,' said a girl's voice. 'I've been looking for you everywhere. They told me you went downtown with the coroner.'

'I never ride with stiffs,' said Chief Ruse. 'Now get your tail out of here, Miss Forbes. This is a police prohibited area.'

The officer at the door said, 'I'm sorry, chief, she just pushed past me.'

Berridge said, 'It's okay, chief. We can let in the star reporter from *The Arizona Flag*, can't we? Maybe she can give us some assistance.'

'Another damned Californian,' grumbled Chief Ruse.

'I'm not, as a matter of accuracy,' said Kathy, unbuckling her black shoulder-bag so that she could check her tape-recorder. She gave Chief Ruse a wide, toothy grin. 'I was born in Tucson, near Randolph Park. I was raised in Phoenix, and I only went to Los Angeles when I was fourteen years old.'

'Thanks for the c.v.,' said Chief Ruse. 'Now, what can you possibly want to know that you haven't already been told? The body's gone, the photographers have gone, the forensic team have made their initial studies and they're going to be back tomorrow to do a little more. Everything's running routinely.'

'Do you have any theories?' asked Kathy.

'Yes,' said Chief Ruse flatly, 'I suspect that Mrs Schneider was murdered.'

Kathy didn't blink. 'How about you, lieutenant? Any ideas?'

'Don't ask him,' Chief Ruse interrupted. 'According to him, Mrs Schneider was decapitated either by someone who didn't want us to know that they'd hit her over the head with some kind of weird object, like a piano; or some kind of sex-magic lunatics who get off on severed heads; or a hit-man who needed a souvenir to prove that he'd done what he was paid for.'

'Is that right?' Kathy asked Lieutenant Berridge.

Berridge drummed his fingers in a complicated tempo on the door-frame. 'Not exactly. But I guess you could say that it's close enough.'

'So I can say that you're looking for a piano-wielding sex-magic madman with a neurosis about being believed by his employers?'

'Miss Forbes –' burst out Chief Ruse. But Berridge raised his hand to quiet him down, and laughed. 'Come on, chief, she's deliberately goading you. You should know that. Miss Forbes, I have to congratulate you on your technique.'

'Lieutenant Berridge is married, by the way,' said Chief Ruse, hitching up his belt again, and sniffing.

'Maybe we'd better go through to the kitchen,' suggested Berridge. 'It's kind of gory right here.'

He took Kathy's arm and guided her through to Margot Schneider's neat wood-panelled kitchen. 'You won't touch anything, will you?' he told her. 'The forensic boys

65

have finished in the murder room, but they have to go over the whole house.'

On the kitchen wall, next to the icebox, was a memo pad with the legend, *'Don't forget brocc! also bank I's check!'* A half-finished cup of coffee had been left on the worktop, still impressed with the pink lipstick of a woman who now had no head. Lieutenant Berridge thrust his hands in his pockets and looked around, and said, 'Pretty strange, isn't it? The last person who came into this kitchen is dead.'

Chief Ruse followed them in, and folded his arms over his belly. 'I don't want to rush you, Miss Forbes, but I'm going to rush you. Three questions and then that's it. I have a duty to *all* of the Phoenix media, not just to *The Flag.*'

'Oh, sure, I understand,' said Kathy. 'Tell me – do you happen to have any photographs of the victim – anything that we could publish?'

Chief Ruse glanced at Lieutenant Berridge uneasily. The question of photographs was one which he would have preferred to hold over until tomorrow, or even the day after tomorrow. The truth of the matter was that they had found no photographs of the murdered woman at all, not even amongst the framed pictures of her family on the sitting-room table. If there were any photograph albums in the house, they hadn't located them yet; and even when they had sent a sergeant around to Luke Air Force Base this afternoon to check on any photographs the Air Force might have on file of social gatherings and parties, they had found no identifiable picture of Margot Schneider in any of them. Plenty of Major Rudolph Schneider, smiling and holding up glasses of champagne. Even one tantalizing picture showing him waltzing with Mrs Schneider – she with her back to the camera. But that was the only one, and it was impossible to make a positive identification from that. It seemed, oddly, as if Margot Schneider had never in her life been photographed. Even her Social Security card was missing.

'Er, we have *some* pictures, but we have to show them

to her next-of-kin first,' Lieutenant Berridge extemporized. 'You understand how it is.'

'May I see one?'

Chief Ruse shook his head. 'Not at this time. And not ahead of any of the other media.'

'Well, suit yourself,' said Kathy. 'But I have to tell you that Mrs Margot Schneider seems to have been the world's least-photographed human being. None of her neighbours have pictures of her. The Arizona Biltmore doesn't have any pictures of her, despite the fact she often used to go to dinners and social functions there. And, of course, we can't even photograph her dead.'

'Right,' nodded Lieutenant Berridge. 'No head.' It sounded like a comic one-line.

Kathy said, 'Hasn't it occurred to you that the murderer might have cut her head off simply to prevent you from finding out who she was?'

'She was Margot Schneider,' said Lieutenant Berridge. 'All the papers prove it. She had pension papers, letters from friends. She was wearing one slipper when she died and that slipper was bought from the Scottsdale Shopping Mall nine weeks ago by Margot M. Schneider. She used her American Express card. Listen, there are theories in homicide cases and there are wild guesses. Sometimes, very rarely, the wild guesses pay off. But if we begin to doubt the overwhelming circumstantial and documentary evidence that the murder victim was Margot Schneider, then we're going to complicate ourselves up our own assholes. Chief Ruse and I don't usually see eye-to-eye on very much when it comes to detective work, but I think we're in agreement about that. The fundamental undeniable fact is that a woman like Margot Schneider has been murdered by decapitation. Now we have to work on the probable theories about *why* she was decapitated. That's what we're doing, and that's all. All I can say in our favour is that we're very good at what we do. We're the best.'

Kathy Forbes was silent for a moment. Berridge looked at her with patronizing interest and thought for the first time how pretty she was. She had dark shoulder-length hair, but today it was tightly tied back with a scarlet-and-yellow silk scarf. Her face was squarish, with high cheekbones and wide hazel-brown eyes. She had one of those nice short, straight noses he always liked, and a wide mouth that looked as if it could smile a lot and talk a lot and kiss a lot. Her figure wasn't anything to complain about, either, in spite of her severe grey linen suit and her sheer grey stockings (seamed, too – he liked that). He thought: 25-years-old, married once and probably divorced, no children, a small-time career girl, Christopher Cross fan and aerobics enthusiast. A feminist until she can find a man who can really take care of her. One hundred per cent wholesome American girl, no dental fillings, closely-depilated underarms, sheer nylon panties, warm well-filled stockings. Breasts that are just a little too large to hold in one hand. At least 10% of US RDA, Ms Kathy Forbes, no doubt about it.

'If you want to discuss the theories in more detail, I can at least do *that* with you,' suggested Berridge. His voice dropped almost an octave. 'I don't think I really want to do it here, though. Maybe a restaurant? I haven't eaten all day.'

'Didn't you order a diet burger?' asked Chief Ruse, sarcastically.

'A diet burger?' asked Berridge, with an uncomfortable laugh. 'What the hell would I need with a diet burger?'

'Maybe you could slim down your head,' said Chief Ruse.

There was another chime at the door and Chief Ruse went to answer it. It was Jackson Dawes from the mayor's office, wanting to talk about the political side of this murder. 'We don't want Phoenix to look like the kind of place where . . .' murmur, murmur. 'Well, you understand what I'm saying, I'm not trying to put a lid on it, but . . .'

Kathy Forbes said to Berridge, 'You're really married?'

'Separated. Considering divorce. Mary never liked the idea of police work. It's the hours, mainly. She's a very

68

systematic kind of a lady, doesn't like her life to be full of surprises.'

'Are you really sure this was Margot Schneider? The woman who got beheaded?'

'You want to see the evidence? There's no question.'

'Then why did they do it? Why did they cut her head off? And why did they kill her, if she was nobody more important than a plain old Air Force widow? All the neighbours said she was sweet. Why should anybody want to kill a woman like that?'

Berridge folded a stick of gum into his mouth, and shrugged. Then, remembering his manners, he offered Kathy a piece. 'Juicy Fruit?'

'No, thanks. I think I'd better be getting back to the office. I want to file my story by ten.'

'You don't want dinner? We could go to Mother Tucker's, it's on the way back to town. They have a terrific salad cart.'

'Well . . . maybe.'

But at that moment Chief Ruse came back into the kitchen, and slapped Berridge on the back. 'There isn't any need for you to stay any later, Lieutenant. I'm sure Stella will be missing you as much as anybody ever can miss you.'

'Stella?' asked Kathy.

'The delectable Mrs Berridge, Ms Forbes. Our ace detective here has one of the tastiest wives on the force. It makes you sick, doesn't it? Sick to your stomach.'

Kathy smiled at Berridge tartly. Berridge, in spite of his bravado, couldn't help blushing. 'Yes, chief,' said Kathy. 'It *does* make you sick.'

'Do you need a ride back to town?' Berridge asked her. '*Without* stopping anywhere to eat.'

'No, thank you. I have my own car.'

'In that case, you can give me a ride. Just wait a couple of minutes while I make sure I've got everything. Chief, do you want to meet for breakfast tomorrow morning – say seven o'clock? I really want to run over this computer thing.'

Kathy waited in the kitchen while Chief Ruse and Lieutenant Berridge arranged meetings for the following day. She felt tired now; she had been up at six, as soon as news of Margot Schneider's murder had broken. She felt like a cigarette, but it was nine weeks since she had smoked her last, and she was determined to keep up her record. This time, it was going to be for keeps. She didn't want to be a slave to anything or anyone.

Lieutenant Berridge had been wrong about her age – she was 29 – but right about her divorce. In Los Angeles, six years ago, she had married an incandescently brilliant young actor, David Forbes, and for four years they had lived a life of fun and laughter and beach-parties and dancing at dawn. Then she had come home from a trip to Arizona to find David in bed with two wide-eyed girls of 13 and 14, and the world had split open like a broken alabaster egg.

Maybe she should have been more sophisticated about it, more Hollywood. After all, men needed their fun. But every single reaction inside her had been negative. She had married David for ever, however old-fashioned that seemed to be, and if it wasn't going to be for ever, then it wasn't going to be for one more minute. She had walked out.

She hadn't asked him for anything, not even a half-share in their Westwood apartment. But he had given her his Mirada, probably on the advice of his lawyer, and, gratuitously, his complete collection of Miró lithographs. That had been the first thing he had ever said to her, 'Come up and see my lithographs.'

While she waited, a police officer came into the kitchen with a large folder. He was slightly-built, round-shouldered, with a moustache, one of those police officers who always seemed to be called Rizzo or Wuschinsky, and who always seem to be apologizing, even when they bust you. He put down a messy collection of magazines and photographs and papers on the kitchen table and said, 'You seen Lieutenant Berridge? I was supposed to hand over all this stuff to Lieutenant Berridge.'

70

'He'll be back directly,' said Kathy. 'He's just talking to Chief Ruse.'

'Oh, right. Well, can I leave these here? You'll make sure that Lieutenant Berridge gets them? I have to get home. It's my birthday, would you believe, and my wife's been planning this surprise party for weeks. They'll all be hiding in the closet bursting their goddamned bladders if I don't get back there and act like I don't know what's going on.'

'Okay,' smiled Kathy. She took the file and shuffled it straight. 'What shall I say your name was?'

'Russo. Officer Russo. They'll know who you mean.'

'Not Rizzo?'

The policeman looked at her strangely. *'Rizzo?'* he asked.

'It's a private joke,' said Kathy. 'I'm sorry. I'll give these papers to Lieutenant Berridge for you.'

'It's the stuff from Mrs Schneider's attic,' said Russo/Rizzo. 'There was nothing else up there, only clothes.'

'All right,' said Kathy.

Officer Russo left and Kathy was alone in the kitchen with Mrs Schneider's papers. There was no question that she wasn't going to look at them: the *Flag's* ace girl reporter? She leafed through them hurriedly, her eyes flicking across insurance policies, invoices, lawyer's bills, garage estimates, a small assembly of news-cuttings about Clark Gable, of all people, fastened together with a rusty paper-clip; a torn review of *The Misfits* (why *The Misfits*, of all movies?); and then something which stopped her cold. A Polaroid photograph, an *old* Polaroid photograph, because it was yellowed and blotchy and black-and-white, of a man who was smiling into the sunshine and just about to push back his thick shock of hair, a man whose face she had seen a thousand times before in news and magazine photographs, and yet never quite in this pose, never quite from this particular angle. It was John F Kennedy, no doubt about it. Smiling, alive, and wearing a white-short-sleeved tennis shirt. So alive, in fact, that he

71

had signed the Polaroid in ballpen: 'For N, special memories, P.'

'P'? she thought to herself. It was certainly John F Kennedy, nobody else. Maybe 'P' stood for 'President', or some other pet name. But who was 'N'? Maybe he had been writing 'M' for 'Margot'. She frowned at the Polaroid for almost two or three minutes before she heard Chief Ruse and Lieutenant Berridge come out of the murder room, and Lieutenant Berridge saying, ' . . . the blood tests tomorrow and then we can check with her doctor. Well, sure.'

She tucked the Polaroid into her suit pocket, and propped her mouth into an innocent smile. Lieutenant Berridge came into the kitchen and said, 'How're you doing? You still going to give me that ride?'

'If you want,' she smiled. 'By the way, some officer called Rizzo left these papers for you.'

'Rizzo?'

'Russo. Same difference.'

Lieutenant Berridge pulled a face. 'No wonder they never spell my name right in the goddamned newspapers. What did the *Star* call me last week? "Burberry." I've had "Bullsbridge" before now.'

Kathy's car was parked outside on the kerb. It was almost dark now, on Oasis Drive, except for a single gleam of sunset over the Phoenix Mountains. Under the evening clouds, the lights of Paradise Valley and Phoenix twinkled and shimmered, grids of diamonds in the desert evening, hope and desperation and hard work and fear, each represented by a single white sparkling light. Lieutenant Berridge opened the Mirada's passenger door, and said, 'Nice night. Mind if I smoke?'

Kathy started the engine, and pulled away from the kerb. 'You really think you're going to catch this joker?' she asked him, as he snapped his lighter and noisily sucked in smoke.

'We'll get him.'

'And you really think that Margot Schneider was Margot Schneider? And that Margot Schneider was the woman who got killed?'

'What other woman could it possibly be?' Lieutenant Berridge demanded. 'Is there another woman who wears your slippers and your nightwear and your make-up, and lives in your house?'

'No. Of course not.'

'Well, do you think it's likely that Margot Schneider had a woman like that in *her* house?'

Kathy made a left into 24th Street. 'It's a pretty heavy murder, all the same,' she said. 'Can you imagine how much strength that guy must have had? To cut her head off like that, in one?'

Lieutenant Berridge shrugged.

'And what does Chief Ruse think about it?' asked Kathy. 'He seems pretty upset.'

'Well, sure he is. Three streets to the east, and the whole thing would have been out of his jurisdiction, and dumped in the laps of Paradise Valley. But, don't you worry, we'll find out who did it. Crimes like this one have a way of solving themselves when you least expect it.'

'They solve *themselves*? Isn't that going to put you out of a job?'

They were passing the King of Beef restaurant, on the corner of Campbell Avenue. Lieutenant Berridge said, 'You're sure I can't interest you in a steak?'

Kathy patted his knee, and smiled indulgently. 'I should go home to Stella, lieutenant, if I were you. She'll be wondering where you are, even if Mary isn't.'

Lieutenant Berridge flipped open the car's ashtray and stubbed out his cigarette. 'Screw you, Lois Lane,' he told her.

Six

Unlike most Western drinking establishments, the bar they called 'Hank's' was not one of those concrete bunkers with freezing cold air-conditioning, plastic venetian blinds and a men's room that looked as if it had recently been used as a setting for a John Wayne fight movie. It didn't even have one of those blue-and-red neon signs in the window saying 'Coors' or 'Bud' or 'Eats.'

It was an old-fashioned parlour, in the only elegant house in the whole of Apache Junction, a gingerbread creation that had been built in the days of the Lost Dutchman Mine by an enterprising but ill-starred madame called Regina Smibbs. 'Hank' was a bald-headed one-time piano salesman called Rufus McNeice, whose wife had never held with drinking. Rufus had lived a double life for thirty years, preaching temperance in public but privately sneaking snorts from a flask which he attached to the underside of his car with magnets. When his wife had died in 1972, Hank had applied for a liquor licence, and opened up a bar where he wanted a bar the most, in his own front parlour.

Daniel was sitting there with Cara when Ronald Reagan Kinishba came in, fully dressed in black motorcycling leathers, swinging his black crash-helmet. He was tall, with a handsome pock-marked face and a nose that looked as if it had been modelled on the beak of a golden eagle. He raised his hand in greeting to Hank, behind the bar, and then came over and put down his helmet on the table in front of Daniel.

'Hi, Ronald,' said Daniel. 'How are you doing?'

Ronald unzipped about ten different zippers, and took off his jacket, hanging it over the back of the chair. Underneath he wore a turquoise T-shirt that was emblazoned with the legend 'Remember Ah-jon-jon.'

'Well, I'm fine,' he said, in his husky voice. 'Are you going to buy me a beer?'

'This is Cara,' said Daniel. Cara nodded, and said, 'Hi.'
Ronald planted his elbow on the table and examined her
with some interest. She was wearing a tight pink T-shirt,
through which her nipples showed as dark and provocative smudges; and an even tighter pair of pink Bermuda
shorts.

'Daniel been treating you good?' asked Ronald.

Cara laid her hand on top of Daniel's and smiled. 'As
good as any man could, thank you.'

'Cara's from South Dakota,' said Daniel. 'What do you
want? Coors Lite?'

'That'll do,' said Ronald. Then, to Cara, 'Are you passing through, honey, or staying?'

'A little of each,' said Cara.

'You be careful of this guy,' Ronald warned her. 'He
has a very weird effect on women. In fact, he has a weird
effect on everybody. The Indians have a word for guys
like him.'

'Oh, yes?' said Cara.

'Sure. They call them "*moksois*." '

'What does that mean?' giggled Cara.

Ronald looked at her with great mock-seriousness. 'Pot-
belly,' he said. Then he laughed out loud.

'Don't take any notice,' said Daniel.

Hank brought them over two Lites, and a pina colada
for Cara. 'Willy coming in tonight?' he wanted to know.

'He was supposed to be here by ten,' said Daniel. 'But,
well, you know what he's like. Gets himself involved.'

'Not just with work, either,' grinned Ronald, dragging
his chair six inches nearer to Cara, and staring at her with
undisguised appreciation.

'You keep your distance,' Daniel warned him.

'Be very careful,' Ronald murmured to Cara. 'He's very
possessive, as well as being crazy. If he catches you even
glancing at another guy, he'll kill you. You don't have any
idea what you've let yourself in for.'

Cara giggled again, and said to Daniel, 'He's cute. Don't
you think so?'

'Cute? Is a sidewinder cute?'

'Oh, come on,' said Cara.

They talked and teased and drank for another hour, until well past eleven o'clock. Then Daniel checked his watch again, and said, 'This isn't like Willy, you know. He's never on time, but he's never as late as this. Particularly when there's drinking time a-wasting.'

'Maybe they gave him extra duty,' suggested Ronald.

'Why *did* your parents call you Ronald Reagan?' asked Cara.

Ronald shrugged. 'They weren't too bright, either of them. Well, they were quite *bright*, but they weren't educated. They thought that if they named me after a famous white hero, I'd find it easier to get on in the white man's world. The only famous white hero they knew was Ronald Reagan.'

'At least they didn't call you Mickey Rooney,' said Cara.

Daniel fidgeted for a while, and then said, 'I think I'll call the base. Maybe he's been held up.'

'Well, why don't you just go do that,' said Ronald, inching even closer to Cara. 'And – please – take as long as you like.'

Pete Burns the deputy sheriff came in, and gave them a wave of acknowledgement. He was a placid, big-bellied man, but he had booked Ronald eight times in two years for speeding, and he had always made it quite clear that he would happily run any citizen of Apache Junction straight into the pokey at no notice flat if he or she even *looked* as if they were doing anything illegal. 'Laws don't get passed to get mocked,' he used to say, too often for it to be interesting. Ronald, just as often, had accused him of 'legislative flatulence'.

Daniel went out into the hall. Hank had fixed a payphone by the front door, next to the elephant's-foot umbrella stand. Daniel thumbed in a dime and dialled 988 2611, the number of Williams Air Force Base.

Inside the parlour, Ronald was saying to Cara, 'What's a foxy-looking lady doing with a nice tame guy like Daniel? Did you ever ride on the back of a motorcycle? Pillion?

76

The wind in your hair, the stars in your eyes, and 749 cc of throbbing engine clutched between your thighs?'

Cara said, 'Daniel's *cute.*'

'Listen, nobody said he wasn't. But I'm talking about four transverse-mounted cylinders, double overhead cams, transistorized pointless ignition and Pentroof heads.'

Cara said, 'You're talking about *what*?'

Just then, Daniel came back in again. He looked perplexed. He sat down and said, 'He's not there. They say he hasn't been there all day.'

'Well, maybe he hasn't.'

'No, he specifically told me he was going to go back to the armoury to run some tests.'

'Maybe he changed his mind.'

'It wasn't the kind of thing he was going to change his mind about. It was something urgent.'

Ronald pulled a face. 'I don't know what to say. If he isn't there, he isn't there.'

Daniel finished his beer. Maybe Ronald was right, and maybe he was just being ridiculous. But he couldn't help remembering what Willy had been telling him so earnestly this morning: all that stuff about missiles that wouldn't work against Soviet radar signatures. All that stuff about 'heads will roll'. And now, he wasn't there.

Cara said, 'You don't have to worry. He's a grown-up man. He's a major in the Air Force, for Christ's sake. I'm sure he can look after himself. Well, I hope to God he can look after himself, when you think that he's supposed to be looking after *us*.'

Ronald suggested, 'How about another beer? Especially if you're buying.'

Daniel bit at his thumbnail. 'Listen,' he said. 'How about a quick ride down to the base, just to make *sure* he's not there?'

'Are you kidding?'

'I'm just worried, that's all. Willy positively and definitely said that he was going to be working in the armoury for most of the day, and that he was going to be round here at ten.'

Ronald leaned back in his chair in exasperation. 'You know what this is, don't you? A cheap way of getting me out of here, so that I won't be able to impress your girl-friend any more with my obviously superior intelligence and clearly superior looks.'

'You're nuts,' said Daniel. 'Do you want to take me down there or not?'

'Okay,' agreed Ronald, reluctantly. 'I guess I wanted to try out my new tune job anyway.'

'And what am I supposed to do, while you're speeding like the Seventh Cavalry to Williams Air Force Base?' Cara demanded.

Daniel leaned over and kissed her cheek. 'You can go back to the diner and tell Mrs Koperwas that she can go home and give Mr Koperwas his Hungry Man dinner. And if Susie's still awake, you can switch off her television and paddle her fanny.'

'Isn't it true about history?' said Cara, finishing her pina colada. 'The men get the fun and the women get to sit around and wait for them to come home.'

But outside the bar, in the darkness, as Ronald went to get his motorcycle, Cara slid her arm around Daniel's waist, and pressed her breasts against him, and kissed him once, twice, three times, with a passion he wouldn't easily forget. 'You won't be long, will you?' she breathed in his ear. 'I'll be waiting for you, when you come back. And I mean, waiting.'

Daniel kissed her back and cupped the firm rounded cheeks of her bottom in his hands. 'You know something,' he whispered back at her. 'You have the finest ass since the Sabine women.'

'All right, cut the groping,' said Ronald, wheeling up his shiny black Nighthawk. 'If there's one thing I dislike more than petty meanness, like not buying me a second beer, it's smugness, like feeling up this delicious red-headed young lady right in front of me.'

'You've got your bike to love, what more do you want?' asked Daniel.

Ronald shrugged. 'It's okay, I guess. It's just that it leaves oil on the sheets.'

Cara blew Daniel a last kiss, and then walked back along the side of the highway to the diner. Under the fluorescent lights, she cast four shadows, one to each point of the compass. 'That's some girl,' said Ronald, straddling his motorcycle and fastening his helmet. 'Just your type, too. Travel-stained, worldly-wise, with a used but pretty face and huge but shapely knockers.'

Daniel climbed on to the high black-leather pillion seat and grasped Ronald tightly around the waist. 'Did anyone ever tell you that Indians were only supposed to grunt, and yodel, and refer to everyone they met as "kemo sabay"?'

Ronald turned around and frowned at him. "Kemo sabay"? What's that? Some kind of wine?'

'Just move your ass,' said Daniel, impatiently.

Ronald kicked the Nighthawk into life. It blared and burbled as Ronald revved it up; and then they were away, bouncing across the dusty roadside, overtaking Cara and giving her a last berrp-berrp on the horn before roaring away westwards on Route 60 towards Mesa.

As far as Ronald was concerned, there were only two speeds on a motorcycle: flat-out and Geronimo. Daniel clung desperately on to his leather jacket as Ronald hurtled into the darkness, insects pattering on his helmet like soft shrapnel. The motorcycle weaved and angled from one side of the road to the other, overtaking trucks, cars, and a vast tractor-trailer carrying livestock. 'Tomorrow's cheeseburgers!' shouted Ronald, as he accelerated past the tractor and topped 110 mph. Daniel closed his eyes and tried not to think what would happen if they hit a stone or a stray animal or an unlit truck.

They made a left on South Lindsay and Ronald opened up the throttle again as they headed southwards towards the community of Gilbert, and Williams Air Force Base. A Hercules transport plane was landing from the south-east, its lights winking as it descended over the desert like a huge black Roc. They touched 100 mph between Southern Avenue and Base Line Road and Ronald let out a wild Indian whoop as they streaked across the intersection without stopping.

At last they were slowing down and turning into the main gates of Williams Air Force Base, with Ronald repeatedly bipping the engine. An Air Force sentry came forward and said, 'Identification, please?' His face under his white steel helmet was as bland as a bowlful of hominy, but there was a tensile twang in his voice which made it clear that nobody was going to get past here without all the proper passes, especially an Indian in black leather and a skinny guy with a face as white as Stan Laurel's from the 100 mph wind.

'I came to see Major William Monahan,' said Daniel. 'He told me this morning he was going to be working in the armoury. Maybe you could call him up and tell him I'm here.'

The sentry said, 'What's your name please? Do you have any identification?'

Daniel reached into his back pants pocket and handed the sentry his Social Security card. The sentry peered at it from beneath his helmet, and said, 'Daniel F. Korvitz?'

'That's right.'

'Okay, then, hold on for just one moment.' The sentry went back to his brightly-lit office and picked up the telephone. He seemed to be talking to someone for almost five minutes, and meanwhile Daniel and Ronald waited for him, still astride the motorcycle, under the dazzling floods which illuminated the air base gates.

'I've been meaning to ask you something,' said Daniel, as they waited.

'What's that?'

'Who's this Ah-jon-jon? The guy you've got on your T-shirt?'

'You never heard of Ah-jon-jon? He was an Assinboin Indian who went to Washington and met President Andrew Jackson. He was so impressed by the white man's ways that he abandoned his buckskins and his feathers and dressed himself up like a dandy. Then one day he beat another Indian with his cane because this other Indian doubted his word. It was the kind of thing that he had seen white men doing. The only trouble was, the Indian came back, quite unlike a white man, and shot him dead.'

'There's a moral in that?'

'I don't know. Maybe. Be yourself, that could be it. Or, don't try to play the game if nobody else knows the rules.'

Daniel cleared his throat. 'That's worth wearing a special T-shirt for?'

'Maybe.'

The sentry finally put down the telephone, and came back out. He handed Daniel back his Social Security card, and stood looking at him as if he couldn't quite decide what to say.

'Well?' asked Daniel. 'Is Major Monahan there or isn't he?'

'He's there, sir, but he's not.'

'What the hell is that supposed to mean?'

The sentry lowered his head so that all Daniel could see below the curved rim of his helmet was his pale-lipped mouth. His mouth said, 'I'm sorry to have to tell you sir that Major Monahan is dead.'

Daniel felt as if he touched a bare electric wire. A freezing, tingling sensation, not quite real. 'Dead? What are you talking about? I saw him this morning. They told me on the phone that he hadn't been around the base all day.'

'Well, sir, I'm sorry, but there must have been a misunderstanding. He has been here all day. But shortly after 1430 hours, there was an accident, involving Major Monahan and a Hughes helicopter.'

'He was flying?'

'No, sir, it was a ground accident. But I'm afraid that's all I've been authorized to tell you. If you leave me your address, somebody from the base will write to you and give you the full details in due course.'

Daniel climbed off the motorcycle. He could hardly stand up. Ronald said to him, 'Daniel, *moksois*, easy now.'

'Easy? This guy's just telling me that Willy's dead. For Christ's sake, what happened?'

The bloodless mouth below the rim of the helmet said, 'I regret that I haven't been authorized to tell you that, sir. But if you leave me your address –'

'Fuck my address, *what happened?*'

There was a long and terrible silence – almost too long, as if it had been written into a bad, Monday afternoon soap opera. A moth whirred and shone in the air between them, and somewhere on the air-base a jet engine suddenly rumbled into life and then died away again.

The sentry said, in a dry voice, 'He didn't see it. He backed into it. The rotors took off his head.'

Daniel stared at the man without saying a word. Then he turned to Ronald and whispered, 'You'd better take me home.'

Ronald's face was strained. His eyes glittered with sudden tears – tears of shock and frustration and sadness. He said, softly, 'Okay.'

They rode back slowly through the night. Even when they reached Apache Junction, they said nothing; but after Daniel had dismounted he took hold of Ronald's wrist and squeezed it tight.

'Remember Ah-jon-jon,' he said, so quietly that Ronald could hardly hear him. 'Don't try to play the game if nobody else knows the rules.'

'You're talking about Willy?'

'I don't know,' said Daniel. He had to purse his mouth together with grief, and the lump in his throat was so constricting that he couldn't answer at first. 'I'll talk to you tomorrow, okay? Thanks for the ride.'

Ronald stayed on his motorcycle and watched Daniel walk across to the diner, fish out his keys, and open the doors. Upstairs, in Daniel's apartment, a light went on.

Seven

Chief Ruse was sitting in front of his giant-sized colonial-style television set, his trousers comfortably open, the clips on his red suspenders unfastened, his boots propped up on a stool. He was watching a late-night movie called *They Saved Hitler's Brain* and drinking warm milk from a mug with Pig-in-Chief printed on it. In spite of the rattling air-conditioning unit under the window, the living room was still oppressively hot, and now and again Chief Ruse tugged out a handkerchief the size of a small bedsheet and dabbed at his sweating face.

His wife Ingrid was upstairs in front of her taffeta-frilled dressing-table, wearing an oatmeal face-pack, her hair tightly wrapped in rollers. His daughter Maisie-Ann was lying on her pink quilted bedspread in her pink quilted bathrobe eating a large bag of M & Ms and reading *The 3-Day Diet Book*.

The door chimes played The Bluebells of Scotland. Ingrid's grandfather had been a Scottish engineer on the Union railroad, and she always liked to think that she had true Scottish blood in her. Chief Ruse tolerated her plaid rugs and her plaid tablecloths, just to humour her, but he had drawn the line at wearing a kilt for her. 'I'm not wearing a dress for anybody,' he had told his deputy. 'I don't know what kind of weird behaviour goes on in Scotland, but it ain't going to spread to Arizona. Not through me.'

'Maisie-Ann, you want to get that door?' he yelled out. There was no reply, but the door chimed again.

'Maisie-Ann!'

Ingrid called, 'She's dressed for bed already! You go!'

Chief Ruse exasperatedly hauled himself out of his armchair, buttoned up his fly, and shambled out to the hallway. 'Women,' he grumbled under his breath. The door chimes rang again, and he shouted, 'I'm coming, for Christ's sake!'

He opened the door. Outside, under the moth-clustered light, stood a thin tall man in a pale-blue suit, and a silver-tipped bolus necktie. His face was hidden by the brim of his Western hat. 'Chief Ruse?' he asked. 'I'm sorry to disturb you so late. My name's Skellett.'

'What's your business, Mr Skellett? Isn't it something that could wait until the morning?'

'It won't take very long, Chief Ruse.' The man reached into his suit and produced a black leather wallet, which he handed over without any explanation at all. Chief Ruse flipped it open and read, 'James T Skellett, National Security Agency.'

Chief Ruse dragged out his handkerchief again and patted the sweat on the back of his neck. 'National Security Agency? You want to tell me what's wrong?'

Skellett took his wallet back, and tucked it into his pocket. 'I'd prefer it if I could come in. This isn't something I want to discuss on the doorstep.'

'All right, then, step inside,' said Chief Ruse, and stood back against the wall whilst Skellett squeezed past his stomach. 'I just hope it ain't nothing too complicated. I've had a day of it, I can tell you. Appropriations committee all morning, the highways department all afternoon, and one pretty damned hair-raising homicide for most of the evening. Came home and my dinner was all dried up. Not that I had too much taste for it.'

They went into the chintzy living-room. Chief Ruse switched off the sound on the television, and then offered Skellett a chair. 'You want a beer?' he asked.

'No, thank you,' said Skellett. 'I don't want to take up too much of your time. The fact is, it's that same hair-raising homicide that I've come to talk to you about. The Schneider case.'

Chief Ruse sat down, and heaved one fat leg over the other. 'Oh, yes?' he said, looking at Skellett narrowly. 'What about it? You know something that we don't?'

Skellett took off his hat. He had thin, wavy blond hair, combed across from one side of his narrow skull to the other to cover his widening bald spot. 'You'll be gratified

84

to know that the FBI discovered the whereabouts of Mrs Schneider's killer, at a little after one this afternoon.'

'Nobody told me that. Why didn't anybody tell me that?'

'Nobody told you because until now it had to be kept under total wraps. But I'm authorized to brief you now because you have a right to know, and also because you have a duty to take all the appropriate action to make sure that it remains confidential.'

Chief Ruse said, 'You want to explain yourself, Mr Skellett?'

From upstairs, Ingrid called, 'Who is it, dear? It's not Mr Weller, is it?'

'It's business!' Chief Ruse shouted back.

'If it's Mr Weller, tell him to come back tomorrow! He can't expect to come around in the middle of the night to mend washing-machines! Tell him that!'

'Women,' breathed Chief Ruse.

Skellett leaned forward, and said in a conspiratorial murmur, 'The fact of the matter is that Mrs Schneider was involved in a little business involving Air Force security. Passing information to folks who had no right to have that information. You get my drift? But – it appears that she failed to do what these folks to whom she was passing this information instructed her to do, or else she passed them some bum information, but in any case they decided to do away with her. You understand? They took off her head because they didn't want anybody to recognize that she was actually a Communist agent called Olga Voroshilov, who came to this country in 1948 with the express intention of meeting and marrying an Air Force officer. She was what we call a 'sleeper'. You've heard of that? An agent who stays dormant for ten, maybe twenty years, building up a respectable background. Then, when they're given the signal, they start passing information.'

'I've heard of that,' said Chief Ruse. 'And she was one of those?'

'That's what she was,' nodded Skellett. 'And that's why you have to keep so much of this secret. Olga Voroshilov

85

was part of a whole ring of Communist spies, many of whom are still in business, and if we make too much of a fuss about her death, they're all going to get nervous, all of these Communist spies, and go under cover. Instead – we want to track them down, and bring them to justice.'

'You say the FBI got the guy who killed her?'

Skellett smirked. 'They didn't get him. They *found* him. He was down at the bottom of a ravine in Deming, New Mexico, in a burned-out pick-up truck. Looks like he probably fell asleep while he was driving.'

'How did they know it was him? I mean, how could they be sure?'

'They found a flexible saw in the truck. She was murdered with a flexible saw, wasn't she? And they also found her head.'

'They found the head?'

Skellett nodded, almost smugly. 'Roasted right down to the bone, but there was no mistake.'

'Well, can I get to see it?' asked Chief Ruse. 'I'd sure like my medical examiners to make a check on it, make sure that it's the *right* head.'

'Chief Ruse,' said Skellett, 'how many men do you think were within driving distance of Phoenix today with a flexible saw and a severed human head in their vehicles?'

'No more than one, I'm sure,' Chief Ruse agreed. 'But I still want to have my ME check it out.'

'I'm not sure that's going to be possible, Chief. In fact, I have a warrant from the National Security Agency for the handing-over of Margot Schneider's body. We'll have a meatwagon around to collect it first thing in the morning.'

Chief Ruse sniffed, and shifted heavily in his armchair. 'You just hold on a minute, Mr Skellett. This was a *prima facie* homicide within the city limits of Phoenix, and as such it's under my jurisdiction, in my territory. Before that cadaver leaves my turf, I'm going to have to be satisfied that it's been properly examined and identified by my medical people, and that all the required paperwork is in order. You got me? This woman didn't just lose her purse, she lost her *head*, and I'm not leaving anyone any openings for saying that I didn't follow the correct and proper procedure. Not with a case like this one, no sir.'

'Chief Ruse,' said Mr Skellett, testy now. 'You have to understand that you're being outgunned here. This is a matter of national security. Far more important than any local investigation.'

'Mr Skellett, I can't ignore proper procedure.'

'The National Security Council warrant will cover your ass.'

'I have a big ass, Mr Skellett.'

'It's a powerful warrant.'

Chief Ruse was silent. He peered into his Pig-in-Chief mug and decided he didn't like the look of the wrinkled skin which had formed on the surface of his warm milk. Skellett got to his feet, and tugged his coat straight.

'That's settled then, Chief?' he asked.

'Not on your life. No sir.'

'You intend to defy a warrant that was issued in the interests of national security?'

'I intend to do my job. My job is to identify that dead woman and to carry out a proper post-mortem examination. Anyone who tries to hinder or obstruct me is going to find their ass in a cell. That's all.'

'You want me to call a judge right now?'

'Not on my telephone, you don't.'

'You want to appear in next week's *Time* magazine as the local yahoo police chief who obstructed the biggest spy operation ever carried out in the United States?'

Chief Ruse stood up, and hitched up his pants. 'I want to tell you something, Mr Skellett. I don't care how I look in the media just so long as I've been doing the job the people of Phoenix pay me to do. And I want to tell you something else. If you had the authority you claim to have, and the legal clout you're trying to pretend you've got, then you wouldn't have to make insulting threats to a local officer of the law who is simply and clearly doing his duty. What's more, if you really *were* engaged in the biggest spy operation ever carried out in the United States, you certainly wouldn't be telling *me* about it.'

Ingrid called down from upstairs, 'He's not trying to fix that washing-machine *now*, is he? He's got a nerve, coming round so late! And now look what he's made me do, crack my face-pack!'

Chief Ruse smiled without any humour at all. 'You heard the lady. You made her crack her face-pack. I think it's time you left.'

Skellett picked up his hat. 'I have to warn you that we'll be round for the body in the morning, whatever.'

'Just try it,' said Chief Ruse, still smiling. 'You'll find an armed guard around the mortuary, and all the TV and newspaper reporters you can handle. You want to drag a headless body out into the street, and try to abduct it? Well, try, that's what I say. You just try.'

'You're making a mistake, Chief,' said Skellett.

'No, Mr Skellett. *You're* the one who's making the mistake. You don't come around to a police chief's private residence in the middle of the night unless you're trying to pull some kind of a number. So, let me tell you something to go home with. Nobody pulls numbers in Phoenix; especially not junior agents for government agencies. Now, get out of here before I try out my boots on your ass.'

Skellett sighed, and positioned his hat on his head with resigned precision. 'You know something,' he said, as he went to the front door, and opened it. 'I really wonder sometimes which side people are actually *on*. You know that? You probably did more to help the USSR in one night tonight than Julius and Ethel Rosenberg did in a year.'

He nodded goodnight, and turned, and at that moment Chief Ruse swung back his Western-booted leg and kicked him so hard in the backside that his feet actually left the doorstep. He tumbled over, tried to stand up, and then fell over the low chain-link fence which bordered Chief Ruse's front path.

'Are you crazy?' he screamed. 'Are you completely out of your fucking mind?'

Chief Ruse stood in the doorway and folded his arms over his enormous stomach. 'You were an intruder, Mr Skellett, and in this state a householder can't be held liable for shooting an intruder, even if he kills him dead. You're lucky you're just sitting on your butt in the front yard, yelling at me. You could be dogmeat. Now, get out of here, and don't come back.'

Skellett stood up and angrily brushed down his suit. 'Have to get the damned thing dry-cleaned now,' he muttered. 'Goddamned $250 mohair.'

Chief Ruse closed the door on him, and locked it. Then he walked through to the kitchen, opened up the icebox, and took out a large cold can of Coors.

'Walter, you're not drinking beer, are you?' demanded Ingrid, from upstairs.

Chief Ruse said nothing, but sucked thoughtfully on the can, leaving the wet impression of his lips on the frosted aluminium top. He thought of the pink lipstick which Margot Schneider had left on her coffee-cup. His ginger cat Redneck came rubbing around his ankles.

'Walter?' Ingrid called again. 'You're not drinking beer, are you? You know how it makes your breath smell.'

'Jesus,' Chief Ruse whispered to himself. 'Women.'

He carried the can into the sitting-room, and picked up the phone. He tried two numbers before he located Lieutenant Berridge. Unhurriedly, he explained what had happened. Berridge, who was obviously in bed with Stella, judging from the rustling and the seductive giggling that was going on in the background, said, 'They want the body? They can't do that! But they've actually found the head?'

'They *say* they have. I haven't seen it. It's been burned, too, according to Skellett. No flesh on it.'

'Still no problem making a firm identification, Chief. Teeth, jawbone, no problem at all. And besides, the sawn-through backbone should exactly match the body we've got down on West Washington.'

Chief Ruse swallowed beer, and belched. Then he said, 'Listen, I'll see you down at headquarters at seven o'clock tomorrow morning. Meanwhile, I'm going to call up Kearney and make sure the whole block is sealed off. I'm going to put people on the roof, too. Nobody is going to take anything out of this town until I'm good and ready, and especially not the remains of Mrs Margot Schneider.'

'You bet, Chief. I'll see you tomorrow.'

'You bet,' said Chief Ruse. He put down the phone, and then stood in the middle of the room, one hand in his pocket, swallowing occasional mouthfuls of cold beer, and wondering if maybe he ought to have handled Skellett a little less precipitously. If he really was an agent from the National Security Council, and if he really did have a warrant for possession of Margot Schneider's body. . . .

'Shit,' he said, to the pink-tinged reflection of himself in the mirror over the fireplace. A big hefty man framed in gilt, in a room crowded with green glass Bambis, and reproductions of snowy mountains in Vermont, and doilies, and chintz, and ugly varnished 'traditional-style' armchairs. Anything that didn't have a frill or a fringe on it was decorated in plaid. Chief Ruse sometimes felt like bringing home an Ingram sub-machine gun from the police armoury and blowing the hell out of the whole lot.

But that, of course, would break Ingrid's heart.

Eight

The news finally broke at 11.30 p.m. A State Department limousine had been blown up at the Elkswood Hotel, in West Virginia, killing two Secret Service agents. The Secretary of State, Titus Alexander, had missed assassination by seconds by deciding to travel in an alternative vehicle. First theories were that the bomb had been planted either by the PLO or by a lone maniac called 'the Great Blast', who had frequently threatened Mr Alexander's life.

Nadine had flown back from Philadelphia at once, to be seen to be close to her husband's side. She was filmed at Dulles in large dark glasses which made her look like a very tall owl. She said she was 'shocked, and outraged, but thankful to God.' She forgot to say she was sorry about the two dead bodyguards.

She arrived back in Georgetown, to their elegant ivy-grown Federal house, to find that Titus was in the library with Joe Jasper, and that the library was thick with smoke. Before asking Titus if he was all right, she stalked across the room and threw open the sash window. Titus said dryly, 'Hello, Nadine. I thought you were seeing your sister.'

'I *was*, my dear, until three hours ago. Three hours ago I had just finished my soup, and was just picking up my knife and fork to eat a plateful of roast duck.'

'Your sister always makes you eat too much. With your height, you should stay thin.'

Joe Jasper glanced uneasily at Nadine, and then back to Titus. 'I can always take a walk,' he suggested.

'Stay,' Titus told him.

Nadine, striking a pose, said, 'Are you all right Titus, darling? You weren't hurt?'

'Do I *look* hurt?' asked Titus. Then, realizing that he was being too hard on her, he stood up, and held out his arms to her, and said, 'I'm fine, thank you. I was lucky and those two poor bastards weren't. Thank you for coming down.'

He held her elbows, and kissed her on the cheek. She looked as disinterested as she could manage. 'Aunt Betty said I should give you her love.'

'That's unexpectedly cordial of her.'

'Well,' said Nadine, with a breathy, whinnying noise. 'She is 72. She's growing senile.'

Joe said, to divert the course of the conversation,

'Would you like me to fix you a drink, Mrs Alexander? There's a jug of martini in the icebox.'

'A dry sherry, if you don't mind,' said Nadine. She unwrapped the white mink stole around her shoulders, and sat down opposite Titus in one of the big red leather armchairs, angling her legs with the same elegance which had once made him think of two adoring swans lying side by side. The damn woman was still as attractive as all hell; even though Titus often woke up and prayed that she might have turned ugly in the night.

'How's Penelope?' asked Titus.

'Penelope? Oh, Penelope's all right. Dowdier than ever.'

'She can't be any dowdier than the last time I saw her.'

Nadine let out a little, annoyed breath. 'That's it. As soon as I'm home, you're criticizing my family again.'

'Nadine, it was *you* who said she was dowdier than ever.'

'Well, I've a right to. She's my sister. What do *you* know about sisterly love.'

'Not a lot, except that it seems to be a small-scale version of the Punic Wars, acted out by two female siblings every August, Thanksgiving, Christmas, and Labor Day weekend.'

Joe Jasper uneasily handed Nadine a schooner of dry sherry. She sipped it, and made a nasty face, and said, 'The usual piss. Why don't you ever buy Croft Original?'

'Because when I *did* buy Croft Original, you made the same face and said, "The usual piss. Why don't you buy Croft Original?" '

'You're lying as usual,' said Nadine, opening her purse and taking out a cigarette. 'No wonder they made you Secretary of State.'

'Nadine, some people tried to kill me tonight.'

Nadine looked at him, her eyes a fraction wider, freeze-framed in the act of taking out a Raleigh. Then she gave a careless one-shouldered shrug, and crossed her legs, and waited for Joe to come over and light her up.

'I'm sorry,' she said. 'I can't really help the effect that you and I have on each other.'

Titus sat down again, and steepled his stubby fingers. His voice sounded very harsh and very serious. 'It may be a coincidence, but only a few hours before this happened, Joe came up with some pretty spectacular material on Marshall. *Leverage.* Something which we could use to affect his entire defence policy, and put RINC on ice.'

Nadine blew smoke. 'Don't tell me that Marshall ever misbehaved himself.'

Joe put in, 'He's like all human beings, Mrs Alexander. He has certain, you know, desires and susceptibilities. Certain, well – '

'Perversions?' asked Nadine.

Titus' face remained slabby and hard. 'That's right,' he told her. 'Perversions.'

'And you mean to use whatever this "pretty spectacular material" is to break down the RINC talks?'

'Only if Marshall fails to see sense.'

'What's sense, to you? That we go on stockpiling nuclear weapons at massive expense and for no reason? You know that I'm not a pacifist, Titus, for God's sake. But we already have enough bombs and missiles to wipe out the world a hundred times over. What's the *point* of it?'

Titus cleared his throat. 'The point, Nadine, is to prevent imbalance. That's the point.'

'*Imbalance*?' mocked Nadine. 'Is that all you're worried about, imbalance?'

'There's also the global obliteration quotient,' put in Joe.

'Ah, yes, that's my favourite,' said Nadine. 'General Housman calls it GOB for short. The number of times that the United States is capable of totally obliterating the world, versus the number of times that the Soviet Union is capable of totally obliterating the world. Poor General Housman was *so* worried about it, the last time I spoke to him. We can only obliterate the world forty-one times over, while the Soviets are capable of obliterating it sixty-three times over.'

'Nadine,' said Titus. 'Please. Save it.'

'Ah, yes, I forgot,' said Nadine. 'As the loyal and devoted wife of the Secretary of State, I'm not really supposed to say things like that. When you're married to a hawk, you have to behave like one.'

Titus said, 'However cynical you are, Nadine – '

'Cynical!' she burst out. She held up her half-empty sherry glass to Joe and said, 'This is terrible. Get me a martini.' Then, to Titus again, 'I'm not cynical, Titus darling. I'm just realistic. And adult.'

'What I was going to say was that I know that I can trust you, cynical or not.'

She stared at him acutely. 'What are you getting at?'

'I'm simply saying that I know that I can trust you.'

'Well, of course you can trust me. I don't propose to give up the chance to be First Lady next year, just for the dubious pleasure of passing around the tedious little details of your grubby little plots. God, Titus, you haven't ever said or done anything worth gossiping about.'

Titus said, 'I want you to do something for me. I can't do it myself, not now. Because of what happened at the Elkswood Hotel, I've got Secret Service men standing three deep all around me.'

'I did notice rather a lot of men with short haircuts and dark suits milling around in the garden.'

Titus finished his martini and flicked the rim of the glass with his fingernail so that it rang. 'Nadine, I want you to take care of our principal witness. The girl with whom Marshall was involved, the one who can help us stop the RINC talks. I want you to meet her, set her up in a safe location, and then keep her happy until we need her.'

'What do I have to do? Read her *The Lives of the Presidents* and feed her on Pepperidge Farm gingernuts?'

'*Nadine,*' cautioned Titus, quietly. Joe Jasper tried to smirk, but found it difficult.

The truth was that the marriage between Titus and Nadine Alexander was one of the spectacles of Washington, to be ranked beside the John Paul Jones statue and the National History Wax Museum. They were fiercely attracted to each other sexually, and yet their politics and their personalities were at complete odds. All they shared, besides their hunger for each other in bed, was ambition. Nadine was a natural-born Southern Democrat (her father had been a warm friend of Herman Talmadge and B. Everett Jordan) while Titus was a bullet-headed Yankee from Illinois, whose father had known nobody but the local tax-collector and a cop called Cummings with whom he had played Saturday-night poker.

Titus and Nadine had met at a cocktail party at the Nixon White House. They had both been drinking too much. Afterwards, they had gone to the Madison Hotel, 'Washington's Correct Address', and made ferocious love all night and all the following morning. They had married because Titus wanted to be President and Nadine wanted to be First Lady. She still browsed through *Architectural Digest*, selecting furniture and tableware and hand-embroidered sheets for the White House. Their marriage, according to Joe Jasper, was straight As – acid, amatory juices, and ambition.

Nadine often thought she should have been a movie star, or a model. She was 5ft 10ins, with thick wavy brunette hair, shoulders like Arnold Schwarzenegger and a magnificent 38-inch bust. Somebody had once said that she would have looked better as the figurehead for a ship. But she wanted the White House more than anything. She had once told her mother that she wanted the White House more than happiness. Her father had died when she was ten, of a coronary, on the top of a flight of stairs, at a birthday party. Since then, birthday cakes had always reminded Nadine of death.

She said, 'This girl, she's a hooker I suppose?'

'Not so much a hooker,' said Joe. 'More of a hostess.'

'You realize that what you're asking me to do is completely against my ethical and moral principles?'

'Possibly,' agreed Titus. 'But not against your personal interests. If Marshall Roberts fails to pull off the RINC talks, then there's no question that he's going to be badly hurt, politically. He may well have to resign before next year's primaries.'

Nadine sipped her martini and stared at Titus thoughtfully. 'It has occurred to you, of course, that Marshall Roberts may have planted the bomb himself?'

'It did cross my mind.'

'He knows how hungry you are for the White House; and he knows that you've promised to do everything possible to break down his détente with the Soviet Union.'

'That's right. I'm not denying it. He's very high up on my list of possible suspects.'

Joe Jasper put in, 'I can't believe it was the PLO. Not after the discussions we've been having with Arafat. It could have been a lone banana, or a fringe group. Some of these '60s underground groups like Yippies and Black Panthers are starting to get pretty restless again.'

'That's because they want a last fling before they get too old,' said Titus, caustically. 'No – my money's on Marshall's Unfortunate Accident squad, or one of those lone assassins. Don't you realize that it's very *fashionable* these days to knock off a famous politician or a legendary rock star; it's the growth profession of the middle '80s. Well – thanks to Marshall's economic policy, the population don't have much else to do, do they?'

Nadine said to Joe, 'Tell me about this hooker. This *hostess.*'

Joe perched one cheek of his narrow buttocks on the arm of a library chair. 'Her name's Colleen Petley, also known as Rita Haze, 25 years old, from Fort Worth, Texas. She left home at the age of 19 after becoming pregnant. She lost the baby, but she didn't go back home straight away. She went to Las Vegas with the idea of becoming a croupier. It wasn't long, though, before she was picked up by a man called Denny DiMarco, a very heavyweight Las Vegas pimp. He groomed her, dressed her, and set her up as a high-class thousand-dollar-a-night hostess. She's the kind of girl who will do absolutely anything a man wants. She's classy enough for him to take out to dinner and pretend that she's his steady date, or even his wife; and yet when it comes to bedtime she'll perform in any way that you can imagine, and in a few ways you can't.'

Nadine edgily tapped the ash off her cigarette. 'And what do you expect *me* to do for this doyenne of latter-day horizontals?'

'It's vital to keep her feeling *important*,' said Titus. 'We're going to fix her up with every creature-comfort she could possibly need; men, dope, you name it. But we can't pay her any money, because that will look too much like bribery, and if she has to go in front of a Congressional committee, I want her to be as clean as possible – at least as far as the reliability of her information is concerned.'

Nadine said nothing. Joe Jasper leaned towards her, and asked, 'Another martini?' but she shook her head.

'You're a well-known, well-publicized, well-admired woman,' Titus told her. 'Colleen Petley, when she sees you, will begin to realize just how serious and how important her testimony is going to be, not only to herself, not only to me, but to the whole of America. If not the world.'

'You really think she's aware of her duties to the United States?' asked Nadine. 'A Las Vegas hooker?'

'That's your job, to make her aware,' said Titus. 'Make her believe that she's going to be famous, and respected. And, above all, make her believe that she's going to be *honourable*. If there's one thing that hookers crave, it's honour.'

'I suppose you have that from first-hand conversations,' Nadine commented, sharply.

'Oh, sure,' said Titus. 'I have enough time and energy to take care of the State Department, argue with the President, act as chairman of the American Legion, be married to you, take care of your snotty kids, fish, exercise, and fuck two or three hookers every night. As well as *talk* to them, by God.'

Nadine crushed out her cigarette. Then she looked across at Titus and her expression had softened. 'I'm sorry,' she said. 'I don't know how many times I've told you I'm sorry – probably just as many times as you've told me the same thing. But I still love you, you know; and I'm glad that you're safe.'

Joe let out a quiet breath of relief. Tonight wasn't going to be so combative after all. And, with any luck, Nadine would help to keep Colleen Petley smiling and co-operative until they were ready to twist Marshall Roberts' arm.

There was a roaring noise outside the window. Titus glanced up alertly, but Joe was already holding the curtains back to see what was happening.

'Relax,' he said. 'It's only Samantha, with her latest boyfriend. You didn't know there were any Hell's Angels in Georgetown, did you? Well, Samantha found one. Hold on, it looks like the Secret Service guys are giving him a hard time.'

'*Titus*,' appealed Nadine.

Titus pulled a face, but when Nadine tilted her head to one side, coaxingly, he knew that this was going to be part of the price of having her take care of Colleen Petley. He picked up the antique-style telephone next to him, and said, 'Wallis?'

'Yes, sir.'

'That simian being who brought my step-daughter home on the back of his motorcycle. He's allowed to escort her into the house.'

'He's tattooed, sir. He has Fuck The World inscribed on his left bicep.'

'Wallis, just let him in, will you? You can hear language like that every day in the Oval Office. There doesn't seem to be any valid reason for excluding it from the State Department. What's good enough for the President is good enough for us.'

'Okay, sir, if you say so.'

'I say so, Wallis.'

Titus put down the phone. 'Those children of yours are totally out of control,' he told Nadine. 'Do you know that?

They're like wild animals. Maybe we should install a cage.'

'Titus, darling,' smiled Nadine. 'I'll do anything you want. But right now, I'm very tired.'

Titus flicked a quick look at Joe Jasper, but Joe had already picked up the message loud and clear. He straightened his notebook and his file, bowed to Nadine, nodded to Titus, and made for the door. 'We'll talk early tomorrow,' said Titus.

'Yes, sir,' said Joe. Then, with a heavy-lidded smile, 'Sweet dreams, Mr Secretary. If possible.'

Nine

Nadine had been away from him for five days, and she was feeling an urgent need for sex. When he came out of the bathroom into the richly-furnished colonial bedroom, with its mahogany four-poster bed and its deep wine-coloured drapes, she was lying on the white hand-woven bedspread naked except for a tiny but expensive pair of handmade French-silk panties, with an insert of Alençon lace through which her glossy dark pubic hair curled temptingly.

He stood at the end of the bed in his pale-blue pyjama trousers, his towel around his neck. He couldn't help admiring her. Even at 40 she had a magnificent figure. Huge, rounded, wide-nippled breasts, a narrow waist, and flaring hips. Legs so long that she could lock her ankles together behind his back when they were making love. And her brunette hair was spread out on the white lace-embroidered pillow like the Lady of Shallott, beautiful and mysterious and doomed, too close to Camelot for comfort.

He sat down on the edge of the bed, and placed his hand on her thigh. His chest was muscular and ridged, with a small diagonal scar under his left nipple. In the light from the white-glass lamp, he looked tired but more handsome than usual; and there was a gentleness about his expression which Nadine hadn't seen on his face for a long time. He had come close to being killed, not by North Koreans or VCs, but by his own countrymen.

The red crest of his penis, already erect, protruded from his open pyjamas; but there was nothing incongruous or crude about it. It was simply the obvious evidence of how much this particular wife attracted this particular husband. Nadine reached down, and opened his trousers wider, and held his erection in her long sharp fingernails.

'Did you miss me?' she said, breathily.

'What do you think?'

'Don't ask me what I think. Tell me.'

He nodded. He didn't smile. 'I missed you.'

'You really think you have the goods on Marshall this time?'

He nodded. 'We really do. I've seen the pictures for myself.'

'What was he doing?'

Titus didn't answer at first, so Nadine clutched his penis and squeezed it tight. 'What was he *doing*?'

'Well, you've heard of golden showers.'

Nadine's eyes widened. 'Marshall Roberts was doing *that*?'

Titus said, 'You wouldn't believe it, would you, to look at him? You wouldn't think that the same lips which have been coming out with all of those holier-than-thou speeches about arms reduction and détente with the Soviets and how we can help the poor. . .'

Nadine leaned forward a little, so that she could reach his pyjama cord with her left hand. She gave it a tug, and it came free. 'Don't let's talk about Marshall,' she said. 'Come here. . .'

Titus said, 'Nadine, I really don't think that I'm up to too much tonight. I have to warn you.'

'Come here,' she encouraged him.

He pulled down his pyjama trousers, and then climbed on to the bed naked and straddled her waist. His erection lay between her breasts; and she lifted her breasts and squeezed them together with her own hands so that he was deeply massaged by soft, warm flesh. He bent forward and kissed her forehead, kissed her cheeks, kissed her mouth with increasing passion, but now she coaxed him upward, until he was kneeling astride her chest. She opened her mouth and took the shiny plum of his penis head between her lips.

Titus closed his eyes, and softly groaned. But Nadine swallowed him deeper, sucking him gently, and licking the underside of his erection with the tip of her tongue, probing the narrow opening which was already slick with juices. She worked him faster and faster, licking and flicking, until he felt as if a volcano were rising up between his thighs.

'Nadine – ' he whispered, a stage whisper by an actor who has long forgotten his lines.

She drew his saliva-glistening penis out of her mouth, and caressed it against her face, against her cheeks, and kissed it and nipped at it with her teeth. She even butterfly-kissed the tip of it with her eyelashes. It was then that Titus shuddered, and ejaculated, and three spurts of thick white semen crowned her forehead, and formed pearls in her hair, and clustered in her lashes.

He kissed her, again and again, and then reached up with his hand to wipe the semen from her face; but she held his wrist. 'I want this,' she demanded. 'And I want more.'

She reached down, and drew aside the thin triangle of silk and lace that covered her. 'Fuck me,' she insisted.

It was difficult. Titus kept softening, and having to push himself into her quicker and quicker to regain his stiffness. But after fifteen minutes, when he was totally tensed up and breathing harshly, and his muscles were glistening with sweat, he felt the irresistible sensation of a second climax. Beneath him, Nadine moved with a fierce undulating rhythm, gasping with every thrust, her nipples crinkled and stiff, her breasts swaying, her eyes squeezed tight in the concentrated effort of a rising orgasm.

She suddenly screamed, and began to shake, and Titus ejaculated deep inside her. It took almost a minute before she was able to stop shuddering, and twitching, and open her eyes. Then, for a moment, he saw in her eyes something that was almost approaching affection. It couldn't be, of course. They had been through too many bitter arguments, and staked their tents too firmly on opposite hills. You can camp over there if you want to, but nothing in the world is going to persuade me to move my tent next to yours, not even love. But Nadine lay where she was, all the same, crowned and anointed with Titus' semen, until the flush began to fade from between her breasts, and her nipples softened, and she sighed and sat up at last and said, 'I suppose I ought to take a bath.'

There was a brisk knock at the bedroom door. Titus found his pyjama trousers and dragged them on. 'Who is it?'

'Titus? It's Carl. I just got back.'

'Fine,' said Titus. 'Maybe we can talk in the morning.'

'Are you okay?' asked Carl, through the door. 'I heard what happened on the news.'

'I'm okay, thanks. A little shaken. But I guess that's only to be expected.'

'I hope you don't mind, ' said Carl, 'I borrowed the Porsche.'

Titus looked meaningfully at Nadine, but all Nadine could do was throw her hands up in imitation of a Jewish momma. He's a grown boy now, what can I do?

'I did specifically tell you that I'd rather you *didn't* use the Porsche, didn't I?' said Titus. 'And you do have the Zephyr.'

'Oh, Titus. Have a heart. I can hardly pull girls in a Zephyr.'

'When I was your age, all I had was a beaten-up Nash 600.'

There was a pause. Then Carl said, 'The Porsche is a little beaten up, too.'

'You beat up the Porsche?' snapped Titus. The veins in his neck swelled up, and he clenched his fists. 'What happened? How bad is it?'

'Well,' said Carl, carefully, 'the front end doesn't look too good. I left it down at the H Street garage.'

Titus stared at the door and decided that for the sake of everything he wanted to do to bring down Marshall Roberts, he had better not open it. Because Jesus Christ, if he opened it, and saw Carl, then he'd beat the living crap out of that boy, and that would be the end of him and Nadine. He tried to think to himself: it's only a car, cars can be fixed. But he knew without being told that it was totally ruined. He was a perfectionist – the slightest scratch was enough to put him off a car completely.

'Okay, Carl,' he said, in a voice like a manhole cover being dragged across a city street. 'We'll forget it this time. Get the car fixed and then we'll talk about it some more.'

Nadine, tall and naked, taller than he was, came across and laid her hands on his shoulders.

'You're a fascinating man,' she said. 'I only wish sometimes that I could really like you.'

He. momentarily closed his eyes, then nodded. 'The feeling's mutual,' he said. 'Extremely mutual.'

Ten

Susie came into the room and stood in a sloping triangle of sunshine watching him solemnly.

'Daddy?' she asked. What's wrong?'

He eased himself around in the cheap creaking basketwork chair. His hair was ruffled and he looked tired. Somewhere outside, a tinny radio was playing *La Cucaracha*. It was 101° at Sky Harbor, one of those relentless Arizona days when even the saguaro appears to throw no shadow, and the horizon ripples with glassy mirages.

He held out his hand for Susie and she came and leaned close to him. She had been eating a Mounds bar and she smelled of candy. He kissed the fine blonde down on her forehead, and said, 'I'll get over it. But I did love him, you know. He was a good friend. A funny, nice person.'

'Will they bury him?'

'I guess so. It depends what his family wants. He came from Omaha; they'll probably fly him back there.'

Susie was silent for a while, stroking the back of Daniel's hand. Then she said, in a small voice, 'I'm sorry. I said a prayer for him this morning.'

'Me, too,' said Daniel. 'Do you remember that old rhyme I used to sing you, when you were very small, when mommy was still here?

'My daddy is dead, but I can't tell you how,
He left me six horses to follow the plow.
With my whim wham waddle ho!
Strim stram straddle ho!
Bubble-ho! pretty boy, over the brow.'

Susie sang it with him; an old tune from long ago. On a very hot day, close to the Superstition Mountains, they sang it together for Willy Monahan. Daniel thought: even today, there is still *some* sentiment left on this jaded planet of ours – still *some* room for genuine grief, and sadness.

Cara came into the room and stood listening to them. She was wearing a tight sky-blue T-shirt and a white pleated miniskirt which she had carefully ironed this morning, before it was light. Neither of them had slept. They had tried to talk, tried to get drunk, tried to make love. But it had been a relentlessly hot night and Willy's sudden death had been too overwhelming for both of them. Daniel had dozed off for five or ten minutes in his bedroom chair, but he had dreamed of Willy's smiling head, flying through the air, and had woken up with a jolt, sweating, trembling, wondering whether Willy's death was real, or just another nightmare. Cara had knelt beside him, naked and soft, and soothed him, but at that moment the night had seemed longer and darker than any other night in the history of mankind.

'Are you opening for lunch?' Cara asked him.

Daniel shook his head. 'You put the card in the window?'

'Sure. But you have to carry on some time.'

He said, 'Yes. I know.'

'Ronald was around this morning,' Cara said. 'He asked if there was anything he could do. He's cute, don't you think?'

'Assuredly. The cutest Indian traffic offender this side of the Mogollon Rim.'

'Dan, Daniel,' said Cara. 'Don't be bitter. It was an accident.'

'Sure,' he said. But there was a phrase which kept turning over and over in the back of his mind, *Just like I said, Daniel, heads will roll.* And he remembered what he had said to Willy in reply. *You're sure it won't be your head? You're sure it won't be* your *head?*

Susie said, 'Can I go play with Lucy, down at the gas station?'

'She's off school too?'

'She's always off school. Her daddy says he doesn't mind if she goes or not.'

'Okay, then, honey. But make sure you're back by three. And don't go near the vehicles. And *don't* go across the highway. You stay on this side, you hear?'

Susie ran off, and Daniel stayed where he was, in the creaking basketwork chair. Cara stayed by the door for a while, watching him, and then went to the window, and looked out at the dusty front lot, at the blacktop highway, at the distant brown ridge of the mountains.

'Did you call the base?' she asked him.

'I called twice. They told me they can't release any details until they've informed his next-of-kin.'

'I'm sorry,' she said.

'Sorry? You don't have to be. Everybody has to die sooner or later. Five hundred years ago, this part of Arizona was populated by the Hohokam Indians. They built canals branching out of the Salt River, they had a whole civilization. But then they disappeared without trace. Who knows what happened to them? Maybe they displeased the gods.'

'Willy didn't displease the gods.'

'I'm not so sure.'

Cara turned around. 'What does that mean?'

'It means I'm not so sure. When he came around yesterday morning, he said he was going to spend the day in the armoury, checking out missiles. He had some theory that missiles fitted to US fighter planes are incapable of destroying Soviet aircraft. Something to do with radar signatures. He said it was going to turn out to be the biggest scandal the Air Force had ever known.'

Cara came across the room, and knelt down beside him. She reminded him so much of Candii: brash, innocently erotic, world-weary, a heroine out of a country-and-western song. Greece may have had its hetaerae; Rome its delicatae; France its lorettes. But America had its Candiis and its Caras and its Belle Coras, its brassy Western girls with their store-bought hair and their white high-heeled boots and their waggling buckskin butts. When Cara knelt down to soothe him, she revealed a freckled cleavage as deep as the Grand Canyon, and her white skirt was raised just high enough to tease but not quite high enough to reveal that she wasn't wearing any underwear, because girls like Candii and Cara never wore any underwear, they dressed to excite their menfolk, regardless of what was fashionable or chic. Until they got married, of course.

'What are you going to do?' she asked him.

'Do?' he frowned at her.

'Well, if you think that somebody did him harm – if you think that somebody might have arranged for him to walk into that helicopter propeller on *purpose* . . . I mean, shouldn't you *do* something?'

'I've called twice.'

'I know. But what have you *done*?'

'I've called! What else can I do? They keep telling me that Willy was involved in an accident, and that he's dead, and that's it. They won't even confirm what the sentry told me – that he'd lost his head. They keep saying that they're trying to contact his next-of-kin, and that until they do, they're not at liberty to release any details.'

'Did you see the *Flag* this morning?'

'The newspaper? No. What's that got to do with it?'

Cara stood up, and walked across to the cheap bamboo table. She unfolded the *Arizona Flag* and showed him the second-lead headline. HEADLESS WIDOW PUZZLE, Police Seek Skull Cult. Daniel said, 'I heard that on the news last night. So what?'

'Did they say on the news that the woman who was killed in Phoenix was an Air Force widow?'

'I don't think so. Is that what she was?'

'Umh-humh. Mrs Margot Schneider, 52, widow of Major Rudolph Schneider, who was killed several years ago on a proving flight from Luke Air Force Base, outside of Phoenix. Daniel – she was beheaded, just like Willy. The only difference is that *her* head they took off with a saw, not a helicopter.'

Daniel looked at Cara thoughtfully. 'You know something,' he said 'You're definitely more intelligent than you look.'

'I don't know whether that's a compliment or an insult.'

'It's a compliment. You look pretty and dumb. In fact, you've turned out to be pretty and intelligent.'

'If that's a compliment, I think I'll ask somebody to cut off *my* head as well.'

Daniel stood up. He said, as a sharp aside, 'Don't joke about it. Do you mind?'

Cara said, 'I'm sorry. I didn't want to upset you. But don't you think it might be an idea to go take a *look* at your friend Willy? Just to make sure that he died the way they say he did.'

Daniel took five or six caged-up steps around the room. Then he stopped; then he walked around some more. Then he said, 'They killed him, you know. That's what I've been thinking all night. He found out about the missiles and they killed him.'

'Maybe they killed Mrs Schneider for the same reason.'

'Yeah,' Daniel nodded. Then he looked up at Cara and said, 'Get me a beer, will you? I'm going to make a phone call.'

He brought the telephone over from the windowsill and punched out the number of Williams AFB. After a long wait, a voice said, 'Williams Air Force Base. How can I help you?'

'This is Mr Korvitz here. I called earlier. Can I speak to Colonel Kawalek?'

'I'm sorry, Colonel Kawalek is away from the base today. Would you like to speak to his assistant?'

'Okay, if that's the best you can do.'

There was an interminable pause, while wires sang and telephones clicked and distant voices said, 'Hello? George? Hello? I can't hear you too well.' At last a crisp-sounding lady said, 'Mr Korvitz? I'm sorry but Colonel Kawalek is away from the base today.'

'They told me that. I just wanted to know how I could get to see the body of Major Monahan. He was a friend of mine, you see, and – '

'I'm sorry, Mr Korvitz. It won't be possible for anyone to see Major Monahan's remains before his next-of-kin have been informed.'

'Haven't they been told yet?'

'I'm afraid that's impossible for me to say.'

'Well, *somebody* must know.'

'I regret that the only officer who might know about it is also off the base today. He won't be reachable until tomorrow at the earliest.'

'Well, can you at least tell me his name?'

'I'm sorry. I'm not at liberty to do that.'

'Who is?'

'Nobody, I'm afraid. Not until Colonel Kawalek returns.'

'Jesus, madam, doesn't anybody know anything?'

'There isn't any need to use bad language, Mr Korvitz. I'm simply trying to be helpful.'

Daniel held the receiver as if he were going to throttle it. Then, without saying any more, he hung up. 'I get the same answer all the time,' he told Cara. 'Colonel Kawalek's away, nobody else can help me, and no, I certainly can't be allowed to see Willy's body.'

Cara said, 'Where did Willy live? Do you think it might be a good idea to go round to his house? I mean, if he was working on some theory about missiles or something, maybe he left something at home. Notes, or a diary, maybe.'

'Well,' said Daniel, 'it's worth a try. I'll just give Levon a call at the gas station, and tell him we're going to be away for a while.'

Willy had lived on Indigo Street, in Mesa, which is halfway between Phoenix and Apache Junction. His house had always been maddening to find, because there are five Indigo Streets, all in a roughly straight line, but disconnected from each other by thousands of yards of open ground, and the Consolidated Canal. Willy had lived on the section of Indigo Street which was closest to the Mesa City Cemetery.

Daniel and Cara drove out there in Daniel's grubby, lopsided Electra. There was a neat row of ochre-painted one-storey houses with shingled roofs and parched lawns. Daniel parked outside Willy's house and put on his sunglasses. He slammed the Electra's door and walked slowly up the concrete driveway, followed by Cara. Above them, the sky was almost navy blue, and the heat was dry and suffocating.

They peered in through Willy's picture windows. It was difficult to see clearly, but it looked as if the house was completely empty of furniture. Even the rugs had gone: there was nothing but shiny woodblock floors.

'Are you sure this was the house?' asked Cara.

'Are you kidding? I came out here once a week for poker and beer. I can't understand it.'

A woman appeared from the house next door in upswept spectacles and a lime-green nylon headscarf. She was wearing a beige double-knit jump suit and a profusion of gold charm bracelets. She said, 'Are you looking for anyone?'

'Major Monahan. I'm a friend of his.'

'He was posted. To Langley, I think they said.'

'Who said?'

'Why, the men who came around to clear his house. They said he'd been urgently posted to Langley, and that they'd come to collect his belongings for him. They said that his furniture would probably arrive at Langley before he did.'

'You can bet it will,' said Daniel. 'The truth is that he's dead.'

'*Dead? Are you sure?* They were quite clear, those men, that he'd been posted to Langley. They were smiling and joking and everything. I don't think they would have behaved that way if Major Monahan had been *dead*.'

'Lady, Willy Monahan was my best friend. I can tell you for certain that he's dead.'

'Well, I hope he enjoys himself at Langley,' the woman replied. 'He's a warm, considerate man. We liked him the moment we first met him.'

Cara took Daniel's arm. 'Come on,' she said, gently. 'Let's go. We're not going to find anything here.'

Daniel reluctantly followed her down the driveway to the car. He climbed in, and started up the engine, with a whinny like an ageing horse. Cara said, 'They've really gotten rid of him, haven't they? I mean, they've made him *vanish*, like he never existed. And if they've told his next-door neighbours that he's going to Langley, maybe that's what they've told his next-of-kin, too.'

'Maybe he's not dead at all,' said Daniel. 'Maybe they've just spirited him away so that he can't make a nuisance of himself any longer.'

'There's only one way to tell.'

'I know,' said Daniel, glancing behind him as he rejoined Route 60, heading east. 'I'm going to have to see his body for myself – if there is a body.'

Cara laid a hand on his thigh, and then leaned over and kissed his cheek.

'What was that for?' he asked her.

'I don't know. Comfort, I guess.'

He kissed her back, on the lips. 'They don't make itinerants like you any more,' he told her. 'You're the last of a fine but dying breed.'

'Don't you believe it,' smiled Cara. 'You just take a look around any city in the west, and you'll be amazed at all those budding 15- and 16-year-olds in high school; they're into double-D cups before they know what an isoceles triangle is.'

'Do *you* know what an isoceles triangle is?'

Cara pursed her lips in amusement, and shook her head. Daniel kissed her, and said, 'Let's go talk to Ronald. Maybe Ronald can figure a way to get us into that air base. He's a professional lawbreaker, you know that?'

Ronald was around at Levon's gas station, two blocks away from Daniel's Downhome Diner; sitting crosslegged on the tailgate of a battered pick-up truck, drinking 7-Up out of the can and discussing with Levon the finer points of torque-reactive anti-dive control. Through the picket fence at the back of the gas station, Daniel could hear Susie giggling and screaming as she played with Lucy. He left his sagging Electra by the side of the workshop, and walked across the sunbaked forecourt with his hands jammed into the back pockets of his jeans. Cara followed, a few paces behind, but not subserviently.

'Levon,' said Daniel, shaking his hand. 'How're you doing?'

Levon Wisby was one of Daniel's favourite characters in Apache Junction. He was rake-thin and laconic as a turkey vulture. He always wore Oshkosh dungarees and, for some reason he would never explain, a Seattle Mariners baseball cap.

'Your little girl and mine been getting on good,' said Levon. 'Would've been a peaceful afternoon save for this jawbreaker here, and all his talk about that motorcycle of his'n.'

'Ronald could bore the ass off a Hell's Angel, when it comes to motorcycles,' grinned Daniel.

'*Salut!* to you too,' said Ronald, and raised his 7-Up can.

'Listen, Ronald,' Daniel told him, 'we just came back from Willy Monahan's place on Indigo Street.'

'Oh yeah?'

Daniel nodded. 'The place is empty, cleaned out. The woman next door said that some men had been around to move all his furniture and all his belongings. But – here's the weird bit – they told her that Willy was still alive, and that he'd been posted to Langley Air Force Base.'

'That's crazy. They never post anyone as quick as that. And in any case, why didn't Willy tell you anything about it? Send you a note, or call you?'

'If he isn't dead, and he's really been posted, he certainly hasn't been posted in the normal way,' said Daniel. 'Maybe the Air Force have put him under some kind of arrest, and moved him out of the state so that they can keep him incommunicado.'

'You really believe he found out something he shouldn't have done?'

'I don't know,' said Daniel. 'But I mean to find out if he's dead or alive and nobody's going to stop me, because if he's dead then someone's murdered him, and if he's alive then he needs help to get himself free.'

'Either way, this is sure going to stir up one whole lot of shit,' said Ronald, philosophically.

'Ronald, I have to see Willy's body for myself. That's the only way that I'm going to be convinced that he's been killed. Or, if he hasn't been killed, I want to know where he is, and why he was whisked away. There are laws in this country; *habeas corpus* and all that kind of stuff. They can't just lock somebody up and throw away the key.'

'Daniel tried to call the colonel again,' put in Cara, 'but it wasn't any good. It's a cover-up, I'm sure of it.'

Ronald raised his eyebrows at Levon, but Levon could only shrug and say, 'Those Air Force characters, they're always screwy, least as far as I'm concerned. Either mad, or drunk, or both, and the way they fly them jets through the mountains, shoot.'

Ronald said, 'What we need to do is get on to the base.'

'Oh yes? And how do you propose we do that? Williams is a tactical base, as well as a training centre. You don't just stroll in through the front gate, whistling *O Sole Mio*.'

'I'm a Navajo Indian. Did you ever hear a Navajo Indian whistling *O Sole Mio*?'

'I heard you singing *Volare* once,' grinned Levon.

'I was drunk,' Ronald protested. 'I only sing *Volare* when I'm drunk.'

'You could dress up as Air Force pilots or something,' Cara suggested. 'I saw somebody do that in a Gregory Peck movie. Well, not pilots, but sailors. Anyway, that was how they got on to a ship when they weren't supposed to.'

'Where the hell are we going to find two Air Force uniforms?' demanded Ronald. 'And, besides, they'd still want to see our identification before they'd let us through the gate.'

'Now, hold on a minute,' said Levon. 'I've got three of them coveralls they wear when they're technician-ing them jets. They was given to me by one of the engineers used to work at Luke. I did him a lube job once for free, and he give me five or six pairs, surplus I guess they were, but they still got the Air Force insignias sewn on them.'

'Well, that's a start,' said Daniel. 'If we could just get into the base, nobody would take very much notice of two stray technicians.'

'Well, you could get *in* there pretty easy,' said Levon. 'That's always provided you could find your own way out again. Jim Pryor goes down there two or three times a week with fresh beef and milk and a whole lot of that frozen Mexican food. Owes me a favour, Jim, gave him a TA tyre with hardly no tread wear, he'll take you in, provided you say he didn't know nothing about you stowing away in the back of his truck if you're catched, and always provided you find your own way out again.'

Daniel glanced at Ronald and he couldn't help smiling. He had always felt that Levon was one of these extraordinary Western characters who can fix anything you can think of: who always know where you can find whatever outlandish spare part you're looking for, or someone who can help you out of whatever bizarre spot you've gotten yourself into. And it was true. Levon was naturally like that. He knew where to lay his hands on duck eggs, irreversible screws, and somebody to splice perfect wooden shingles. He knew to the day when the cactus wrens would start nesting in the saguaro, and he knew to the minute when dust storms would start blowing.

Cara said, 'What will you do?'

'It's easy,' said Ronald. 'We'll get into the base, find the sick-bay, or the morgue, or wherever Willy's body is likely to be; then take a look at him if he's there, and satisfy ourselves that he's dead, and how he died.'

'Then how do we get *out*?' asked Daniel.

'We'll bluff. Go to the front gate and run like hell.'

'And supposing they catch us, and arrest us?'

'It won't matter by then, will it? We'll already know the truth about what happened to Willy.'

'Oh yes? And what possible good is that going to do *us*, if we're jailed for trespassing on restricted property, and for impersonating US Air Force personnel?'

'Relax,' said Ronald. 'I'm beginning to hatch a *plan*.'

'You and your goddamned plans,' complained Daniel. 'It was *your* plan that we picked up those two guys in that broken-down Cadillac last March, and played poker with them. Sitting targets, you said. Rubes. Some rubes. Two goddamned professional gamblers on their way back to

Nevada. I'd have myself a new icebox now if it wasn't for you and your goddamned plans.'

'You're talking like Willy,' said Ronald.

Daniel turned away and looked across the highway, towards the Goldfield Mountains. The day was so hot that the store across the street looked as if it were dancing. He said, 'I miss him, that's why. And I'm worried about him.'

Ronald flipped his empty 7-Up can into the air; then knocked it with his elbow so that it described a perfect parabola and clattered into the gas-station trashbucket. 'Everything's going to be fine. How many times have I told you, Daniel Korvitz, that I'm a *genius*?'

'About a thousand. But how many times have you *proved* it?'

Susie came out of Levon's back yard, carrying her Sindy doll. She held it up to Daniel and there were tears smudging her cheeks. 'She's busted,' she said.

'What's happened?' Daniel asked her, holding out his hands.

Into one of his hands, Susie laid the Sindy doll's naked body. Into the other hand, she laid the doll's detached head.

Eleven

From the moment he had opened his eyes at five o'clock that morning, Chief Ruse had been nursing the gritty suspicion that he had seriously underestimated James T Skellett. He was unusually edgy as he took his place outside the Phoenix city morgue, a few minutes after the sun had risen over the top of the 40-storey Valley National

Bank; and when Lieutenant Berridge came across and asked him if he'd heard anything about a Diamond I jet going down last night in the Dead Horse National Park with millionaire Clinton Charles on board, he gave nothing but a disinterested hmmph, as if men like Charles deserved to drop out of the sky from 12,000 feet and be pulverized among the cactus and the copper-dust and the petrified jasper.

There were thirty armed police around the morgue, as well as ten patrol cars, eight motorcyclists, and six sharpshooters up on surrounding rooftops, on KOOL radio and the Grace Court School. There were roadblocks on the Maricopa Freeway going south-east and the Canyon Freeway going north, as well as ambushes on West Indian School Road and Van Buren at 24th Street. It was all a little theatrical, but then Chief Ruse had always preferred a little theatricality to any kind of violence. 'Better to ham it up than shoot it out,' he had told his deputy, more times than his deputy had cared to count.

Lieutenant Berridge came up and said, 'You really think we're going to have trouble?'

Chief Ruse shook his chins. 'I'm putting on a show, that's all.'

A girl came strutting across the street in indecently tight denim hot-pants and a Hawaiian-style top, tied in a knot at the front. 'Some show,' remarked Lieutenant Berridge, as she waggled her way around the parked police cars. 'I think you deserve an Emmy for that.'

A young black man was scrabbling on the road in front of Chief Ruse's car, picking up parcels. Chief Ruse grunted in amusement. 'One look at that ass and he dropped the lot.'

Skellett arrived on Washington Street alone, a few minutes before seven o'clock, in a shiny white '80 Eldorado. He climbed out of the car, closed the door carefully and almost noiselessly behind him, and then walked across the sidewalk with his hat tugged low over his forehead, and his white city shoes clicking on the sidewalk. A small

116

crowd of onlookers watched him from behind a police barrier with curiosity.

'Chief Ruse,' he said, politely.

'Mr Skellett,' responded Chief Ruse.

'Chief Ruse, I have here a warrant issued by the Chief Judge of the State of Arizona requiring you to release the remains of Mrs Margot Schneider into the custody of the National Security Agency. I also have papers from the National Security Agency requiring you to do the same. I have to tell you that unless you comply with these warrants, you will be in serious breach of the law, and in contempt of the Arizona District Court.'

Chief Ruse sniffed and noisily cleared his throat. 'I have to tell *you*, Mr Skellett, that Mrs Schneider's body is not going to leave the Phoenix city morgue until I am personally satisfied that her body has been properly identified and that the cause of death has been established by a full autopsy carried out by *my* medical examiners.'

'Chief Ruse, these warrants –'

'Mr Skellett, you can roll up those warrants and stuff them up your ass.'

Skellett was silent for a moment, his lips pursed. He looked a little white around the eyes. Then at last he adjusted his hat, and said, 'Okay. You're adamant?'

Chief Ruse nodded. 'You bet.'

Skellett looked at his heavy gold Rolex wristwatch. 'I'll come back here in exactly one hour. I'll bring an ambulance with me. If you're prepared to release Mrs Schneider's remains by then, we'll say nothing more about it, and I won't take the matter any further. If you're *not*, however. I'll have to take steps. You understand that, don't you?'

Just then, Kathy Forbes pushed herself forward, holding up the microphone of her Sony tape-recorder. 'Sir?' she asked. 'Can you tell me why you're so anxious to remove the remains of Mrs Margot Schneider from the Phoenix city morgue? Is there some kind of threat to national security involved?'

Skellett gave her a tight, impatient grimace. 'I don't have any comment to make to the Press at this time.'

'But this *is* a matter of national security?' Kathy persisted.

'We do have to evaluate certain possible infractions of US military integrity, yes.'

'What does that mean in English? You're trying to tell me that Margot Schneider's death may have had something to do with a military security leak?'

'I can't make any further comment on that right now.'

'When *will* you be able to comment? And why do you have to take Mrs Schneider's remains?'

Skellett turned and stalked briskly away across the sidewalk, but Kathy came after him, closely followed by two other newspaper reporters and a cameraman from KPHO television. Skellett raised his hand in front of his face to prevent the cameraman from focusing on that pale vinegary scowl of his, but the cameraman ducked and weaved around him and caught on video tape an expression which the KPHO anchorman later described as 'noticeably less than jolly.'

'Did Margot Schneider have anything to do with Cuba?' asked Kathy.

Skellett, already halfway into his Cadillac, froze and stared at Kathy as if she had cursed out loud. 'Cuba?' he demanded. 'What made you say Cuba?'

'*You're* supposed to be answering the questions, not me,' Kathy told him.

'I want to know why you said Cuba.'

Kathy said, 'I don't have to tell you that. You're the public servant. I represent the people.'

'Get in the car,' said Skellett.

'Not a hope.'

'You want to hear the truth about this? Get in the car.'

Kathy glanced anxiously behind her. Chief Ruse was talking loudly to Lieutenant Berridge, and by now the other reporters had turned back to hear what he was saying. 'Absolutely no way that Mrs Schneider's remains are going to be released until – ' She hesitated for a moment, but then she walked around the front of Skellett's Cadillac, and climbed into the passenger seat. Skellett slammed his door, started up the engine, and swung the car westwards with a sharp squeal of tyres.

'Now then,' said Skellett, 'what's this about Cuba?'

Kathy turned around in her seat. A beige Pontiac was following them, only twenty yards behind. 'They're tailing you,' she said. 'You know that, don't you?'

'Of course I do. They've been tailing me ever since I left my hotel this morning. They're just trying to intimidate me, that's all.'

'Chief Ruse is a hard nut. He won't budge unless he really has to.'

Skellett shrugged, and turned on the car radio, twanging country-and-western music. '*Don't forget me when the sun goes down. . . .*' He made a right at 11th Avenue, and headed northwards in the direction of University Park. Kathy said, 'I can't honestly remember when I ever saw Chief Ruse so upset.'

'I'm treading on his favourite bunion, that's all.'

Kathy was silent for a while. Then she said, 'There's something very important happening here, isn't there?'

'Important?'

'Well, they wouldn't have sent anyone from the National Security Agency if it hadn't been important.'

'No,' said Skellett. 'They wouldn't.'

'So what's going on? The whole of downtown Phoenix is bristling with armed police. Chief Ruse is blowing a gasket. Tell me what's going on down here.'

Skellett glanced up at his rear-view mirror. The beige Pontiac was still there, cruising steadily through the morning traffic. The sky above the buildings was a light, dry blue, the colour of southern harebells. The temperature was already up to 71°, and the radio was forecasting another hot one.

'You're a pretty girl,' said Skellett. 'I know that you're also a reporter, and that ever since Watergate, every reporter has been trying to break the national scandal to end all national scandals. But, let me tell you, this isn't any Watergate. This is straightforward, routine security, a simple operation to make sure that the military technology at Luke Air Force Base remains confidential.'

'You're trying to tell me that Mrs Schneider was passing out secret Air Force information?'

'I'm not trying to tell you anything, except that you'd be making a mistake if you tried to blow this story up into anything special. So, Chief Ruse lost his temper? How much of a story is that? I have warrants for the remains of Mrs Margot Schneider to be turned over to the National Security Agency. Chief Ruse will have to give in eventually.'

Kathy felt oddly prickly and frightened sitting next to Skellett. He drove with one long-fingered hand draped over the top of the steering-wheel like the crab-creature in *Alien* which implanted itself in John Hurt's facemask. There was something casual but alarming about him; as if he would be just as happy strangling a dog as he would be cooking up spaghetti bolognese for his friends. A man with no perceivable conscience.

Kathy said, 'You got upset when I mentioned Cuba.'

'Upset? No, I wouldn't call it upset. But interested to know why you said it.'

'It was a guess, that's all. Can you believe a guess?'

Skellett flicked his eyes up towards his rear-view mirror again. 'Unusual kind of a guess,' he commented.

'Not unusual at all. Phoenix has some pretty heavy Cuban exiles these days. Antonio Mantanzas, Juan Casilda. Ever since Marshall Roberts was elected, they've been talking about having another crack at overthrowing Castro. I thought maybe that Margot Schneider had gotten herself involved. You know – lonely widow, nothing else to do.'

'Are you serious?' asked Skellett.

'Of course I'm serious. We had a case just two months ago, an old lady from El Mirage joined up with a gang of bank robbers. She helped them turn over two banks before she was arrested. Said she was bored.'

Skellett said, 'You're bullshitting me, young lady.'

'Would I bullshit you? I'm trying to get a story out of you.'

'No, you're bullshitting me. No question. I know when someone's trying to bullshit me, and that's what you're doing. Cuba wasn't any guess. You know something, or else you've deduced something, and I want to know what.'

Kathy said, 'Well, you're out of luck.'

Skellett looked at her for the first time. His eyes were peculiarly vacant, as if he were staring right through her, and across the street somewhere. 'Are you going to tell me the truth or what?' he wanted to know.

'Is that a threat?' Kathy demanded. 'If that's a threat, you can stop this car right now and let me out.'

'I'm not stopping this car, young lady and you're going to tell me why you mentioned Cuba.'

'I'm getting *out* – ' snapped Kathy, and wrenched at the door-handle, but Skellett calmly touched the central locking switch, and the door refused to budge.

'Will you stop this car and let me out of here?' Kathy insisted. She was genuinely scared now. Skellett was so calm and inhuman, still piloting his car with one hand on the steering-wheel as if he were cruising along Main Street Mesa on a Saturday afternoon looking at used Oldsmobiles. He smiled at her, and when he smiled, she had no doubt at all that he would kill her, if he had to.

She twisted around in her seat again and the beige Pontiac was only a block behind. 'The cops are still tailing us,' she said. 'You want me to attract their attention? Tell them you tried to rape me?'

Skellett shrugged. 'You can do what you like. I'm in charge of this situation and you're not. I just want to know what led you to mention Cuba. Or *who*.'

'I'm an accredited journalist!' Kathy shouted at him. 'It doesn't matter who you are or what government agency you're from, you can't do this! My paper will have your guts!'

'Scripps-Howard, isn't it, the *Arizona Flag*?' asked Skellett, matter-of-factly.

'No. It's still independent. The Rosner family.'

'Ah, that's right. The Rosners. Nice old folks who wouldn't like to do anything to upset the President. I shouldn't think the Rosners will stir up too much of a fuss, even when one of their girl reporters goes missing.'

'Are you *crazy*?' asked Kathy.

Skellett shook his head. 'Just doing my job.'

He had reached Woodland Avenue, opposite University Park and the Arizona Museum. He flicked down his traffic signal to turn left, but when the lights changed he gunned the Eldorado's engine and swerved right, provoking a hostile chorus of car-horns, and an upraised finger from a cab driver. The beige Pontiac was momentarily snarled up behind them, but then it bounced over the corner of the sidewalk, and came in fast pursuit.

Kathy shouted, 'Stop! For God's sake, *stop!*'

But Skellett took no notice, and deftly swerved the Eldorado left, on squittering tyres, and roared north-westwards on Grand Avenue, which followed the line of the Aitchison Topeka and Santa Fé Railroad, and which was the only diagonal street in the whole of Phoenix. Kathy wrenched at Skellett's right shoulder, making him swerve, but he pushed her away flat-handed, and snarled, 'Don't make me hit you, because I will. You stupid bitch.'

He streaked up Grand Avenue, past West Roosevelt Street and the Arizona State Fair Grounds, running one stop light after another, with the Pontiac close behind him. Kathy gripped the edge of her seat as they bounced at 75 mph across the intersection with Encanto Boulevard, and set up another flurry of horns. 'You're out of your *mind!*' she told him. 'You're going to kill us!'

Skellett said nothing, but kept his foot flat against the Cadillac's floor. He swerved around a bus, narrowly missing its rear bumper, and then zig-zagged between a string of cars. Kathy heard a siren behind them, and turned around to see that the Pontiac which had previously been trailing them incognito was now sporting a red flashing light, and was officially in hot pursuit.

She thought for a moment that Skellett was going to

turn north on to the Canyon Freeway, where he would be bound to be stopped by one of Chief Ruse's roadblocks. But he sped straight over the freeway and kept going northwest on Grand Avenue, crossing Indian School Road on a green light at nearly 80 miles an hour.

Kathy turned around again, and she was just in time to see a huge unmarked tractor-trailer pull out of the side of the road, and begin to crawl diagonally in front of the police Pontiac that was chasing them. What followed was like a very slow-motion movie, and she stared in horror as every movement unfolded in front of her at half-speed, tragic and unstoppable.

The Pontiac collided with the tractor's offside front wheel, and rolled over sideways in a shower of glass and hubcaps and torn-off windshield wipers. Kathy could see the driver rise through his shattered side window like a bloody Aphrodite rising from the waves, and cartwheel across the road. Then the car screeched and skidded and rolled again, and crashed straight into the window of a liquor store on the opposite side of the street, bringing down shelves of whiskey and wine and champagne, and thrusting a middle-aged woman customer straight through the glass front of the icebox, cutting off half of her face. Her nose and her forehead flapped up like a carnival mask.

Kathy didn't see any more: Skellett immediately took a right on Camelback, then a second right on 35th Street, and began to speed due southwards.

'You had that arranged,' she said, in a white and shaky voice.

'I'm a professional,' said Skellett. 'And meanwhile you know more about Mrs Margot Schneider than you've been telling me.'

'What are you going to do?'

'I'm going to take you back to a safe house, outside of town, and I'm going to ask you a few searching questions. Do you mind? Or would you rather answer them here and now?'

'What about Chief Ruse? He'll be wanting to know where I am.'

'Don't you worry about Chief Ruse. I've taken care of him, too.'

'What do you mean?'

Skellett took another swerving turn on Thomas Road, and began to head east. 'I told you. I'm a professional. I do things thoroughly and properly.'

'You're out of your mind. You've just killed people. Did you see that woman's face – ?'

'I wasn't looking.'

'*You're out of your mind!*' screamed Kathy.

Skellett stared at her coldly. 'Listen,' he told her, 'I'm an agent for the United States government. I have the highest authority to do whatever I find expedient to do. That accident back there was a failsafe, in case I needed it, which I did. If Ruse's men had kept well away, and let me do my job unhindered, it wouldn't have been necessary. I didn't want to hurt anybody, policemen or bystanders. But there are some government affairs which have to be dealt with secretly and quickly and conclusively. Don't think that what you saw back there was unusual.'

'This is like a *nightmare*,' said Kathy. 'I don't know anything about Margot Schneider at all. Why is she so important?'

'I didn't say she was. In any case, all that's important about her as far as *you're* concerned is why you connected her with Cuba.'

'I told you, it was a guess. I was fishing.'

'Too many people are fishing these days,' said Skellett, cryptically. 'A little less fishing, a bit more happy co-operation, we'd all get along with each other a darn sight better.'

'I didn't know government agents were permitted to philosophize,' said Kathy, regaining some of her confidence and sharpness, especially now that Skellett had slowed down.

Skellett gave an offhand smile. 'To apply a philosophy, you have to understand it. Blind obedience isn't enough.'

'Will you let me out of the car, please?' asked Kathy.

Skellett looked ahead, looked in his rear-view mirror, and then looked across at Kathy. 'No,' he said, quietly but quite emphatically, and she knew that it wouldn't do her any good to ask again.

Twelve

Chief Ruse was just leaving to find himself some breakfast when the mayor's official limousine drew up by the kerb, and the window was rolled down. Chief Ruse said, 'Wait a minute,' to Lieutenant Berridge, and walked across to bid good morning to Mayor Gardens.

'Good morning, Walter,' said the mayor. He was a thin, sun-wrinkled man with hair as crisp as Shredded Wheat. 'Harris tells me you've been having some difficulty with the NSA.'

'Nothing we can't handle,' said Chief Ruse, leaning on the Cadillac's black vinyl roof, and affording the mayor a close-up view of his enormous belly. 'A little difference in judicial focus, that's all.'

'I never thought I'd see the day when *you* started talking that bureaucratic jargon, Walter,' complained the mayor. 'What the hell's "judicial focus"?'

'It's the way you look at the law, Andrew. The NSA look at it one way, and I happen to look at it another way.'

The mayor drew back his lips over his clenched teeth. He always did that when he had to say something awkward. His words came out like chopped meat. 'The problem is, Walter, that Judge Fredericks happens to share the NSA's way of looking at it, and so do I, and that kind of leaves you way out on a limb.'

'Andrew,' warned Chief Ruse, leaning forward. 'There was a very nasty homicide here in Phoenix, a lady losing her head, and I don't mean to release her cadaver until I'm absolutely sure that I know what's going down around here. Because, you mark my words, *something* is.'

The mayor tried to smile, but couldn't manage it. 'I can understand your reservations, Walter. I sympathize totally with all of your feelings. But the NSA have gone through all the proper channels, and sought all the proper authority, and there isn't any way in which we can legally defy them. We're supposed to uphold the law, Walter, not obstruct it; and in this particular matter it seems that our own local priorities have been overwhelmingly superseded by national priorities.'

He hesitated, and then he said, 'Besides, I don't like all these sharpshooters and guard dogs around. It makes the city look like an armed camp.'

Chief Ruse drummed his podgy fingers on the roof of the mayor's car. Then he stood up straight, and hitched up his belt. 'I'm going to tell you something, Andrew. The only way they're going to remove the remains of Mrs Margot Schneider out of that morgue is over my dead body.'

'Walter, I'm appealing to you,' said the mayor.

'You're appealing to me, and you can't even be bothered to get out of your limousine?'

Mayor Gardens immediately opened the door of his car and stepped out on to the sidewalk. It was only when he was standing next to Chief Ruse that the remarkable difference in their heights became apparent. Mayor Gardens was only a fraction of an inch over five feet tall, whereas Chief Ruse was well over six foot two. Usually, Mayor Gardens managed to arrange his meetings with Chief Ruse so that he was standing on a dais, or at the top of a flight of stairs, or sitting behind his enormous mayoral desk. He knew that Chief Ruse was challenging him to show his sincerity by coming out on to the sidewalk; to show that he really meant what he said.

'Now,' said Mayor Gardens. 'I'm appealing to you. Do you understand me? I don't want to have to take any action that one or other of us might regret.'

Chief Ruse took out his handkerchief and dabbed at his big, sweaty face. 'I hope you're not trying to say what I think you're trying to say.'

Mayor Gardens grimaced again, and looked embarrassed. 'How long did he give you? Skellett?'

'An hour,' said Chief Ruse, placidly. 'More like forty-five minutes now.'

'Well, in forty-five minutes I want you to release that cadaver. Do you hear me? I want you to do it because it's legal and because it's right and because I don't want Phoenix to get a reputation with the National Security Agency for being unco-operative and negative. We're going to need them some day, Walter, need their help, and this isn't the way to go about getting it.'

'Andrew,' said Chief Ruse, 'I am not letting that body go. Now, do you mind if I go get some breakfast?'

Chief Ruse walked away, his large backside swaying rhythmically beneath his baggy pants. Mayor Gardens watched him go, and then yelled after him, 'Walter! You meathead!'

When Chief Ruse got back to his car, Lieutenant Berridge was taking a radio report from police headquarters. 'The chief's right here,' he said, 'I'll tell him. Okay. Over and out.'

'What's going on?' asked Chief Ruse.

'It's Skellett. Wilson and McKenzie tailed him uptown, up Grand Avenue. Apparently he took that girl reporter with him, what's her name, from the *Flag*.'

'Kathy Forbes,' said Chief Ruse. 'You spent half of yesterday evening trying to get into her pants, and you didn't even find out what her name is?'

'Wilson and McKenzie had an accident,' said Lieutenant Berridge, seriously. 'Hit a truck at eighty, and rolled over.

Wilson's down at the County General right now, broken legs, badly concussed. McKenzie died.'

'Shit,' said Chief Ruse. He was silent for a moment, standing with his hands on hips, looking down at the ground. Then he rubbed his face, and said again, 'Shit.'

'Skellett got clear,' added Lieutenant Berridge. 'Da Vito and Haskins thought they saw him driving south on 35th, but after that nothing.'

'He went north and then he went south?'

'Seems like it. Probably hung a right on Camelback or Bethany.'

'Hmm,' said Chief Ruse. 'He's got to be back in a half-hour or so, in any case, to pick up Margot Schneider's body. Or to *try* to pick up Margot Schneider's body.'

'There's nothing we can actually pin on him,' said Lieutenant Berridge. 'Speeding, maybe, but that's all.'

'What about the truckdriver?'

'What truckdriver?'

'The truckdriver in the accident with Wilson and McKenzie. Somebody took the trouble to ask him one or two questions, I hope?'

'Oh, sure,' said Lieutenant Berridge. 'But it doesn't seem like he was tied in with Skellett in any way.' He licked his thumb and turned back two or three pages of his notebook. 'His name's Gordon Farito, from Tucson. Clean record, apart from a couple of minor trucking offences, insecure loads, that kind of thing.'

'Insecure loads,' said Chief Ruse, reflectively. 'Insecure fucking loads.'

Lieutenant Berridge didn't quite know what to say. He closed up his notebook and tucked it back into his inside pocket. 'It just reminds me of something the Ziff brothers used to do. You remember the Ziff brothers, used to run stuff across the broder at Nogales and Sonoita? They'd always have an ambush set up someplace, in case of pursuit. A van or a truck that would just accidentally happen to pull out in front of the police after the Ziffs had gone by. Well – the Ziffs is what *this* reminds me of.'

Chief Ruse said, 'Make sure we know where we can

find Mr Farito, in case we want to talk to him some more. Meanwhile, let's go eat. I don't relish the idea of losing my job on an empty stomach.'

He climbed into the passenger seat of his car, and told his young police driver, 'Rita's, okay? And make it fast. I have exactly twenty-eight minutes to eat a plateful of corned-beef hash and eggs and get right back.'

'Very good, sir,' said the driver, and twisted the key in the ignition.

Chief Ruse knew what had happened at once. It was the slamming sensation against his ears, the way the entire world shrank into a pressurized pinprick, right in front of his eyes. And then came the unrelenting blast of fire and grit and glass and twisted fragments of metal, and the car doors flew off and tumbled away across the road.

He actually thought to himself: they've blown me up. This is what it's like to be blown up. And out of the shattered windshield he saw something which looked like a bloody carcass of beef turning over and over in the air, and realized it was his driver's torso, and that his driver's legs were still beside him in their wrecked and tattered seat, still poised for a journey to nowhere at all.

He heard the bang, or the echo of it from the surrounding buildings. He heard a pattering sound, and thought at first it was rain, but it was the sound of running feet. He thought for one ridiculous moment: I'm unhurt. I've been blown up, and I'm completely unhurt.

He heard the breathy roaring of a fire-extinguisher, as someone put out the flames. He heard someone else saying, 'Don't touch him, don't move him. He's still alive,' and he thought to himself, that's quite correct, I *am* still alive. Still alive, and what's more, unhurt.

'Lieutenant Berridge,' he tried to say, but he could only speak inside his mind. This is absurd, he thought to himself. I can articulate the words inside me, but I can't say them. It must be the shock. That's it. I'm unhurt, but I must be suffering from shock. I've seen it happen in road accidents. Nothing that a strong cup of coffee won't cure.

He thought it would be a good idea to close his eyes for a while. Rest was another excellent cure for shock. But he was surprised to find that he couldn't do that, either. It was almost as if he didn't have any eyelids. It was irritating, because his eyes were beginning to feel very sore.

He looked up, towards the sky. It must have been some hefty explosion: there was no roof on the car any more, only a blackened framework hung with red ribbons. He lowered his head again. He had no way of understanding that the red ribbons were all that remained of his face. His skull was showing white through his cheeks, and his bulging eyes were rolling and turning in their sockets like those of a gruesome doll. He looked so ghastly that to begin with nobody would step near him: they couldn't believe he was still alive.

Mayor Gardens was the first. He came forward, brisk and quick, and stripped off his coat. 'Walter,' he said. He knelt beside the police car's twisted chassis. 'Walter, you're going to be fine.'

Chief Ruse tried to focus on him, and gave a bloody snarl from his lipless mouth.

'You hear me, Walter? Everything's going to be fine. The medics are right here.'

'Skellett,' Chief Ruse tried to say, but he couldn't manage anything more than a thick choking noise. He tried to lift his arm, and take hold of Andrew's hand, but even an action as elementary as that seemed to be quite impossible. Damned stupid shock, he thought, I never felt so stupid in my whole life. His arm, still wearing his broken wristwatch, lay in the gutter more than fifty feet away.

He began to feel cold. His head began to droop. He looked down and saw that someone had been inconsiderate enough to leave yards of fire-extinguisher hose in his lap. Yards and yards of it, glistening and wet. You would have thought that they might have treated a shocked man with more respect than that.

Andrew Gardens covered him with his coat. 'Walter?

130

Do you hear me? Everything's going to be fine. You want me to say a prayer for you? Would you like a prayer?'

Chief Ruse could hear the mayor's voice like a distant telephone call from somewhere very cold. Why was Andrew telephoning him from the Arctic? It seemed quite absurd, enough to make a man laugh. He knew that he was perfectly all right, but he felt very cold, very distant.

Andrew Gardens said, 'God be merciful to us, and bless us: and show us the light of his countenance, and be merciful unto us.'

The cameraman from KPHO videotaped the mayor's tears, in close-up, but kept his lens away from Chief Ruse. Chief Ruse died unphotographed, a few minutes later, still believing that he had escaped the explosion unhurt.

Thirteen

High above the street, the black smoke from the bomb still hung in the windless sky like a dead soul that refused to be on its way to purgatory. Walter Ruse's nemesis, the hooded reaper of the terrorist age. And only thirty yards away, in distinct profile, wearing a crumpled tan safari-suit, his hands in his pockets, stood Henry Friend. A woman standing close to Henry with a white poodle in her arms was saying, 'Oh my good Lord. I never saw anything like that before, not ever. That poor *man*. Blown to pieces. I never saw anything like that before.'

Henry lit a cigarette. He didn't look towards the wreck at all: not because he was squeamish, but because he didn't need to. He hadn't personally planted or wired up the explosives himself; he never touched explosives unless he had to. Not after his friend Franco Presto had accidentally blown himself up with a napalm device in a 25th-floor elevator in Chicago. Franco's incinerated skeleton had been found wearing a helmet of melted aluminium from the elevator's ceiling. Nice funeral, lots of flowers, but not the way that Henry wanted to go. Henry wanted to go peacefully. That was why he had done nothing more than supervise this particular hit: the timing and the logistics and the supply of equipment and transport.

He rubbed his eyes, and stung them with the nicotine on his fingers. He was very tired, and he needed a bath. Two days ago, only six hours after he had arrived back in Los Angeles from Phoenix, and had triumphantly deposited Margot Schneider's head in a locker at Santa Monica Municipal Airport at Clover Field, they had instructed him to return immediately to Arizona.

He had been sitting in the Black Whale restaurant in Marina del Rey, the first time that he had sat in a restaurant to do nothing more than eat and relax in twenty years; the first time that he had been able to concentrate on his own drink and his own food, instead of having furtively to check the identity of his fellow diners. He had ordered a giant-sized Bloody Mary and a heaping plateful of Alaskan King Crab, the Black Whale's speciality. And just as he had sipped his drink and closed his eyes in exhaustion and peace a hand had tugged at his sleeve. The same, familiar tug.

'You have to go back,' a young, half-broken voice had whispered. A voice like an adolescent numbers-runner.

'Go back?' he had said, without opening his eyes. 'Go back *where*?'

'Phoenix. There's trouble.'

'They've found out who she is?'

'Unh-hunh. It's something else altogether. Don't ask me what.'

Henry had at last opened his eyes and stared at the young man in the checkered linen suit and the upslanted sunglasses, and thought to himself, a creep. Why did they always pick creeps? Well, maybe the kid was purposely trying to look that way. You never knew these days.

Trying to look like a zod or whatever they called it in Valspeak.

'I'm not sure I haven't had enough of Arizona,' he had replied, as carefully as if the words he chose could really make the difference between going back and not going back. He had already caught sight of the waiter bringing over his pink-and-white mountain of iced crab.

'Nonetheless,' the young man had said.

Henry had thought: *Nonetheless? Who says nonetheless?* But nonetheless, he had caught the next Western Airlines 727 from LAX to Phoenix, without even telephoning his brother or his bookie, or unlatching his Gucci valise. He had stared out of the airplane window as the dry beige western desert of Arizona reappeared beneath him, and his eyes had been as glutinous as freshly-opened clams. It never ended, this job. You killed one, and you always had to kill more, as if every human life was part of an intricate network which trembled whenever one of the lives was deliberately extinguished. 'Sweeping-up,' the Mafia had always called these extra killings. 'You sweep up for me, gumba, hah?' 'For sure, Piretti, for you I sweep up.' Five or six killings for the price of one.

An ambulance came whooping and warbling across Washington Street, and blocked Henry's view of the smoking wreck. He waited for a minute or two, and then pushed his way as politely as he could out of the crowd, and began to walk southwards on 6th, to the corner where he had parked his rented car. He felt unexpectedly depressed, not because of the carnage he had created, not because of the violent loss of two human beings, but because this whole job seemed to have become unnecessarily messy and complicated. To a man who had spent so long in motel rooms, living out of suitcases, untidiness and disarray were anathema. In every Holiday Inn or Howard Johnson's, he had placed his bottle of English Leather to the right-hand side of the dressing-table mirror, his new copy of *Reader's Digest* on the left-hand side of his bed. He had lived systematically and unobtrusively, a real professional: and that had been his pride. It had worked, too: after twenty years of self-effacement, he had found the woman who called herself Margot Schneider and killed her. The trouble was, her death seemed to have stirred up some kind of psychic vibration, some dark ripple of memory and consciousness that meant bad news.

He reached his green Mercury, opened the driver's door, and climbed awkwardly in. The young black man was already waiting for him, calm, unexcited, his peacock blue shirt collar neatly folded over the lapels of his cream weave sport coat.

'Worked a dream, hunh?' the young man asked, as Henry settled himself into his seat, and started the engine.

'You didn't expect it to? You're working with a lifetime professional now, young Boyd.'

'*Lloyd*, Mr Friend, not Boyd.'

Henry pulled carefully out into the traffic. He sniffed. 'Perhaps we can all go home now.'

'I don't know, Mr Friend. Mr Skellett didn't say.'

Henry testily drummed his fingertips on the wheel. '*Skellett*,' he said to himself, in the tone of a man who has suddenly remembered that he has left his wallet at home. 'Was that a good job or was that a good job?'

'Perfect, Mr Friend. Timing, perfect. Charge, perfect. Total effect, perfect.'

'Better than that damned mess they made in Virginia,' said Henry, concentrating on making a left into Jackson, past the Union Railroad Station.

Lloyd didn't say anything, but propped his elbow on the windowsill and stared out at the street. Henry glanced at him, and said, 'Were *you* involved in that one?'

'You're not supposed to know that.'

'I see,' said Henry. 'And it never occurred to you that Mr Alexander might possibly change cars? You didn't have a contingency plan?'

'I can't discuss it.'

Henry gave a soft, unamused chuckle. 'Skellett,' he said again, acidly. 'Skellett couldn't pour piss out of a shoe if the instructions were written on the sole. I think Skellett always wanted to be a cowboy. Clint Eastwood. Did you see that song and dance today? The way he riled up those local badges so that they came pouring out on to the street with guns, and sharpshooters, and TV cameras and Press? This whole business was *supposed* to be kept completely secret.'

He paused for a while, driving with care through the morning traffic. 'If you ask me, Skellett's going to be lucky if he lasts the month,' he reflected, as they made another left towards the Greyhound Bus Terminal.

Lloyd said, 'Who knows? I don't get into discussions. I just plant the packages.'

'You did well today. That took a little nerve, planting that one.'

'It was nothing, man. The timing was perfect.'

Henry smiled to himself in satisfaction. There had been no way of discovering in advance where the Chief of Police would be parked, or even which vehicle he would use. That was why Henry had chosen a 7½-lb high-explosive charge in a vinyl briefcase. He had learned years ago how easily people's attention could be distracted, even the attention of police officers and security guards. And the big-breasted brunette in the tight denim hotpants he had picked up at Sky Harbor hotel the previous evening had certainly earned her hundred dollars by turning every head in the street – just at the moment that a young black 'office-worker' with too many packages in his arms had crossed the road in front of Chief Ruse's parked car and scattered everything all over the road.

As he had made a clumsy performance of trying to collect his packages, the young black 'office-worker' had thrust the vinyl briefcase up behind Chief Ruse's front bumper, into the open cavity between the car's front grille and the radiator. There had been six wire hooks on the back of the briefcase, made out of hotel coathangers: it had needed just one of them to catch on to the radiator's criss-cross support bars to hold the briefcase securely out of sight.

The explosives had been triggered by a short-range electronic receiver which responded to the frequency of automobile starter-motors. Henry had once bought four of them, $30 each, in Cleveland. A bargain, as it turned out.

Henry supposed that he could have waited until later to eliminate Chief Ruse. Tomorrow evening perhaps, when everything had settled down. He could also have done it much more quietly. But if Skellett could grandstand then *he* could, too; and Skellett had explicitly told him to do the job right away, without delay. He didn't like Skellett and he had sorely wanted to show him just how frighteningly efficient he could be, when he was called to.

There was something else in the air, something that Henry couldn't quite pin down. A feeling that some very heavy political manoeuvring was going on, a deep shift in the power structure. Maybe that was the reason why Skellett had taken such a risk in confronting Chief Ruse direct, to get himself noticed by his superiors. Henry didn't know very much about the NSA, but he had been briefed and debriefed by enough NSA agents to have realized that there was a constant struggle within the agency for political influence, especially now that Ikon was growing so old and infirm. Henry didn't know very much about the NSA, but he knew very much more than he was meant to. If they had discovered just how much, they would have killed him. Instantly. Outright. He knew that for sure.

He left Lloyd at the bus terminal. Lloyd leaned back into the car and said, 'Maybe we'll work together again some day, how about it?'

Henry shook his head.

'Just have a drink, then, maybe?'

'Maybe,' said Henry, and reached over to close the passenger door. Lloyd watched him drive away and picked his teeth with the edge of his thumbnail. There was something scary about Henry Friend. The man seemed to possess his own personal voodoo.

On the way back to downtown Phoenix, Henry was passed by a howling ambulance and a keening chorus of police motorcycles, speeding in the opposite direction, towards the county hospital. Chief Ruse, on his second-to-last ride.

Back at Chief Ruse's house, Ingrid opened the front door and was surprised to see Lieutenant Berridge standing there. Lieutenant Berridge was distressed to see that Ingrid was wearing a face-pack. It was going to be particularly difficult to tell a woman with a face-pack that her husband had just been blown to bits.

'Mrs Ruse,' he said, 'would you please wash off the face-pack?'

She stared directly at him. Then she stared *past* him, at the white police-car parked by the kerb, its red lights revolving.

A wet line slid slowly down her chalk-white cheek from the side of her left eye. She said, 'There's been an accident, hasn't there? It's Walter.'

'Yes,' nodded Lieutenant Berridge. 'It's Walter.'

Fourteen

Joe Jasper drove Nadine to Dulles Airport that afternoon, in Titus' freshly-dented Porsche. Titus had inspected the damage at five o'clock in the morning, before he left for the State Department, and had said nothing at all. But Joe had been able to tell from the flinching muscles in his cheeks that he never wanted to drive the car again.

Nadine was silent for most of the drive across the Potomac. It was a grey, humid day. The eastern seaboard was overcast from Boston down to Norfolk, and thunder was forecast for the rest of the afternoon and most of the evening. Nadine wore a yellow silk headscarf and a grey silk blouse, and Italian slacks. Most of her face was concealed behind large mirror-lensed sunglasses. Even Titus would probably have walked past her in a crowd.

She felt tired, but she wasn't dissatisfied. Apart from a night of lovemaking with Titus, which always unwound her, she had actually achieved that most subtle of successes: which was to have given Titus so much confidence in her that for the first time he had actually persuaded her to participate in one of his clandestine plots.

It hadn't been easy. It had taken years to make him believe in her sincerity. Not her sexual sincerity: that was something else altogether. Sexually, she found him as stimulating and as necessary to her daily happiness as a narcotic drug; and he knew it. What was more, he was probably as deeply addicted to her as she was to him. There wasn't any part of each other's bodies that they hadn't explored, both with tenderness and fierce excitement.

No, the difficult part had been building up the friendship, and the utter trust. She had been obliged to argue with him and fight with him just to make him believe in her, and to treat her as something more than a Washington wife. It had taken five-and-a-half exhausting years, but now it had paid off. Nadine couldn't help smiling to herself as Joe turned into the airport entrance, and made his way towards the short-term parking-lot.

'Something funny, Mrs Alexander?' asked Joe.

'I don't think so. It's just this heavy disguise.'

Joe nodded, two or three times more than was really necessary. 'If your friends at the bridge club could see you now, huh?'

'That's right, Joe.'

Joe found a parking-space, and wrestled the Porsche into it; although he finished up so close to the car parked next to him that he couldn't open his own door, and had to struggle across to Nadine's side. 'I'm not very good with manuals, you know? I'm too busy worrying about the shift to think where I'm pointing.'

They walked towards the terminal. Joe took his sunglasses out of his coat pocket and put them on, feeling very undercover and clandestine. Nadine said to him, 'You'll recognize this hooker when you see her?'

'Sure. But you shouldn't call her a hooker, Mrs Alexander. At the very worst, hostess.'

Nadine ignored him. 'What is she like, as a person?' she asked. 'You've met her, haven't you, and talked to her?'

'I liked her, as a matter of fact,' said Joe. 'Mind you, I like most people. I'm not what you might call socially discriminating.'

'Oh. Thanks a lot.'

'I didn't mean *you*, Mrs Alexander,' Joe apologized. 'I didn't mean to suggest that —'

'Oh, for Christ's sake, stop cringing,' Nadine snapped at him. 'And take off those ridiculous sunglasses. They make you look like an albino.'

Joe took the sunglasses off and pushed them back in his pocket. He had to skip a little to keep up with her. 'Colleen Petley is class, as hostesses go. Nice background, and it shows. Well brought up. And of course she's pretty well off these days. A thousand a night for three hundred nights of the year, plus gratuities and other assorted goodies.'

The flight from Dallas-Fort Worth was already in; and Colleen Petley was waiting for them outside the terminal, by the cab-rank, silently escorted by one of Joe Jasper's helpers, a taciturn ex-pugilist called Crack Nielsen. The meeting between Nadine Alexander, tall and svelte and supercilious, and Colleen Petley, small and pouting and obvious, was one of the classic encounters of modern politics: but, like the death of Chief Ruse, it went unphotographed. It did, however, turn heads.

Colleen Petley aka Rita Haze was blonde, curly, busty, and stunningly pretty, with wide blue eyes and a mouth like smashed strawberries. She wore an off-the-shoulder Mexican-style blouse in frilly blue, a wide white PVC belt, and pale-blue satin pedal-pushers that looked as if they had been sprayed on to her naked body by Kustom Kars of Redondo Beach. Crack Neilsen, short and heavy, his face as immovable as a heap of concrete that had been allowed to dry unshovelled on a sidewalk, carried her white airline bags and her white fun fur.

Joe Jasper took Colleen's arm and leaned towards her ear. 'This is Mrs Alexander, Colleen. The wife of the Secretary of State. Now, all you have to do is shake her hand and say hi, and don't make a performance, and then we'll be on our way.'

'Hello, Colleen,' Nadine greeted her. 'Welcome to Washington.'

'Well, delighted,' replied Colleen, in a high Texas accent. Then, to Nadine's complete amazement, she curtseyed. Her enormous breasts bulged dangerously from the elastic of her Mexican blouse.

'The car's in the parking-lot,' said Joe. 'I just hope we can squeeze everybody in.'

They drove northwest along the Washington Memorial Parkway in awkward intimacy. Nadine said to Joe, 'I don't know why the hell Titus ever buys these ridiculous foreign imports. Sixty thousand dollars for a car that wouldn't even pass the federal housing regulations on overcrowding.'

Colleen chipped in, 'I knew a guy in Vegas who owned this amazing stretched Lincoln. He had television, brocade seats, and a real wolfskin rug. It was just amazing.'

'Very nice,' replied Nadine. Then, to Joe, out of the corner of her mouth, 'I thought you said *class*.'

Joe gave an embarrassed shrug. 'It's a question of comparisons. It *seemed* like class in Vegas.'

'Have you been to Washington before, dear?' Nadine asked Colleen.

'I never did. Is that the Lincoln Memorial?'

'That's right. Maybe in a day or two you'll have a chance to see the sights.'

'I've got to tell you,' said Colleen, 'I'm very nervous. I mean, I'm not at all sure that I'm doing the right thing. I mean, he is the President, and all.'

Nadine smiled at her, and reached around to pat her comfortingly on the hand. 'Don't you worry. You're doing the most honourable and courageous thing that anybody possibly could. You realize that your name will probably go down in history?'

Colleen gave an uncertain smile. 'I know. Mr Jasper told me that. But, you know, I'm kind of concerned. Flattered, for sure. But, you know, concerned.'

'That's why we're all so proud of you,' said Nadine. 'Because you're *concerned*.'

They arrived at last in Rockville, Maryland; in a quiet tree-lined back street where the most vicious enemy was crab-grass on the lawn, and where status was measured not in political power but in late-model Oldsmobiles and push-button garage doors. There was a humid wind blowing as they climbed out of the car, and Joe went up to the single-storey house that he had rented under the name of 'Smithson', and opened the front door. Nadine said to Colleen, 'Go ahead. Step inside. It's your home.'

Inside, the house was stale but comfortable. Thick shag-pile rugs, leather-upholstered furniture, televisions in the living-room, kitchen and dining-room. On the cream-painted walls, the kind of non-committal orange-and-brown abstract prints usually found in Loews hotels. A glass-fronted bar, a breakfast den, and a patio door with a view of a small, untidy back yard, with a rusty wire leaf-burner.

'No jacuzzi?' asked Colleen, disappointed. 'I always spend *hours* in the jacuzzi.'

'You want a hot tub?' asked Joe, before Nadine could say anything at all. 'We'll have one fitted in. No problem.'

'Well,' said Colleen, walking fom room to room, her tight pedal-pushers shining in the mid-afternoon gloom like freshly-caught bluefish, 'I guess it isn't *too* bad, for a hideout.'

'You mustn't think of it as a hideout,' insisted Joe, writing down 'hot tub' on the back of an envelope. 'It's a temporary refuge, that's all. As soon as all of this problem is over, we'll be getting you some place far better. Hot tubs in every room, if that's what you want.'

'I could use a drink,' said Nadine. 'I don't suppose you

happen to have mixed up any of those martinis of yours, Joe?'

Joe tucked away his pencil. 'I do believe we have a jug or two in the icebox. I came up here last night, just to check that Colleen would have everything she needed.'

'If you once taste Joe's martinis, you'll never need anything else again,' smiled Nadine.

Joe poured drinks, then went to the phone to sort out arrangements for tomorrow's press conference. Crack Nielsen, stolid as ever, was keeping watch out of the window. Colleen said, 'I think I'll take a bath. I feel like I've been travelling for ever. Do you want to come and talk, Mrs Alexander?'

'Call me Nadine, for God's sake,' said Nadine, following her into the bedroom suite.

Colleen covered her face with her hands, so that only her wide cornflower eyes were showing. 'You know something, I've been trying not to show it, but when Joe Jasper called me last night and told me that you were going to take care of me personally . . . well, I couldn't believe it. I promised myself I was going to be so *blahsay*, you know? But I've read so much about you in the magazines; and I saw you with Johnny Carson. Wasn't that just hilarious when he asked you to show him how a man should seduce a really tall woman?'

'Hilarious,' agreed Nadine, sitting on the end of the bed and crossing her legs.

'I have to say it, I really admire you,' said Colleen. 'All the things that you've been doing for women's rights; and everything you've been saying about nuclear weapons. That was very courageous of you, you know, considering who your husband is.'

'Everybody has to take a moral stand somewhere,' Nadine told her.

'Well, for sure, and that's why I said that I'd come along to Washington. When you consider that he's supposed to be the *President* . . . Well, a man like that, a man with those sex habits, you wouldn't even ask him to run a concert party, let alone a country, you know?'

Nadine spread her hand and made a show of inspecting her long red fingernails. 'How did Joe Jasper find you?' she asked.

'I'm not really sure. But I told a guy I know called Jackie Opa all about the President, you know, what he did during the primaries, and I guess Jackie Opa must've sold the information for whatever he could get for it. I mean, you can't *blame* him. Jackie Opa, I mean.'

'No, sure. I can't blame him,' said Nadine.

Colleen tugged off her Mexican-style blouse, revealing big soft breasts that were cradled in a Frederick's-of-Hollywood quarter-cup bra. Nadine had always considered that her own figure was Valkyrie-like; but Colleen's was centre-spread quality, golden and curvy, a living breathing Little Annie Fannie. Nadine watched her as she stood in front of the looking-glass and unfastened her tight satin pedal-pushers, and thought to herself that, in spite of her sexual brashness, in spite of her own elegance and fame, they were sisters of a kind, sisters both of fate and of political expedience.

'I didn't bring too many clothes with me,' said Colleen, sliding her pants down her bare hips. 'I have a *huge* wardrobe back in Vegas; so many dresses I have a card-index. And *shoes*.'

'We'll find you some clothes,' said Nadine. 'I'll take you out shopping if you like. Now you're in Washington, maybe we'll be able to find you something more chic. A tailored suit, maybe; and some formal evening gowns.'

'You're really kind,' said Colleen. 'I just *know* that we're going to be friends.'

'I hope so,' said Nadine. She was being polite when she said it, but then Colleen turned around and stood in front of her wearing nothing but her uplift bra and a cute smashed-strawberry smile, and Nadine felt an upsurge within her that she hadn't felt for years and years, not since she had been at school, on that freezing whirling winter's day, and she and Tania had wrapped themselves up naked in a huge bearskin rug and –

She looked away. She found herself guiltily trying to

143

remember whether the bedroom door was locked. Colleen sat down perkily beside her and began to file at her nails. Close up, she was even more unreal: her skin was flawless except for a Southern Cross of moles on her left shoulder, her little nipples were sugar-pink. Everything about her was shiny and bright and larger than life. No wonder she made a thousand dollars a night.

Nadine said, 'You won't be making much money while you're here.'

'Oh, I don't care about *that*,' smiled Colleen, wiggling her fingers. 'I haven't taken a day off in two years. Can you believe that? Two years. Then it was only a weekend at Lake Tahoe, and that was with four guys. Four! Mind you, only one was a real tiger. The rest were, you know, eager but easily tired.'

'Do you really enjoy it?' asked Nadine. It was one of the questions she had promised herself that she wouldn't ask. But now that she had met Colleen, she couldn't resist it. She would never be able to form any kind of relationship with Colleen, as friend or helper or protector, until she understood what could possibly motivate a girl to do anything a man wanted. Especially a girl as pretty and vivacious as this.

Colleen blinked her big blue eyes. 'Enjoy it? What do you mean?'

'Do you enjoy doing what you do? Being a hostess?'

Colleen thought about it with obvious seriousness. Then she said, 'Yes. I guess I do.'

'Even when you have to do the kind of thing that Marshall Roberts made you do?'

Colleen shrugged, and went on filing her nails. 'It's all a question of what your threshold is, I guess. I mean your threshold of tolerance. I mean some girls get upset if their husband says he wants to wear their dirty panties to work. They think he's a pervert or something. Then again some girls want to do things themselves but don't know how to tell their boyfriends or husbands without feeling like they're whores or something. The only reason I'm in business is because ordinary people don't relate to each other, you know? If a wife wants to tinkle all over her husband, and he doesn't mind, then what difference does it make? Anyway, Marshall Roberts didn't *make* me do anything. Nobody does. They ask for what they want, and I tell them the price.'

Nadine didn't know what to answer to that. She sat staring at Colleen for a while; and Colleen stared back. It was a strange, decisive moment.

'I'd better take that bath now,' said Colleen.

'And I'd better get back to Georgetown,' said Nadine, looking at her watch.

Colleen stood up. She reached behind her back and unhooked her bra. Her breasts swayed a little as she took it off. She had fine blonde pubic hair, closely trimmed, and the candy-pink lips of her vulva pouted through it like some wholesome but forbidden sweetmeat. Nadine looked up at her, and attempted a dismissive smile, but somehow her face seemed frozen. She kept thinking of Tania and that deep warm bearskin rug, and that snow that fell outside the window like lost memories, torn-up love-letters. . . .

'You know something,' she said, 'when I was at school. . . .'

Colleen held out her hand. Nadine, feeling foolish, but unable to refuse, accepted it. Colleen knelt down on the rug in front of her. Her nipples were pink and tight.

'Every woman feels it,' Colleen said, gently. 'I've had women too, you know. They pay me just like the men do. There's nothing wrong with it. Sometimes they're perfectly ordinary housewives. They come to Las Vegas to let go a little; experience something new. They gamble, have a few drinks. Then they spend a thousand dollars on a night with another woman. I don't know, I think they find it more reassuring to their femininity than going to bed with another man. Less *threatening*. And, most of the time, do you know what they want to do?' She released Nadine's hand, and squeezed her breasts so that the soft flesh bulged through her fingers. 'They want to feel another woman's breasts. Kiss another woman's nipples. It's not the way that men think it is at all. It's not like one of those lesbian porno movies, all panting and gasping – and wriggling around like grunion. It's soft, and it's gentle, and most of the time it's beautiful.'

Nadine leaned forward, only a fraction. Colleen, naked, ran her fingers into Nadine's thick brunette hair, and kissed her. It was an open-mouthed kiss, but the tips of their tongues explored each other only gently, nerves touching nerves.

'Lie back,' coaxed Colleen, in a voice so soft that Nadine could almost have imagined that she had heard it inside her head. She hesitated, but then Colleen murmured again, 'Lie back,' and she lay on the bed and looked up at the ceiling and made a deliberate effort to let herself go.

She felt, rather than saw. Once or twice she looked down, but mostly she closed her eyes, or stared at the jigsaw cracks on the ceiling above her.

She felt the zipper of her Italian slacks being opened; then they were pulled down from her hips. She rarely wore underwear under trousers, and she immediately felt the coolness of the air against the moistness of her sex. I'm excited, she thought. It's madness, but I'm actually excited. I don't even know if either of us remembered to lock the door, and both Joe Jasper and Crack Nielsen are sitting in the next room, separated from the most hair-raising scandal in Washington for five years by nothing more than an inch-and-a half of deal.

She felt Colleen's fingers running up the inside of her thighs, and she shivered. Then she felt Colleen's curly blonde hair against her skin, and the electric feeling of Colleen's tongue between her legs.

Colleen lapped her and teased her, her tongue-tip parting her flesh, arousing her clitoris with an expert immediacy that made Nadine blush; then probing into the opening of her urethra, teasing, tingling, and at last plunging suddenly and deeply into the slippery well of her vagina.

Nobody had ever aroused Nadine like this before, not

even Titus. Colleen's tongue flew over her sex like a wet and fluttering butterfly, making her shiver and bite at her knuckles in ecstasy. Now she didn't care whether the door opened or not, her mind was too crowded with erotic fantasies. She stretched her legs wide apart, so that Colleen could reach every crevice of her, and twisted the bedcover around herself as if she were burning or drowning or both.

Very near to the end, Colleen moistened one finger, and slid it promptly into Nadine's anus, as far as it would go, and when that happened Nadine felt as if the ceiling were collapsing on top of her, as if the world were a dynamited kaleidoscope, flying with fragments of coloured glass.

When she opened her eyes it seemed as if it were hours later, although it was only minutes. Colleen was in the bathroom, running a tubful of hot water, and scenting it with the Chanel bath oil which Joe Jasper had left for her. Nadine slowly pulled up her pants, fastened the belt, and got up from the bed. She ran her hands through her hair to fluff it up.

'I hope you realize that you've just committed a very indecent act with the woman who could be America's next First Lady?' she asked.

Colleen said, 'It had occurred to me, I have to admit.' Her tone seemed different now. Harder.

Nadine leaned against the bathroom door, watching Colleen swish the bath with her hand. 'You're not saying that you seduced me on purpose?'

'You're worried?' smiled Colleen.

'I don't know. *Should* I be worried?'

'I'm not going to take advantage of you, if that's what you mean. But a girl always needs some insurance. Like Marshall Roberts. I asked Denny specially if I could service Marshall Roberts; and don't you think it's paid off?'

Nadine said nothing while Colleen stepped into the bath, and sat down. 'Would you pass me that backbrush?' asked Colleen. 'That's right. The one with the swan's neck. Don't you think that's just *cute*?'

With the studied gestures of a drama-school student, Nadine sat down on the edge of the tub and watched Colleen while she soaped herself. 'I suppose I was a fool, then, to let you do what you did.'

'Not particularly. There weren't any witnesses.'

There was a silence between them, punctuated only by the slopping of bathwater. Then Colleen smiled and said, 'You've got me all wrong, you know that? And you've got *yourself* wrong, too. You should have more confidence in yourself as a woman. I made love to you because I *wanted* to make love to you, not because I wanted to blackmail you, or bring you down, or demand money.'

Nadine looked uncertain, but Colleen reached out of the water and took her hand. 'I was just trying to show you that I could have blackmailed you if I'd wanted to. I could have taken pictures. A whole roll, all of them clearly showing Mrs Nadine Alexander with her pants down. But I didn't, and I won't. I respect you, and the only way that I know how to show somebody that I respect them is to make love to them.'

'Well, it won't happen again,' said Nadine, in a brittle voice.

'It might,' Colleen opined.

'It won't. I'll make sure of that.'

'But you're supposed to look after me. Satisfy my every need, with the sole exception of money. Isn't that it?'

'Yes, that is it.'

'Well, that's what I want. That's my every need.'

'What are you talking about? What's your every need?'

'*You*, Mrs Alexander. *You're* my every need. You're beautiful and you're famous and you have the quickest climaxes I ever came across.'

Nadine thought: what the hell have I gotten myself into? If this is another of Titus' nasty double-plots . . . But it didn't seem possible. It seemed far more likely that this Vegas-trained young hostess had simply discovered the secret of becoming wealthy without doing anything that was remotely like work. Fucking the famous, and then coming out with the true, unexpurgated inside story, weekly fodder for the *Star* and *National Enquirer*. The trouble was, games like that could quickly and easily become dangerous. Nobody likes to be taken for a sucker, and nobody likes to be robbed. Even more, nobody likes to be ridiculed.

'Colleen,' Nadine said, 'what do you actually want?'

'I told you. I want *you*. That's for as long as I decide to stay here in Washington. I also need some money, and I want some fun. I know what Joe Jasper said about keeping me locked up here, but who needs it? I'll be good. I even promise to come home by midnight.'

Nadine said, 'Have you any idea how risky it's going to be for you to dance around in the open? You're the only girl in the world who can bring down the President of the United States simply by opening her mouth.'

'So?'

'So what you don't seem to understand is that this particular President of the United States, like very many others before him, is hard and uncompromising and is quite likely to have you badly hurt if you try to unseat him. And when I say badly hurt, I mean badly hurt. You value your eyesight, do you? Your breasts?'

Colleen rose from the bath, and reached for a towel. She wrapped it tightly around herself, staring at Nadine suspiciously. 'I wasn't trying to hustle you,' she said. 'I was only showing off.'

Nadine took her in her arms, and held her. Then she kissed her on the forehead, and on the nose, and on the lips. 'Let's keep this our secret, shall we?' she whispered. She slipped her hand inside Colleen's towel, and massaged her big slippery breast, until the nipple tightened between her fingers. Colleen kissed her cheek, and then her mouth, hungrily.

Unknown to both of them, a silent camera was squeezing its eye at them at intervals of exactly 8.3 seconds; and Joe Jasper was already on the phone to an address on Pennsylvania Avenue, speaking quickly and pointedly, and occasionally glancing towards the closed door of Colleen's new bedroom.

Fifteen

Just after 11 o'clock in the morning, the remains of Mrs Margot Schneider were removed from the Phoenix city morgue in a black plastic body bag and handed over formally to James T Skellett of the National Security Agency. Skellett refused to make any comment to the Press. The mayor of Phoenix, Andrew Gardens, said that the city was simply obeying a directive from a higher authority, in the interests of national defence.

'I'd prefer to think about Chief Ruse today, rather than Mrs Margot Schneider,' he remarked. 'Wouldn't you?'

Sixteen

Daniel was wiping up the tables after lunch when Ronald Reagan Kinishba came in with an untidy parcel under his arm, and beckoned him over to the table on the far side of the diner. Pete Burns the deputy was sitting at the counter, finishing off a lemon Danish, and Ronald was anxious that they shouldn't be overheard. These days, Ronald would only have to wear a loud suit in a built-up area and Pete Burns would run him in.

Cara, who was wiping up the counter and stacking away the dirty dishes, looked across and saw what was going on; she turned to Pete Burns with a smile and a bounce and said, 'How about some more coffee, deputy? Another Danish?'

Pete Burns turned majestically on his counter-stool and remarked to Daniel, 'The help's improved around here,

Daniel. Must say I like your taste. Always had a penchant for redheads.'

Ronald gave him a quick wave and a wink. He was obviously about to say something cutting in reply, but Cara said, 'Sweet'n'Lo, deputy?' and distracted him.

'What's happening?' Daniel asked Ronald. He nodded towards the parcel. 'Are those the coveralls?'

Ronald nodded. 'Jim Pryor's coming by in an hour's time. Levon said he wasn't altogether too happy about smuggling us into the base, but he'll do it.'

'I wish to hell you'd tell me what fancy plan you've cooked up for getting us out.'

'You really want to know?' asked Ronald.

'It's that bad, is it?'

'It's bad, and I mean ba-a-ad.'

Daniel drew back a chair and sat down. 'You'd better tell me. If I'm not going to live to see sundown, I think I'd prefer to know about it in advance.'

Ronald leaned his head forward, and in a conspiratorial murmur said, 'It's like this. Jim Pryor's truck is large enough to take my motorcycle, hidden under a few sacks and boxes. Now, I rode around the perimeter of the base early this morning, and found just what I was looking for. There's a rocky outcrop, quite close to the perimeter fence, on the Higley side. So what we do is – once we've checked out Willy's body – we cross the base on the motorcycle – speed up when we reach the outcrop – and literally fly right over the fence. Evel Knievel can eat shit: we're going to do it pillion.'

Daniel slowly rubbed the side of his cheek. He was silent for so long that even deputy Burns turned around again to see what had caused such a lull in the conversation.

'That's bad,' Daniel commented, at last. 'That's *bad*.'

'I told you. But what a way to make an exit. The ground's level and hard, the fence is only ten feet high. That outcrop makes a natural ramp. We'll clear the top wire by two, three feet. And if anybody's chasing us, they

151

won't be able to follow because the nearest gate in the fence is more than a half-mile away. We'll be home free.'

'That's if we're still alive.'

Ronald puffed out his cheeks, and shrugged. 'You want to take a look at Willy, you got to take some risks.'

Daniel stood up. 'You know something,' he said. 'I now have a clear understanding of how and why the Indians lost the west. If they'd have had motorcycles, instead of horses, they would have lost it even quicker.'

'Then you'll do it?' grinned Ronald.

'Do I have a choice?'

When Pete Burns had finished his third Danish and left, Daniel followed Cara into the kitchen, where Susie was helping Mrs Koperwas stack the dishwasher. Mrs Koperwas was a fussy, motherly old biddy who had helped Daniel with the cleaning and the housework ever since he had first opened the diner up for business. She had immediately impressed Susie because she could remember the last gunfight at Apache Junction, in 1907, when Robert 'Chicken' McTeague had shot and killed Edward Bailey right in front of the dry goods store. 'I can see Mr Bailey's one boot standing up by itself in the street, clear as if it happened this morning.'

Cara said, 'You're going *now*?'

'As soon as Jim Pryor comes by.'

She grasped his hands, and kissed him. 'I know it was my idea, dressing up as Air Force people and everything . . . but you're sure you want to do it? I mean you're sure you ought to?'

'I don't think there's anything else I can do.'

She held him close. 'You keep yourself safe then, you hear?'

'I'm not usually known for my suicidal nature. Not like this Navajo kamikaze biker here.'

Ronald grunted with amusement.

'There's just one precaution you can take,' Daniel told Cara. 'If we're not out of the base in two hours, then call Pete Burns and tell him everything that's happened. If we're okay, he'll probably throw our tails in prison; but if we're not, then somebody in authority needs to know.'

They went upstairs and changed into the USAF technicians' coveralls that Levon had lent them. 'They don't smell too good, do they?' commented Ronald. 'You don't think that Levon sews himself into them for the winter, do you?'

Levon had also managed to dig out a couple of blue peaked drill caps, and a battered USAF tool box. Daniel prized the box open and saw that it contained three rusty octagonal spanners, the metal clips from a pair of Osh-Kosh dungarees, and a torn copy of the Seattle *Post-Intelligencer*. 'I always knew there was something funny about Levon and Seattle,' Ronald remarked.

They shared a cold Coors, which they drank too quickly and too nervously. Then, at five after two, they heard the bullfrog croak of Jim Pryor's truck horn. Daniel tugged on his cap and asked Cara, 'How do I look?'

'Scared,' she said.

Jim Pryor was waiting for them impatiently, in his tall sweat-stained stetson hat and his red checkered shirt, chewing a massive mouthful of gum. His blue Ford panel truck was parked on the highway nearby, its doors wide open and its tailgate down.

'I can tell you straight, I wouldn't be taking you guys at all if it wasn't for Levon,' he said, and spat into the dust. 'I always thunk you two were a couple of weirdos.'

Ronald slapped him cheerily on the back. 'There's something else, as a matter of fact. I was wondering if you could be kind enough to take my bike along, too.' He nodded his head towards the Nighthawk, and smiled.

'The bike?' asked Jim Pryor, incredulously.

'Come on, Mr Pryor. Levon told us you owe him one.'

'Jesus wept,' said Jim Pryor.

Between them, while Susie watched solemnly from her upstairs window, the three of them manhandled the motorcycle into the back of Jim Pryor's truck, wedging it in between a stack of canned beets and a side of bacon wrapped in muslin. Then they locked up the tailgate, climbed into the cab, and drove off. Susie knelt on her chair watching the empty highway for almost five minutes before Cara came in, and laid a gentle hand on her shoulder.

'Daddy's going to be all right, isn't he?'

'Oh, for sure.'

'You're not lying to me?'

'Why would I lie?'

'Because *you're* worried, too.'

Cara sat down on the bed. 'Your daddy is quite capable of taking care of himself, if only he'd realize it.'

'I don't know what you mean,' said Susie.

Cara smiled. 'I don't believe that I know myself. But he's a strong man, much stronger than he thinks he is. He still loves your mommy, you know that?'

'He says that if mommy came back, they'd only argue.'

'Maybe he's right.'

Susie looked at Cara with big round eyes, and her mouth was pursed in distress. Cara touched her cheeks, and two large tears rolled out, the kind of tears which smudge the ink of hopeless letters, or fall into a cold reflecting river on a winter's afternoon.

In the truck, meanwhile, Ronald was determinedly singing *O Sole Mio*. Daniel was sitting with his feet up on the dash, and Jim Pryor was driving as if he had a permanent migraine. There were six or seven air fresheners dangling from the knobs of the truck's radio, every scent from mountain pine to huckleberry; and on the inside of the cab roof, there was a large picture of Chesty Morgan, the lady with the 72" bust.

Jim Pryor said, 'You guys are going to have to get your carcasses out of this cab in a minute or two, and hide in the back.'

'Ten-four,' said Ronald.

'Don't know why the hell you want to sneak yourselves into an airbase anyway. You're not set on stealing one of them swing-wing fighters, are you? Flying it to Moscow?' He pronounced it 'swang-wang farter', a real Apache Junction accent.

'No,' said Ronald. 'Something better than that. We're going on a panty raid. Stealing the officer's thermal underwear.'

'I always thunk you two was weirdos,' said Jim Pryor.

They pulled up by the side of the road. It was a hot, clear afternoon, no traffic in sight for miles, except for a lone Indian driving a diesel earth-mover about a quarter of a mile away, in a nearby field. Ronald and Daniel heaved themselves up into the back of Jim Pryor's truck, and wormed their way in between the supplies until they found a stuffy niche behind a case of canned peaches. Jim Pryor locked the tailgate again, and climbed back into the cab.

'I just hope he doesn't decide to get smart,' said Daniel, as the truck pulled away. 'Try to tip off the sentry, anything like that.'

'Well,' said Ronald philosophically, 'there's always that risk. But Levon wouldn't like it too much; and I don't think Jim Pryor's going to go out of his way to upset Levon. Not if he wants spare parts, and gas, and good service.'

'I don't know,' said Daniel. 'I'll trust him when we're inside the base; not before.'

It seemed to take a whole afternoon of jostling and bumping before the truck pulled up in front of Williams Air Force Base. Daniel and Ronald sat crouched and sweating in the darkness and listened to the sentry approaching the cab and asking Jim Pryor to produce his pass documents.

'Bacon, canned fruit, canned vegetables, potatoes, broccoli, cooking oil,' recited the sentry, from Jim Pryor's docket. 'Anything else? Any liquor? Beer? Perfumeries?'

'What you read on that docket is what there is,' said Jim Pryor.

'Well, that's what *you* say,' replied the sentry. 'But the way *I* hear it, you've been bringing in some of them videos, *Debbie Does Dallas* and suchlike, and some of them magazines, *Fifteen* and *Anal Fun* and *Private*.'

'Young man, you certainly hear some weird stuff,' said

155

Jim Pryor. 'Now, give me that docket back, and let me get on with my deliv'ry.'

'I'm entitled to search your vehicle,' said the sentry. 'I'd be obliged if you'd step down from the cab, and open the tailgate. Then maybe we can take a look, see what you're hiding in there.'

'I'm behind time as it is,' Jim Pryor complained.

'That's too bad,' said the sentry. 'Because it's my duty to make sure that nothing gets on to this base that shouldn't; like firearms, or dope, or cameras, or questionable movies.'

'This is crazy,' said Jim Pryor. 'You ain't never searched me before.'

'I ain't never heard that you were bringing in unsavoury movies and magazines before.'

There was a pause. Daniel felt the sweat running down the side of his face, and his back was beginning to creak with stiffness. Ronald murmured some obscure Indian invocation under his breath; a call to the gods of desert and mountain to cleave the sentry in half. They heard the sentry's boots walking around the truck towards the back, and they heard Jim Pryor's door open.

This is it, thought Daniel. He's going to sell us to the Air Force, as the price of his own neck. He's going to turn us in. But then he heard Jim Pryor say, 'Listen, okay, we can be reasonable, can't we?'

'What's your definition of *reasonable*?' the sentry wanted to know.

'Here, look here. Couple of good video movies. Let's say they're a private arrangement, kind of a commission.'

There was another pause, longer. Daniel wiped the sweat from his forehead with the back of his sleeve. Ronald whispered, 'Take them. For Christ's sake. Take them.'

Jim Pryor and the sentry walked out of earshot, although Daniel and Ronald could still indistinctly hear them discussing the merits of *Busy Bodies* and *World of Pleasure Part III*. An F-15 Eagle thundered overhead, blotting out all conversation and all sensible thought; but when it had gone, there was complete silence. Ronald

156

said, 'What's happening out there?' but Daniel could only shake his head.

The next thing they knew, Jim Pryor had climbed back into his cab and started up the truck's engine. They heard him say, 'Have a good evening. Don't overdo it. There's plenty more where that came from.' Then the truck was jouncing through the gates, and swinging around towards the stores, where Jim Pryor would unload his supplies. As he shifted gear, Daniel could hear him cursing the sentry out loud.

The truck jolted to a halt, and Jim Pryor came around and lowered the tailgate. 'It's all right, you can come on out,' he grumbled. 'But don't ask me for no more favours because I'm not in the goddamned mood. That punk of a sentry. If I hadn't had you two guys stashed in the back, I would've told him to go shove his dick up some airplane's tailpipe. Goddamned twenty dollars apiece, those videos cost me. And now I've got to give him a couple every time I go through the goddamned gate, less'n he gets suspicious.'

Daniel dusted off his coveralls. 'Don't worry about it, I'll pay you back. Levon didn't say anything about porno movies.'

'You have to make a living, you know? Whatever these fly guys want, I provide.'

'And where do *you* get them?'

'Are you kidding? There's a whole goddamned video-copying industry going on out at the Fort Apache Indian reservation. Whole barns crammed with video machines, sixty or seventy running at a time.'

'This great nation of ours,' said Daniel, sarcastically.

'The Indians had to do *something* after the white man stole their lands,' protested Ronald. 'Maybe porno was the best thing. Cochise's Revenge.'

'Why don't you stop talking crap and help me get this goddamned motorcycle out of the back of my truck,' Jim Pryor complained.

They hefted the cycle over the tailgate and set it on the ground. Daniel said to Jim Pryor, 'That's it, okay? You're no longer responsible. You never smuggled us in through the gates, and we never saw you before in our lives.'

Jim Pryor took off his stetson, and raked his thinning hair across his scalp. 'You tell Levon I don't owe him no favours no more, that's all. That Levon, he's some god-damned smartass, I can tell you. You tell him I don't owe him no more favours.'

'Double negative,' Ronald commented.

'Kiss off,' Jim Pryor retorted.

Daniel and Ronald left the disgruntled Jim Pryor to unload his supplies, and went in search of the base hospital. Ronald wheeled the motorcycle a hundred yards along to the shade of a stunted foothill paloverde; and parked it there ready for their eventual getaway. A flight of three F-15s screeched low behind the rows of huts, and for a moment it was impossible for them to hear each other speak. At last, as the jets began to climb towards Chandler and the Gila River Indian Reservation, Ronald took Daniel's arm and said, 'You go that way, okay? That looks the most promising direction, all those concrete buildings. I'll check out the huts along here. We'll meet back here in five minutes, unless you find what you're looking for. But in any case I'll be here waiting for you, whatever.'

'Take care,' said Daniel.

Ronald said, 'You too, okay?'

Swinging Levon's bashed-up old USAF toolbox as casually as he could, Daniel walked towards the main administration buildings and the control tower. He had forgotten his sunglasses and so he had to half-close his eyes against the glare of the white-painted concrete blocks, and the dazzling glass of the control-tower windows. There was a heady, heated smell of aviation fuel in the air, mingled with that dry desert aroma which is always Arizona's. It was a baking hot afternoon, and there was hardly anyone around, except for a tall black airman in fatigues, painting the air base flagstaff.

Daniel walked around the main administration block, pretending to whistle through lips that were too parched

158

to make a sound. A door suddenly opened, and a young Air Force captain came hurrying out, so abruptly that Daniel didn't have time to do anything but snap what he thought was a reasonably authentic salute. The captain flapped a dismissive hand at him, and then disappeared around the corner. Daniel stopped, and took a breath. His lungs and his heart felt as if they all had twisted up together in an impossible knot.

Locating the base hospital turned out to be ridiculously easy. As he walked around the last block, he saw a clearly-stencilled array of signposts, pointing the way to such arcane destinations as the General Support Annex and the Procurement Office. The hospital block was right across the road in front of him, surrounded by a white-painted chain-link fence.

He glanced quickly from right to left. Apart from a couple of technicians working on the nose radar of a distant F-15, the area was deserted. He began to walk across the road, his head lowered so that his face would be shadowed by the peak of his cap.

He was almost across when he heard the whine of an approaching Jeep. He tried to walk faster, but he was still five or six paces from the hospital block driveway when the Jeep squealed to a stop beside him. A harsh voice said, 'Hey, you!'

He stopped, and looked around. Sitting in the driver's seat of the Jeep, his freckled sunburned arms perched on top of the steering wheel like curing Virginia hams, was an Air Force master sergeant. He stared at Daniel out of impenetrable sunglasses, and chewed gum between his back molars as regularly as if there was an Air Force ordinance on the exact rate of correct mastication.

'What's your name, airman?' he demanded.

'Korvitz, sir.'

'Well, Korvitz, what the hell do you think you're wearing?'

Daniel said, 'Huh?' and then looked down at his filthy coveralls as if he had never seen them before in his life. 'These, sergeant?'

'That's right, Korvitz. Those.'

Daniel opened his mouth but no words seemed to feel like coming out. The master sergeant stared at him and chewed, and stared at him and chewed. The identification badge on his sharply-pressed shirt said 'WELLS, HB'

Suddenly, Daniel found himself speaking. His voice sounded as if it were coming from the throat of a child's jack-in-the-box, springy and peculiar. 'It's the hospital, sergeant. The head's backed up. I've got to clear it out. They told me to wear something that they could burn afterwards.'

The master sergeant chewed thoughtfully for almost a minute. Then, with considerable relish, he said, 'You're going to get smothered in shit, is that what they meant?'

Daniel nodded, trying to look as unhappy as possible.

'Ha!' barked the sergeant. Then, 'Ha! ha! ha! ha!' And then he thrust the Jeep into gear and drove off, still laughing. Daniel watched him go, and felt the sweat trickling down the sides of his body. Thank the Lord for the small-minded cruelty of the military sense of humour.

He walked up the driveway to the hospital block, up the steps, and pushed open the door. Inside, the hospital smelled of fresh paint and formaldehyde, and it was shadowy and cool. There was a desk near the entrance, but nobody was sitting there. A post on the wall extolled the virtues of a daily diet with plenty of bran. 'Moral Fiber Is Not Enough.'

Cautiously, he walked along the corridor, peeking into the porthole windows in every door. In one room, he caught sight of a young officer with his leg in traction, frowning at *Groovie Goolies* on television; in the next, a cleaner was noisily wax-polishing the floor. At the end of the corridor was a closed windowless door marked *Private*. He hesitated in front of it; then turned the handle and found that it was unlocked. Beyond it was another corridor, running at right-angles, painted a particularly unpleasant shade of pea-green. Daniel closed the door behind him, and walked quietly along this second corridor, until he reached another door marked *No Admittance to Unauthorized Personnel*. He opened that, too, and found himself in the morgue.

It wasn't much of a morgue. Twelve feet square, with nothing more than two medical trolleys, parked side by side as casually as if they had been left there by a supermarket attendant; a dripping sink; a shelf crowded with bottles of antiseptic, sodium chloride, arsenic, and surgical alcohol; a *House & Garden* calendar for two years ago; and a rattling, growling refrigeration unit.

On one of the trolleys rested a US Air Force body bag, which obviously contained a body. Daniel stared at it for a very long time before he stepped any further into the morgue. His pulse-rate seemed to have dropped to a slow, thunderous drumbeat, and the sweat chilled on his forehead and under his arms as if he himself were close to death. He stepped up to the trolley and stood beside it with his head lowered, half in homage and half in utter terror. The refrigeration unit coughed and banged, and he began to think of every horror movie he had ever seen: movies in which corpses suddenly sat upright and clutched at your throat. Knowing that this particular body might be Willy didn't make it any less alarming; in fact it made it worse. People in zombie movies were always being attacked by their erstwhile friends.

There was a label tied to the zipper of the body bag. Daniel picked it up and looked at it, but all it bore was a pencilled number 755368. He knew that he was going to have to open the bag and examine the body. He felt as cold as if he had been waiting for a train in Alaska; his fingers seemed to have turned to frozen bananas. But he reached for the zipper tag, and began to tug it down.

It took forever just to draw the zipper down to chest level. The slider kept sticking, and he had to ease it back up again, and then try opening it a little further. But at last the corpse inside the bag was exposed to the light, and Daniel could see for himself what had really happened to Willy Monahan.

There was no head, but he knew it was Willy. He recognized on the corpse's right collarbone the L-shaped scar which Willy had always boasted to Daniel that he had sustained in a rapier-duel with a Prussian count. It was nonsense, of course – he had fallen off a motorcycle when he was a cadet, and jabbed himself with the brake lever. But it was Willy's scar; and the chest and shoulders were Willy's chest and shoulders; and in Daniel's mind there was no doubt at all. Willy was dead.

What was really horrifying, though, was that Willy had quite obviously not been decapitated by a helicopter rotor. Even the thinnest rotor would have left a bruised, mangled neck stump. But Willy's neck had been sliced, or sawn. It was cut off cleanly just above the larynx; and although it was thick with crusts of congealed blood, it had been as neatly severed as if he had been executed by a surgeon. Even more chilling: there was no sign of his head. Whoever had killed him had taken his head as a souvenir.

Numbly, Daniel recited for Willy the *Kaddish*, in Aramaic. It was all he could do. He and Willy had shared such a closeness of character that they had never spoken to each other as much as they should have done. They had drunk a lot, played cards, laughed, watched television. But Daniel would have done anything now for one last serious conversation with Willy, one last questioning bull-session with beer and pretzels just to find out who Willy Monahan had actually been, and to answer all those questions which even husbands and wives who have lived together for twenty years never get around to asking each other.

'Who were you, Willy?' he whispered. But there was nobody to answer him in that close, claustrophobic green-painted morgue; only a headless corpse. There was no air to be breathed that wasn't tinged with the smell of decomposing tissues, or that sweet abattoir odour of blood gone bad. There were no thoughts to be thought that weren't potential nightmares. Only memories, and horror. He zippered up the body bag again, so hastily that he caught his fingers. Then he backed towards the door with the unbalanced, firmly-planted steps of a drunk leaving a New York bar. He closed the door loudly behind him. Bang. And then the real world again.

'Lord God,' he said to himself, and tasted bile in his mouth.

He made his way back along the pea-green corridor, and pushed his way through the door marked *Private*. He was beginning to feel the extraordinary coldness of shock; and a panicky need to escape from the hospital block, and get out into the sunshine again. As he walked back into the entrance area, however, he was confronted by a woman corporal, sitting behind the reception desk with a tightly-waved hairstyle and an expression like a freshly-opened box of paperclips.

'*Airman!*' she rapped, at the very instant he raised his hand to push open the hospital door.

'Yes, ma'am!' Daniel responded. But he stayed where he was, his hand still pressed against the glass. Outside he could see blue sky and hot concrete and freedom. Inside, there was nothing but nausea and death.

'Who gave you permission to enter the hospital block dressed in that disgusting coverall?'

'Master Sergeant Wells, ma'am.'

'What have you been doing here? I didn't see you come in.'

'You were temporarily absent from your desk, ma'am. I did wait. But they told me it was urgent. The head was blocked.'

'The head, airman, is *that* way.'

'Yes, ma'am. But I was just checking the outfall. I like to do the maintenance thorough, you know?'

'Just a minute,' the corporal told him, and picked up her telephone. Daniel stayed where he was, an inch away from that 90° afternoon, an inch away from escape. He heard the corporal say, 'Get me Sergeant Wells, please. Corporal Knobla.' Then she clamped one hand over the receiver and said to Daniel, 'You stay there. You stay right where you are.'

Daniel didn't move. Another F-15 flew over the base, making the doors rattle and vibrate in their frame, but all he could think about was Willy's sawn-off neck, the pipes and the tubes and the white protruding spine; and the sweat slid down his back like chilled blood.

'Sergeant Wells? Is this Sergeant Wells? This is Corporal Knobla, sergeant, over at the hospital block. Yes, sergeant, I'm sorry; but I have an airman here who *claims* that he's been cleaning out the head. A blockage of some kind. Well, he says that *you* sent him. Yes, sergeant. You personally. I *know* he's wearing disgusting fatigues. I know that. Well, that's why I stopped him. Yes. But I think we ought to check his identity, don't you?'

There was a long silence, punctuated only by the tiny voice of Master Sergeant Wells speaking from the sergeants' mess. Daniel sweated and waited and almost prayed. But then Corporal Knobla suddenly said, 'You'll send over the SPs? Very well, I'll keep him here.'

Without a word, Daniel pushed open the hospital door. The warm air flowed around him like an opened-up bread-oven. Then his vision was jiggling in *cinema vérité* as he ran down the hospital driveway, past the chain-link fence, across the wide roadway, and around the corner of the administration block. His sneakers flapped on the baking concrete. His breath roared inside his head as if it were the breath of someone close behind him.

He almost collided with Ronald coming the other way. He panted. 'They called the SPs! For God's sake let's get out of here!'

Ronald said, 'You found the hospital?'

'I saw the body. I saw Willy's body. Now, let's go.'

They ran heavily back towards the tree where Ronald had parked his bike. There was no alarm; and no sign of anybody chasing after them. But Daniel didn't want to take any chances. He wanted to be back in his own bed tonight, with Cara lying next to him, and Susie sleeping down the hall. He certainly didn't want to be locked up in an Air Force cell, answering questions about Willy Monahan and guided missiles that wouldn't work and headless corpses that obviously hadn't been decapitated by helicopter rotors, and most certainly hadn't been posted to Langley AFB.

They reached the Nighthawk, and climbed astride it. It took Ronald two or three kicks before he could get it started, because it had been lying on its side in Jim Pryor's truck, and flooded. But at last it burped and burbled and roared into life, and a cloud of blue smoke rose up through the branches of the paloverde, and they were away.

'You're sure this jump stunt is going to work?' yelled Daniel, as they swerved between two PX buildings, and out into the open beside the airfield perimeter.

'You want to be sure of anything, you should never take any risks!' Ronald shouted back.

They jolted and blurred past a row of firetrucks, two huts, a long wire fence, and a parked collection of partially dismembered airplanes, a Super Sabre and a Delta Dart. Out to their right, two or three F-15 Eagles were taxiing for take-off, their gleaming outlines wavering in the heat-haze which rose from the runway. Then, above the roar of jet engines, Daniel heard the *whip-whip-whip* of a siren. He twisted around and saw two Jeeps speeding towards them with flashing red lights, quickly joined by a third Jeep.

'They're chasing us!' he shouted, close to Ronald's neck.

Ronald leaned his head back. 'They don't have a fucking chance! Watch this!' He twisted the throttle wide open, and the Nighthawk blared at nearly 110 mph along the edge of the runway apron, jolting so much that Daniel felt as if all his teeth were being shaken out of their roots. He turned around again, and the Jeeps were almost a quarter of a mile away, but still coming.

'If you can't get over that fence, you know what's going to happen, don't you? Bread and water for ten years, if you're lucky.'

Ronald shouted, 'What the hell are you worried about? Trust me!'

Suddenly, they heard a crackling noise. Daniel looked around to their left. Another Jeep had joined the pursuit, and an Air Force security policeman was standing up in the back seat with a rifle resting against the rollbar.

'Get this goddamned bike moving!' he screamed at Ronald. 'They're shooting at us!'

A bullet hit the mudguard just behind Daniel's protruding backside, and moaned off into the dust. Another one whizzed hotly through the air an inch or two in front of his face. He suddenly understood that this was serious, and that they could die.

Ronald yelled, 'This is it! Look! The fence!'

Daniel bobbed his head up over Ronald's shoulder and saw ahead of them an ochre-coloured outcrop of rock. Beyond that was the airbase's ten-foot-high perimeter fence, double mesh with barbed wire on top.

They were committed: there was no time to stop and consider if it was a good idea to leap ten feet in the air over a high-gauge wire security fence, or how the hell they were going to land when they reached the other side. Ronald twisted the accelerator to give himself the very last ounce of power, and Daniel hugged Ronald's waist and crouched down on the pillion seat and clenched his teeth so tight that he broke one of his porcelain crowns. Then they were streaking up the flat table of rock with the Nighthawk's engine screaming at top pitch, an A-natural that could have brought down the windows of half-a-dozen cathedrals in one devastating shower of glass.

Ronald let out a war-whoop that made Daniel's hair prickle up, and he knew as they flew up into the air that they could never make it, that the Nighthawk was too heavy with two people astride it, that the natural ramp of rock wasn't angled up high enough, and that Ronald had probably never even meant to escape at all, not seriously. Ronald was more of a Navajo than Daniel had given him credit for: fiercer, and more suicidal; and this assault on Williams Air Force Base had given him the justification he had always been looking for to go out in a thunder of glory. Daniel thought of all the times they had slammed along Route 60 together at 100 miles an hour, and realized that he was probably fortunate to have lived as long as this.

The front wheel dropped in mid-air; and then the whole bike was somersaulting. Daniel tried to hang on to Ronald but his grip was torn away, and the next thing he knew he was being hurtled over the ten-foot fence as if he had been tossed by a bull, tearing his hand open on the barbed wire. He was slammed on to the hard ground on the other side, and rolled over and over with his arms and legs flailing, breathless, his ribs pummelled by rocks, his face lacerated by dry branches.

Ronald was not as lucky, but then perhaps he hadn't wanted to be. As the bike nosedived he was thrown head-first into the wire fence, at nearly 90 miles an hour, and his face was mashed instantly into a bloody purée. Both of his eyes shot out on red ribbons of optic nerve, and as he collapsed to the ground, they slithered down the links of the fence and ended up staring at Daniel, still attached to their bloody string of tissue. It took him only thirty seconds to die, blinded and shocked, and whatever he was thinking it was enough to keep him silent, paralysed, his hands raised in the air as if he were still grasping the controls of an invisible motorbike.

The four Air Force Jeeps skidded to a halt by the fence, raising a high cloud of dust. Two of the SPs ran right up to the wire and looked intently for Daniel, while the rest of the detail stood around Ronald's wrecked Nighthawk as if they had discovered a pterodactyl which had suddenly dropped out of the sky. Daniel, winded and bruised amongst the desert brush, stayed motionless. Almost unconsciously, he said a prayer to thank God that he was still alive; and a prayer for Ronald Reagan Kinishba, who was now dead.

He heard a voice say, 'He must've run off. I don't see him there.'

'There's enough damn brush around here to hide an elephant.'

'Find the nearest access gate and go get him. You don't

bring that guy back to Colonel Kawalek, dead or alive, he's going to have your balls.'

A quick rifle shot snapped into the dry ground only twelve feet away, and the bullet sang into the afternoon air, but the SPs didn't fire again. Daniel slithered backwards through the brush, down into a gully, and then ran and hopped until he reached a deeper gully fifty yards to the west, one of the old Indian canal-beds. He was gasping so loudly that he was sure that everybody could hear him for miles around. His ankle was twisted, and he could only jump and hobble and roll. He wished to God that he hadn't come. He wished to God that it was all a nightmare, and that Ronald was still alive. He wished to God that the sight of Willy's headless neck wasn't so deeply imprinted on his mind. He sat down for a minute or two beside a giant saguaro and wiped sweat and grit from his face, and caught his breath.

There was scarcely any sound now, in the scrub. Only the distant rumbling of jets, and the chirruping of crickets. The Air Force police must have given up the search, or gone the wrong way. He thought he heard someone shouting, but it soon faded. He lay back and closed his eyes.

Seventeen

It was dark when Kathy Forbes opened her eyes. An illuminated digital alarm-clock beside the bed told her it was 23:17. She felt stunned and drowsy, and for a long moment she wondered if she might have been involved in a traffic accident, and been anaesthetized. She reached instinctively downwards to feel if her legs were still there.

She turned over, and then she tried to sit up. Her head was pounding, and she found it difficult to focus her eyes. She sat there for more than five minutes; but her dizziness and nausea were too overwhelming, and at last she fell back on the pillow again.

She remembered James Skellett asking her questions. She remembered a thickly-carpeted living-room, with sunshine illuminating the tightly-drawn calico blinds. She remembered a rocking-chair that creaked with every movement, and a reproduction of Picasso's *Guernica*. She remembered somebody else, too, a man in a white shirt with an expensive wristwatch. He had sat well back, smoking a cigarette that had a strange aroma to it. Now and then, he had made a remark to James Skellett in a language which she failed to understand.

'Do you think she really has any understanding about what happened?'

'I don't know. But it is necessary to find out.'

'Necessary for what reason? You could kill her immediately; or ask your loathsome Mr Friend to do it for you. Then you would have no problem whatsoever.'

'You don't think so? Supposing she has already told someone else? Supposing Mrs Schneider confided in her before she died? She could be the most dangerous woman on this planet.'

'You always over-dramatize. You should have gone into the theatre, Skellett, not the security services. One day your stage-whispers will find you out, and then you'll be sorry. That nonsense today in Phoenix. Couldn't you find a more discreet way of removing that police chief than *dynamiting* him? Ikon was furious.'

'Ikon wasn't here. He didn't know the difficulties. Besides, I didn't really plan it that way. I simply asked Friend to get rid of him, as promptly as possible.'

'I hope that Friend wasn't overstepping his brief.'

'I can handle Friend.'

'Can you? I didn't see much evidence of it today.'

A silence; calculated rather than hostile. Then: 'Friend is no problem. A little exhibitionistic, perhaps. But then, he is a genius at what he does. He found Margot Schneider, didn't he? He eliminated her, and kept her elimination a complete mystery.'

'A mystery which you have done very little to *keep* a mystery.'

'I don't have any duty to justify my actions to you.'

There had been more conversations; different men. Then somebody who had lifted her arm, swabbed it with surgical alcohol, and injected her with something that had put her to sleep within seconds. Her dreams had been populated with distorted faces, and echoing laughter, and a feeling that she wasn't here at all, but living years and years ago, speaking, talking, on a Saturday afternoon in 1962. A voice had said, 'Jack? Jack Kennedy? Jack Kennedy? Jack Kennedy?' and another voice had joined in to say, 'Yes! Ford Galaxie have three wagons for 1962, with Country Squire featuring walnut-grained steel panels and Cruise-O-Matic drive!'

Now she was awake; alert; and pricklingly frightened. The bed was a reasonably comfortable divan, with clean sheets. There were maroon velveteen drapes over the windows through which two or three streetlights shone; and even in the darkness she could make out the shapes of white-painted furniture. There was a hint of cigar-smoke in the air, but otherwise the room smelled clean. She could hear the mutter of a television somewhere in the house, and someone coughing.

She tried to sit up again. She was dressed in nothing but bra, panties, garter belt and stockings, and all her jewellery had gone, even the ring that Ken had given her at Lake Tahoe. Her head felt as if it were wallowing on a slack incoming tide, and there was the taste of something bitter in her mouth. From the next room she heard more coughing, and then a woman's voice saying, 'It won't be possible until tomorrow. No, of course not. I won't be able to get one until daylight.'

She reached out towards the bedside table to help herself climb out of bed. But the bed suddenly rose and tipped beneath her, and she fell heavily sideways, knocking the digital clock and the bedside lamp and a glass of water on to the rug. She lay back, panting. Whatever they had used to put her to sleep, it had completely unbalanced her inner ear.

The bedroom door opened, and a man stood silhouetted against the light from the next room, watching her. She couldn't focus her eyes properly but she was sure that it was Skellett. After a while he came forward and stood right beside her. He made no attempt to pick up the clock or the lamp.

She said, hoarsely, 'How long have I been asleep?'

'Two or three hours, that's all. You were supposed to sleep until morning.'

She said, 'I'd like some water, please.'

'In a moment.'

She turned her head away, and squeezed her eyes tight shut in an effort to clear her mind. She wished she didn't feel so sick or so fuzzy. She had never been seriously ill in her life, and she hated to depend on anyone for anything. Just like her father. Stubborn and independent to the point of self-destruction. It formed the central part of her character, this hardness; and any caring or kindness or little attractive softnesses she showed were achieved in spite of it. She always felt a sense of pride when she remembered to do something nice for one of her friends, like sending flowers or phoning up on anniversaries; and yet she always felt guilty, too, because she believed that she should have done them naturally, without even having to think about them.

Skellett stayed where he was, watching her.

She said, 'You can't keep me here for very much longer. Chief Ruse –'

'Chief Ruse is dead.'

She opened her eyes and stared at him. 'What do you mean? What do you mean Chief Ruse is dead?'

'Exactly that. A bomb was planted in his car, only about ten minutes after you last spoke to him. There wasn't enough left of him to feed to your family pooch.'

Kathy pressed her hand against her mouth. 'Oh, God,'

she said. She felt as if the whole world had suddenly revealed itself to be an utterly different and nightmarish place; as if everything she had believed about people since she was a child had turned out to be a hideous misapprehension.

Skellett said, 'If it's any consolation, that wasn't the way I wanted it. But Chief Ruse was being obstructive; unnecessarily and ignorantly obstructive; and when it comes down to a question of national security. . .'

'What question of national security can possibly justify you killing Chief Ruse?' Kathy demanded.

Skellett clucked mildly. 'Come on now, Miss Forbes. Don't over-excite yourself. You've had a heavy shot of chloral hydrate.'

Kathy took a deep breath to steady herself, and to restore her sense of equilibrium. Skellett walked across to the window and parted the drapes slightly, looking out over the street with absent-minded satisfaction. He said, 'Chief Ruse deliberately ignored a warrant issued by the National Security Agency and an order made by Arizona's Chief Judge. It was urgent that the remains of Mrs Schneider should be removed from the Phoenix city mortuary and taken to Washington for special examination. Urgent, before any further deterioration could take place. Chief Ruse was adamant that he was not going to release the body, and therefore the only possible course of action was to remove him. I have to tell you that it was quite likely that Chief Ruse was part of a large and influential Communist espionage ring.'

'Chief Ruse? You're joking. He was the biggest redneck I've ever met.'

Skellett smiled wanly. '*Red*neck may be the right expression.'

'But did you have to kill him? Couldn't you just have had him arrested?'

'That would have meant charging him, and at the moment we're not ready to alert the entire espionage ring by making formal detentions. Besides, we wouldn't have been able to hold him for very long. We have very little watertight evidence. We could have set our whole counter-espionage operation back by five years; and risked some of our own people's lives.'

Kathy said, 'Why are you holding me? What have I got to do with it?'

'That's exactly what I intend to find out.'

'But I don't know anything about spy rings or Communist agents. If your intelligence is any good at all, surely you must realize that.'

Skellett let the drapes fall back into place, and came across to stand by Kathy's bedside again. 'I've never been so arrogant that I've claimed my intelligence setup is 100%. For all I know, you could be a Soviet sleeper. I'm having your background checked out now. Didn't you once belong to the Socialist Discussion Group, of Palo Alto, California?'

'You're being absurd. That was at college.'

'Absurd? Well, maybe. I'm not a witch-hunter. Not unless there are any real witches to be hunted.'

'What do you want me to say? I've told you everything I know, and that's precisely nothing.'

'You still haven't explained why you asked me about Cuba.'

'I've explained. It was an odd shot, that's all.'

'I don't believe you. Something made you connect Mrs Margot Schneider with Cuba and I want to know what it was. You went up to her house, didn't you, after she was murdered?'

'Of course I did. It was my job.'

'Did you find anything there; or see anything there; or did anybody mention anything there that might have led you to assume that Mrs Margot Schneider had any connection with Cuba?'

Kathy shook her head. 'Nothing.'

'Maybe Chief Ruse suggested it to you.'

'What does it matter?' she said, acidly. 'He's dead now.'

'*He's* dead but *you're* not.'

'So what are you going to do about that? Kill me, too?

I'm being just as obstructive as Chief Ruse. At least, you seem to think so.'

Skellett paced around the bed thoughtfully. Then he said, 'You mentioned Jack Kennedy in your sleep.'

'Who?'

'You heard me. Now, why would you talk about Jack Kennedy, unless he were somehow on your mind? And why would Jack Kennedy be on your mind? Can you answer me that?'

Kathy frowned at him. 'Why are you so concerned about Cuba and Jack Kennedy? That all happened twenty years ago. What on earth is so important about Cuba and Jack Kennedy that makes you want to keep me here? It's ancient history.'

'History can be ancient but still relevant.'

'I wish you'd stop this cheap philosophizing. Where are my clothes? I want to get dressed.'

Skellett said, 'That won't be possible.'

'It had better be possible.'

'I want to know why you said Cuba. Then maybe we can talk about getting dressed.'

'Mr Skellett, I don't *know* what made me say Cuba. I simply don't know. It was a silly idea, I admit. But there have been so many stories about Cuban exiles trying to persuade the President to – '

Skellett swung his arm and slapped her face, so hard that she let out a sharp cry of pain and surprise. She tried to get up, but he slapped her again, even harder, and drew blood from the side of her mouth. Her cheek felt as if someone had clamped a hot steam-iron against it. Her eyes were bursting with tears.

'Don't you mention Cuban exiles to me again,' he said. His voice was as cold and as even as before. 'All this talk about Cuban exiles is shit. You know as well as I do that Margot Schneider had nothing to do with any Cuban exiles. What I want to know is, what connection do you believe she *did* have with Cuba?'

Kathy didn't answer, but wiped the tears away from her face with the corner of her pillowslip. Skellett waited a minute or two longer, and then said, 'You're not going to tell me? Very well. That's it.'

He walked back into the next room and half-closed the door. Kathy heard him talking; and then the door opened again and he returned. With him now were the man in the white shirt she had seen earlier on, and another taller man whom she didn't recognize. The man in the white shirt rolled up his sleeves, a cigarette dangling from between his lips. He looked like a corrupt twin of Alain Delon. The taller man had high Slavic cheekbones, small glittering eyes, and a large strawberry-mark across the left side of his face.

Skellett said to Kathy, 'I'm going to explain something to you. It is necessary to the security and safety of the United States that you tell me what it is that led you to connect Mrs Margot Schneider with Cuba; and why it was that you mentioned Jack Kennedy in your sleep. There are 226-and-a-half million people in the United States. You are only one. I am authorized to do to you whatever I feel necessary in order to safeguard the rest of those human lives. I can torture you and I can kill you. It is entirely my decision, and if you leave me with no choice, then I will.'

Kathy said, in a choked voice, 'That's murder. You can't murder me.'

'You don't understand. I *can* murder you, if the security situation warrants it. We call it DE5, in the NSA. Disencumbrance, on a scale of five. DE1 is simply arranging for a change of location within the continental United States. DE2 is forcible expulsion from the country. DE3 is imprisonment, for as long as necessary. DE4 is injury or physical persuasion forcible enough to guarantee complete co-operation. DE5 is disencumbrance in the last resort.'

Kathy stared at him. She had never in her whole life felt so vulnerable and so helpless. But that Forbes hardness made her even more determined to resist. As long as she refused to tell Skellett anything about Mrs Schneider and Cuba, then she was reasonably safe. It was obviously vital to him that he knew, otherwise he wouldn't have gone to all the trouble of detaining her here. He might try to hurt her, but as long as she kept her mouth shut, he wouldn't kill her.

She didn't imagine that he might frighten her so much that she would beg him to let her go.

'This is one last chance,' said Skellett. 'Tell me what you know, and we won't touch you.'

Kathy said, 'I don't know anything.'

Skellett made a mock-disappointed face. Then, without any hesitation, he said, 'Walsh, let's get her tied down.'

'If you even try – ' snapped Kathy. But Skellett slapped her face again, and then again, stunning her into silence. The big strawberry-marked man called Walsh came forward with a handful of scarves and teatowels, and lashed her wrists and ankles to the head and the foot of the bed, so that she was spreadeagled.

'This is *primitive*,' Kathy wept. She was furious at herself for crying. 'You're supposed to be taking care of American civilization, and yet you're behaving like wild beasts.'

'It's your own fault,' said Skellett. 'The information that you're holding back from us is vital. Don't you see how unpatriotic you're being? We don't *want* to do this to you. But what alternative do we have?'

The big man came forward again, and this time he was carrying a ten-inch carving knife. Kathy's stomach tightened in terror, but he did nothing more than lean over her, seize her bra, and slice it open with a single upward cut. Skellett looked at her bare breasts appreciatively, and smiled. The man who looked like Alain Delon said nothing, but stayed in the corner, smoking, and watching.

'You're perverted,' said Kathy. 'You're perverted and sick.'

Skellett said, 'I've no choice. I'm sorry, but that's the way it is.'

Now Walsh slid the carving-knife under the elastic of her panties, and separated them with another upward slice. He didn't bother to cut her garter-belt or her stockings. It was enough that she was naked and exposed, enough that her legs should be lashed wide apart and that all three of them could sit staring at her as pruriently and as intently as they liked.

Skellett said, 'Walsh, bring me one of those needles. That's right, the hypodermic needles. That's it. Thanks.'

He sat down on the bed beside Kathy and smiled down at her as benevolently as a family doctor. 'I'm not going to ask you any more questions,' he said. 'I'm simply going to start working on you, and when you decide that you've had enough, you tell me. All right?'

Kathy shivered, 'You're crazy. You're completely out of your mind.'

'I'm practical, that's all,' said Skellett.

Without any further discussion, he picked up the hypodermic needle, grasped her left breast, and pushed the needle straight into the pink flesh of her nipple. She screamed out loud, couldn't help it, and tried to writhe and twist against the bonds which held her to the bed, but Skellett kept the needle where it was, and kept on smiling at her as calmly as if he were doing nothing more than taking her temperature.

He was true to his word: he didn't ask her any more questions. But he continued with deadly cruelty to stick the needle into her breasts and nipples, until she felt that they were ablaze. If she cried out too much, he slapped her face again and again. If she was silent, with her teeth clenched against the pain, he could coax her out of her silence by pushing the needle right through a nipple from one side to the other, and twisting it around as if he were winding a clock.

She had never known anything so agonizing. Her nerves seemed to shudder and rebel against every needle-prick, and she prayed out loud for Skellett to stop. But she knew that Skellett wouldn't stop until she told him what she knew about Mrs Margot Schneider, and she also knew that if she did tell him, he would probably kill her. The thought of that was all that kept her from pleading for mercy.

Some time in the early hours of the morning, Skellett

got up from the bed and left the room. Walsh stayed there, and so did the man in the white shirt, but they didn't make any attempt to touch her. She kept her eyes closed and tried to imagine that she was somebody else, and that she wasn't here at all. It occurred to her that she didn't even know where 'here' was. It was probably close to Phoenix: she was sure they hadn't driven out too far. But they may have moved her to another address when she was asleep. This didn't feel like the first house to which Skellett had brought her: this house seemed more permanent, better furnished, as if it were permanently occupied.

She nearly managed to sleep, in spite of the pain in her breasts. The effects of the chloral hydrate had still not completely worn off, and she went into a shallow dreamless doze. When she woke up, it was light, although the drapes were still closely drawn, and Walsh and the man in the white shirt were still there, watching her. She looked down at her breasts and saw that they were mottled with red, and swollen.

Skellett came back in again, eating a Swiss cheese sandwich. He said to Walsh, 'There's some coffee in the kitchen. Help yourself.' Walsh went out, and after a moment or two, the man in the white shirt followed him.

'Well,' said Skellett, 'any change of mind?'

She turned her head away. She didn't even want to look at him. Skellett sat on the end of the bed, chewing his sandwich, and said, 'None of this self-sacrifice is worth it, you know. You're going to suffer like hell, and in the end you're going to tell me what I want to find out.'

He finished his crust, and took out his handkerchief to wipe his hands. 'You should have heard Chief Ruse, how heroic *he* was. Full of fire. Full of determination. But fire and determination don't help when you're fundamentally wrong, when you're fighting for the wrong cause. In the end, you always have to admit your mistakes, and give in. I can tell you, Miss Forbes, you're not helping anybody by being so stubborn, especially not yourself.'

178

Kathy kept her head turned away. 'Why don't you go *fuck* yourself?' she told him.

Skellett pursed his lips and thought that over. Then he said, 'You're still not understanding me. What I'm going to do to you next is going to drive you half out of your mind. I'm trying to avoid the necessity of having to do it. Do you get me? I'm not a cruel man, by nature; but this is cruel.'

'You can't do any worse than you've done already.'

'Hmh! You want to bet?'

'Oh, do whatever you damned well like, if it turns you on.'

Skellett said wistfully, 'I only wish it did.'

Walsh came into the room, carrying a small cardboard box. The man in the white shirt followed closely behind, smoking a fresh cigarette. The cigarettes had an odd foreign pungency; and Kathy realized somewhere in the back of her mind that it must be the same smell that she had previously mistaken for cigars. *Balkan*, she thought, for some inexplicable reason.

Skellett took the small cardboard box and set it down on his lap, holding the lid closed with his thumbs. 'Have you ever heard of *Heloderma suspectum*?' he asked Kathy.

'I imagine you're going to tell me.'

'Of course. Even the ugliest of guests deserves a proper introduction. *Heloderma suspectum* is the scientific name for the lizard known as the Gila Monster, the only poisonous lizard which frequents the deserts of Texas, New Mexico, and Arizona. But, of course, being a native of Arizona, you are quite well acquainted with him already.'

'The Gila Monster only attacks birds and small animals.'

'Of course. You couldn't call him much of a danger to humans. Except, of course, under special circumstances.'

'What do you mean by special circumstances?' asked Kathy, nervously.

'Well, for instance, if a man were to swallow a live Gila Monster whole, and it went down into his stomach. Or, if a Gila Monster were to penetrate the human body in any other way.'

179

For the first time, Skellett glanced down between Kathy's thighs, and drummed his fingers against the side of the cardboard box.

Kathy breathed, 'You *can't*.'

'I beg your pardon?' said Skellett. 'You forget that I can do anything I want. You forget that I have official sanction to cut you into tiny pieces, if I think that it's required.'

Something shifted inside the box, making a scratching noise. Kathy couldn't keep her eyes off it. She said, breathlessly. 'It's nothing to do with official sanctions. It's to do with human decency.'

'Human decency? You want to debate the subject of human decency? Well, I'm very good at that. I know quite a lot about human decency; yes, and human indecency, too. I would say that for you to withhold what you know about Mrs Margot Schneider is pretty indecent, and I would say that what I am going to do to you now is justifiable in the interests of the security of this great nation of ours.'

'You're out of your mind. You can't possibly – '

Skellett jerked his head as a signal to Walsh that he should untie one of Kathy's legs. Kathy gasped and struggled and arched her back, but Walsh was too strong for her.

'Bastards!' shrieked Kathy. 'Bastards! Let me go! Bastards! Let me go!'

With an amused smile, Skellett opened the cardboard box. With a scuffling sound, a blunt, snakelike head appeared, and this was followed by one slowly-flailing claw. Skellett reached inside, and lifted out a seven-inch Gila lizard, only a young one, its scales speckled with black and orange. Its long tail thrashed from side to side, and its tongue flickered out of its black lips like a whip.

Walsh gripped Kathy's thigh so tight that his fingers dug into her flesh. She screamed and screamed at a shrill, unending pitch, but Skellett ignored her, and slowly presented the Gila monster's head to the parted pink opening of her sex.

'Do you still refuse to talk about Margot Schneider?' Skellett asked her.

Kathy was too hysterical to do anything but twist her body around, and scream in horror. Skellett parted her vulva with his fingers and held the Gila lizard so close that its flickering black tongue touched her flesh.

'This is your last chance,' he told her, his voice as chilly as ever. 'If you don't tell me what you know, I'm going to push this lizard right up inside you, and then I'm going to bind your legs together so that you can't get it out.'

Kathy let out a moan of absolute defeat. 'I found a photograph,' she wept. 'I found a photograph of President Kennedy. It was dedicated to N. I couldn't think why at first . . . but there were a whole lot of Press cuttings about *The Misfits* with it . . . I wasn't even sure that I was right.'

Skellett kept the Gila Monster where it was for more than twenty seconds. Then he lifted it up in his right hand, and squeezed it tight, until its bones crackled like breaking twigs and its tail slashed furiously from side to side. He did nothing to put the creature out of its agony, but held it up while it shuddered and squirmed, and blood ran darkly out of its mouth.

'You guessed then,' he said. 'Or, you *thought* you guessed.'

Kathy looked away. She couldn't bear to watch Skellett crushing the Gila Monster with such terrible deliberation. She felt the tears pool against the side of her nose as she haltingly whimpered out everything she had discovered and everything she had guessed about Margot Schneider's murder. In the corner of the room, the man in the white shirt lit another cigarette with a Zippo lighter, and regarded her impassively. Her tear-stained face, her straggled hair, her sex wide open as if it were a symbol of her complete submission and surrender. Walsh, now that the tension of extracting a confession was over, thrust his hands into his pockets and almost inaudibly hummed the old Groucho Marx song, '*Everyone says I love you . . .*'

Kathy said, 'The photograph of President Kennedy was

181

a Polaroid. Not official. A snapshot taken by somebody's pool. You couldn't have worked out where it was, not unless you'd known the place, or come across it by accident. But I just had a feeling . . . and I went through the picture morgue at the office; and then through half-a-dozen books which my flatmate owns. And there it was. The same pool. The same changing-hut. It was Marilyn Monroe's pool at Brentwood.'

Skellett stood up, and walked across to the far side of the room. He dropped the dead Gila Monster into the metal wastebasket with a scaly clang. Then he said, 'You still haven't explained Cuba.'

'I was telling you the truth,' said Kathy. She closed her legs now, suddenly aware of her vivid nakedness. 'Cuba was a guess. There were so many theories about Marilyn Monroe, why she was supposed to have died. Norman Mailer said that the FBI might have gotten rid of her, to protect the Kennedys' reputation. Other people said she was killed by the Mafia. But nobody ever suggested that she might not have died at all; that she might still be alive.'

Skellett waited for a while, and then said, 'Go on. I want to hear it all.'

'There isn't very much more to tell,' said Kathy. 'Most of it was supposition. I guessed that N was Norma; and that P was President. I guessed that if Marilyn Monroe really were alive and well and living in Phoenix, Arizona, under an assumed name, then out of all the photographs she'd ever possessed, she would try and hold on to that one. Except maybe a picture of Bobby, but I didn't see any of those.'

'So you thought that Margot Schneider wasn't Margot Schneider at all, but Marilyn Monroe? You thought this dark-haired frowzy widow was the greatest screen goddess of all time?'

'Yes,' said Kathy, 'I did. And how do *you* know that Mrs Margot Schneider was dark-haired? Have you ever seen any pictures of her? Because *I* haven't. Maybe you've seen her *head*?'

Skellett said nothing, but stared at her frigidly, his hands held in front of him like a male ballet dancer waiting for his cue in *Daphnis et Chloë*.

Kathy said, hesitantly, 'There are so many theories about what happened to Marilyn Monroe, whether she was murdered or committed suicide, or whether she simply took too many Nembutals. There were two or three people who could have saved her, that night that she was supposed to have died; and I began to wonder if maybe somebody did. Maybe she *did* have a row with Bobby Kennedy that night; maybe she *did* take too many pills. But maybe somebody actually answered one of her telephone calls, and came round to help her. She had a lot of friends, as well as a lot of enemies. Maybe somebody realized what trouble she was in, and spirited her away, to save her.'

'This is fantasy,' said Skellett.

'I told you it was only guesswork. There was a body, after all. But there were several strange things about the body, like the odd way it was lying, and the fact that her stomach was completely empty, as if it had been pumped. One witness said that when she was dead, Marilyn looked "remarkably young". But if you look at Bert Stern's nude pictures of her, taken that same year, she looks lined and old; even her hands look old. It occurred to me that somebody who was influential enough to have her spirited away could also have been influential enough to substitute a look-alike body.'

Skellett was silent for a long time. Then he said to Walsh, 'Cut her loose. Get her a robe. Then bring her into the living-room.'

It was five minutes before Kathy was ushered into the living-room, wrapped in a grubby beige towelling robe. Walsh pushed her towards one of the armchairs. In the opposite armchair, Skellett was clipping his fingernails. It was bright morning now, and the room was patterned with sunlight. The furniture was uncompromisingly 1960s – black plastic chairs, circular shaggy rugs, coffee tables

183

with black-painted metal legs. There was even a spindly LP rack, with red wooden balls for feet.

Skellett said, 'You have to understand that you're wrong. You've been doing what every young reporter tries to do these days, trying to dig up a sensational political scandal where none exists. Well, you're wrong. I should know. I've been working for the National Security Agency for eight years, and I've seen all the files. There's no scandal.'

'Then why were you so worried about my connecting Margot Schneider with Cuba?' Kathy demanded. 'Why did it mean so much to you that you were prepared to kill me?'

Skellett ignored her question, and said, 'Did you tell anyone else what you thought?'

'No,' said Kathy. 'I didn't tell anybody else. I wanted to gather in some more evidence before I discussed it with anybody. All I had was that one Polaroid of President Kennedy.'

'Tell me why, exactly, you thought that Mrs Margot Schneider had anything to do with Cuba,' Skellett insisted.

Kathy said, 'You hurt me. You know that? You hurt me so badly.'

'You don't think you deserved it?'

'Deserved it! You bastard!'

Skellett shrugged. 'There are plenty more Gila Monsters out in the desert.'

She was silent. Then she said, 'You would, too, wouldn't you? You'd do it?'

'Of course. My only priority is national security.'

Kathy hugged her arms over her breasts. They were so sore that she could have cried, but she was determined not to. She had already shed too many tears for Skellett. She said, slowly, 'I thought that Margot Schneider was Marilyn Monroe, or could have been. If she *was* Marilyn Monroe, then she was in hiding, under a false name, and there could only be one reason for doing that – because she was afraid. So what was she afraid of? I asked myself.'

184

Kathy paused, and then she said quietly, 'She could have been afraid of the scandal which would have followed the public revelation of her affairs with Bobby and Jack Kennedy. But then I thought, no, she wasn't the kind of woman who worried about things like that. She was worried about her pride, and about her identity, but not her reputation. The only thing that really would have worried her would have been the threat of mutilation or murder; and in those days the only people who would have been likely to kill her or hurt her would have been the people who really wanted to get at the President. Right-wing activists who were afraid that the Kennedys were going to let in a tide of left-wing legislation. Hardline Southern Democrats, racialists, or Ku Klux Klan. Maybe Lyndon Johnson, who knows. Or Cuban exiles, who felt that they'd been let down at the Bay of Pigs. Maybe the Kennedys wanted to get rid of her themselves. Maybe she knew too much about what they were doing; how badly they'd failed when everybody thought they were heroes. You can't hide much from a woman when you're in bed with her. Maybe Jack and Bobby told her just a little too much.'

Skellett said, 'You didn't tell me this to begin with.'

'No, because I thought that it might be true. And the angrier you became, the more convinced I was that it was true, or partly true. Margot Schneider was Marilyn Monroe, wasn't she? However she got to live in Phoenix, however she managed to change her identity, she *was* Marilyn Monroe, wasn't she?'

Skellett shook his head. 'No, she wasn't. I'm sorry to disappoint you. It sounds like the scoop of the millennium, doesn't it? But Margot Schneider was nobody more than Margot Schneider, and the truth was that she was selling off technical data about US planar-array radar to a Soviet espionage ring. Nothing spectacular; nothing that would seriously threaten national security. But enough to be treasonous.'

He carefully clipped off his long left thumbnail. 'The way I see it, she tried to press for a little more money.

Tried to get clever. Or maybe she passed some dud information. Whatever happened, she was assassinated by a KGB hit man. That was why we had to rush her body back to Washington, to check for prints, and to compare the *modus operandi* with other Soviet hits. It was urgent. Chief Ruse tried to get in our way; and that's why he had to go. Then *you* started asking awkward questions; and that's why I had to find out exactly what you knew.'

'She wasn't Marilyn Monroe?' asked Kathy. 'She really wasn't?'

'No,' said Skellett.

'Well, where did she get that photograph of Kennedy? Why did she keep so many reviews of *The Misfits*, and pictures of Clark Gable?'

'We'll be looking into it, don't you worry,' Skellett assured her. 'But remember that thousands of people took photographs of Kennedy; and that thousands of people own the same kind of changing-hut that Marilyn Monroe owned at Brentwood. A Criterion. You can buy them anywhere.'

'How do *you* know what kind of changing-hut she owned?'

'We've been to your apartment, Miss Forbes; and checked the Polaroid for ourselves. We're very thorough. We have to be. By the way, that wasn't a bad hiding-place, inside the coffee-jar. But not particularly original.'

Kathy stared at him blankly. 'You knew all the time? You tortured me like that and you knew all the time?'

Skellett grinned. 'We may be cruel, Miss Forbes, but we're not dumb.'

Eighteen

Few people would have recognized Titus in his horn-rimmed spectacles as he sat in the back of his chauffeur-driven limousine that morning, heading south on 23rd Street from Washington Circle towards the Department of State, through sunlight and shadow and reflected light. He was trying without much success to read a sheaf of reports on Israel and Lebanon, while Smetana's *Die Moldau* played with suppressed grandeur on his in-car stereo. He flicked his eyes up now and again to check which street they had reached: I Street, H Street, G Street, so that he knew to the second how much time he had left to digest all this jargon-riddled nonsense which his staff had prepared for him on the latest struggles between the Phalangists and the Moslems.

Religion, God damn it, he thought. Religion was nothing but trouble. The only faith worth believing in was holy pragmatism.

Somewhere between 'the re-divisionalization of West Beirut' and 'socio-religious interfaces', his mind wandered to thoughts of Nadine. Last night she had come home with her breath smelling of whiskey, laughing, alight, and insisted on taking him straight to bed; even though Carl and Samantha had both been there, lounging unlovably on his antique sofa in their dirty sneakers and drinking his best brandy, and had watched their mother drag their stepfather upstairs with eyes as unappreciative as four cigarette holes burned in a white linen pillow.

Nadine had been incoherent for sex. She had torn the buttons off his shirt, and pulled out his penis even before he could take down his pants. She had sat astride him with her pink silk cocktail-dress bunched up around her waist, and ridden him with almost insatiable ferocity. Near to her orgasm, she had taken him out of herself, and rolled him furiously against her pubic hair, until he had shouted out loud and spattered her dress and her stomach and her tautened thighs.

During the night, she had reached out for him again and again; and it was dawn before she had slept. He had quietly eased himself out of bed and tiptoed downstairs to his library to make telephone calls to London and Bonn. For the first time in almost two years he had lit a cigar before breakfast and smoked it thoughtfully.

'I'll pick you up at ten, Mr Secretary,' his chauffeur said, as the limousine drew up outside the Department of State, and the door was whipped open by one of Titus' security guards.

'Thanks, John. How's your boy? Recovered yet?'

'Much better, thank you, sir. Thank you for asking.'

'Umh-humh.'

Joe Jasper was waiting for Titus in his office. So was a tray of hot black coffee and a plate of Titus' favourite pecan cookies. Also, two roses boxed in cellophane, one white and one red.

'The flowers are from Nadine,' said Joe, with a sly smile.

Titus picked them up and examined them. 'One white, one red. The symbol of lost virginity.'

'Is that appropriate?' asked Joe.

Titus glanced at him, and then tossed the box on to the desk. 'It's none of your goddamned business, that's what it is.'

Joe said, 'Colleen Petley seems to be settling in quite well. You know? She's relaxed, and ready, and not complaining too much, although she did ask for a hot tub. She's very flattered that Nadine is looking after her personally. That was an excellent idea of yours, sir. Excellent.'

Titus poured himself some coffee, and dipped one of his cookies into it. He wasn't particularly hungry, but it was a ritual from his Army days, when he had insisted on making surprise breakfast inspections, and sharing coffee and cookies with his leathernecks. One of his many Army nicknames had been 'Dunker.'

'What's the news on RINC?' he asked Joe. 'I called Senator Rodney this morning and he seemed to think that Marshall may be trying to outflank us by calling in support from Droxard and Smith.' Hugh Droxard was the chairman of the Armed Services commission; Nestor Smith was the deputy chairman of the Finance commission. Both were heavyweight Southern Democrats whose views could substantially affect Congress when it came to voting on nuclear reduction.

Both would be happy to see Titus lynched from the flagstaff outside the Department of State, and slowly, slowly turning in the wind.

Their sudden enlistment to Marshall Roberts' cause was a clue that Marshall was thinking of re-starting the RINC talks sooner than Titus had expected. An unexpected chess-move, two white bishops going off in diagonally opposite directions.

Joe said, 'My guess is that the President's going to announce this morning that RINC II is all ready to start; and that RINC I had better be ratified as soon as the summer vacation is over.'

Titus reached for another cookie, and dipped it. 'He's pushing it, isn't he? Faster than I thought he would. Well, maybe we're going to have to show him our hand right now. I didn't particularly want to use Colleen before we saw which way the RINC talks were going to go; but if Marshall's going to start hustling them through like a junior-league football-game . . . maybe it's time we blocked him.'

'He's never going to forgive you, you know,' said Joe, with detectable relish.

'I've survived one of his hits; I can survive another. Besides – if he tries anything like that again, I can make it absolutely crystal clear that I'm going to release those videos, those pictures, everything. I'll release them posthumously if that's the way he wants to play it, but I'll bring him down, one way or another, dead or alive.'

Joe's face went through twenty different subservient expressions, from simple respect to complicated kow-towing. 'You're a tough man, Mr Secretary. Nobody can say that you're not.'

Titus sat down at his desk. 'What else?' he wanted to know. 'I was reading all that shit on Lebanon this morning. Why the hell can't Gemayel keep a hold on that situation? He's like a goddamned child.'

'Fejahl is coming in later this morning, around eleven.'

'And what about Sköping? Is he coming in?'

'I don't think so.'

'Well, *demand* it. Goddamned Swedes. I want this submarine business knocked on the head as soon as possible. Did you hear from the Office of the Joint Chiefs of Staff about it?'

'There's an OJCS memo on your desk.'

Titus was still sorting through his paperwork when his intercom made a noise like a flatulent corncrake. His secretary said, 'It's Senator Rodney, sir. He asked if you could possibly spare him two or three minutes.'

'All right,' said Titus; then, when it was apparent that the line was still open, 'Send him in.'

Senator Rodney entered the office blowing his nose. He was a short, white-haired man, with flappy trousers and a gold pocket-watch chain hung across his dark houndstooth vest. In appearance, although not in politics, he always reminded Titus of John L Lewis, the 1930s labour leader. The same bushy eyebrows, the same deeply-cleft chin.

'Ken,' Titus greeted him. 'Take a seat. We were just discussing this morning's Presidential talk-in.'

Senator Rodney pulled over a chair. 'You've got the woman?' he wanted to know.

'Safe and secure,' Titus assured him. 'Have some coffee.'

'I will, thanks. Do you have some whiskey? This damned summer cold's been killing me. Listen, from what I hear, you're going to have to put the squeeze on Marshall pretty damned soon. Never mind the niceties. He's been disconcertingly busy during the past couple of days; bribing, threatening, gathering up enough support to ratify the final clauses of RINC I and to start the preliminary discussions of RINC II. He's going to push for some early results, too: that cute little number in his publicity office called up Jerry Rosen late last night and said that she'd already seen some dummy brochures for Marshall's 1984 electoral campaign.'

'Can she be trusted?' asked Titus.

'Jerry trusts her. Sexually, if not politically. She said the heading on the brochure was '*America: Roberts Country*'. I guess that's convincing enough, don't you? Nobody else could possibly be that corny.'

Titus said harshly, 'That was one goddamned promise that Roberts always used to make. You remember that? In Denver he made it; in Seattle he made it; in New York he made it. "I'm in this race for one term and one term only. I'm too old for repeat performances." The lying bastard.'

'What you going to do?' asked Joe.

'I'm going to sic him,' said Titus. 'I'm going to stop him in his tracks. I wanted to save Colleen Petley for later – use her to block his tax budget, maybe. But it doesn't look like he's left me any choice.'

'All I can say is, be careful,' Senator Rodney warned him.

'Are you kidding? After that last little Fourth of July display?'

Senator Rodney said, 'Marshall Roberts has a mean streak so deep that you couldn't touch bottom with a bathyscaphe. You thwart him, Titus, and he's going to do everything and anything he can to have you ousted; and when you're ousted, killed. There's no question about it, as far as I'm concerned. Marshall Roberts is a sore loser.'

Titus stood up. 'Marshall Roberts is going to be thrown out of the White House faster than any President ever was; including Nixon. And I'm going to be the man who makes sure that he does. I know he's vindictive, but he's also vain. The Proud President, he called himself once. You remember that? But pride cometh before a fucking great fall.'

Titus and Senator Rodney talked for nearly fifty minutes about the upcoming RINC meeting; and about the way in which Titus was going to start building up his political presence as a likely runner for next year's Presidential primaries. They agreed that he would have to keep himself as far away as possible from Marshall Roberts' decline and fall – in case he was implicated either as a political conspirator or as a man who had known all along about the President's sexual tastes, and for his own political ends had chosen to ignore them. No Mid-Western voter was going to support a Secretary of State who could turn a blind eye to blatant sexual perversion.

Joe Jasper drank a last cold mouthful of coffee out of Titus' dirty cup, and said, 'Whatever happens, Mr Secretary, you always have to look as if your hands are clean.'

'And your ass,' put in Ken Rodney, with characteristic crudity.

At ten o'clock, Titus left the Department of State for the White House. Marshall Roberts had convened the RINC meeting in Titus' favourite room, the Lincoln Sitting Room, partly for its quietness and its comfort, and partly because he enjoyed rubbing it into Titus' face that he would never be able to live here. There was no doubt in anybody's mind that today was going to see a prickly confrontation between a once-hawkish President who had inexplicably gone soft on disarmament, and a military commander who had made his reputation as the hardest and least compromising politician since John Foster Dulles. But Marshall was deliberately late, and kept his Cabinet twitchily chattering to each other for almost fifteen minutes before he made his entrance. Only Titus appeared calm.

Marshall Roberts had always been imposing. Today he looked grander than ever. Tall, suntanned after a week's vacation near Big Sur, with a forehead that overhung his determined eyes like a cliff, and a sculptured wave of steel-grey hair. He wore a dark plaid sport coat and grey slacks, and a crimson silk handkerchief that spilled out of his breast pocket (in Senator Rodney's words) 'like fake blood from an artificial heart'.

'Good morning, gentlemen,' he said, easily, and went directly to his chair. 'We'll be having some coffee shortly.'

The doors were closed and everybody settled down. As if by natural selection, the military men and nuclear hard-liners had grouped themselves on the right-hand side of the room, an assembly of close-cropped haircuts and relentlessly shiny shoes; while the more liberal representatives had scattered themselves around on the left, in their unkempt bow-ties and scuffed suedes. Marshall Roberts waited for the shuffling and throat-clearing and document-rustling to die away, and then he said in that distinctive voice of his, chocolatey but completely self-assured, 'I'm not going to beat around the bushes this morning, I'm going to inform you straight away that I intend to re-open the talks that we've been having with the Soviet Union for the reduction of nuclear weapons as soon as Congress has reconvened after the summer vacation. Now, as you're aware, we cannot continue with these talks until the House ratifies the last two clauses of RINC I, relating to the withdrawal from British bases of cruise-type missiles. These two clauses have become a sticking-point far out of proportion to their real political or strategic implications.'

Marshall cast his eyes slowly around the members of his Cabinet and the officers from the Joint Chiefs of Staff. Several of them grinned uneasily.

'There are some among you who have opposed the ratification of RINC I right from the beginning, either covertly or openly. Well, I'm going to tell you gentlemen here and now that those agreements are going to be approved whether you like it or not; with you or without you. My Presidency is going to be recorded in history as an administration that was strong, but also intelligent. Powerful, but also humane. I have always been the first to advocate military integrity in the face of Communist expansionism; but we stand for life as well as for liberty, and it is my considered opinion that if we continue seeking the *measured* reduction of nuclear weaponry, particularly in the European theatre, then we will be doing the world the sanest and most responsible service that any administration has done in 206 years.'

John Gibbons, the bald-headed Secretary of Defence, raised his propelling-pencil and said sharply, 'Mr President, we all appreciate your humanity. But some of the outline proposals you've been circulating for RINC II come dangerously close, in my view, anyway, to unilateral disarmament. They certainly don't constitute mutual and balanced nuclear reduction.'

Marshall cleared his throat. 'John,' he said, in a soft voice which carried in its softness a clear threat of later retribution, 'there is no such concept as complete mathematical mutuality when it comes to nuclear disarmament. Our weapons systems are quite different from the Soviet weapons systems. So is our view of nuclear strategy. An installation which *we* consider relatively unimportant can appear to the Soviets as a grave threat to their national integrity. So to strive for a one-for-one reduction in nuclear weapons is not only misguided but unnecessary. The notion of complete mutuality has been standing in the way of nuclear reduction for decades. It's up to us, in ratifying RINC I, and in proceeding as expeditiously as we can with RINC II, to break the logjam.'

'Pardon me, Mr President,' put in General Paul D Immerman, one-time Army Chief of Staff and now Chairman of the Joint Chiefs, 'the JCS are very sensitive to your viewpoint on disarmament. But we've already had our strategic study group run the proposals for RINC II through the computer, and there isn't any doubt at all that if even the least contentious of them are agreed and ratified, the United States will be put irreversibly into a nuclear no-win situation. If we pull back as few as half of our ALCMs from Britain, and limit the deployment of the neutron bomb by as little as a third, the Soviet Union will have a 63.9% chance of occupying the whole of Europe within five days. I agree with you about an obsessive concern with mutuality standing in the way of sensible reduction. But I can't go along with you when you suggest national suicide.'

Titus shifted in his high-backed antique chair, and Marshall turned towards him and asked, 'Titus? What's your view?'

There were tense glances around the room. Everybody knew that Titus was irreconcilably set against any nuclear disarmament whatsoever; and that the moment had now come for him to face up to the President toe-to-toe, or compromise everything that he had ever said about 'let America melt'.

Titus neatly collated the papers on his lap, and smiled. 'Mr President,' he said, 'it appears to me that before we go chasing after nuclear rainbows, we should seriously appraise whether this is the same defence policy which this administration was elected in 1980 to carry out. The same, or even *remotely* similar.'

Marshall leaned forward angrily. It was obvious that he felt like whipping back at Titus, but he held himself under control. He wanted Titus to say everything that he had come here to say; he wanted Titus to wind himself tightly in the shroud of his own sarcasm; and then he wanted to bury Titus alive, in full view of the entire Cabinet, and later in front of the media. If only Titus had half a glimmer of the agony which Marshall had been going through since his inauguration. The media always remarked on the way in which incumbent Presidents aged so dramatically during their first year in office; and in spite of his suntan Marshall felt like a man more than a decade older than his 66 years. If only that smug-faced bastard knew. If only he had the humanity to *sense* it. But he didn't, and he wouldn't, and that was why Marshall wanted him entombed.

With deliberate long-windedness, Titus went on, 'It seems to me, Mr President, that you have been overly concerning yourself with your lustrous international image as a peacemaker, and forgetting the price which your fellow countrymen are going to have to pay to keep your halo shiny.'

'Titus – ' Marshall started to interrupt him, but Titus smiled and raised a hand.

'Please, I'd like to finish. A great deal hangs in the balance today. Not just our own political ambitions; not just the defence of America; but the safety of the entire planet. And while you have obviously considered the Geneva principles in considerable detail, Mr President, have you perhaps forgotten the Nevada protocols?'

Marshall Roberts frowned at Titus darkly. 'The *what*?' he growled. He knew that Titus never said anything irrational or frivolous. Every word that Titus spoke was like one of those damned ingenious anti-personnel devices, that blew up if you touched them and then blew up if you didn't.

'I think you'd better explain what the Nevada protocols actually *are*, Mr Secretary,' said General Immerman. 'We're not all *au fait*.'

'Oh, my apologies,' smiled Titus. 'The Nevada protocols were based on a purely informal political meeting at the Futura Hotel in Las Vegas, Nevada, shortly before President Roberts was nominated by the GOP.'

'Can we know who was there?' asked John Gibbons. '*I* certainly wasn't.' He didn't have the faintest idea what Titus was talking about, but he was beginning to sense in Titus' voice and in Titus' posture that the old hunter-killer of the State Department had scented blood. He could also see that Marshall Roberts had been unexpectedly silenced, and that his usually bullet-hard eyes were betraying some interesting suggestions of genuine anxiety.

Titus said, 'President Roberts was present at these discussions; as were certain personnel especially chosen for their *refreshing* political views. It was generally agreed that if President Roberts were to be elected, he would soon be entering a new golden age.'

Now Marshall Roberts knew for sure. His face was fixed as tightly as if his teeth had been clamped together. His eyes wavered away from Titus' face to Titus' casually-crossed knees, and then down to the yellow-patterned carpet. Titus monotonously swung his foot, and kept on smiling. His polished black shoe swung in and out of Marshall's line of vision like an irritating memory that refused to go away.

I can even remember her name, he thought. *Rita. And the way she opened up her thighs and climbed on to me, and then sat over my face and said, 'Care for a cocktail, sugar?'*

Titus said, with undisguised triumph in his voice, 'The President will recall that the Nevada protocols clearly expressed the GOP's determination to give the Joint Chiefs of Staff all the support they would need within the scope of the available Federal budget to implement as fully as possible the recommendations of JSOP II. In other words, to provide the United States with the optimum defence capability as envisaged by the military services themselves.'

There was a very long silence. Marshall Roberts was still staring at the carpet. Titus added, in the gentlest of tones, 'I was only suggesting that the President, in his zeal for wholesale disarmament, might have omitted to remember how his own party feels that international peace might be more readily and more safely achieved.' He bowed his head towards Marshall with unmistakable sarcasm. 'I do hope that I have been of real assistance.'

Marshall Roberts looked up at last. 'Well,' he said, and his deep Hershey-coloured voice sounded suddenly tired, 'It appears that the Secretary of State has raised some very fundamental policy matters which require my further attention.'

'Mr President, with respect, Mr Alexander still hasn't made it quite clear what the Nevada – ' began General Immerman, but Marshall Roberts gave a quick, displeased shake of his head that silenced the chairman of the JCS instantly. General Immerman turned to Admiral Carstairs and gave him a baffled shrug.

'This meeting is adjourned,' said Marshall Roberts, and stood up straight away and left the room. Everybody else gathered up their papers and their briefcases in complete confusion; all except Titus, who remained where he was, still smiling his saintly smile. John Gibbons came over and said, 'You really got your teeth into him that time.'

Titus nodded. 'It seems like it, doesn't it?'

'Don't suppose there's any chance you might give me some slight inkling what these Nevada protocols actually are?'

'Use your brains, John. There are only two commodities in Las Vegas, money and sex. So it's either one or the other.'

John Gibbons' eyebrows rose up his bald forehead. 'Well, now,' he said. '*You're* playing with fire, aren't you?'

'You need fire to fight fire.'

'Let me buy you lunch,' said John Gibbons. 'Let's talk about this some more.'

'Not yet, John. In any case, I'm dieting.'

Just as John Gibbons turned away, the far door of the Lincoln Sitting Room was opened, and Rosemary Wuppers, the President's personal secretary, gave Titus a discreet beckoning wave. Titus stood up, brushed down his suit, and then followed her into the small book-lined room next door which Marshall Roberts had turned into his private den. Marshall was standing by the window, his hands in his pockets, silhouetted like an ageing lion against the blurry summer sunshine. He said, 'Come on in, Titus. Close the door.'

Titus came in, and laid his papers down on Marshall's leather-topped desk.

'You want a cigar?' asked Marshall.

Titus said, 'No, thank you, Mr President. I'm trying to be a little more ascetic these days.'

Marshall was silent for a while. Titus watched him, standing up smartly and confidently, with the bearing of a soldier. Then Marshall said, 'It's difficult for me to explain to you, Titus, just what a serious mistake you're making.'

'Oh?'

'You've gotten hold of some photographs, I expect?'

Titus looked quickly around. 'This room wired?'

Marshall shook his head. 'It wouldn't matter if it were,

198

would it? If you've gotten hold of some photographs, I'd scarcely be likely to want to advertise the fact, would I?'

'Well, there's more than photographs,' said Titus. 'There are video-taped confessions, pictures, and, of course, real live witnesses.'

'The girl herself?'

'It's conceivable.'

Marshall came away from the window and stood very close to Titus, so close that Titus could feel the President's warm, even breath against his cheek. 'I have to advise you of something, Titus; it will not be a good idea to attempt to interfere with the RINC talks.'

'What are you talking about, Marshall? The RINC talks are giving away so many strategic concessions to the Soviets that they practically constitute a crime against the Republic.'

'Believe me, they're the lesser of two evils. At least they're gradual.'

Titus stared at him. 'What the hell do you mean, *gradual*? What's gotten into you, Marshall? You and I, we used to be the closest of friends. The closest of allies, too. You don't believe in this strategic arms reduction any more than I do. You would have nuked the Soviets over Afghanistan, if you'd had the chance. So how can you stand in front of me now and tell me you want to pull back our cruise missiles out of Britain, and still seriously believe that you're capable of continuing your administration with any kind of honour at all?'

'Honour?' asked Marshall, as if he scarcely knew what the word meant. He turned away from Titus and sat down heavily at his desk. 'Honour is a rare bird these days, Titus. Especially when you start looking for it on the top of the mountain.'

Titus said, 'I didn't want to have to do this, you know. This Nevada business. Playing dirty isn't something I particularly enjoy. But RINC is too much of a national risk, Marshall, and you're becoming unstable and irrational, and, let's face it, weird.'

'*Weird?*'

'You don't think it's weird for a President to double back on one of his strongest election promises? You don't think it's weird for a President to take part in peculiar and perverted sex acts? You don't think it's weird for a President to attempt to waste his own Secretary of State?'

Marshall raised his head. 'You think that I had anything at all to do with that bombing? You actually believe that I intended to have you killed?'

'Someone did, Marshall, and you're my prime suspect. I know what happened to Fred Coggins back in '76, when he tried to squeeze you out of that Asquehanna Power Project. And I *still* believe you had a hand in that Sybil Coles affair.'

'You're crazy Titus, you know that? I may be weird, but *you're* crazy.'

Titus smiled. 'Nevertheless, Marshall, you're going to do what you're told. You're going to put RINC I right on the back burner, and you're going to forget about RINC II for good. Do you understand me loud and clear? Otherwise, the videotapes will be handed out wherever they'll do you the most harm; and the girl will be fanfared to the media. Can you imagine facing Margaret Thatcher again, after you've been publicly accused of urolagnia?'

'I'm, uh, obviously going to have to consider this for a day or so,' said Marshall. He sounded suddenly very tired. 'You must give me a little time.'

'No time, Marshall. The answer is yes or the answer is no; and I want it right now.'

Marshall drummed his fingers on the desk. 'It wasn't me who tried to kill you, you know. I want you to believe that.'

'Marshall, I want an answer.'

Marshall suddenly banged both hands flat on his blotter. His forehead was crimson with rage and frustration. 'I can't *give* you an answer, for Christ's sake! I can't postpone those RINC talks for anyone or anything! They're way behind time already! For the love of God, Titus, don't you see what I'm trying to tell you? I'm not *allowed* to!'

Titus felt an extraordinary prickle of uncertainty, right

up his spine to the nape of his neck. The last time he had felt anything as unpleasant as that was in Nam, when he had woken up one morning to feel a sharp, spidery sensation right inside his pants. He frowned at Marshall and said hoarsely, 'You're not allowed to? Am I hearing you straight? You're the *President*.'

Marshall sat wearily back in his seat. 'I can't tell you anything else, Titus. I've told you far too much already. But, believe me, if you try to delay or upset these talks, you're going to be digging many more graves than just your own.'

'Are you under some kind of threat? Blackmail?'

'Only the blackmail threat that *you're* making against me. And, of course, the daily threat of seeing the entire United States collapse like a house of cards.'

'I don't know what you mean. What do you mean, collapse like a house of cards? For Christ's sake, Marshall, talk sense!'

Marshall shook his head. 'You're just going to have to take what I'm telling you on trust, Titus. You know that I've never been a man to beg favours, and I hope you can understand that I'm not telling you to back off just to save my own skin. I'm quite prepared to take full responsibility for everything I've done, political and sexual, when the time comes. But not now, Titus. Please not now. If you stop RINC II, or if you force me to resign from the Presidency on moral grounds, then believe me a burden is going to fall upon your shoulders greater than you will ever be able to bear.'

Titus was silent. He had never seen Marshall like this before. He had seen him threaten, cajole, bully, and flatter. He had seen him bargain. But he had never seen him *plead*. Not in such bursts of anger and fear; not with his eyes darting about under his eyebrows like trapped and frightened fish. He didn't know what to say: whether to insist that Marshall should put a stop to RINC II regardless, or whether to give him a little more time, in the hope that he might explain himself more fully. The trouble was, there were high practical risks in giving a man like Marshall Roberts more time. In a day or so, Marshall could track down Colleen Petley, and make sure that she was in no position to speak out against him. In a day or so, Marshall could stage a politically embarrassing incident anywhere in the world, like revealing that Titus was secretly sending military supplies to Ecuador, and drastically undermine Titus' power-base. In a day or so, Marshall could ensure that the bombing attempt which had failed in West Virginia was restaged, this time successfully.

At last, Titus said, 'You've got an hour. That's all I'm prepared to give you. Call me at the State Department and let me know what you've decided. I might be prepared to do some kind of a deal which would leave you with the minimum of egg on your face. Say, pretending to defer RINC II for a year or so. But if you don't call, or if you call and say no, then I'm going to bring you down. Do you hear me? By the time I'm through with you, Warren Harding is going to be remembered as a saint, by comparison. And I mean it.'

Marshall said nothing. But as Titus buttoned up his coat and turned to leave the den, he saw Marshall's clenched fist quivering as if it were a human hand-grenade that was just about to explode.

Nineteen

Lieutenant Berridge was sitting at his desk eating a grapefruit yogurt when Sergeant Corso came in to tell him that Skellett's car had been identified outside a house in Palmcroft Drive, in Tempe.

'Who identified it?' Berridge wanted to know. Then,

'Shit,' as he reached for his jacket and knocked yogurt all over his paperwork.

'The Tempe fire department. They were called to a fire there about an hour ago, suspicious circumstances. Somebody set light to the bedroom drapes.'

'Let's get out there. Where the hell's Norris?'

'At the hospital. His old lady's having twins.'

'Well, get Pulaski then. I want somebody who can *drive*.'

Within four minutes, Lieutenant Berridge and Detective Pulaski were screeching out of the police garage in their bronze Chevrolet, siren whooping and red light flashing on the roof. Pulaski had once been a stocker, and he drove with hair-raising precision, sliding the car around the corner of 7th Street towards the Maricopa Freeway as if it were on rails. He overtook a huge refrigerated truck on the inside, stood on the brakes, and spun the car neatly in front of the truck's huge oncoming bumper and across the street.

'I suppose that's one way of crossing an intersection,' remarked Lieutenant Berridge, trying to sound casual. His feet were pressed so hard against the floor that he was getting cramp.

'There's another way?' asked Pulaski.

Pulaski may have been a hot-rod driver, but his knowledge of Phoenix's maze of suburban streets was decidedly patchy. He managed to get them on to Palm Road, but then he lost five vital minutes roaring around Loma Vista Road, Broadmor Drive, El Parque Drive, and Del Rio Terrace, passing the same smart little houses over and over, and leaving the smell of burned rubber in the summer heat. At last he found Palmcroft Drive, and howled to a dramatic halt beside three firetrucks and four patrol cars from the Tempe police department. Lieutenant Berridge stiffly climbed out, and walked across the street like a man who has narrowly avoided a fatal accident.

'Lieutenant,' said Bill Hagerty, Tempe's police chief, by way of greeting. 'That's where they've holed themselves up, number 1226.'

Number 1226 Palmcroft was one of the larger properties in the area, a shingle roofed one-storey building on a low landscaped hill, closely surrounded by dense flowering bushes. On the sloping driveway was parked Skellett's Cadillac, one tyre flat. Around to the side of the house was an open bedroom window, its drapes hanging in burned tatters, its glass blackened with soot, and a dark smudge above it on the grey stucco.

'They're still *in* there?' asked Berridge.

'Sure. Three of them, a girl and two men.'

'The girl's probably Kathy Forbes, from the *Flag*.'

'We've tried talking to them,' said Hagerty. 'So far they haven't answered. The phone's off the hook, and they've ignored the bullhorn.'

'What do you think about the fire?'

'If the girl *is* Kathy Forbes, then it wouldn't surprise me if she started it herself, to attract some attention. She was lucky the fire department was able to put it out from outside the house. She could've been roasted in there. *All* of them could've been roasted.'

'Have you seen them yet?'

'Not me, but the firemen did. When they broke down the front door, trying to get in to tackle the blaze, the two men were waiting in the hall. A big guy and a medium-sized guy, both armed. They fired three shots, all .45 calibre. The fire chief told his men to back off and stay off, and I can't say that I blame him.'

'Who saw the girl?'

'That fireman right over there. He saw her briefly at the bedroom window before the smoke got too thick.'

'Nobody's seen her since then?'

'Unh-hunh.'

'So she may be dead?'

'It's possible, yes. We've got no way of telling.'

An officer came up and said, 'Chief Hagerty, sir? We've been questioning the old couple directly opposite. They swear they saw three men going into number 1226 last night, three men and two girls. They were kind of ashamed to admit it at first, but they spend most of their time by the front window, spying out over the neighbourhood. The wife's in a wheelchair. Last night they positively saw three men, and two girls. They believe that one of the girls left the house earlier on this morning and as far as they know she hasn't come back.'

'Thank the Lord for nosy neighbours,' Chief Hagerty intoned.

'The third guy is probably Skellett,' said Lieutenant Berridge. 'Has anybody called the National Security Agency, and asked what the hell he thinks he's playing at?'

'I've had a call in for a half-hour,' said Chief Hagerty. 'So far the response has been underwhelming, to say the least. They keep quoting 'special prerogatives' to me. This country is going to choke itself on jargon one day.'

'What do you intend to do?' asked Berridge.

Chief Hagerty gave a quick, barking cough. 'Play it cool, that's what. There's no particular need to rush in there like the Seventh Cavalry. We've no immediate indication that the girl is in mortal danger, that's if she's still alive. I'd rather wait it out, let them sweat. They know they can't escape.'

'You don't mind if I stick around?'

'Be my guest. I've sent for hot-dogs, if you're hungry.'

They waited around for the rest of the afternoon, while the sun slowly burned its way westwards; hours of coffee-drinking and smoking and leaning against hot glaring police cars and talking about baseball. Lieutenant Berridge talked a lot about Chief Ruse, but he said nothing about his conviction that the chief's murder had been nothing more than a quick and callous way to extinguish his opposition to the removal of Margot Schneider's remains from the Phoenix morgue. The official line, as put out by Mayor Gardens, was that Chief Ruse had been conducting an in-depth investigation into Mafia corruption in Arizona, and that his execution had borne 'all the hallmarks of a quasi-Sicilian revenge killing'.

Chief Hagerty kept directional microphones pointed at 1226 Palmcroft, and police marksmen concealed all around the perimeter of the grounds; but if there was any conversation going on inside the house, it was being conducted in very low whispers, and none of the occupants made any attempt to poke their noses out. The house might just as well have been empty.

'I want generators, okay, and floods,' instructed Chief Hagerty, as darkness began to fall. He came up to Lieutenant Berridge and said, 'This could be a long one. You want to go home, come back later?'

'I'll stick it out for another hour.'

'Suit yourself.'

It was at one minute after sunset, at 6.42, that the broken front door of the house was suddenly pushed half-open, and a man's voice yelled out, 'I'm coming out! You hear me? I'm coming out and my hands are way up! I'm unarmed!'

Immediately, there was a scurry in the street, as officers ducked and dived behind their cars, and raised their weapons. Chief Hagerty shouted for the floodlights to be directed at the front door, and almost immediately the blue-white halogen beams picked out the figure of a man in a white shirt with rolled-up sleeves, his hands stretched up over his head.

'Is that Skellett?' Chief Hagerty asked Berridge.

Berridge shook his head. 'That one I've never seen before in my life.'

The man came halfway down the front path of the house, and stood blinking at the floodlights as if he had emerged from a week trapped in a pothole. Lieutenant Berridge said, 'What's the matter with him? Why is he just standing there?' Chief Hagerty picked up his bullhorn and demanded, '*Walk forward another ten steps. Then lie down on the road, face downwards, with your arms and legs spread. Do you understand me?*'

Hesitantly, awkwardly, the man did what he was told. As soon as he had lowered himself on to the road-surface, his left ankle was seized by two police officers who were crouched behind a parked car, and he was roughly and speedily dragged into cover. One of the officers kept a

Python revolver pressed to the man's head while the other searched him for weapons.

'Looks like he's clean, sir.'

'Okay. Handcuff him.'

The man's arms were twisted around behind his back and locked with handcuffs. Then he was hoisted on to his feet and hurried at a knees-bent run across the road, behind a police panel-van.

Chief Hagerty left his own position behind his car, and joined the officers in the cover of the van. Lieutenant Berridge followed him, but kept a foot or two behind. He was very conscious that this was Chief Hagerty's territory, and that a small gesture of police etiquette would win him more co-operation than all the big-city assertiveness in the world. Chief Ruse always used to say to him, 'Policemen are more damned territorial than coyotes.'

The man was pushed up against the van and both his arms were held. Chief Hagerty approached him closely, and stood with his hands on his hips staring at him. The man was sweaty, unshaven, and smelled of foreign cigarettes. The pupils of his eyes were dilated, as if he was high on narcotics.

'Are you going to talk to me?' Chief Hagerty asked him.

'There's no use,' the man told him, in a thickly-accented voice.

'Oh, you don't think so? Three or four of you are holed up in that house there, and you let fly at a detail of perfectly innocent firemen with .45 automatics, and you don't think there's any use in talking? What's your name?'

'Andrej.'

'Andrej? What kind of a name is that? You foreign, or what?'

'Czech.'

'I shall, don't you worry.'

Lieutenant Berridge put in, gently, 'Chief, I think he said "Czech." You know, like Czechoslovakian.'

Chief Hagerty looked briefly annoyed. 'Is that right?' he demanded. 'You're a Czechoslovakian?'

The man nodded.

'Naturalized American, or what?'

'I don't have to tell you anything.'

'You fucking do, buddy. There's two of your friends in that house, along with a kidnapped girl, and if you don't start talking and talking quick you're going to wind up with telephone numbers.'

The man looked completely baffled.

'You know what telephone numbers are?' asked Lieutenant Berridge, as diplomatically as he could. The man shook his head.

'Jail, buddy,' explained Chief Hagerty. 'Jail for the rest of your natural life.'

At that moment, there was the sudden snap of automatic fire from the house. A large-calibre bullet shattered the panel-van's windshield, and groaned into the bushes nearby. The floodlights swung and flickered, and there was a heavy rattle of shooting from the police marksmen crouched behind their cars. Somebody shouted, 'They're making a run for it!'

What happened next would return to everybody who saw it for years to come in nightmares. The man in the white shirt suddenly twisted away from the two policemen who were holding him, and butted Chief Hagerty straight in the forehead. Chief Hagerty went down flat, like a man hit by a baseball bat. Then the man dodged and shouldered his way past Lieutenant Berridge and ran around the front of the van with his hands still securely handcuffed behind his back. One of the patrolmen had already drawn his gun, but Lieutenant Berridge shouted at him, *'Don't shoot!'*

The man timed his run perfectly. Just as Skellett and Walsh appeared in the front door of the house, both of them waving Colt automatics towards the police, the man crossed Palmcroft Drive at a long diagonal, straight across the police marksmen's line of fire, and exploded.

Lieutenant Berridge stared in total horror as the man's head leapt ten feet in the air, still attached to unravelling strings of nerves and tendons. His arms flew away in opposite directions, and then his guts spiralled around in a grisly splattering corkscrew. Blood and fragments of liver and lungs showered the policemen like rain, and then there was nothing but smoke and fire, and a sound like a wet thunderclap.

In the confusion, Skellett and Walsh ran into the next-door yard, clambered over the fence, and disappeared. None of the policemen even bothered to fire at them; they were too busy staring in horror at the sickening remains of the man in the white shirt, which had splattered their faces and uniforms like some grotesque and hideous practical joke.

Chief Hagerty, still lying on the ground, stared up at Lieutenant Berridge wide-eyed. 'The guy blew up,' he said. 'The guy just *blew up*.'

Lieutenant Berridge sat down on the kerb, took out his handkerchief, and smeared blood away from his face and hands. He was so shocked that he could hardly speak. Chief Hagerty humped himself over to where he was sitting, and propped himself up beside him, nursing the bruise on his head.

'He must've been a walking bomb. Jesus. A walking bomb. We searched him, but he was still packed full of explosives. Up his ass, it must have been. Who'd have thought of that?'

'Can you imagine what a *fanatic* he must have been?' Lieutenant Berridge replied. 'His whole goddamned rectum must have been chock full of gelignite; and a timing device, too.'

'Jesus,' said Chief Hagerty.

One of the officers came over, looking distinctly pale in the light from the halogen lamps, his shirt jigsawed with blood. 'I'm sorry, sir. We lost the other two. They went over the fence and along the culvert, as far as we can make out. Nyman thought he saw them, but we can't be too sure.'

Chief Hagerty managed to stand up, swaying on his feet. 'I think you're forgiven this time,' he said. Then he suddenly retched, and held his hand over his mouth.

'You all right?' Lieutenant Berridge asked him.

'Sure. Just that knock on the head. Spanier, find a hose will you, and sluice this crap out of the street.'

'Yes, sir. Sir?'

'What is it?'

'Do I really have to, sir?'

'Yes, Spanier, you do. Ask Montez to help you. He used to work in a processed-meat factory. He won't mind.'

'There's still the girl,' said Lieutenant Berridge. 'We'd better go in and take a look.'

'Supposing the girl's booby-trapped, too?'

'Are you kidding?'

'Look at that mess on the street and tell me this is all a joke.'

'This is all a joke. Now, let's go and see what's happened to the girl.'

They found Kathy Forbes bound and gagged in the living-room, wearing nothing but a garter-belt and stockings. She was bruised, and her breasts were mottled with scarlet wounds, but otherwise she was unhurt. Lieutenant Berridge knelt down beside her as one of the officers cut her free, and said, 'It was Skellett, wasn't it? He got away.'

'He got away?' whispered Kathy. 'I heard the gunfire; I thought you'd killed him.'

Lieutenant Berridge shook his head. 'They used a decoy. The guy in the white shirt. You heard that bang, a few minutes ago? That was him. Blew himself up.'

'He was Czech,' said Kathy, as if that made any difference. 'He told me this morning he came from Pradubice. He said he missed his brothers. Isn't that ridiculous?'

'It is now. They're washing him away with a garden hose.'

One of the officers brought Kathy a blanket from the bedroom, and she shakily wrapped herself up. When they brought her out into the night, there was a dazzle of TV and newspaper lights, and Lieutenant Berridge had to jostle her across the road towards the ambulance. 'No questions now,' Berridge insisted. 'Just keep back, will you? The lady's hurt. How badly? I'll tell you tomorrow. Now keep back.'

Kathy lay back in the ambulance, listening to the shouting and the arguing and the scribbling sound of sirens, and shivered like someone who has seen their own tombstone. Lieutenant Berridge squeezed himself in beside her, and said, 'I'll come to the hospital with you, okay? I have to ask you some questions.'

'All right,' she said dully. She realized that she was nearly asleep. Shock, she supposed. Shock always sends you to sleep. 'What do you want to ask me?'

'It was you who set fire to the bedroom drapes, right?'

'That's right. I was desperate. I thought they were going to torture me again.'

'They tortured you?'

She nodded. The ambulance had started off now, and she felt the unreal swaying of the suspension as it turned out of Palmcroft Drive into Terrace Road and then into Loma Vista. 'They stuck needles in my breasts. I mean Skellett stuck needles in my breasts. They wanted to know about Margot Schneider.'

'You know they killed Chief Ruse. At least, I believe they did.'

Kathy nodded. She could hardly keep her eyes open. 'They were worried, you know. They were worried that I'd discovered their secret. They were going to push a Gila Monster up inside me. Can you believe that? They had a Gila Monster, and they were going to push it up inside me.'

'Listen,' said Lieutenant Berridge. 'What secret?'

'That's why they killed Chief Ruse, don't you see? They were frightened that he was going to find out. They were frightened that he was going to guess the truth.'

'And what *is* the truth? What were they so frightened about?'

Kathy stared at him through slitted eyes. 'I don't know. There is a truth, but I can't remember it.'

'Miss Forbes, you've got to tell me.'

'I can't think. Lieutenant, I can't *remember*.'

'For Christ's sake, this is a homicide investigation. A *double* homicide investigation, plus whatever you call someone who packs their backend with gelignite and paints the town red.'

'Recticide,' said Kathy, with a wan smile. Then she fell deeply asleep.

Twenty

At five o'clock in the morning, just as the moon rose, Daniel abruptly sat up in bed and said, 'What the hell's that? Did you hear that noise?'

Cara muzzily snuggled in closer to him, and said, 'What noise? I didn't hear any noise.'

'There was a noise. Like somebody prowling around outside.'

'It's probably dogs. Or coyotes. Go back to sleep.'

Daniel swung out of bed, and walked across to the window. Outside, on the moon-blanched parking-lot, he saw two stray hounds scavenging in the garbage-can which old man Tremlett next door had left out for the trash collectors. He watched them for a while as they snapped and fought over the remains of a TV-dinner tray, then came back to bed and eased himself between the sheets.

'Dogs?' asked Cara, putting her arm around him, and pressing her bare breasts against his side.

'Dogs. I guess I shouldn't be so goddamned jumpy.'

'Do you want some coffee? Or a soda maybe?'

He turned towards her and kissed her on the forehead. 'Just a little comfort, thank you. I've got to get up in an hour anyway.'

'Are you opening the diner today?'

'Why not? Either they know who I am, or else they don't know who I am. I'm not going to run. I can't afford to. You have to be wealthy to be a fugitive these days. Especially when you've got a child and a girlfriend to take with you.'

Cara was quiet for a moment, stroking his shoulder. Then she said, 'They killed Willy. They might kill you.'

'They killed Willy because he was just about to blow the whistle on the biggest armaments scandal in ten years. That's what I think, anyway. Somebody got a contract to build missiles and missile guidance systems and the damned things don't even work properly. Do you know what the finance for those contracts runs into? Billions. Hundreds of billions. Somebody's making a whole lot of backhanders out there; and we're not even being protected from enemy attack.'

'Daniel, they must know that you were Willy's friend. And they're only going to have to identify Ronald to realize who was with him. Pete Burns could easily tell them, without even understanding that he's putting you at risk.'

'What do you expect me to do? Pack my bags and jump on the first bus? Drive west? Drive east? I didn't manage to salvage very much of my existence when my marriage broke up; what I've got here is all that's left. I'm not leaving this behind, too.'

Cara propped herself up on her elbow and looked at him closely. The moonlight illuminated the soft curve of her back, the roundness of her bottom. She had bought some Indian perfume yesterday at the Navajo store on the way to Tortilla Flat, and she smelled like fresh cactus and spice. She kissed him, again and again and again, and whispered, 'You've found it, you see. Your courage.'

'Courage? Well, maybe. I don't think I actually know what courage feels like, even when you've found it. But I'm staying, if that's anything to do with courage; and I'm going to find out how Willy was killed, and who did it, and why.'

'Make love to me,' she said.

They made love simply and slowly, while the moon appeared through the upper left-hand quarter of the bedroom window with all the brightness and blandness of an alien voyeur. He thrust rhythmically into the coppery curls of her pubic hair, and caressed her big soft breasts in his hands until the nipples stiffened between his fingers like buttons. She shuddered in orgasm a moment before he did, and her shuddering brought him to his climax, too; and then they both lay side by side in silence, staring at each other with fondness and friendship and the warm accomplishment of a plain but almost perfect act of love.

'Do you want me to leave?' she asked, after a long interval.

'Leave? What makes you think I want you to leave?'

'Sometimes the time arrives, whether you want it to or not.'

He laid his hand flat on her stomach; the way he had laid his hand on Candii's stomach when she had first told him that she was pregnant with Susie. 'I don't want you to leave. Not now. Maybe not ever.'

'I'll never marry you.'

'I don't want you to marry me. But, for now, I want you to stay.'

Cara came close to him, and ran her fingers into his hair. 'You're a good man, Daniel.'

Later, he went downstairs to the kitchen to make coffee. Susie came down and said she was hungry, and he gave her a bowl of Donutz and a glass of orange-juice. Daniel switched on the FM radio to KSTM, and whistled along with 'Joleen'.

In a small voice, Susie said, 'Cara told me that Ronald was dead. Is that true?'

Daniel swallowed. He was still trying to keep back his own grief about what had happened yesterday. 'Yes,' he told her, as if he had a thistle in his throat. 'Yes, that's right. Ronald's dead.'

'Is he going to have a funeral?'

'I guess so.'

'Are we going to go? To the funeral, I mean?'

'I don't know, honey, it all depends.'

'It all depends on what?'

'I don't know. Don't ask me. It all depends on . . . I don't know, fate.'

'What's *fate*?'

'Ask Cara, will you? I don't know what fate is. Fate is what jumps out of the closet at you when you're expecting nothing but jeans and T-shirts.'

Susie frowned at him, but didn't ask him any more questions about Ronald. She had lived alone with her father for long enough to understand when he was upset. He finished making the coffee, and then he leaned over and kissed the parting of her hair. 'Finish your Donutz, okay?'

The radio announcer said, '. . . right now, at the top of the hour . . . and first we have more news of the dramatic siege yesterday evening in Tempe, when a terrorist deliberately blew himself up in full view of police officers and horrified local residents in order to provide a grisly and spectacular diversion to two escaping colleagues in crime. . . . Rescued from the siege was *Arizona Flag* reporter Kathy Forbes, who was working on an equally grisly news story . . . the mystery of the Air Force widow Mrs Margot Schneider who earlier this week was beheaded by an unknown intruder at her North Phoenix home . . . Miss Forbes was captured by the terrorists the day before yesterday, and held captive in a plush Palmcroft Drive home, where she was stripped, tortured, and threatened before her rescue . . . Miss Forbes says she has no idea what the terrorists wanted from her, or what information they hoped to extract. . . .'

Daniel turned up the volume, but the news story was finished, and the announcer started reading out dust-storm firecasts. Susie looked up at him and said, 'Blew himself up? Like a *balloon*?'

Daniel shook his head. 'No, honey. Like a bomb. Bang, splat. You know?'

'Yuk,' said Susie, and enthusiastically scooped up the last of her Donutz.

Daniel took the coffee upstairs and sat down on the end of the bed. Cara was buried in the sheets at first; but soon she raised her tangled head and said, 'What is it? What's the matter?'

'I just heard a news story on the radio. *Half*-heard it. You remember we were talking about that woman who had her head cut off?'

'Well, of course, that was the whole reason you – '

'Right. But the girl reporter who wrote the story was kidnapped by terrorists or something, and apparently they were torturing her to try to get information out of her. It was on the news just now.'

'Where was this?'

'In Tempe, that's all. Just a couple of miles away. They said that some guy blew himself up so that his friends could escape.'

Cara stared at him. 'It was the same reporter?'

'That's what they said. She was working on the Margot Schneider story and they kidnapped her. I don't know how she got away.'

'And somebody blew himself up?'

'That's what they said.'

'Daniel,' said Cara, in an unsettled voice, 'is there something bad going down here or not? I mean, what's going on?'

Daniel sipped his coffee, and then wiped his mouth with the back of his hand. It was growing light outside now, and the moon was fading behind the peaked façade of Apache Junction's main hotel. 'I don't know,' he said. 'But that woman had her head cut off with a wire saw, right, and there's no question at all that Willy's head wasn't cut off by any helicopter. A helicopter would have – Jesus, *smashed* him. The top of his neck, it looked just like it was *cut*, or *sawn*.'

'Don't,' said Cara.

'But that's two people in the Phoenix area in just a few days . . . Willy and Margot Schneider. And now the re-

216

porter gets kidnapped by terrorists. I don't know what the hell goes on here, but it all sounds too damned interconnected. You know? I get the feeling that one thing happened because of some other thing, and Willy died because he shouldn't have known what he knew, and maybe this Margot Schneider did too. I don't know.'

'Well, why don't you ask this girl reporter?' suggested Cara.

'What's the use of that? She's not going to tell me anything, is she?'

'They do deals, don't they, in the movies? You know the real truth about Willy and she doesn't, so offer to trade.'

'You run your whole life according to what you see in the movies?'

'In South Dakota, what else can you do?'

Later that morning, Daniel opened up the diner as usual, and even Pete Burns came in for his breakfast and sat perched on his stool and said nothing to Daniel except that it looked like another hot one, maybe close on one hundred and something, like that June in 1954 that his daddy had told him about, when it was 122 and folks had put eggs out on the sidewalk in frying-pans and the eggs had cooked and sizzled by themselves. Two Air Force cars had driven past, one of them from Luke and the other from Davis-Monthan, and an Air Force truck had parked outside for almost ten minutes, but there was no sign of the military police.

'Seen Ronald today?' asked Pete Burns, as he put on his cap to leave.

'Ronald? Can't say that I have.'

'When you do, tell him his hearing's been fixed for the 23rd of next month.'

'Oh, sure. What's the charge?'

'Driving like a frigging lunatic.'

Daniel stood in the doorway wiping his hands on his striped apron and watching Pete Burns climb fatly into his police car. 'Hey, Pete,' he called. 'Did you hear about that siege last night, over at Tempe?'

'You bet. We had to put up roadblocks for most of the night.'

'What do you know about that?'

Pete Burns put on his sunglasses, and started up his engine. 'What's it to you?'

'I don't know. Just curious.'

'Well, don't ask me. Read the what's-it's-name, the *Flag*. The very determined lady reporter declined to answer any questions from the police and instead is going to publish the full story in her lousy newspaper, in *episodes*, would you believe, for the next three days.'

'Can she do that? Isn't that obstructing justice or something?'

'Her lawyers don't seem to think so. The Phoenix police department is going up the wall. Chief Ruse, and then this. But she's determined, this lady. Chief Hagerty at Tempe said she was lace on the outside and barbed wire on the inside. Glidden's Winner.'

Daniel said, 'Okay, Pete. Thanks for your custom. See you tomorrow.'

'You bet.'

Pete Burns drove off and Daniel went back into the diner. Cara was pouring coffee for two tired-looking truck-drivers with her right hand and wiping the counter with her left.

'He tell you anything?' she asked.

'He didn't know much. The *Flag* girl refused to talk to the police; instead she's going to print her story in the newspaper.'

'I *told* you to call her,' said Cara. 'Call her, and see if she'll make a deal.'

'Well, okay.'

Daniel went upstairs to the bedroom and eased himself back on the unmade bed. He propped the telephone on to his chest and dialled the offices of the *Arizona Flag* on East Van Buren Street. The newspaper had a computer-ized answering system, and it seemed as if today they were more than just busy. It took five minutes of schmal-tzy music before a nasal girl's voice said, '*Flag*.'

'Oh, good morning. Listen, my name's Daniel Korvitz. I want to speak to the girl who did that Margot Schneider story. You know, the woman who had her head cut off?'

'Ms Kathy Forbes? I'm sorry, Ms Forbes isn't taking any calls right now.'

'Will you tell her this is important? I have some important information to discuss.'

'I'm sorry, you'll have to call back later.'

'Will you tell her I know about another one? Another beheading?'

'Another what?'

'Beheading, you know what beheading is?'

'You mean *beheading*? Another *beheading*?'

'That's what I said.'

'Will you hold on please?'

There was another lengthy wait. Daniel was almost tempted to hang up, to forget about the whole frightening and ridiculous business, to pack up his case and take Cara and Susie and spend the rest of his life in Chicago or Denver or New Orleans, grow a beard, wear dark glasses, and never speak about missiles or Willy or headless bodies ever again; but then the schmaltzy music abruptly stopped and a sharp woman's voice said, 'Mr Konvitz?'

'Korvitz.'

'This is Kathy Forbes. My secretary tells me you know something about another homicide.'

'That's right.'

'Have you told the police?'

'No. And I don't think I'm going to, either.'

'Why not? Is this some kind of a hoax? I'm a little tired of hoaxers this morning, thank you.'

'No hoax, Ms Forbes,' said Daniel. 'Just listen to me for one minute and one minute only, and hear what I have to say; and if you think it's a hoax you can hang up and never worry about it again. But I don't think you're going to. Because nobody could invent anything like this, Ms Forbes. Any more than anybody could invent what happened to you.'

He didn't actually know what had happened to Kathy

Forbes, except that her captors had tortured her. But it was enough of a line to keep her attention while he told her all about Willy and his radar-signature theories, and all about Ronald Reagan Kinishba and what had happened at Williams Air Force Base. He even told her about Ronald's eyes, and then she believed him. He could hear it in the tone of her voice.

'You think there's some sort of a conspiracy, Mr Korvitz?'

'I don't know. What do you think?'

'Meet me, we'll talk about it.'

'At your office?'

'No, that would be too conspicuous. You're out at Apache Junction, right?'

'That's right. But if you came out here, somebody would be bound to notice. We notice strangers around here.'

'There's a movie ranch out there, isn't there? Apacheland? Why not meet me there . . . say, at three o'clock. Carry a copy of the *Flag* or something, I'll know you.'

'Okay,' agreed Daniel. 'Three o'clock. Under the gallows.'

He hung up the phone and went downstairs again. Susie was buckling up her school sandals, and Cara was helping Mrs Koperwas with the morning's dishes.

'Why are you being so good to me?' Daniel asked Cara, with false jollity, patting her tight-bottomed shorts and kissing her ear.

'You should have a *wife* like this,' said Mrs Koperwas, pointedly.

'I did once,' said Daniel. He poured himself another cup of coffee and stood drinking it and staring out of the window. Then he turned to see Cara looking at him, hurt, and he said, 'I'm sorry. That was a crappy thing to say. I'm worried, that's all.'

'You called her?'

He nodded. 'I'm meeting her at three, out at Apacheland.'

'What does she want to do, play cowboys and Indians?'

Daniel put down his coffee cup and shrugged. 'I'm

220

beginning to think that cowboys and Indians is what this is all about. Except that *we're* the ones who stand to get scalped.'

Susie said, 'Can I come? It's *ages* since I went to Apacheland.'

'*You've* got to get yourself to school,' Daniel insisted. 'You think I want some kind of half-educated moroness for a daughter?'

'What's a moroness?'

'You don't know? Then that's what you are.'

It was a busy day at the diner, with a constant traffic of travellers and truckdrivers stopping in for beer and shakes and Daniel's special three-deck Downhome Burger, with mushroom sauce. Daniel was edgy and didn't feel like talking too much: but Cara made up for his reticence by bouncing around in one of her tightest T-shirts and flirting with every truckdriver who stopped by.

'Nice place you've got here,' remarked a tattooed gas-truck driver from Idaho. 'The help sure looks good. Tastier'n the burgers.'

In the kitchen, Daniel hissed at Cara, 'Will you stop jiggling your jugs so much? You'll get us closed down for indecency.'

'Jealous?' grinned Cara.

Daniel shrugged, and pouted. Cara reached over and kissed him, first on the cheek and then on the mouth. 'Don't be,' she said. 'As long as I'm with you I'm with you.'

'That sounds like a bad country'n'western song,' Daniel complained, and then squeezed her close, and laughed. He didn't feel like laughing. He kept imagining Ronald's eyeballs sliding down that chicken-wire fence like some glutinous nightmare by Salvador Dali.

At a quarter to three, Daniel left Cara in charge of the diner and drove off eastwards in his beaten-up car towards Apacheland. The heat was so intense now that the Superstition Mountains rippled and wavered in the distance, and the car's air-conditioning spluttered as unhappily as a run-over turkey. Two US Air Force jets thundered and scratched their way across the sky, and Daniel thought of Willy, too, as well as Ronald, and the feeling of dark unexplained coincidence began to disturb him even more deeply than it had before.

'It's a one-in-a-million flaw,' Willy had said. 'A one-in-a-million flaw. And I discovered it.'

God, Willy, if only you hadn't.

Apacheland was at the end of a half-mile track between Highway 60 and the foothills of the Superstition Mountains. Daniel's car stirred up a high trail of ochre dust as he drove between the brush and the stunted saguaro, and his suspension jolted in every pothole. Then he turned into the parking-lot and there it was: an old-style Western town with a fort-like entrance, the background for scores of cowboy movies, and now a tourist attraction for anyone who wanted to remember what an American community was like before inside sanitation and freeze-dried coffee.

The Main Street sloped upwards, towards the Marshall's Office and the livery stables. Outside the saloon, two actors dressed as old-time prospectors were staging a mock gunfight for the benefit of a small crowd of tourists, and the afternoon popped with blanks. There was laughter and applause as one of the actors fell back in the dust with his legs sticking up in the air. I live in a country that finds death hilariously funny, thought Daniel; and then told himself not to be so morbid. For God's sake, don't be so morbid.

She was waiting for him, as she had promised, under the gallows. She was sitting on the sun-warped steps, and the shadow from the noose swung slowly from side to side, across her face. She was wearing large rose-tinted sunglasses and a seersucker dress with puffed sleeves, the pale colour of arrowroot. In case there was any mistake, she carried a freshly-printed copy of the *Flag*.

'Mr Korvitz?' she said, as he approached.

'Hi,' said Daniel, and shook her hand.

'Just in case you aren't *quite* what you claim you are, I brought a friend along,' said Kathy. She nodded towards the livery stable, where a heavily-built man in a loud plaid coat was waiting, his hands in his pockets, steadfastly chewing gum. 'My editor insisted.'

Daniel made a face. 'That's understandable.'

'You want to tell me who you are, and what you know?'

'Well, I'm not anybody, in particular. I mean, I'm nothing to do with murders or criminal syndicates or terrorists. I run a diner at Apache Junction. It's a living, and the big terrible world usually leaves me alone. At least, it did until now.'

He told her everything that had happened over again, trying to remember as much of the technical detail that Willy had explained to him as he could, standing with his arms folded, his left eye screwed up against the glare of the sun, his sneaker tracing semi-circles in the dust. She listened without interrupting him, without taking notes. When he had finished, she glanced towards the body-guard she had brought with her, and then looked back at Daniel with an expression that he was unable to read.

'Do you know why I refused to answer all the questions the police put to me?' she asked.

Daniel shook his head. 'Our local deputy thinks it's because you wanted to keep the story exclusive to the *Flag*. But if that wasn't the reason, then, no, I don't know.'

'I didn't answer their questions because I was scared to. If an agent of the National Security Agency was all mixed up in this, why not the police? And, if I were to tell them what I knew, or at least what I'd *guessed*. . . .'

'What did you guess? What are you trying to tell me?'

Kathy took off her sunglasses and folded them up. There was a slight reddish bruise under one of her eyes. 'Maybe I'm going off my head,' she said. 'Maybe that kidnap got to my psyche. You know? They always say that kidnap victims begin to have delusions after a while. It's something to do with having to rely on somebody else for everything – food, water, communication with the outside world, life itself.'

'I wouldn't have thought you were kidnapped for long enough.'

'No,' said Kathy, 'nor would I. Maybe I'm suffering

from plain old paranoia instead. Maybe I'm getting to be like one of these old ladies who always keeps the plugs in the washbasin because she thinks that the utility company is spying on her through the wastepipe.'

Daniel said, 'What are you trying to tell me? You're trying to tell me that you think some kind of *conspiracy* is going on? That the National Security Council and the police and the Air Force are all mixed up in it? Is that it? And you don't want to tell anybody in case they start thinking you've lost your marbles?'

Kathy looked up at Daniel and took a deep breath, as if she were desperately anxious to say yes, but couldn't quite manage it.

Daniel sniffed, and wiped sweat from his chin with his sleeve. 'If it's any consolation, I feel exactly the same way,' he told her. 'First there was Willy and his missiles; then there was Ronald; then Margot Schneider and Skellett – that was his name, Skellett? And that police chief who got killed in Phoenix, and the guy who blew himself up in Tempe. Normally you'd think they were separate, unconnected incidents, right? One of those weird runs of violence you sometimes get in the summer, when it gets too hot and everybody goes bananas. But somehow it's different, all of this. It seems to have a peculiar kind of logic behind it. It seems to have a *meaning*.'

Kathy said, 'Thank God.'

'Thank God for what?' asked Daniel.

'Thank God that somebody else believes that there's a conspiracy. Mr Korvitz, you've made me feel sane for the first time in days.'

'Wait a minute. You may not be. Maybe *I'm* crazy too.'

'Crazy people very seldom agree. Besides, look. Sit down, and see what you think of this.' Daniel sat down beside her on the edge of the gallows platform, and she opened her buff leather pocketbook and took out a dark Xeroxed copy of a Polaroid photograph. 'It's kind of blurry,' she said, 'I wanted to make some proper photographic copies but Skellett's people broke into my apartment and stole the original before I could get them done. All the same, you can see who it is.'

'For sure. This is a picture of President Kennedy. Why should they want to steal a picture of President Kennedy? They could get one anywhere.'

'Not *this* picture of President Kennedy. This is the only one there is. This shows President Kennedy sitting beside Marilyn Monroe's swimming-pool in Brentwood, Los Angeles. Late summer of '61, I'd guess, or maybe spring of '62.'

'Well, come on, everybody knows that Jack and Bobby Kennedy were both seeing her. I mean, that's common knowledge, isn't it?'

'Oh, yes. But where do you think I *found* this picture? Tucked in amongst Margot Schneider's possessions, the day after she was murdered, before the police had a chance to go through them. I'm still not sure why I took it. Maybe it struck me as kind of peculiar. You know, that an Air Force widow living in Phoenix should have an original Polaroid of President Kennedy. I thought maybe there was some kind of interesting angle. Some warm, human, woman-who-met-the-President story. But Skellett sure jolted me out of *that*.'

'Tell me,' said Daniel. 'Come on – if you can't trust the guy who runs Daniel's Downhome Diner in Apache Junction, Arizona, you can't trust *anybody*.'

'Well,' shrugged Kathy, 'maybe I can't. But when I took the Polaroid home, the night after I'd found it, I got to thinking. Why did Margot Schneider have this picture among her private possessions? You can't read it here, on the Xerox, but it says on the photograph, *'To N, special memories, from P.'* I thought P could have been President, and maybe N could have been Norma Jean.'

'I guess that makes sense.'

'Surely . . . but what was Margot *Schneider's* reason for having this picture? She didn't *collect* pictures of President Kennedy, or anything like that . . . this was the only one. It didn't seem like she collected movie memorabilia, either. There were a few reviews of *The Misfits* along with the picture, but not much else. It could have been a one-off souvenir; something she found; something she bought at one of those stores that sell old political campaign buttons. Photographs come into people's possession in the oddest ways. My aunt used to have a family snapshot of Harry Truman. I think she found it in a bus-station wastebasket.'

Daniel gave her a long, expectant look. He began to realize what she was going to say next, and why she was hesitating. The simplest of all reasons for Margot Schneider owning the Polaroid carried the looniest of all implications; and once they spoke the lunacy out loud, they were going to have to accept that recorded history and political logic had for years been standing on their heads.

Kathy said, with a slight catch in her throat, 'Then, of course, I had to consider the most *obvious* reason. Margot Schneider owned the picture because it belonged to her; because it had been given to her by President Kennedy. Maybe she had taken it herself.'

'She was supposed to be an Air Force widow, so what had she been doing in Hollywood taking Polaroids of President Kennedy?'

'Exactly. She was supposed to be an Air Force widow, a normal middle-aged lady living on a military pension, leading a routine, unexceptional life. Yet she had no Social Security card that anybody could find; there were no pictures of her anywhere, not even in the files at Luke Air Force Base, where her husband used to fly from; and for no apparent motive she was murdered by an unknown man or woman in the most gruesome way you can think of. She wasn't raped and she wasn't robbed. Her head was removed so that nobody could identify her; and within twenty-four hours the National Security Agency sent an agent down to remove the rest of her, too – an agent who had *carte-blanche* to kill anybody he liked, just so long as he got the body back.'

'Why didn't the guy who killed her take the body in the first place?' Daniel wanted to know. 'He could have dumped her in the desert somewhere and nobody would have found her for *years*, if at all.'

'I thought about that, too. But if Margot Schneider had simply disappeared without trace, the police would have started making much more intensive inquiries into her background; where she came from, who her relatives were, that kind of thing, instead of accepting the apparent fact that here was poor Mrs Margot Schneider and here she was dead.'

Kathy paused, and then she said, 'She was the right age, she had the right kind of physique, and the police found hairs in the bathroom wash-basin which corresponded with her natural hair colour, before she bleached it. There was a circular mark on the back of her right arm, too.'

'You really believe it was possible? I mean, you really believe it was *her*?'

'I'm – what, 75 per cent sure of it. Eighty per cent. Why else did Skellett react so violently when I asked him if she was connected with Cuba? I couldn't fit the bricks together but I could tell that they all came out of the same box. Kennedy – Monroe – Margot Schneider. If Margot Schneider *hadn't* been Marilyn Monroe, why would Skellett have bothered to torture me? He tried to tell me that Margot Schneider was part of a Soviet spy ring or something like that; but he completely failed to explain why the very mention of Cuba in connection with Margot Schneider was enough to make him speed through Phoenix at 90 miles an hour, kill two cops, and then behave like a medieval torturer. And I can tell you something – whatever Skellett knows about Margot Schneider, or Marilyn Monroe – it was sufficiently devastating to make it worthwhile blowing one of his own men into tiny little pieces, just to help him get away.'

Daniel said, 'Why *did* you ask him about Cuba?'

'No particular reason. Reporter's nose for trouble, I guess. It was the biggest political storm that was brewing at the time, in 1962. I just took a shot at it. I've been reading through most of the books on Marilyn Monroe's death, and trying to form some opinions about the various theories on why she died, and how; and I couldn't find any idea that was actually solid enough, actually concrete enough – either to justify somebody killing her, or to justify her going into hiding in Arizona for the rest of her life.'

'Didn't somebody once say that she was killed by agents of the Communist party because she was threatening to expose Bobby's plans to legalize a whole lot of left-wing political organizations?'

Kathy Forbes shook her head. 'There are *scores* of theories, most of them cranky. Hardly any of them stand up to the simple test of asking yourself, would Marilyn Monroe really have done that? She wasn't a politically active person, neither was she vengeful. No, it's *my* view that she simply overheard too much from Jack and Bobby; listened to one too many of their political problems. And one day they realized that she knew so much about one *particular* political problem that her life could be in danger. *Their* lives were in danger, too, as we know from what happened in November, 1963, and in June, 1968, and it makes much more sense to me that all three of them – Marilyn, Jack, and Bobby – were under threat from the same people. Skellett's people, whoever they are.'

She replaced her sunglasses, and then she said, 'Whether Marilyn died in 1962 or not, and I really believe now that she *didn't*, she was killed because of something she knew that was crucially important, and as far as I could judge, Cuba was the only crisis big enough. What's more, if Margot Schneider really *was* Marilyn Monroe, the crisis was long-lasting enough to make it worthwhile somebody murdering her after twenty years. Now, which crisis can you think of that Jack and Bobby were faced with which is still going on today? Which crisis could still harbour a secret dangerous enough to *kill* people for? The Mafia, possibly; spies, not likely. No, I chose Cuba, and Skellett's reaction proved me right.'

'Now there's Willy,' said Daniel. 'Where do you think *he* fits in?'

'I don't know,' said Kathy. 'I've been swivelling the whole thing around in my mind like a Rubik's cube, ever since you telephoned me this morning.'

'I never could solve Rubik's cube.'

'Well, I've only done it five times. But let's try some theories out and see if they fit. Or half-fit, at least. The first thing we know for sure is that your friend Willy was killed in a very similar way to Margot Schneider, in the same general locality, within three days. And the method of killing was sufficiently unusual to make it quite likely that he was killed by the same individual. I mean, you don't get too many flexible saw murderers.'

Daniel wiped sweat from his face. 'I could use a beer,' he said. 'Do you think we could continue this discussion down at the saloon?'

'Sure,' Kathy nodded. 'Do you mind if my friend comes along? He looks tough, but actually he's very harmless.'

'That's what they all say,' Daniel remarked, and then wondered if he had sounded too macho.

Twenty-One

They sat at a dark corner-table drinking beer by the neck while the local 'cowpokes' entertained the tourists with gun-twirling and pretended drunkenness. Kathy's heavy-weight bodyguard dragged his chair back a few feet out of earshot, and tossed peanuts into his mouth by the monotonous handful. The buxom girl behind the bar gave him a sassy wink or two, but he remained expressionless and unmoved.

Kathy said to Daniel, 'I have about four main theories why Willy Monahan was killed by the same man who killed Marilyn Monroe. None of them may be completely right. For instance, we have to allow that he may have been disposed of by somebody at Williams AFB who cut his head off in the same way as Marilyn's for no other reason except to throw us off the trail. The two homicides might be completely unconnected. But my feeling is that if the murderer wanted people to think that both murders were committed by the same individual when in actual fact they *weren't*, then he or she wouldn't have kept Willy's death such a secret. Whoever killed Willy didn't particularly want anyone to know what had happened to him; unless they were devious enough to make it all *seem* like a mystery, so that anyone who had actually twigged what was going on, like you and Ronald Kinishba, would be flushed out into the open. Maybe that's *too* devious. I don't know.'

'It wasn't difficult for me to get *into* the air base mortuary,' said Daniel. 'Getting *out* was the tough bit.'

'Well, that's something to bear in mind,' agreed Kathy. 'Now – we have to think what Marilyn Monroe could possibly have known about Cuba that related to what your friend Willy Monahan had learned about the missiles at Williams AFB. So, let's shift the Rubik's cube around and see what we come up with. Monroe – Kennedy – Cuba – missiles. Nuclear missiles were the principal point of contention in the Cuban crisis of 1962; so maybe what Willy Monahan discovered was something to do with a disarmament agreement that was reached between Kennedy and Khruschev. We all know about the treaty of July 25, 1963, which prohibited all nuclear tests except those conducted underground; and that was a direct result of the crisis over Cuba. But maybe there were other agreements, secret agreements which only a few people ever got to hear about.'

'You mean those missiles that Willy discovered weren't ever *supposed* to work against Soviet planes? That Kennedy might have agreed with Khruschev that US planes wouldn't be able to shoot down any Soviet aircraft?'

'It's a theory.'

'But surely subsequent Presidents would have done something about it. I can't see Marshall Roberts allowing US fighter planes to fly around with useless weapons.'

'A couple of years ago, I couldn't see Marshall Roberts agreeing to the RINC talks.'

Daniel sat silent for a moment, then took another swallow of cold beer. 'It seems incredible.'

'That's what I thought. But the more I went over the idea, the more I rearranged it in my mind, the more sense it seemed to make. That could be dangerous, of course. Journalistic theories have a habit of fitting all the known facts, and still remaining preposterously untrue. But if there *had* been a number of secret nuclear agreements between Kennedy and Khruschev; if the price of getting the Russians to take their missiles out of Cuba and back to Russia *had* been much higher than the rest of us poor suckers were led to believe at the time, then Marilyn Monroe's murder would begin to make sense, so would Willy's, and so would Jack and Robert Kennedy's. Skellett's behaviour still seems a little peculiar, to say the least. I don't know why he had to make such a three-ring circus out of recovering Marilyn's body when she was already safely dead. All he did was draw everybody's attention to the murder, when it could easily have remained as another one of those nasty unsolved mysteries, for ever and ever. But maybe we'll find that out later.'

'You don't think we ought to go to the police?' asked Daniel.

'No, *sir*. If even one-half of this bears any relation to the real facts, then we're dealing with some very heavy people indeed; and the fewer people who know what we know, the better. I don't very much fancy being beheaded, do you?'

'I thought you were going to publish the whole inside story in the *Flag*?'

'All I'm going to publish in the *Flag*, Mr Korvitz, is "My Kidnap Ordeal by Kathy Forbes" with all the salacious details of what they tried to do to me. I haven't told anyone about my Marilyn Monroe theory yet, except you, and Skellett, and that was only because Skellett tortured me. I really think it's too early and it's too damned dangerous. Unless, of course, you're one of Skellett's agents, in which case you're probably going to take me out right now and string me up from the town gallows.'

Daniel finished his beer. 'What do you think we can do? Any ideas? Any *sane* ideas? Maybe it's best if we don't do anything. Pretend it never happened. I mean, what possible effect can you and I have on the history of the entire world?'

'Are you kidding?' asked Kathy. 'If Kennedy made a secret disarmament deal with Khruschev that US missiles should be totally ineffective against Soviet airplanes, and if President Roberts is still sticking to the terms of that agreement today – you know what a news story that would be? We'd be famous for ever. And rich. You want to run a *diner* all your life?'

'I want to stay *alive* for all my life, that's all.'

Kathy said briskly, 'Well, it's up to you. I've got to investigate it, because it's my job. My instinct, too. If you don't want to help me, well, that's it, don't help me. But I'll have to make you promise not to blow the story to any other newspaper. I think after what I've been through I'm entitled to an exclusive, don't you?'

'You're really going to start poking your nose around in this? You're serious? After the way they've been killing people off, blowing people up, sticking goddamned – *needles* in you?'

'Mr Korvitz – '

'Please, Daniel.'

'Daniel, I have to. It's my vocation. This is the kind of break that every newspaper reporter has dreams about.'

'So what are you going to do?'

'First of all, I'm going to Los Angeles. I want to talk to as many people as I can who saw Marilyn Monroe in the last few days of her life, and particularly on the night of her alleged death. I want to talk to the mortician who laid her out and everybody who saw her body. If there's even the slightest suggestion that the body they buried at Westwood isn't Marilyn . . . well then, we'll know that we're on to something.'

Daniel rubbed his eyes, tiredly. 'It would be easier, you know, if it didn't all sound so goddamned far-fetched.'

'Mr Korvitz, Daniel, the whole trouble is that it *isn't* far-fetched. It's actually *less* far-fetched than all the accepted historical explanations about Marilyn Monroe and the Kennedys and the Cuban Missile Crisis. It fits the facts better, and it could account for all kinds of apparently inexplicable trends in the way that this country has been governed for the past twenty years.'

'If you say so,' said Daniel, unconvinced.

'Let me spend some time in Los Angeles, and then get back to you,' said Kathy. 'Maybe we can talk it over again.'

'All right,' Daniel agreed. Suddenly it didn't seem so important to find out why Willy had died, or how. Suddenly it seemed more important that Willy should be left to rest in peace, and not have his sleep troubled by distant rumbles of thunder from 1962. Daniel had heard how violent thunderstorms could bring corpses rising out of the fresh earth in country graveyards; as well as cause women to miscarry, and milk to turn sour.

They said goodbye to each other in the dusty parking-lot. Daniel was fairly sure that he would never see her again, this snappy and over-enthusiastic lady reporter, although he would probably take the trouble to read her story in the *Arizona Flag*, and follow her investigations into the Cuban Missile Crisis. He shook hands with her politely and went back to his car. He sat down behind the steering-wheel, and sorted through his keys, and didn't know why he felt so down.

He was just about to start up the engine when Kathy came across again, and leaned into the open passenger window.

'You know what you're feeling now, don't you?' she asked him.

He didn't answer. He didn't know what to say.

'You're feeling fear, that's what,' she told him. 'And do

you want to know something, I *respect* you for it. It means you've got enough imagination to recognize that what I'm saying to you is true, or could be. I know you've got a little girl, Daniel. I know you're the kind of guy who wants to be left alone. But just remember you had enough guts to break into that airbase to find out what had happened to Willy; and you had enough guts to come here and talk to me about it.'

Daniel said, 'You're the second person today to tell me how gutsy I am. I'm beginning to feel like Audie Murphy.'

'I'll be in touch, okay?' said Kathy, and left him. He shrugged to himself, and started up his car. The engine coughed, backfired loudly, and died away with a whine like a broken washing-machine.

Kathy, who had been halfway back to her own car, walked over again and looked in at the passenger window. 'You don't happen to need a ride?' she asked him.

As they drove back to Apache Junction, they began to relax with each other. Kathy told Daniel how she had gone to California, and then come back to make her name on the *Flag*. 'I thought I was going to win the Pulitzer Prize the first year I was there.' Daniel told her about Candii and Susie; and about the attractions of living a simple and uncomplicated life in the shadow of the Superstition Mountains.

'Are you afraid of life? Afraid of success? Or what?' asked Kathy. 'I'm not being rude. It's just that you seem to want things out of life that don't actually exist, like women out of country-and-western fantasies, and complete peace and quiet. There isn't any such *thing* as complete peace and quiet. Life will never leave you alone. And all the women I've ever met who look like country-and-western fantasies are pretty as cotton-candy on the outside and hard as reinforced concrete on the inside.'

Daniel said, 'I don't lack confidence, I can tell you that. I don't lack determination, either. But I look around me and begin to wonder what all that confidence and determination is going to bring me. Money? I'm eating okay. Happiness? I've got my daughter, and my occasional girlfriends. Fame? I'm famous with the people who know me. You may think I'm backing off, opting out, but I don't seriously think so. What I want is what I've got, and I think the real strength comes in saying to yourself, that's it, I'm happy.'

'The trouble is,' said Kathy, 'I don't believe that you *are*.'

They drew up in front of Daniel's Downhome Diner. Kathy said, 'I noticed this place on the way out here. Do you think you could spare us a cup of coffee, and a muffin maybe? Neither of us had time for lunch.'

Daniel hesitated, and Kathy said, 'You could send the cheque to my paper. They'll pay you.'

Daniel grinned. 'Come on in,' he said. 'I think I can just about afford to treat you.'

But the second that Daniel walked into the place he realized there was something wrong. Pete Burns was in there, and two Highway Patrol officers, and three or four other regular customers, but none of them was eating. Then he saw Cara's legs on the floor, in between the chair-legs, and he felt as if everything was suddenly rushing in to meet him with the velocity of a locomotive, faces, chairs, tables, walls, and Pete Burns was turning to say something with an expression which he knew in that first explosive instant meant bad news.

'There were two guys. They came in here about a half-hour ago. Neil says they asked for you.'

'She's not dead, Daniel. Daniel, she's not dead. Okay? She's going to be fine. They hurt her a little, that's all. But the doc put her under a sedative, and she's fine. Listen, will you calm down?'

'They asked for you by name. That's what Neil says. Jimmy here heard them too. They said, where's Daniel Korvitz; and when Cara said you were out, and she didn't know where, they started pushing her around, you know? One of them hit her with something; nobody saw what it was, but it lacerated her face and her shoulder. Maybe a broken bottle. The ambulance is coming, anyway. The thing is, Daniel – '

Daniel stared at them blurrily. Somebody jostled against him and he turned around; but then Pete Burns said, 'The thing is, Daniel, Susie was coming home from school right then – '

'Susie?'

'Well, it was pretty bad luck. A couple of minutes later and she would've missed them completely. But they were just leaving and the school bus turned up, and when she came into the diner and said, you know, where's my daddy – '

'Don't know what the hell they hit her with. Will you look at those cuts?'

'Pete, what happened? Where's Susie?'

'Daniel, I'm real sorry about this. I was only about thirty seconds away from here myself. It was bad luck, that's all. You know what I mean? A crappy combination of circumstances.'

Charlie McEvers said, in his gravelly gold-prospector's voice, 'She's kidnapped, Daniel. That's the meat of it. They just picked her up and carried her out and there wasn't a damned thing that any of us could do about it.'

Daniel looked around. By the door, Kathy Forbes was watching him with sympathy and pain. *There isn't any such thing as complete peace and quiet. Life will never leave you alone.*

Somebody brought Daniel a chair and he sat down. He kept saying to Pete Burns, 'You've got to find her, you understand? I want her found. And, by God, if anybody touches one hair of her head, I'm going to kill them. I warn you now, Pete. I'm going to kill them stone dead.'

'Sure, Daniel. Nobody blames you.'

The ambulance arrived outside, its siren moaning in the afternoon heat. The medics lifted Cara on to a stretcher, and carried her past Daniel as if she were just another victim of the disaster he called his life. She was deeply sedated, her eyes closed, her mouth open. But Daniel could clearly see the rows of parallel lash-marks that lacerated her cheek and her collar-bone. She looked almost as if she had been clawed by a tiger.

Pete Burns said to Daniel, 'How about some coffee? A shot of brandy, maybe?'

Daniel shook his head.

'You don't know what these guys *wanted*, do you?' asked Pete. 'What I'm trying to get at is this: what would they want from *you*?'

'I don't know,' said Daniel. 'I don't have any idea. I sure don't have any money worth speaking of.'

'You haven't been threatened recently? No mafiosi hanging around? Sometimes somebody's Sicilian brother wants to open a liquor store or a restaurant, and then everybody around gets leaned on, just to make sure that nobody objects.'

'Nothing like that,' said Daniel.

Kathy came up and laid her hand on his shoulder. 'Are you okay?' she asked him. 'Is there anything I can do?'

One of the customers was saying, 'Kind of skinny guy, one of them, but the other was big. Real gorilla, with a red birthmark.'

Daniel raised his eyes and looked at Kathy with angry intensity.

'Skellett,' she whispered, and Daniel nodded, and for the first time in his life he felt like killing a man.

Twenty-Two

She met Ikon in a private dining-room on the sixth floor. He rarely went out these days; even though he still harboured a longing for the *sole fourree tzarine* at the Montpellier restaurant on 15th and M. He had grown old in a particularly Russian way, as if all the gravity to which his thickset body had been subjected in the 82 years of his life had cumulatively dragged him down, pouching his eyes and jowling his chin, and spreading his stomach until it pressed against the rim of his antique dining-table. He spoke thickly, and took frequent sips of the rare Tokaj wine which was specially imported for him from Hungary. In the dark, densely-carpeted room, with the drapes drawn so closely that only a tall two-dimensional triangle of summer sunlight could penetrate, he looked like one of the decaying provincial gentry from Mikhail Saltykov's novel *The Golovlev Family*.

'You looked tired,' she told him, as she squeezed lemon on her Sevruga caviare.

'Well,' said Ikon, 'I *am* tired. Those who have to struggle will always have to pay the price.'

'As long as you can carry on for two or three months; long enough for Marshall Roberts to get the RINC talks restarted.'

Ikon shrugged heavily, and reached for one of the small buckwheat pancakes which were always served to him with his caviare. He spread the sturgeon's eggs as thick as a child would spread bread with peanut-butter, and then ladled sour cream on top, and took a quick and unexpectedly avaricious mouthful.

'Marshall had better act soon, otherwise he may very well sink both of us.'

'He's doing his best. But you can understand what a difficult situation he's in.'

'Of course,' said Ikon, wiping his mouth with his napkin. 'But he is the President, *niet*? And the President should be capable of dealing with any problem which confronts him. That is what Presidents are *for*.'

'Your English improves every day,' smiled Nadine.

'Hmmph,' said Ikon. 'I never get out as much as I should. I should go to parties, and receptions. I am beginning to speak like an American television anchorman. I even understand what 'what's coming down,' means. Now, there's a colloquial rarity for you, 'what's coming down.' In Russia, we would say "what is it that flows this way".'

'Did you see the doctor?' asked Nadine.

Ikon looked at her with unconcealed fondness. In all the years he had been in Washington, in all the days and nights he had lived in this building, he had never come across anyone so alive and so determined as Nadine. He had never come across a woman who combined so successfully the values of Leninism with the enthusiasm of the modern age. If only he were forty years younger; if only he could show her what he had been like in his pre-war days, as one of the *udarniki*, the shockworkers; or as a political commissar during the war. She was such an ideal, sexual woman. Tall, and proud, and intelligent. The sort of woman who could look any man commandingly in the eye.

'The doctor?' he said. 'The doctor is as pessimistic as ever. I believe that all doctors are born pessimists; or perhaps all pessimists become doctors. In any case, my leukemia is as virulent as ever, and I shall be lucky to see next May Day.'

'Nikolai Nekrasov,' said Nadine, and reached out her hand. Ikon touched her fingers with his, and then withdrew them.

'You must eat, enjoy yourself,' he told her. '*Your* problems will come next. And there will be many.'

'My problems have already started. Titus has warned Marshall that if he persists with RINC II, then all this business with Colleen Petley will be made public immediately. He's given Marshall a little time to think it over. First of all, he gave him only an hour, now he's agreed to give him a day. But that day will be over in an hour or so. And, believe me, Titus is serious.'

'That was always Titus' trouble, wasn't it?' remarked Ikon, spreading more caviare. 'So *serious*. It will lead to his downfall, you know.'

Nadine put down her knife. 'I'm waiting for your instructions. You know that, don't you?'

'Well,' said Ikon. 'It seems as if there is only one course open to us. The RINC talks must continue; otherwise everything we have been working for will collapse. I know that gradualism is tedious; I know how much the young administrators champ at their bits for progress. But only gradualism will lead the American people towards an eventual understanding of their true situation without bloodshed, or riot, or civic resistance. Can you imagine what would happen if you told them *now*? The country would burn from end to end. There would be fighting, barricades, organized resistance. Thousands of people would die. And this is in the 1980s, when people are supposed to have become far more liberal and understanding. You can just picture what would have happened if they had known about it in 1962.'

Nadine said, 'What do you want me to do?'

Ikon stared into his glass. His shaggy eyebrows reminded Nadine of a thoughtful bear. He said, 'Colleen Petley will have to go, that is all. Can you arrange for it? And the chambermaid at the Futura Hotel . . . she will have to go, too.'

'You want *me* to – '

'Nobody else can get close enough without arousing suspicion. Besides, I have the ideal method.'

Nadine laid her caviare spoon on to her serving-plate. 'You're quite sure? You want me to *kill* her?'

Ikon placed a finger over his lips and said, 'Ssh. We don't usually mention such subjects here. Not . . . disposal. Not in such terms.'

'How do you expect me to do it?'

'It will be very easy. You will simply tell Miss Petley that she has to have an injection against influenza so that there is no risk of her being unwell when the Congressional hearing is convened. The dose of medicine which you inject into her arm or her buttock will look like this – ' Ikon held up a small glass vial of straw-coloured fluid, and then laid it carefully on the vine-leaf ashtray. 'It is a mixture of water, simple sugars, and a single drop of hydro-cyanic acid. Death will be almost instantaneous, seizure of the heart.'

Nadine stared at him. The old, Slavic mask of his face. He could have been made out of latex rubber, like Yoda, or ET. He had asked her to perform many strange and disagreeable tasks in the past; out of all of them, courting and marrying Titus Alexander had probably been the most complex and the most self-sacrificing. But he had never required her to *kill* anyone before; and it was particularly unnerving that he should have asked her to kill Colleen Petley, the first woman in years with whom she had formed a warm and immediate sexual relationship. She had dreamed of Colleen when she had been making love with Titus. She had dreamed of plunging her tongue into Colleen's salt-and-sugary cleft. She had dreamed of kissing Colleen's breasts.

Now, he was asking her to kill Colleen's body stone-cold, with the most lethal poison known to man.

'I can see that I have disturbed you,' said Ikon.

Nadine pushed back her plate of caviare, and stood up. She walked to the window, and looked out through the inch-wide gap in the drapes, her face unnaturally illuminated by the single shaft of sunlight which fell through it into the room.

'You shrink from the thought of killing for your country?' asked Ikon. He took another mouthful of pancake and sour cream. 'Soldiers are required to do it as a matter of course; yet nobody thinks that what soldiers have to do is disturbing, or exceptional.'

'Colleen Petley is . . . well, Colleen Petley is different,' said Nadine. 'It's difficult for me to think of her as an enemy.'

'She *is* an enemy, nevertheless. She is worse than an enemy. She could have remained neutral, and yet she was prepared to sell her information for money.'

'That, Nikolai Nekrasov, is what a girl like Colleen Petley would call 'turning an honest buck'.'

'You're *refusing*?' asked Ikon, and there was a rumble of displeasure in his voice.

Nadine turned back towards him. She wore today one of the softest of Bill Blass ensembles, a black watered-silk blouse with wide sleeves and a narrow tailored waist, and a canary-yellow taffeta skirt; and for a moment Ikon would have forgiven her anything, absolved her from any kind of duty or duress. But, the times were too threatening. Everybody had to be used to keep the *Peredoviki* from taking over once Ikon himself had gone; everything had to be sacrificed to keep the world in political balance for at least a generation longer. And that meant love, and self-indulgence, and kindness itself. 'You are kind,' he had read, in the works of the American poet Gregory Corso, 'because you lead a kind life.' Ikon knew that he had never led a kind life.

'There was a time,' said Ikon, without waiting for Nadine to reply, 'there was a time when I, too, was in love with a member of my own sex. It was in 1937, when I was working for Goelro, the State Commission for the Electrification of Russia. We were building a new power-station at Saratov, in the Privolskaja Vozvysennost. We were shockworkers, you understand, young men who backed their belief in Communism with intensively hard work, seven days a week, twelve or thirteen hours a day. We could build in a month a factory that, these days, it would take a year to complete. Well, there was a fellow there, a bricklayer; and for some reason I fell in love with him. He was devastatingly handsome, muscular, and yet innocent, too. What he could have done in Hollywood! One day, after we had finished a record day of building, we went to bed together almost completely exhausted, he and I, and made love. Yes, sodomized each other; but with pride and fellowship, and the genuine affection of two men who have worked side-by-side for the same political and industrial ideal.'

Ikon was silent for a little while, and drummed his fingertips on the white damask tablecloth. Then he said, 'I understand, you see, what you may be feeling about Colleen Petley.'

'You don't know anything about me and Colleen Petley.'

'I don't, no,' Ikon admitted. 'But I have known for some years about the affair you had with Charlotte Kane, and I recognize the look you have. You have the look of being infatuated. Not in love, maybe, but infatuated, and I know for sure that it cannot be Titus.'

'You've grown far too American,' Nadine complained. 'Do you know that? You're so American I can't believe it.'

'You will still do what I ask, with Colleen Petley.'

'You mean, murder her?'

Ikon raised his finger to his lips again; a reminder that here, in the hushest and darkest of the rooms of power, such words as death and killing and disposal were never spoken out loud. It was an indulgence that Nadine should even be allowed to eat here; and to speak to Ikon in person. It was a special favour that she should be allowed to address him by his name, Nikolai Nekrasov; the first four letters of which had been twisted around to form his code-name, Ikon. Everybody else in the building had to call him 'Premier Ikon.'

It was a typically ironic Russian joke that the foremost representative of Communism in the Western hemisphere should be named after a symbol of religious veneration; and that a man of such stoutness should be associated with works of art which were traditionally two-dimensional.

Nadine said, 'Has it occurred to you that you might be asking too much of me?'

'I am dying,' Ikon told her. 'I can ask as much as I like of anybody. Do you want to see the *Peredoviki* tear down everything for which I have worked? Do you want to see bloodshed, and chaos? I was not sent here to preside over the wholesale destruction of the United States. I was sent here to maintain the balance. To keep the world intact. One life, even if it happens to be the life of the woman you love, is never going to be worth as much as that.'

'Did you hear what happened in Arizona?' Nadine asked him.

'Oh, yes,' nodded Ikon. 'And have no fear, I have already spoken to Kama about it. Kama, of course, was polite. "I was only doing what I thought fit, Comrade Ikon. I was only acting expediently, Comrade Ikon." But we should have no illusions about Kama, and what he is trying to do. He is trying his very best to bring the whole Supervisory Committee into the open, in such a way that he is not personally blamed for the revelation. He is trying his very best to dig up old corpses, and turn the world into a charnel-house! But, we have managed to keep him at bay for seven years; and we can continue to keep him at bay until RINC II is ratified. That is – if you agree to support me, and do what you have to do with Colleen Petley.'

Nadine sat down on the far side of the room, on a walnut side-chair. She kept her head lowered, as if she were thinking, or praying. Ikon watched her, occasionally reaching for his wine, or spreading more Sevruga caviare on his pancakes, his breathing harsh and unpleasant, rattling in the fluid-filled recesses of his lungs.

'If I don't agree to get rid of her, I suppose that you'll ask somebody else to do it?'

'Of course.'

'Then I think that I'd prefer to do it myself. At least I'll be facing up to myself, and what I am, and what I've done to her.'

'Well, I knew that you would say yes. Why don't you sit down and finish your caviare? Do you know how much it costs these days, in America? The best Sevruga?'

Nadine sat down at the dining-table again, with a rustle of yellow taffeta. 'You know something, Nikolai Nekrasov, the strange thing about you is that you're not a bad man at all. I think history may see you as a saint.'

Ikon wobbled his jowls in disagreement. 'Moderates are never canonized. You have to be an extremist to be a saint. You have to poke your own eyes out, or set yourself alight. You know from experience that I am not that kind of a man. A fruitcake, the Americans say. I prefer to live, and eat, and survive, and make sure that all around me do the same. Men such as me are never remembered; but we do the most good.'

They finished their meal in complete silence; eating, drinking, and thinking. Then they went into the conservatory that overlooked Pennsylvania Avenue, and one of the staff put Prokofiev's *The Love For Three Oranges* on the stereo. 'Beautiful music,' said Ikon, one hand thrust into the pocket of his enormous pants, the other holding a glass of strawberry vodka. 'It makes me cry, sometimes, because the world cannot be ordered like an opera. Life cannot be scripted, or scored.'

'Are you afraid of Kama?' asked Nadine.

'You always have a knack of asking the most direct questions.'

'I have to know. You may be dead by next May; but I won't.'

'Kama was one of Brezhnev's protégés. He has always supported Brezhnev's doctrine on polycentrism. But where Brezhnev was prepared to let the situation in the United States take an apparently natural course; not pushing too quickly, nor too fast, Kama believes that we ought to announce the 16th Soviet Socialist Republic overnight. A thunder-and-lighting man, Kama. Sweep away the old, sweep in the new! Damn the consequences! Unfortunately, he made sure that he took control of all the executive agencies which would give him the power to enact such measures. The National Security Council, the Council of Economic Advisers, the Office of Administration. You cannot underestimate him, my dear Nadine. He is the second most powerful administrator after me; and even though I am superior to him, I cannot possibly keep him in check.'

'So he *wanted* that woman's body to be identified.'

'Of course. He must be deeply chagrined that the media have been so slow to understand what his agents were doing. All these stories of "Cadaver Kidnapping" and "Fanatics Torture Girl Reporter." The American press never look further than the first pair of breasts. No wonder Marilyn Monroe was such a heroine. Personally, I thought she was a plump little cow. Fit for milking, not much else.'

The evening began to die. They drank more strawberry vodka, and Ikon told her about his boyhood in Zarajsk, on the Os'otr River, in the days of the Tsar; and how he had picked cherries and lain back on the haycarts as they trundled home through the long warm evenings of August, seventy-two years ago.

At seven o'clock Nadine said, 'I have to go now. We have a party at the British Embassy. Sir Leonard Grosvenor.'

'Very well,' said Ikon. He made no attempt to rise from his chair.

Nadine collected her wrap, and her pocketbook, and the staff saw her out to the elevator. Ikon waited for five minutes before he eventually eased himself up, and walked with a slightly dragging step into the dining room. He went across to the table, and peered into the vine-leaf ashtray, where earlier that evening he had laid the capsule of hydrocyanic acid.

To his satisfaction, he saw that it was empty.

Twenty-Three

Titus, that evening, was in a wolfishly ebullient mood. As a rule, he hated going to the British Embassy. 'The British speak like they're carrying their rolled-up cricket socks in their cheeks.' But he grasped Sir Leonard Grosvenor's hand as if he were greeting a long-lost buddy from the Class of '38, and he bussed Lady Grosvenor on the cheek with an enthusiasm which led the *Washington Post*'s social correspondent to remark that 'the special relationship seems to be looking up. *Up*, I say.'

Nadine didn't need to ask Titus why he was feeling so buoyant. She could guess what had happened. During the afternoon, shortly after three o'clock, Marshall Roberts had telephoned Titus at the State Department and reluctantly agreed to postpone RINC II 'certainly for the time being, if not indefinitely'. No announcement had yet been made to the media, but Titus had insisted that the President should quickly make his acquiescence public. The White House press department were working on a statement which would satisfy both Marshall and Titus; and which wouldn't appear too sudden and too bizarre when announced to the White House press lobby.

The British Embassy party was alcoholic and fatuous. There was a roar of jingoistic talk about the Falklands; and heaps of fatty roast beef; and two young British actresses with breasts like half-set blancmanges sat on the laps of as many long-suffering middle-aged diplomats as they could and giggled endlessly. At the end of the evening, there was an hour-long demonstration of Morris dancing, which Titus watched with the glazed expression of a man who suddenly wishes that he was at home; in bed; and thinking back on Morris dancing, rather than experiencing it first-hand.

Sir Leonard Grosvenor leaned over his chair, and said, 'I must say, Titus old boy, you've done such an enormous amount to keep the old *je-ne-sais-quoi virgo intacta*.'

'Yes,' said Titus. Then, 'Yes?'

'Fascinating, this Morris dancing,' Sir Leonard told him. 'Comes from *Moorish* dancing, don't you know. Bells on the ankles, that kind of thing.'

'Yes,' said Titus.

On the way back to Georgetown, in the sudden frigidity of their air-conditioned Cadillac, Nadine said, 'You've heard from Marshall, haven't you?'

Titus, who had been rubbing his eyes, suddenly stared at her. 'Yes. As a matter of fact I have. How did you know?'

'Titus, my dear, you can't fool me. Up until they started that ridiculous folk-dancing, you were as chipper as fifteen beavers. And only *one* thing that I can think of could make you feel like that.'

'You're right,' said Titus. 'Marshall called me mid-afternoon, and conceded. RINC II is dead as a doughnut.'

247

There was a long silence, and then Nadine said, 'Titus, I have to talk to you.'

'Sure. Go ahead.'

'Serious talk, Titus. Professional talk.'

'All right. Serious talk. Tell me. What is it, your children are leaving home? That can't be true. God wouldn't smile on me twice in one day.'

'Titus, I want you to call Marshall Roberts tonight, tell him it was all a mistake. You know, an error of judgement.'

'You want me to what?'

'I want you to call Marshall Roberts tonight, and – '

'You want me to *what*???'

'Titus, it's vital.'

'You bet your *ass* it's vital. Marshall was just about to concede every last strategic defence we ever had in the European theatre. No neutron bombs, no ALCMs, no third-generation missiles of any kind. Have you *read* what he wants to do? The guy's crazy! He wants to open us up like a fucking oyster, all ready for the Soviets to swallow us down!'

'Titus,' said Nadine, with extraordinary calmness. Her hair shone intermittently in the light from the passing street-lamps. 'What would you say if we'd *already* been swallowed?'

Titus sniffed, and harrumphed, and stared at her. 'What are you talking about? What do you mean, *already* been swallowed?'

'Just that. Supposing we had?'

'B-b-b-but by *what*? By *whom*? What are you talking about? Damn it, Nadine, what the hell are you talking about?'

'I'm sorry, Titus. You're drunk. I didn't mean you to be drunk when I told you.'

'What the hell do you mean, I'm drunk? All right, I'm drunk, I admit it, but I still don't know what you're talking about. Now, tell me what the *hell* you're talking about.'

'Titus, wait until we get home. Look, we'll be home in ten minutes.'

'Nadine, what the hell are you talking about – swallowed?'

'Let's wait until we get home.'

'No, God damn it, we'll talk about it here. *Swallowed*, what the hell are you talking about, *swallowed*? John, stop this goddamn car. Here! That's right, here! Anywhere! What the hell.'

The chauffeur pulled the car into the kerb on Constitution Avenue, just across the road from the lake in Constitution Gardens. It was a warm, well-lit night, one of those odd summer nights when sleep seems almost unnecessary, except at dawn, and even though it was nearly twelve o'clock, people were still promenading along the sidewalks, or trying to photograph the floodlit Lincoln Memorial with Kodak Instamatics, or walking their dogs, or smoking and talking as easily as if it were daylight.

Titus and Nadine walked down to the lake, and stood beside the wind-rippled waters, two or three feet apart, Titus in his tuxedo and black tie, Nadine in a long pleated evening gown of turquoise crêpe.

Nadine said, 'I knew that I was going to have to tell you this one day. Well – you would have found out anyway, if you were ever elected President. But things have changed. Events are becoming critical. It's partly your fault, of course, although you weren't to know. If you hadn't blackmailed Roberts into postponing his disarmament talks . . . well, perhaps we could have carried it off. But there doesn't seem to be very much hope of that now, not unless you agree to back down.'

'Nadine,' said Titus, in a phlegmy, uncontrolled voice, 'I want to know what the *hell* you're talking about.'

'I'm trying to tell you. I'm *trying*, Titus. But it's important for you to understand, as well as listen. Everything you ever imagined to be solid, irrefutable truth; every political and constitutional guideline by which you've worked; everything, Titus, that you've believed to be real . . . well, it just *isn't*. The world is a completely different place from the one in which you think you've been living.'

Titus glanced behind him. His secret service men had

parked their car close up behind the limousine, and were now standing fifteen or twenty feet away, their heads raised as if they were blindly sniffing the air for snipers or explosives, their hands nervously perched inside their coats.

'Nadine,' Titus said, more soberly now, more gently, 'did anybody give you anything to *snort* at that party?'

Nadine brushed back her hair with her hand. 'You think I'm high? Is that what you think?'

'I think you're talking like you're so spaced out you're not going to come down till Thanksgiving.'

'Titus,' she said, 'it's absolutely *vital* that Marshall continues his RINC talks.'

'Do you want to tell me why?'

'You want it straight from the shoulder? The reality?'

'Shoot. I'm not standing beside this fucking lake all night.'

'The truth is, Titus, that the United States has been administered for the past twenty years not by Congress, nor by any of its Presidents, but by a committee of Soviet caretakers.'

She waited to see how Titus would react, but Titus said nothing, just stared at her narrowly with one eye slightly closed, as if he were trying to focus on some very distant landmark.

'In Moscow, the United States of America is actually known as the ACOA, the Autonomous Capitalist Oblast of America. The caretaking committee is made up of thirty senior Communist party officials. You actually know quite a few of them already. Yevgeni Saratov, from the United Nations delegation? Anton Sviridov from the Russian Arts Council? And the chairman of the committee is a one-time friend of Leonid Brezhnev, a man whom the Russians codename Ikon.'

Again, Nadine hesitated. Titus was giving no indication either that he understood her, or that he believed her. But he said, 'Go on,' in a flat, toneless voice, and waited for her to continue.

'Ikon has been governing America for the past twenty

years,' said Nadine. 'Every President, on the evening of his Inauguration Day, has been told exactly what I'm telling you now. He's been told that the general style of his administration must remain true to his own character, but that everything he does . . . politically, economically and militarily . . . must conform to Ikon's overall plan.'

'Yes?' said Titus.

Nadine crossed her arms over her breasts, as if she were cold. Quietly, she said, 'Ikon, whatever you think of his Marxist beliefs, is a wise and sensitive man. He's been doing his utmost to convert America *gradually* towards complete social democracy, without sacrificing any of the spirit of self-determination that made America what it is. Or, what it *was*, before Ikon took power.

'One thing that Ikon's always argued against is a sudden public revelation that America is a conquered nation. He argued against announcing it in 1962 and he's still arguing against it. His idea is that America should be allowed to prosper and grow in her own way; and that the *appearance* of international conflict between East and West should be kept up. That is all part of his fundamental thirty-year plan. He's a socialist, you see; but he's also a social realist, and a humanitarian. "You must never take the struggle out of people's lives," that's what he says. "Once you take away the necessity to struggle, you take away the reason to live." '

Titus turned towards the lake, and grimaced at it, as if he were facing an ocean, rather than a still ornamental pond.

Nadine said, 'Everything you believe about the cause-and-effect of US policy over the whole of the past two decades, in every area of government, is wrong. Ikon controls it all. And every policy that Ikon implements is aimed towards the gradual acceptance by the American people that they are world citizens, that the Soviet people are their friends and their comrades, and that Communism is the *only* way in which men can be free. *All* men, not just a grotesquely wealthy elite.'

'I see,' said Titus, with preternatural self-control. 'And

how has Ikon been working this social and political miracle?'

'Through the US economy, mostly,' said Nadine. 'Ikon's been using Russia's influence on the Middle-Eastern oil-producing countries, as well as Russia's leverage in the world banking system, to force the economy of the United States into a false decline. His aim has been to eat away the power-base of the capitalist system and to encourage the American working-man to start turning towards new political alternatives. A man can sometimes only accept the truth when he needs to.'

'And where does RINC come in?' Cold, colder, colder still.

Nadine said, 'RINC is one of the last of Ikon's long-term measures to go for nuclear disarmament. He drafted all of the SALT agreements and was pleased with them, but RINC was his special pride, especially since it won the support of so many of Europe's politicians and military men – even General Rogers, the Supreme Allied Commander for Europe. RINC, when it's ratified, will mean the end of what NATO calls the "flexible response", the notion that the West might strike with nuclear weapons first. It will also mark the beginning of unopposed Soviet superiority in Europe. And peace, too, in time.'

'I can't believe I'm hearing any of this,' said Titus.

'I know it's difficult,' said Nadine. 'But you have to listen and you have to make an effort to understand, because it's crucial. You made it more crucial yourself, by your own belligerence. Ikon is old now, and very ill. He may not survive six months. At least two other committee members want to see him ousted, and most of the committee already believe that America should be openly declared a subject people of the USSR. Ikon wanted to preserve the United States, to keep her traditions and her folklore and her colour, not to mention her sanity. But Kama in particular, the Commissar in charge of National Security, is hungry to see the Red Flag flying over Washington, and all the trappings of capitalism swept away in a tide of scarlet. Kama's the leader of the *Peredoviki*, the innovators, the revolutionaries.'

Nadine went on, 'If RINC succeeds, the American public may gradually be brought to believe that true mutual disarmament is not only possible but imminent. Can you imagine the feeling of relief, after thirty years of cold war? The *hope* that people will feel, if they realize that all nuclear weapons are at last going to be dismantled? Moscow has been impatient with Ikon on more than one occasion. They've pushed him to assert an overt Communist rule over the ACOA at almost twice the historic speed at which he first planned it. He's managed by the skin of his teeth to keep control; he's managed to assure the Kremlin that RINC I and RINC II *can* be ratified, and that along with all his other measures, America can be safely Sovietized within the next decade.'

'But?' demanded Titus.

'But, if RINC fails, the *Peredoviki* will almost certainly take control. Kama and Ilyushkin will force Marshall Roberts to announce that America is an administrative *oblast* directly answerable to the Communist Party of the Soviet Union. And then, all hell will break out. I promise you, Titus, all hell. We will see the H-bombs dropped yet. America will certainly melt.'

Titus hunkered down on the grass and stared for a very long time at the wavering reflections of the passing promenaders, and the Lincoln Memorial. One of his security men came a little closer, not too close, and called politely, 'Whenever you're ready to leave, Mr Secretary. We're kind of nervous about the security aspects around here.'

Titus stood up again, and cocked his head towards Nadine. Then he said, 'We're leaving now. Directly. Come along, Nadine. Let's finish this little discussion at home.'

They drove back to Georgetown in silence. Titus drummed his fingers on the grey hide of the Cadillac's interior, and coughed from time to time, sharp, barking coughs, but he didn't look once at Nadine, and wouldn't respond to her even when she said, 'Titus? Are you okay?'

In the living-room, Carl and Samantha had spread their

record albums all over the floor, and were playing the soundtrack from *Fame* at a volume which made the Waterford crystal chandeliers jingle in horror. Titus stalked into the room and said, 'Turn off that goddamned noise and get the hell out of here.'

'I'm sorry, Tight, I can't hear you too good,' said Carl. 'This music's too loud.'

'Turn off the goddamned noise!'

'Aw, come on, Tight, the loudest noise I can hear in here is *you*.'

Titus skirted around the coffee-table at the speed of a head-waiter who has suddenly caught sight of a customer trying to duck under the velvet rope. He hefted the Trio record-player up off the English walnut sideboard on which it was kept, and there was a ripping blurt of noise as the stylus slid sideways across the record. Then Titus wrenched out the wires which connected the record-player to the amplifier, and hurled it clear across the room. It struck the marble mantelpiece, knocking the head off a Staffordshire shepherdess and smashing part of the gilded mirror behind it.

'Now get out of here,' quaked Titus, his eyes protuberant with anger. 'Get out of here before I do the same to you.'

Carl and Samantha sheepishly gathered up their records, and left the room in uncertain silence. They left the door ajar, until Titus yelled, '*Door!*'

Nadine said, 'I'm going to bed. I'm not going to put up with your ridiculous bursts of temper. I've risked my life tonight to tell you the truth, and all you can do is rant and rave like a petty-minded drill sergeant.'

'You're not going anywhere,' snapped Titus. He went to the liquor cabinet, slammed open the doors, and found the bottle of Glenmorangie malt whiskey, ten years old.

'If you're going to start drinking – '

'*Don't* – ' roared Titus, jabbing his finger at her, ' – lecture to me!'

'Very well,' said Nadine. 'Since you're there, you can pour me a Campari-soda.'

'You're sure you don't want a Stolichnaya?'

'I *am* Russian, if that's what you're trying to suggest.'

'Oh, you're *Russian*, are you? And I suppose Carl and Samantha are Russian, and the dogs are Russian, and the servants are Russian, and all this time I've never suspected it. Nadine, for Christ's sake, I'm the Secretary of State. I'm the goddamned Secretary of *State*.'

He sat down heavily in his favourite chintz armchair, crossed his legs, and took two or three furious swallows of whiskey. 'Jesus Christ,' he kept saying.

Nadine sat on the rug opposite him, her hands in her lap. Her expression when she looked at him was very sorrowful.

'I didn't know what else to do,' she told him. 'I couldn't see any other way out of it.'

'You couldn't see any other way out of *what*?'

'Titus, I had a choice. Either I told you everything, and convinced you to withdraw your opposition to the RINC talks, or else I killed Colleen Petley.'

'Now I *know* you're bananas,' said Titus.

'Titus, please, you have to understand that I – '

'I understand already! I understand perfectly! I understand that my loyal, supportive wife is prepared to come with some obscene and unpatriotic bullshit just to try and make me feel guilty about stopping Marshall Roberts going ahead with those disarmament discussions! Come on, Nadine, I'm not utterly stupid. I know an allegory when I hear one. An allegory, that's what it was, wasn't it? An Aesop's fable, about America. A story to make me feel that I was selling out on tomorrow's hope of a bomb-free world.'

Nadine was aghast, no colour in her cheeks at all. Titus jabbed his finger at her again and said, 'Let me tell you something, my lady, you're a very beautiful woman. You've got everything it's ever going to take. But when you start snorting coke at embassy parties, and when you start trying to get at my moral conscience by making up crappy bad-taste un-American stories like that – that's when you and I are going to fall out. And when you and

I fall out – boy, I can tell you, you're going to know about it.'

'Titus,' she whispered. 'For God's sake. Don't you *realize*?'

'I realize that I married a princess with the brain of a witch, that's what I realize. But can anyone tell what this princess is going to do? Well, I'll tell you. This princess is going to take off all her clothes, and this princess is going to grovel on the floor and kiss my feet, and tell me she's sorry, and that she apologizes abjectly not only to *me*, but to the United States of America, and the proud heritage which made this nation great.'

'Titus, you're incredibly drunk.'

'Oh, no, Nadine. Not drunk. Intoxicated, maybe, poisoned. Poisoned by everything you've told me. But not drunk. Not any more. No man could stay drunk, not with you around. You're the most sobering influence since Fernet Branca.'

'Titus – '

'Fuck you, lady!' roared Titus, and smashed his glass of whiskey against the fireplace. Then with two savage wrenches, he pulled open the front of Nadine's evening-gown, baring her breasts, and stripped it right down to her waist.

'How dare you tell me such shit,' he trembled. 'I've fought for this country and sweated for this country all of my adult life. I've seen my friends disembowelled; I've seen my family go crazy with grief. I've given everything and anything for that flag of stars and stripes and for the American constitution.'

He stood up. He was so drunk that he had to grab for the arm of his chair to steady himself. Then he began to sing, in a loud, flat voice, the last verse of *The Star-Spangled Banner*.

'Oh! thus be it ever, when freemen shall stand
Between their loved home and the war's desolation!
Blest with victory and peace, may the heav'n rescued land
Praise the Power that hath made and preserved us a nation.'

Nadine clung at his sleeve, and said, 'Titus, please.' But Titus slapped her away, and stood in the centre of the room, his eyes crimson and swollen with alcohol, and sang at the top of his lungs,

'Then conquer we must, when our cause is just,
And this be our motto: 'In God is our trust.'
And the star-spangled banner in triumph shall wave
O'er the land of the free and the home of the brave.'

Nadine said, 'Titus, please. You have to listen.'

'I've listened enough, damn it! I've known ever since I've married you how much of a goddamned pacifist you are. I couldn't have failed to, really, the way you've always taunted me. Nuclear imbalance, you said, like it was some kind of joke. And now all this. The American Capitalist Oblast. You think that's funny? You damn well think that's *funny*?'

'Titus!' screamed Nadine. 'It's true! But I don't want to have to kill Colleen! Please! Listen! If you don't listen, I'll have to kill Colleen! Titus! *Titus!* Damn you, Titus! God curse you, Titus, I love her!'

Titus swung around and punched Nadine with his closed fist, right in the jaw. She fell back with a sound like a malt-sack falling from a second-storey window. Then Titus fell down beside her, on his knees, and ripped apart her gown until she was almost naked, except for her self-support stockings and her silk eau-de-nil panties.

'Jesus, you're a bitch,' he snarled at her. She opened her eyes, concussed, and stared at him as if she didn't know who he was. 'Titus?' she asked him.

He dragged down her panties, baring the vivid pink slit of her vulva. He jostled himself out of his own clothes, except for his shirt, and his straying starched collar; and then he clambered on top of her. She didn't resist, couldn't. He was too heavy, too powerful, too enraged, too insistent, too drunk. His penis was like a nightstick, masculine, thrusting, but somehow inanimate. He jammed it into her again and again and again, raping her, because she didn't participate and she didn't consent; and then he turned her over and jammed it into her again, into her bottom, and her hands gripped the thick pile of the Persian rug and tore it out in agonized handfuls. He shuddered, and came, deep inside her tightest place, and she closed her eyes and tried to hope that this would be her ultimate sacrifice to everything she had been born and trained to believe in. She couldn't give any more, except for her life.

Titus stood up, swayed, and tried to focus on her, triumphant and lewd. 'You're *nothing*, you know that? A Washington whore. A political groupie. You know that? You make me sick.' Then, with the inaccurate gait of Jacques Tati, he made for the door.

Nadine sat up amongst the rags of her torn evening-gown. There were vivid red fingermarks on her breasts, and on her stomach. Her head ached with a sharp, shrill, endless pain. She lowered her head in sexual defeat and tiredness, and watched as a white dewdrop was squeezed out of the scarlet rose of her anus. Titus had invaded her soul and her privacy, both erotically and politically, without care, without any feeling at all; as if she were there to be used, and nothing else. He had denied her where Colleen had aroused her and accepted her, he had given her coldness and clubs where Colleen had given her kisses and understanding. And yet the irony was that it was Colleen whom Ikon had asked her to kill; and Titus whom Ikon had asked her to care for.

Titus came back into the room, pushing the door open so hard that it banged against one of the occasional tables.

'Are you coming to bed?' he demanded.

'No,' she said. Then, 'Yes.'

'Listen,' he enunciated. Then, more softly, 'Listen, I'm sorry I hit you. Sorry I hurt you. You just – made me lose my temper.'

He looked down and saw the white dewdrop on red flesh and the flicker in his eyes told her that he was aroused again. Titus was a soldier, after all. His success had always been measured by the pain which he had been able to inflict on other people. That was what soldiers were for. He had hurt her; badly; and yet he felt triumphant.

Later, in bed, just before morning, he whispered in her ear. 'That stuff about Russia.'

'Yes?' She could imagine her voice rising to the high moulded ceiling like an airship filled with chilled helium.

'Well, that was bullshit, wasn't it?'

'If that's what you want to think.'

'The American Capitalist Oblast? I mean, that's a joke, right? A sharp, intellectual joke. A little too sharp for a regular patriotic guy like me.'

'You're still drunk.'

'No, I'm not. There wasn't one single officer in Nam who could drink me under the table. Not one. Not one single officer. And in those days we were drinking Chivas Regal with Singha Beer chasers. You ever drunk that Singha Beer? Comes from Thailand. Two – just *two* of those – would wipe your average American beer drinker out completely. Two.'

Nadine said, 'Titus, it's true. Ikon is true. The American Oblast exists; and has done, for twenty years.'

Titus squeezed his eyes shut. 'Nadine,' he said. 'You and I are going to talk about this in the morning. You got me? And another thing we're going to talk about is your fucking children, all right? Got that? Meanwhile I'm going to go crash out on the library couch.'

'Thank God for that,' she told him. The bitterness in her voice was like lime-peel under the fingernails.

He stood and watched her as she painfully got up from the floor, gathering her torn clothes, and limped towards the stairs. He couldn't even begin to understand at that moment the agony she felt; not just physically, from what he had done to her, but mentally. There was no alternative left to her now but to poison Colleen Petley; no hope but to destroy the one person in whom she had felt able to invest her romantic trust.

'Oblast, for Christ's sake,' said Titus, as she passed him.

It was only at five o'clock in the morning, when Titus

woke to find his cheek pressed against the shiny brown hide of the library couch, and a slick of dribble coming out of the side of his mouth, that he thought for the very first time that Nadine might not have been joking; and that Ikon's administration might for twenty years have been a hideous reality. He sat up: the library clock chimed five. He thought: Jesus H Christ.

Upstairs, Nadine's bed was empty, cold, and unslept-in. Titus stared at it for almost five minutes. Then he picked up the telephone and dialled Joe Jasper.

Twenty-Four

It had taken furious arguments; slammed doors; and moments of silent pain and unexpressed agony; but at last Kathy Forbes had persuaded Daniel to come with her to Los Angeles. It had taken two days without a telephone call, two days without a ransom note, two days without anything but knots in his stomach and two nights without sleep.

And always, that remembered rhyme,

'My daddy is dead, but I can't tell you how;
He left me six horses to follow the plow.
With my whim wham waddle ho!'

Against Kathy's direct advice, Daniel had told Pete Burns that Susie was missing, and Pete Burns had solemnly put out a Missing Child poster, with a black-and-white photograph of Susie on the day that Daniel had bought her that blue spotted frock for Thanksgiving, and Daniel had been so proud of her, and thought she looked so pretty, until he had heard her talking to Levon's daughter out in the back yard, saying, 'Can you believe this dumb dress? Daddy thinks it's so cute, so I have to wear it. But can you believe it? It looks like an anteater's nosebag.' Daniel had said nothing at the time, but a week later, when they had gone out visiting, and Susie had asked him what she should wear, Daniel had said offhandedly, 'Oh, just throw on the old anteater's nosebag.'

Pete Burns, as a matter of course, had passed on the details of the case to Lieutenant Berridge in Phoenix. Under 'Possible Suspects', was the name 'Skellett'.

Daniel had left a forwarding address; and on the last Thursday in August they had flown out of Sky Harbor, eastwards at first, and then curving around to the southwest so that he could see the whole criss-cross landscape of Phoenix spreading out towards the New River Mountains.

He had thought of Cara. She was still in hospital, with twenty-six stitches and three fractured ribs. Then he had glanced at Kathy, sitting next to him, and she had smiled sympathetically and he had felt at least that he was not alone.

Now he and Kathy were installed in a quiet rented cottage just off Sunset Boulevard, and were spending most of their time trying to talk to anyone who could remember Marilyn Monroe. Some agents and actors ate the lunches they bought at the expense of the *Arizona Flag*, and told them apocryphal stories about the night that Marilyn died, or about imaginary arguments between Marilyn and Ralph Roberts, or anything that came into their heads. But most of the Hollywood professionals just shrugged, and averted their eyes, as if Marilyn's going was still a personal embarrassment, as if all of them were individually responsible for that week when she had failed to turn up on the set of *Something's Got To Give*. As if all of them had gathered together and crammed Nembutals down her throat, to extinguish that bleached-blonde *angst* forever, and give them, who knows, some kind of haunted peace from the sexual spirit of the late 1950s.

Every one of them said, 'She'd be 56 years old now, if she were still alive, you know that? Fifty-six years old. She would have *hated* it.'

And most of them said, 'You want to know about Marilyn? What for? It's all over. It's all dead and buried.'

Then, by chance, they met Rollo Sekulovich.

It was on the morning of the third day. They were eating breakfast at the Sunset Hyatt, and Daniel had just come back from the pay phone, checking with Pete Burns to find out if there was any news of Susie. The restaurant smelled of burned coffee and bacon; and there was that jangled conversation of businessmen who have just woken up; wives who are just about to go out shopping; waitresses who refuse to serve anything that isn't written on the menu. 'It says two eggs, right? You have to have two eggs. No, I'm sorry, you can't have one egg and pay for two. I have to give you the two eggs, in case you complain.'

Kathy said, 'No news?'

Daniel shook his head. 'Nothing. Not even a ransom note.'

'That isn't a bad sign.'

'It isn't a *good* sign, either.'

'I know. I'm not going to pretend that everything's fine and dandy. It's not my style.'

Daniel sat down, and stared at his plate of Canadian bacon and eggs. 'You think they've killed her?' he asked.

'No,' said Kathy. 'Everything points away from it. I mean, why would they kill her? If they want money, they'll keep her alive, if they want a hostage they'll keep her alive. If they want *you*, they'll keep her alive.'

'Why would they want me?'

'Maybe a little Air Force bird told them that you'd been snooping around the morgue at Williams Air Force Base. Maybe that's the whole reason they kidnapped her.'

'If they want me, why don't they contact me? It's this damned *silence*. I don't even know if she's dead or alive. I don't even know where she is, or what they might have

262

done to her. And she's *mine*, you know? My daughter. My responsibility.'

Kathy reached across the table and touched his hand. 'You've got to stop blaming yourself. It wasn't your fault.'

'Nobody else was responsible. Not even her mother.'

'Have you gotten in touch with her mother?'

'Candii? What for? She wouldn't care. Too busy whooping it up somewhere with some poor man's Howard Keel.'

It was then that a man in a loud purple blazer sat down next to them, and said, 'Okay if I join you people?'

'Go ahead,' said Daniel. Then, to Kathy, 'Who have we got on the list today? Did you manage to get in touch with MGM? Isn't there anybody else who might have known what Marilyn did on that last night? The police, maybe, or doctors?'

'Excuse me,' said the man in the purple blazer, 'are you talking about Marilyn Monroe?'

Daniel and Kathy looked at each other, and then Daniel said guardedly, 'That's right. We're, uh, journalists. Writing a book on famous scandals in Hollywood.'

'Well, there's always plenty of material,' the man grinned. He reminded Daniel of Ed Koch, only shorter. Same bald dome, same prominent Yiddish nose, and something of the same experienced glitter in the eyes. 'But when you talk about Marilyn, then you're talking. That was a scandal, all right. You talk about Marilyn and half the people in Hollywood start shitting their pants, even today, if you'll excuse my Hebrew. I knew Marilyn. Sure, you don't have to look surprised. I knew Marilyn just about as well as my cousin Fruma. And, to tell you the truth there wasn't much in it, except Fruma has a bigger chest.'

Kathy said, 'You saw Marilyn the night she died? Or that week?'

The man said, 'Better than that. Or more *interesting* than that. But, listen, I should introduce myself. Rollo Sekulovich, I'm an agent. Most people call me RS. You've heard of Christy Welcome? She's one of my girls. Girls, I handle mainly. New girls, giving them some kind of movie work without the necessity to screw producers, excuse me. Call me a one-man social mission, if you like. But Christy Welcome didn't have to sleep with Don Oppenheim to get that lead part in *Triple Murder*; and Jean Prisnik didn't have to sleep with Jim Martin, although she did. Well, she liked him, he's a nice guy. But let me tell you something else: I have the same surname as Karl Malden, did you realize that? Malden Sekulovich, that's his real name. Can you imagine the *Streets of San Francisco* with Malden Sekulovich? And Kirk Douglas was born Issur Demsky; so Michael Douglas would be Michael Demsky. Can you imagine that? A TV series with Sekulovich and Demsky?'

Kathy forked up the last slice of her tropical-fruit salad. 'You want to tell us about Marilyn?'

'Marilyn, sure. It's an interesting story. Maybe you won't believe it, who knows? But you can always check. Maybe the Brentwood police know somebody who remembers that night, one of their officers. It was twenty years ago, right? But I can remember it clear like today. You want to know why? I had a new girl called Vera Rutledge. What a name, you know? Vera Rutledge. Sometimes I think people become actors just to get rid of their crappy names, excuse me. Did you know that Robert Taylor was born Spangler Arlington?'

'What about Vera Rutledge?' Kathy persisted.

'She was terrific,' said Rollo Sekulovich. 'She was blonde, natural blonde, and she looked exactly like Marilyn. Marilyn had a nose-job, you know that, but Vera didn't need anything like that. She looked like Marilyn *should* have looked like, only her big disadvantage was that Marilyn happened to have looked like that *first*. Ten years earlier, I could have made Vera a big-name star. She had that luminous look about her skin, you know, like Marilyn had; and that kind of innocent-sexy come-hither look in her eyes. Vera Rutledge, one of the great names that never was.'

'What happened to her?' asked Daniel.

'This is the point,' said Rollo Sekulovich. 'Vera Rutledge

was invited to a party the same night that Marilyn died . . . a party that Marilyn was expected to go to, too. I tipped off my friends on the *Times* that there was going to be a good look-alike picture if they could get Vera and Marilyn together – you know the kind of thing I'm talking about – 'Marilyn meets Marilyn' – or 'The Twin Monroes' – or something like that. Well – about midnight I'm still working on a new contract for one of my latest girls – Darlene Hughes, I think it was – yes, right, I'm sure it was, Darlene – and this guy Rick Montez calls me from the *Times* and says neither Vera nor Marilyn showed up at this party, and of course he's pissed about it, excuse me.'

'It's a matter of history where Marilyn was,' said Kathy. 'So what are you telling me that's new? A starlet called Vera Rutledge didn't show up to the same party twenty years ago that Marilyn Monroe didn't show up to?'

'No, listen to me,' said Rollo Sekulovich. 'Neither of them was ever seen alive again. Marilyn Monroe was said to have taken an overdose of sleeping-pills, Vera Rutledge disappeared without trace. I hired two private detectives to look for Vera but they had to give up after six months. They found some strays, all right, and how many corpses of young girls, you'd be amazed. Two murderers were prosecuted as a result of that investigation, and one of them went to prison for life. But I never found Vera. She just vanished, piff, the same night that Marilyn died, just like she was a ghost or something; just like she and Marilyn were part of the same person.'

Kathy said, 'Where did Vera live, Mr Sekulovich? In Los Angeles?'

'She lived with her mother in Van Nuys. Not far from where Marilyn used to live with Jim Dougherty, when she was first married. Her mother always used to say that the Rutledge family were friends with the Doughertys, but I believe that was just a story. Her mother lives there still.'

Daniel finished his breakfast and pushed away his

plate. 'Mr Sekulovich,' he said, 'why did you tell us all this?'

Rollo Sekulovich made a silly, sentimental face. 'You want to know the truth? That Vera Rutledge was always a fantasy to me. I never took her to bed. I was true to my wife, God rest her soul. I always thought I had principles. But Vera Rutledge was special; much more special to me than Marilyn ever was. If you could have made Marilyn perfect, and bright, then that's what Vera was. And I sent her off to that party that night. "It'll be good for your career," I told her. "Just go." And so she went, and I never saw her again. Never. She could be on Mars.'

Daniel thought of Susie, that Susie could be on Mars, too, for all he knew. Vera Rutledge and Marilyn Monroe and Susie Korvitz, fellow wanderers on an alien planet; scared faces under scarlet skies.

That afternoon, they drove out to Brentwood. Before they went to Mandeville Canyon Road, where Lieutenant Lindblad lived, they took a left off Sunset Boulevard and drove slowly past the rows of exclusive cul-de-sacs called Helena Drives. There are twenty-five Helena Drives, eighteen of them south of Sunset, and on Fifth Helena Drive, Marilyn Monroe used to live, and was supposed to have died.

They stopped. It was a hot, smoggy afternoon; and the sun was screened by lunchtime pollution. The engine of their rented Monaco burbled and whistled, but on Fifth Helena Drive that was the only sound, apart from a distant radio playing, with almost absurd irony, *Candle in the Wind*. It occurred to Daniel that it could actually have been possible for Elton John to have known Norma Jean; if only anyone had realized that she was hiding in Phoenix in fear of her life, under the assumed name of Margot Schneider.

Kathy said, 'That's the Monroe house. Not much, is it?'

'It doesn't look like anything at all. A cement-brick hacienda.'

Kathy said, 'Please have courage. I'm sure Susie's all right.'

'Courage? What the hell does courage have to do with it?'

'I'm not sure. But it'll help.'

'If you say so.'

Lieutenant Lindblad lived in a small white combed-stucco bungalow with red Mexican tiles on the roof and a wrought-iron sign on the wall announcing that this was La Casita Mia. He was sprinkling the lawn when they drew up, a thin 67-year-old in a white short-sleeved shirt and light grey slacks, the kind of man from whom all the flesh seems to have shrunk, leaving nothing beneath his darkly-tanned skin but sinews and bones and arteries. His clip-on sunglasses were raised, revealing eyes that were faded by years of sun and years of detective work. He raised his hand in greeting as they approached, and Daniel could see his bicep muscle rolling around on top of his humerus. A walking anatomy lesson.

'You folks care for some guacamole? My wife made some fresh. Makes the best guacamole in Greater Los Angeles, I can tell you. Rosa, come out and say hi.'

A pretty, plump Mexican woman came out of the house, her hair stuck up in combs, and smiled and shook hands and said, 'hi,' and 'hi,' and that was about all. She wore a bright crimson-and-yellow frock that just about managed to contain her enormous breasts and her huge haunches, and she jiggled back into the bungalow as if every part of her body was dancing to a different maracas-player.

'She's a terrific woman, Rosa,' said Lieutenant Lindblad. 'My second wife. Just the sort of woman I always wanted. My first wife was thin and mean and sour as hell. I wanted a woman I could get hold of. You know what I mean? Never had so much damned fun in my whole life.'

They sat inside, in the cool, around a glass table with black wrought-iron legs, and ate guacamole with fresh-baked taco chips and drank Budweiser out of Budweiser glasses. 'I came from Wisconsin originally, did my training in Milwaukee. Can't touch this Western beer, not for nothing.'

Daniel said, 'They told us round at the police station that you were concerned with the Vera Rutledge disappearance. Well, they checked it in the files.'

Lieutenant Lindblad steadily ground up a taco chip between his dentures. He took a swallow of Bud. Then he said, 'Vera Rutledge, hunh? I thought you said you were writing a book on famous Hollywood scandals.'

'Wasn't Vera Rutledge a scandal?'

'Vera Rutledge was a disappearance, that was all.'

'Routine, yes? Nothing special about it?'

'Not that I remember.'

'I'm surprised you remember it at all,' said Kathy. 'It was more than twenty years ago, after all. Just one case in a hundred thousand.'

'She disappeared the night Monroe died, that's all. That's why I remember it.'

'And she looked like Monroe?'

'I guess so. That was one description.'

There was a very long silence. Lieutenant Lindblad looked from Daniel to Kathy and then back again. 'Is that all you want to know?' he asked them.

'It depends whether that's all you're going to tell us,' said Kathy.

'What's to tell? I was on duty that night; I was given a report that some blonde young starlet had gone missing. Then it came over the radio that we were supposed to go round to Fifth Helena, because Marilyn Monroe was suffering from some kind of an overdose. That's all. That's all I remember. We put out the usual searches for Vera Rutledge. We found quite a few bodies, quite a few stray starlets, but then you always do when you comb Hollywood real thorough. You could do it today and you'd find the same. But we never found Vera Rutledge.'

'What time was Vera Rutledge reported missing?'

'Ten o'clock maybe. I don't exactly remember.'

'And what time was Marilyn reported to have OD'd?'

'Listen,' said Lieutenant Lindblad, sharply. His dentures made a loud clicking noise. 'You want history, you go to the history books. Don't bother me about it. I was only doing my job.'

'The history books are full of lies and discrepancies,' Kathy insisted. 'You know they are, because you were actually there, and you know what happened.'

'What are you trying to say, that something happened different?'

'I *know* something happened different.'

'Well, there's no use in asking me. I don't remember too much about it. It was one of those nights, you know? Pretty confused. Lots of publicity, lots of confusion. And everybody lying their asses off to protect their reputations.'

Daniel said, 'We know that Marilyn Monroe didn't die that night.'

Lieutenant Lindblad stared at him. 'Are you crazy?'

Daniel shook his head. His heart was bouncing like a dolphin at Sea World, but he was determined to stick to his story. 'Marilyn Monroe didn't die that night, but somebody did. Some girl who hadn't eaten supper, like Marilyn had. Marilyn ate supper that night with Bobby Kennedy and Peter Lawford, as well as Pat Newcomb, and her housekeeper Mrs Murray. But the autopsy on the girl's body showed that her stomach and her intestines were completely empty. Only her blood was thick with barbiturates.'

Kathy said, in her gentlest voice, 'On the same night in 1962, Marilyn Monroe was supposed to have died in mysterious circumstances; and a girl who looked almost exactly like her disappeared without trace. Twenty years later, in Phoenix, Arizona, a woman was murdered; a woman who in all probability is Norma Jean Baker, aged 57. So what kind of a conclusion can you draw from that?'

Lieutenant Lindblad said, 'What are you trying to suggest? Why don't you say it straight?'

'You want me to?' said Kathy.

Lieutenant Lindblad sucked thoughtfully and anxiously at his dentures. Then he said, 'I don't know why you

269

want to dig all this up. It's all dead and buried, twenty years ago. It doesn't make no difference, not now. If that woman who was murdered was Norma Jean; well, what of it? What difference does it make? They're both dead now; and so are Jack and Bobby, and that's the end of it.'

'Lieutenant, that isn't the end of it. That's just the very beginning. Marilyn Monroe was hustled out of Brentwood in 1962 because she knew something she shouldn't have known – wasn't she? And maybe Bobby Kennedy was trying to protect her. But he couldn't protect her after he was dead; and after twenty years someone found her and killed her. And if what she knew was important enough for someone to look for her for twenty years; then believe me it must have been damned important. I don't know *how* important, I'll admit that. But people don't get sacrificed for nothing, not even by Kennedys.'

Lieutenant Lindblad put down his beer, stood up, and went to the door. His wife Rosa was cheerily cooking in the kitchen. He gave her a little finger-wave and then closed the door. Then he went to the window and looked up and down the street. 'You don't have no microphone, do you?' he asked Kathy. 'I don't want no record of this; not in my own voice.'

Kathy raised her hands to show that she was clean. Daniel did the same.

'How much is this worth?' asked Lieutenant Lindblad.

'What's the bottom line?' Kathy wanted to know.

'Two thousand, cash.'

'Fifteen hundred, that's all I've got.'

'Okay, then,' said Lieutenant Lindblad. 'Money first.'

Kathy opened her purse, took out the large roll of bills which the *Flag* had given her for buying street information in Los Angeles, and stripped off $1,500. It left her with nothing more than two $20s, and a $5. Lieutenant Lindblad took the money and pushed it into his back pants pocket without a murmur.

He poured out three more beers, and then settled down in his armchair.

'I'm going to say this once only, okay, and I'm not

going to repeat myself. You don't take notes, got it, and you don't make no recordings; and if you ever ask me again if this is what I've said, then I'll deny it. I'll deny that I've even seen you, and so will Rosa. So don't try to get funny. I've still got plenty of friends on the force, and I still carry my own gun, I'm entitled. So don't try to get funny.'

'I promise you that neither of us will try to get funny,' said Daniel.

Lieutenant Lindblad gave him a wary look. But Daniel managed to keep his face deadly serious; and at last Lieutenant Lindblad said, 'Right. This is the way it happened. Way back in August, 1962 . . . this is the way it really happened.'

Twenty-Five

Joe Jasper carefully hung up the phone and ran his hand through his hair. On the other side of the room, on a makeshift cot, Crack Nielsen was still swaddled in a pink blanket, his mouth gaping open, snoring his way through sixty cords of good dreamland lumber. Joe looked at him for a while, pursing his lips, then got up from his own bed and went through to the living-room and opened the drapes.

Colleen was already up, although it was only a minute or two past seven o'clock. She was wearing a pale-green baby-doll nightie in flounces of transparent nylon, through which her nipples showed with unremitting prominence. Joe ignored her. He was not a sexual creature in the conventional sense; he was not aroused by America's naked big-breasted babies, or by women in general, or in particular.

Joe Jasper was aroused only by humiliation; and by hurt. If he had any credo in life, it was probably that the obedient and the masochistic will eventually inherit the earth.

'You're up early,' he told Colleen.

'I haven't been to bed yet.'

'What time did you get in?'

'Four.'

'Crack was with you?'

'Most of the time.'

'You realize you're running a risk, going out so much?'

'Fuck it, Joe, Nadine said I could. Besides, I'm not *The Prisoner of Zenda*.'

'I didn't say you were. But you've known all along that you'd have to do this some day. Stay inside, keep yourself safe. That's valuable evidence you've got there.'

'Don't you keep reminding me. It was me who had to swallow Marshall Roberts' piss. Not you. Or maybe you would have liked to.'

'What was the difference between Marshall Roberts' piss and any other man's piss? You do it all the time.'

'I do it when I feel like it. That's all. With Marshall Roberts, I did it because he said he wouldn't pay me, else.'

'Such a hardship.'

'Asshole.'

Joe Jasper went to the drinks cabinet and poured himself a large DOM liqueur. It was dry and strong and if you were going to drink first thing in the morning in the company of transparently-clad whores, it was probably the best drink going. Colleen watched him, and said, 'I don't even know what the hell this is all about.'

'You're not supposed to. Nobody is supposed to. Not even *I* know what it's all about. Not completely.'

'Well, that shows what a cretin *you* are.'

Joe took a mouthful of liquor, and closed his eyes. In actual fact, he was desperately worried, although he was trying his utmost not to show it to Colleen. If Titus believed for one moment that Nadine was right, and that the United States really *had* become the American Capitalist Oblast in the summer of 1962; then there was a strong possibility that Titus would allow Marshall Roberts to go ahead with RINC II, and seriously threaten Kama's chances of taking over from Ikon as chairman of the Oblast committee. Titus was a hawk; and he hated Marshall Roberts for giving so much away to the Russians in the RINC talks. But Titus was also a patriot, fierce and dogged; and if he was brought to perceive that RINC was the lesser of two threats to what was left of the American nation; if he actually understood that RINC would mean only a gradual decline in American influence, while Kama wanted an immediate takeover on all levels, then Titus would withdraw his opposition at once, and leave Joe holding the tar-baby.

On the phone this morning, Titus had said that he was 'anxious, to say the least' about the things that Nadine had told him. Joe had denied any knowledge of an American Oblast. In fact, he had laughed out loud. Was Nadine *serious*? How could the United States possibly be run by a Soviet committee? It was just a gag; a way of making Titus feel uncomfortable about putting such an immediate stop to the RINC talks. They both knew how strongly Nadine felt about nuclear disarmament. She was a liberal, wasn't she? That was the kind of thing you had to expect from liberals.

But all the time, Joe had detected in Titus' voice a lack of sureness; a suspicion that Nadine would never have told him such a preposterous story if something about it hadn't been true. I mean, the *Russians* running the United States for twenty years? Did she really expect a hardnosed soldier like Titus to swallow anything so patently stupid? You only had to look at America, didn't you? Free, prosperous, and as nutty as ever. Would the Russians allow Times Square sleaze; or whores in hotpants on Hollywood Boulevard? Would the Russians allow drugs, and booze, and profiteering, and the Hunt Brothers? America hadn't changed, or had it? Look at all the money we've been spending on defence. What was the point of *that*, if Russia was in charge? Would the Russians finance MX, or B-1 bombers, or cruise missiles that were targeted straight towards the heart of Moscow?

Except, of course, if the Russians had theorized that the United States was too large and too hostile to be conquered in the usual way in which nations are conquered; that perhaps the easiest way of taking over a prosperous and opinionated continent of 220 million people would be simply to reach out and grasp the reins of finance and power and leave the body of the nation to continue to grow in its own characteristic way, at least for the time being.

Except, of course, if the Russians had theorized that a balance of armed conflict was necessary for global stability; and in particular for stability within the Soviet Union itself, and its satellites. For who within the Soviet bloc would knuckle down to the Communist regime if there was no threat from the West? Who would tolerate a life of repression and deprivation, of lines and boredom and no fresh meat, if there was no corrupt capitalist ogre at the gates, waving his nuclear club?

Joe knew Titus well enough to guess that thoughts like these must at least have flickered through Titus' mind; and that Kama's succession to the committee could immediately and substantially be threatened. Joe had been tempted to argue with Titus, but he had managed to control himself sufficiently to say nothing more than, 'Well, sir . . . it all seems pretty far-fetched to me. I mean, I haven't seen anybody on Constitution Avenue with snow on their boots.'

Colleen said, 'I'm hungry, Is anybody going to fix breakfast?'

'What do you want?' Joe asked her, with considerable self-control.

'I don't know. Eggs, maybe. Bacon.'

'Why don't you fix it yourself?'

Colleen looked up at him. There was nothing in her

eyes at all, no sympathy, no friendship, nothing. She was a whore and she knew her value, that's what he thought. She knew when she was needed and she knew when she wasn't needed; and exactly how much. Right now, Joe Jasper needed her badly. She didn't understand what it was all about, but she could smell fear the same way a child can; or a cat. Joe Jasper was frightened. His glands gave him away, like a polecat.

'Okay,' said Joe. 'I'll see what I can rustle up. You want muffins with it? Juice?'

Colleen didn't answer, and after a moment or two, Joe Jasper turned around and marched himself stiffly into the kitchenette. Fuck it, he thought, as he tied on a vinyl apron. Fuck all women to hell. He opened up the Tupperware box in the refrigerator and took out a pack of bacon. If he didn't need that woman so badly he'd slice her from cunt to chin, and feed her to the State Department dogs.

There was a chime at the front door. He wiped his hands and went to answer it, but Colleen had reached the lobby first. To Joe's horror, it was Nadine, in a severe white linen suit, with a smart white feathered hat, with a net veil.

'Joe,' Nadine nodded. 'I like your apron.'

Joe looked down at himself. It was one of those aprons with a woman's curvaceous body printed on it, complete with heavy-duty bra and black frilly garter-belt. Colleen laughed, and her breasts jounced up and down beneath the garishly-green nylon of her nightie.

'How do you do, Mrs Alexander,' said Joe, trying to twist his mouth into something like a smile of welcome. 'The Secretary was on the phone a little earlier asking about you.'

'I left the house early, that's all, before he woke up,' said Nadine, and stalked confidently into the centre of the living-room, where she rolled off her white net gloves. 'Are you making breakfast? I'd adore some coffee.'

'How do you like it?' asked Joe, with humiliated wrath.

Nadine handed him her gloves, in a small white snowball, and then her hat. 'Impenetrably black,' she said, in an exaggeratedly husky voice.

While Joe began to grill the bacon and perk the coffee, Nadine and Colleen went through to the bedroom. Colleen was erotic and immediate: she tugged her baby-doll nightie over her head, so that she was naked, and then came up and held Nadine close, and kissed her, full on the mouth.

'I've missed you,' she whispered. She pressed her bare breasts against Nadine's immaculately-tailored white suit. She kissed her again, and then touched her mouth with her fingertips, as if she could scarcely believe that her kisses were real.

'You've been out,' said Nadine. 'A friend of mine saw you last night at Ulvaro's.'

'You can't keep me in prison,' said Colleen.

'I think that from now on I'm going to have to. The situation is getting very dangerous.'

Colleen kissed her again, and again, so fiercely that she smudged her lipstick. Nadine tried to pull away, but Colleen gripped her arms and held her tight. 'Make love to me,' she insisted.

'Now? What about Joe?'

'That's what you came for, isn't it, to make love to me?'

'I came – ' Nadine hesitated. She turned her head away, and looked down at the white kid purse in her hand; the purse which contained the poison which Ikon had given her. She had almost let it slip out, completely frankly, 'I came to kill you.' She had been thinking of nothing else all night and somehow it seemed quite natural; to blurt it out. That was why she hadn't slept. She said, 'Yes, I came to make love to you.'

'My darling,' smiled Colleen. Her eyes darted from side to side as they took in the pleasure of Nadine's face. 'My famous, elegant, sophisticated darling.'

Colleen lay back on the rumpled quilt of the bed, as if she were diving backwards in slow-motion into a private swimming-pool. The quilt was pale green, silk, and could have been shimmering water. She parted both her lips

276

and her thighs as she fell back, her lips licked and moist, her sex open and slippery as a morning flower. Perhaps she had made love to a man last night; perhaps her slipperiness was simply the result of heated dreams. Whatever it was, Nadine knelt at the end of the bed and pressed her face deeply into it as if it were a fleshly oxygen mask, as if she needed to breathe it as well as taste it.

'Nadine,' Colleen gasped. Then, *'Nadine. . . .'*

She lifted her legs high so that Nadine could explore every crevice of her; and it was then that Nadine reached across with one blind hand until she found her purse, and twisted it open, and took out of it the syringe of cyanide which Ikon had given her.

Colleen was panting, tugging at Nadine's hair, pulling Nadine's face as close as she could, writhing, tossing her head from side to side, feeling Nadine's endlessly lapping tongue against her peaked-up clitoris.

'Nadine, what you do to me. . . .'

Nadine held the hypodermic in her right hand like a dagger. It only needed one stab; one single drop would be enough. She drew back her arm and closed her eyes and prepared herself to dig the needle deep into Colleen's upraised thigh.

It was then that the door racketed wide open and a high-pitched voice screamed, 'Freeze! Freeze! You touch her with that needle and I'll blow your goddamned head off!'

Nadine lifted her head with a breathless gasp; her cheeks flushed and her mouth glistening with fluid. At that instant, Colleen rolled away across the bed.

Joe Jasper was standing in the doorway with a huge .357 Magnum held in both hands, pointed straight at Nadine's neck. His eyes were wide and his mouth was contorted into an Edvard Munch grimace. The revolver was so heavy that he could scarcely keep it still. Colleen reached for her bathwrap and struggled into it, tying the belt tight around her waist, glancing quick and scared from Joe to Nadine and back again.

'All right, Mrs Alexander, you drop the needle, you

understand me? You drop it. Right there, on the rug. That's it. Now, get up, please and back off right to the wall.'

Nadine brushed straight her skirt as she stepped back against the bedroom wall. She left the hypodermic on the thick white rug, glistening in the morning sunlight. Joe Jasper came forward and picked it up.

'What's this? Strychnine? Cyanide?'

Nadine didn't answer. Joe held the hypodermic up towards Colleen, and said, 'This is how much your precious Mrs Alexander has been looking after you. Making love to you with one hand, and getting ready to murder you with the other. So what do you think about that?'

'That's *poison*?' asked Colleen, in shock.

'It's just a sedative,' said Nadine. 'All I wanted to do was to make sure you stayed in the house today.'

'A sedative?' asked Joe, disbelievingly. 'All right, if it's a sedative, why don't you show us yourself? Here . . . inject this into your own arm. Then we'll see just what kind of a sedative it is.'

Nadine said, 'Don't be ridiculous. I'm only trying to keep Colleen from going out. Titus wanted to make sure that she was around today.'

'Mr Alexander called me this morning before you got here,' said Joe. 'That wasn't the story *he* told me. Mr Alexander was worried you might be thinking of doing something stupid.'

'That's a sedative, nothing else. A solution of chloral hydrate.'

'Then prove it.'

'I don't have to.'

'Oh yes, you do. Crack! Get out of that cot and give me some help! Crack! Do you hear me?'

It was a little while before Crack Neilsen appeared in the doorway, in undervest and jockey-shorts, rubbing his face as if it were made out of the same heavy silicon syrup as a Stretch Hulk. 'What's going on here? Oh, hi, Mrs Alexander. Hi, Colleen. What's the matter, Joe?'

Joe waved the Magnum towards Nadine. 'Mrs Alexander here wants some help with an injection. Here's the syringe. All you have to do is make sure that she jabs it right into herself. That's it. Right into a vein.'

Crack frowned at Joe and then at Nadine. 'Have you people had some kind of an argument?'

'Will you stop asking questions, Crack, for Christ's sake, and just take the syringe and make sure that Mrs Alexander gets her injection.'

Crack hesitated, and then shrugged. 'Whatever you say, Joe.' He took the syringe and held it up between one stubby finger and one stubby thumb. 'What is it, anyway? Dope, or something?'

'Nothing like that. Just a little sleeping potion. That's what Mrs Alexander says, anyway.'

Crack came up to Nadine and lifted up her arm. Nadine stared at Joe with an expression that was cold as Barre granite, and just as unreadable. In response, and maybe in fear, Joe raised the muzzle of the Magnum a little higher. If the hypodermic really contained poison, she would die almost instantly. But if it didn't, he would be faced with the prospect of having to kill her. It wasn't an easy choice to have to contemplate: apart from the repercussions from police and security services, and from Titus himself, he would have to explain himself to Kama and Ilyunavich. Besides, a .357 Magnum was a completely unsuitable weapon for killing a woman in a white-carpeted bedroom. The whole room would have to be redecorated, ceiling and all.

Crack Neilsen turned to Joe, and asked, 'Now?' and in the instant Crack turned, *Jesus*, Joe could see it happening, he could see it taking place right in front of his eyes but Crack was too close to Nadine for him to think of pulling the trigger, apart from all the reservations inside of him which said don't pull it yet, wait, it's going to cause too much trouble, too much mess. But Nadine seized Crack's wrist, the wrist of the hand which held the hypodermic, and thrust it upwards into Crack's face, so that the needle stuck right up into the fleshy underside of his nose, right up to the chromium hilt, and then she pressed the plunger halfway in before Crack even had time to screech out.

Crack said, 'Shit,' and tugged the hypodermic out, and threw it across the room. Then he lifted his eyes and realized that everybody was staring at him. Joe, Nadine, and Colleen.

'Well,' he demanded, 'what's so fucking funny?'

Joe said to Nadine, 'If he dies, I warn you. I'm going to kill you right where you stand.'

Colleen moved around the bed, but Joe waved the revolver in her direction, too, and said, 'You stay back, lady, or the same thing's going to happen to you.'

'If he *dies*?' Crack demanded. His face looked suddenly and remarkably blue. His lips could have been two small fish, seen through the glass wall of an oceanarium. 'What are you talking about, if he dies? What do you mean, if he *dies*?'

The hydrocyanic acid was diffused through Crack's nervous system with frightening speed. He suddenly choked, and tried to reach up to feel his face, but dropped heavily on to his knees. Then, before anybody could touch him or help him, he fell flat on his face, and lay there shuddering and twitching, and then died.

They knew he was dead. His eyes glassed over, and his bright turquoise tongue slid out from between his parted lips as if it were some disgusting parasitic worm making an unsuccessful attempt to escape from its expired host.

Joe Jasper raised the Magnum again, but Nadine knew now that he wasn't going to shoot her. Not straight away, at least. Not here. Not unless she did something too quick and too foolish.

'They taught you well, didn't they?' he asked her. 'But let me tell you here and now, you're not going to get away with it.'

'I always had a suspicion that you were one of the *Peredoviki*,' Nadine replied. 'You were always much too subservient, much too helpful. Nobody could treat anyone like that unless they believed that, ultimately, they were going to be able to rub it all back in their face.'

Joe didn't answer, but said to Colleen, loudly, 'You see what she really is, Colleen? A traitor. Look at poor Nielsen there. That's what she meant to do to you. Cyanide. You would have been dead by now, like he is.'

Colleen stepped back, well away from both Joe and Nadine, her bathwrap clutched around her as if she had been physically chilled by what she had seen, one breast bare, her hair awry.

'Nadine Alexander,' Joe told her, loudly, waving the gun with a flourish. 'In reality, Nadiana Katia Voroshilova, one of the finest sleeping agents of modern times. Said to have been born as the illegitimate daughter of Kliment Voroshilov, who was the titular head of Russia after Stalin's death; and who is still a symbolic hero from the revolutionary past. Brought to the United States at the age of seventeen, and planted in the Mayhew family, of Back Bay, Boston, as their adopted daughter. First married to the young, energetic president of Sparling Aeronautics; feeding back to the Soviet Union the complete details of some of America's latest advances in missile guidance. Then, after a discreet affair with General Titus Alexander, and an even more discreet divorce, married to the leading military officer in the US Army and later, of course, to the Secretary of State. Perhaps, next year, to the President. An impressive career. And a very elegant lady. If somewhat dangerous.'

Nadine said, 'What are you going to do now? I presume that you've decided not to kill me.'

'That particular option is still open to me, Mrs Alexander,' said Joe. His face was white and glossy with sweat. 'But, right now, I'd prefer to keep you alive. For one thing, I don't want any trouble with the police. And, for another, I want you to go back and tell the Secretary that everything is fine; and well under control; and that everything you told him about Ikon was nothing more than a little bit of left-wing feminist fantasy. Just a way of making him feel bad about stopping the RINC talks.'

'You don't seriously think that I'm going to do that, do you?' asked Nadine.

Joe lowered the gun. He looked at it, gently released the hammer, and then laid it on the bedroom side-table.

'Mrs Alexander,' he said, taking out his handkerchief, unfolding it, and carefully dabbing the sweat away from his face, 'this room is fitted with a two-way mirror. Everything you've been doing in here with Ms Petley and I mean *everything*, has been photographed and recorded.'

Nadine looked quickly at Colleen, but Colleen did nothing but shrug in apparent mystification.

'It was always your weakness, wasn't it?' smiled Joe. 'It was your weakness at school; and later, of course, when you first moved to Boston. That's right, we have records of what you did at school. The girl's name was Petya. Remember Petya? She's married now, lives on a farm in Jasnogorsk. Fat, I shouldn't wonder, not like the girl she used to be when you fell in love with her. And then there was Charlotte Kane, in Boston. Very pretty, just your type.'

Nadine pressed her hands together in front of her mouth, as if she were thinking deeply, or praying.

Joe said, 'I don't really have to threaten you with a gun, do I? If any of this gets out, Titus' chances of becoming President will evaporate instantly; and any influence *you* ever had in Washington will evaporate, too. It will have to be the biggest female gay scandal since Billie Jean King. Worse. You won't get invited to Girl Scout cookouts any more, let alone White House banquets.'

Nadine turned her face away. She should have realized that Joe Jasper had always been too good, or too slimy, to be true. But the Soviet infiltration of American politics was so complex that often it was impossible to tell if you were talking to an infiltrated Russian or not. Self-mockingly – using the title which had once been given to aristocratic administrators both military and civil in the days before Peter the Great – the infiltrators called themselves *boyars*; and their administration the *boyars' duma*. Percy F Nash, the Comptroller of the Currency, was a *boyar*. So was the Chairman of the Board of Immigration Appeals, Frank Runcie. The Ikon administration had spread across the entire breadth of the United States on many different levels; in twenty years it had penetrated thousands of political and bureaucratic offices like an undetected cancer. Often, the head of a government or local department would be 'straight', a genuine American, unaware of Ikon's control; while his subordinates would all be *boyars*. With particular exceptions, Ikon's policy had been to extend his influence through the executive stratum, rather than try to replace chairmen and presidents and public figures. And it had all been achieved in almost complete secrecy.

Nadine said, 'I suppose I should be grateful that you didn't shoot me straight away; and that your simian friend here didn't manage to inject me.'

'I doubt if Ikon will be pleased,' grinned Joe. 'Come to that, I don't suppose Kama will be very well pleased, either.'

'What should I do now?' asked Nadine.

'Go home, that's all. Apologize to Titus for being so hysterical. Explain that it was all a mistake. Then call me, and tell me that it all went well.'

'You're quite a rat, you know,' said Nadine.

Joe raised his hands, as if in surrender. 'It's the part I play the best. They trained me for four years at Severo-Zadonsk, where Lee Harvey Oswald was trained. You probably would have liked me before.'

'I doubt it,' said Nadine, frostily. 'As you so rightly point out, my real weakness is for other women.'

'Those pictures would fetch a fortune on 42nd Street,' Joe mocked her. *'The Lady and the Tramp.'*

It was only when Joe moved towards her that Nadine realized how Colleen Petley had been edging her way around the bedroom behind him; and how Colleen was now only a foot away from the table where the revolver was lying. She stared at Colleen and her eyes widened; but Colleen gave her a stare in return which defied her to say anything, defied her to do anything but stay where she was. She looked back at Joe, and Joe was just opening up his handkerchief again, his face slightly contorted in preparation for blowing his nose, and every split-second seemed like thunder.

Colleen lifted the Magnum off the table, and raised it up in both hands cocking back the hammer as she did so. She took up the stance of an educated shootist, ignoring the way that her bathwrap fell away and revealed her naked body. Nadine half-lifted her hand; Joe flicked up his eyes and saw the expression on her face; and then the Magnum went off with a bang like a jet airplane breaking the sound barrier, and Joe's pants exploded in a spray of blood and nylon locknit.

Still clutching his handkerchief, shocked, goggle-eyed, Joe looked down at his burst-apart crutch. What remained of his penis dangled by a single shred of flesh; the rest was a crisis of blood and muscle. He said, 'Wha – ' and then Colleen fired again, and this time the bullet walloped into the back of his head, expanding his face for one fraction of a moment as if it were a Joe Jasper party balloon. Then everything blew apart, and he toppled around sideways, leaving a mist of blood in the air, and a blue twist of gunpowder smoke, and bounced dead on to the bed, and then on to the floor.

Colleen threw the gun down beside him. She made no attempt to fasten her wrap. Nadine stared down at the body; then across at Crack Nielsen; then back at Colleen.

'It seems as if *you're* not everything you've been pretending to be, either,' said Nadine.

'Not all Americans are innocent,' said Colleen. She gave a wry, quick smile. 'We've known about Ikon for years.'

'Who *are* you?'

'I'm Colleen Petley, that's all you have to know. I should kill you, too, except that I have specific instructions to make sure that you're safe. Compromised, but safe.'

'Supposing *I* tried to kill *you*? I did, after all, didn't I?'

'Yes,' said Colleen. She ran her hand through her hair, the gesture of somebody who hates what has happened, but has to be resigned to it. 'Yes, I could be dead by now. So could you. But I suppose that both of us are used to taking risks, in our own particular way.'

'You belong to some kind of resistance movement? Is that it?' asked Nadine.

'You could say that.'

'Well, we've always felt that there might be some kind of organized opposition. I mean, it's difficult to tell, this country being so *naturally* violent. But those bombs that were found in Greenwich Village last year – we seriously suspected that *they* were going to be used against Soviet targets.'

Colleen walked around Joe Jasper's body and stood silent for a moment. Then she said, 'We started off as rebels against America. You know that, don't you? Black Panthers, the Weather Underground, the Symbionese Army. We wanted to see an end to capitalism and the absolute death of prejudice. Then we realized that this country we were fighting against wasn't the country we believed it to be. Our Presidents were puppets; our whole way of life was a carefully-preserved sham. And nobody seemed to understand – or if they did understand, to *care*! None of us knows how it happened, or when exactly; but we guess that it was some time in the '60s. And America went on producing *Playboy*, and Cadillacs, and *The Waltons*; but not in the same way as it had before. Something happened in the '60s, and it was like national shock; the same sort of shock that a human body suffers when you shoot a bullet into it. An alien intrusion, you know? Something that sends shudders to every quarter of your body, down to your toes. That intrusion was Ikon. And as soon as we found out what it was all about, we amalgamated ourselves together, Black Panthers and Weather Underground and all, and we made up our minds that you bastards weren't going to get away with it, not easily, anyhow; and that if nobody else was going to carry the torch for liberty, then we would. We call ourselves Free Columbia. You know?'

'You're a terrorist,' said Nadine.

'Of a kind. This is the first time I've ever killed anybody.'

'But all this blackmail business with Marshall Roberts

. . . you don't mean to tell me that it was all planned by *you* . . . by whatever you call yourselves, Free Columbia?'

'We were almost duped ourselves,' said Colleen. She sat down on the end of the bed, well away from Joe's twisted body. 'We had girls going to bed with as many candidates as we possibly could at the last election; and all of their sessions were filmed. The idea was that we would try to blackmail whichever candidate was elected President, and see what kind of response we got; see what defence mechanisms we could flush out into the open; see if any heads popped up that we could shoot at.'

She was silent for what seemed like whole minutes. Then she said, 'I had to set myself as a real Las Vegas hooker. Can you imagine that? I had to invent a background, find myself a pimp, and *be* a hooker. I think it probably wiped me out as far as men are concerned. I think *forever*. That was why I made love with you . . . well, not totally. I did want to put you into a position where you'd be forced to let me go out now and again, so that I could go out and rendezvous with other people from Free Columbia.'

She paused again, and then she said, 'We didn't realize that there was such an internal struggle within the Soviet administration. We didn't know anything about Kama, or the *Peredoviki*. We simply thought that Joe Jasper wanted to get hold of our videotapes and photographs and destroy them, to protect the President. That's what he *said* he wanted to do. We thought we'd be doing nothing more than flushing out a few Soviet infiltrators, so that we could waste them.'

Another pause. Then, 'Kama would be worse than Ikon, wouldn't he? Kama would rip this country apart from top to bottom.'

'That's right, ' said Nadine. 'Kama would be hell. Back to the days of the Terror.'

Colleen looked at her questioningly. 'What are you going to do now? Are you going to try to persuade Titus to let RINC continue?'

'I doubt if he'll listen. I've told him far more than I should have done.'

'But surely he'll take notice of what you're saying if you tell him about the *Peredoviki?*'

'I don't think so.'

Colleen suddenly realized that she had left the gun lying on the carpet, right beside Joe Jasper's body. And she also realized that if Nadine was so deeply pessimistic about her chances of persuading Titus to let RINC go ahead, there was only one positive way left to her to release Titus' grip on Marshall Roberts, and make sure that the disarmament talks went ahead. To kill Titus' principal witness – her. And after all, hadn't Nadine come here this morning with the intention of killing her anyway?

There was a flash of recognition between the two women that was almost electrical, like the crackling current of a Van der Graaf generator. Both of them dived towards the gun at the same time; Nadine snatching the grip, but Colleen slapping it out of her hand so that it tumbled heavily across the room.

They wrestled fiercely on the floor, Nadine twisting Colleen's hair and forcing her head back. But as Nadine tried to reach out again for the gun, Colleen grabbed at her white skirt, and wrenched it, and there was a tearing of cotton and silk lining. Beneath her skirt, Nadine wore nothing but a white lacy garter-belt and white stockings, and Colleen tore her skirt away even further as she rolled her over and pushed her violently against the bed. Colleen scrabbled for the gun now, but Nadine threw herself on top of her, and for minutes on end the two women struggled and scratched and tore at each other. They didn't scream, like women fighting out of jealousy or anger. They both knew that only one of them was going to survive.

Abruptly, Colleen banged her head against the bridge of Nadine's nose. Nadine jerked back in pain, and that moment was all that Colleen needed. She wriggled her naked body out from between the tight clench of Nadine's silk-stockinged thighs, and grasped the gun.

Nadine held on to Colleen's wrist with both hands, keeping the gun in the air. Colleen fired once, and the bullet hit the ceiling and showered them both in stucco. They fought and rolled on to Joe Jasper's body, smothering their arms in his blood; then rolled back again across the white carpet, leaving gory tracks. Gasping, Nadine pressed her head close against Colleen's bare, sweaty breasts, and gritted her teeth, and tried to summon up every last strain of energy

But gradually, in a series of gasping jerks, Colleen brought the gun across her chest so that the muzzle was pointing less than an inch away from Nadine's head. Nadine grunted with strain, but the muzzle was so close now that she could smell the burned gunpowder. She was flooded with the terrifying understanding that she was just about to die.

She did the only thing she could think of. She pushed back against Colleen's gun-wrist as forcefully as possible, and buried her teeth deep into Colleen's nipple. She tasted blood, a sudden mouthful of it, and realized with shock as Colleen screamed that she had actually bitten it right off. There was a brief, bloody wrestle. Nadine wrenched the gun out of Colleen's hand, staggered back from her, and pointed it directly at her head.

Colleen's face was like a mask of herself. She said something like, 'Whatever you do – ' and then Nadine pulled the trigger and Colleen's head exploded like a can of red paint.

Slowly, stiffly, Nadine stood up. She stayed where she was for a while, shivering. Then she walked with dragging feet into the living-room, and sat down on the sofa. Apart from the chambermaid in Nevada, Titus' attempts to blackmail Marshall Roberts were finished; and it was unlikely that the chambermaid's testimony would satisfy a Congressional committee. The videotapes were all here, in the house, in a floor safe which Joe Jasper had arranged to be installed at the same time as Colleen's hot tub.

She reached for the phone beside the sofa, and dialled Ikon's action number. A calm woman's voice answered her, and said, *'How can I help you?'*

'This is V. A matter of utmost urgency. Do you understand that? There's been an incident at the Rockville house. Three down with severe headaches. I need clean-up people, also a locksmith. And the first priority is to call our contacts at the Rockville police to keep them away. Somebody must have heard the firecrackers.'

'Is that all?' asked the woman's voice, unruffled.

Nadine looked down at her blood-smeared hand, and her torn skirt.

'That's all,' she said.

She put down the phone. She sat with her head bent while the clock ticked loudly and cheaply over the fireplace. Then, she began to weep; silent tears at first, followed by deep, agonized sobs.

Twenty-Six

Ikon met Kama at the Smithsonian Institution, in front of the black-painted X-15 aircraft; and they solemnly shook hands. Neither man was alone: there were two dark-suited young bodyguards following Ikon at a discreet but watchful distance; and a man in a grey houndstooth jacket following Kama. Ikon wore a camelhair overcoat, even in the summer heat, and looked heavy and unwell. Kama was leaner, taller, and younger, although his head was completely bald and he wore magnifying spectacles which enlarged his bright blue eyeballs until they looked like those miniature globes which schoolchildren use for pencil-sharpeners.

It was the first time that Ikon had been out for a month, and he was already coughing and labouring for breath. But there was an understanding now that he and Kama could only meet on neutral territory; the rift in the Supervisory Committee was too wide and too intricately stratified for Ikon to be able to assert his authority across it. He had long ago begun to lose his strongest supporters in the Kremlin; either through death, or old age, or political unpopularity; or through desertion. Kama, after all, was the younger and the stronger man. Kama had powerful contacts in the international KGB and the Central Committee. And, what was more, Kama was ferociously dedicated to the idea of publicly announcing that the United States had been overthrown by Russia, almost to the point of obsession. 'The American Capitalist Oblast is *ours*,' he used to repeat. 'It has been ours for twenty years. We should treat it as ours.'

Ikon thrust his hands into his coat pockets and contemplated the black slender shape of the X-15. 'America's first thrust into space,' he said. 'Even before we took over. You have to admire their technology.'

Kama gave a non-committal nod. Ikon was still the titular head of the committee; and Kama wasn't rash enough to disagree with him outright. Kama's whole political career had nearly collapsed in 1961 when he had expressed out loud his support for Khruschev's isolation of China. Even Khruschev had refused to support him; and it was only his friendship with Leonid Brezhnev that had saved him from permanent exile.

The two men walked side by side through the echoing museum. In the next hall, a party of black schoolchildren were giggling and shuffling as their teacher tried to show them around. The light that filtered through the windows had a strangely wintry quality, as if they were back in Moscow.

Kama said, 'It was good of you to come out and meet me here. I thought it more discreet.'

'Occasionally, I can benefit from the exercise,' said Ikon.

Kama gave a tepid smile. 'You're thinking of retiring soon, of course.'

'As soon as I'm convinced that the American Oblast is in capable hands. And as soon as I'm sure that RINC II is near completion.'

Kama said, 'You'll have to forgive me, Nikolai Nekrasov, but I do think that these RINC talks are an unnecessary pretence. I may be naive, of course. You're so much wiser and more experienced. But what *is* the use of them, when no American nuclear warhead is capable of being fired? America is already disarmed. Why make such trouble over nuclear reduction talks?'

Ikon raised one bushy, bear-like eyebrow. 'You have a great deal to learn about social psychology, Comrade Kama. A whole nation cannot be dragged kicking and screaming into a new philosophical age, not without grave repercussions that can last for decades afterwards. The Soviet Union is a classic example. We have *still* to recover from the October revolution morally, or politically, or economically. It will take a hundred years before we do.'

'That sounds remarkably like heresy,' smiled Kama.

'Heresy is usually nothing more than the simple truth,' Ikon retorted.

They jousted and prodded at each other for another ten minutes; and then Ikon suggested they leave the Institution and take a walk outside. He felt trapped, and suffocated, as much by Kama's relentless opportunism as he did by the Smithsonian. They crossed Jefferson Drive and then walked across the grass of The Mall, towards the Washington Monument, while red and white kites flew around them, and traffic nudged and beeped and growled on either side like a herd of impatient cattle.

Kama said, 'You've heard, of course, that Marshall Roberts has decided to *postpone* the RINC talks?'

Ikon checked his watch. Colleen Petley should be dead by now. He had no guarantee of it, of course. Nadine may have run into difficulties with Joe Jasper. But she was an efficient, elegant woman, an extraordinary agent, the very cream of the KGB. There hadn't been a female agent to touch her since Maria Denisova, who had used her sexual abilities to turn the tables against both Churchill and Roosevelt at Yalta, and had later supplied Moscow with some of the most important details of the hydrogen bomb.

Ikon said, 'I believe that the President had some temporary difficulty, yes.'

'Temporary? If RINC II fails to go ahead, the Sovietization of America could be put back for ten years.'

'You exaggerate,' said Ikon. 'Perhaps five.'

'Nikolai Nekrasov, it is essential that the Soviet Union asserts her authority over America *now*. America is still too much of a corrupting influence; American culture is like rabies, driving everybody mad. The whole world will be mad until America is revealed to be subordinate to Moscow – until everybody realizes that political sanity has at last prevailed.'

'You want a national massacre?' asked Ikon, brushing back his windswept hair with his hand.

'Of course not, although a certain amount of spilled blood will be unavoidable. America is full of lunatics who say that they would rather die than let the Soviet Union take over. Better dead than Red. But once most of them perceive the conquest as a *fait accompli* . . . well, I truly don't believe that we will experience half the trouble you seem to think we will. The Americans are a tired nation, Nikolai Nekrasov; the fire has gone out of their veins, and has been replaced by cholesterol. Now they want to do nothing else but sit down in front of their television sets and be left alone.'

Ikon paused. Out of the corner of his eye, he had seen one of his bodyguards begin to walk diagonally towards him across the grass. The man turned away when he was still fifteen or twenty paces distant; and went with exaggerated thoroughness to peer into a pale blue Chrysler which somebody had parked nearby on a red line.

'An American car enthusiast, hunh?' asked Kama, sarcastically. 'Or perhaps he's concerned that somebody might be trying to do to *you* what *you* tried to do to Titus Alexander.'

'An American car enthusiast,' Ikon asserted, without any expression in his voice at all. He didn't tell Kama that the bodyguard's walk towards him was a pre-arranged signal which meant that the bodyguard had received direct news on his walkie-talkie from Rockville. A turn to the left would have meant bad news. A turn to the right had meant that everything was satisfactory, and under control.

Nadine must have been able to kill Colleen Petley. Now the horse was answering to a different driver. Ikon turned to Kama, and he was unable to suppress a grandfatherly smile.

Kama said, 'I came here to suggest that we could come to some arrangement, you and I. The ideological differences between us seem to grow wider every day. But they needn't. You are old, Nikolai Nekrasov, you have to admit your years. And while I am always respectful of age, and the wisdom that comes with it, I believe that you have been neglecting the natural progress of America towards her inevitable acceptance of what she really is: a Soviet possession.'

'Well?' asked Ikon. 'What is your suggestion?'

'I suggest your resignation,' Kama told him. 'You have achieved tremendous things; but it must be time for you to go. The failure of RINC II shows that gradualism is no longer the answer. But, if you agree to resign, I believe that you should be allowed to stay in the American Capitalist Oblast as a figurehead, as a grand old man to whom the American people can turn in their hour of disillusionment and surprise. We can announce you as the man who has personally taken care of the American republic for over twenty years; the man who took on to his shoulders the enormous burden of preparing America for the day when she would have to be told that the Soviet Union has been in effective control of her government since August 6, 1962. Red Monday.'

Ikon carefully adjusted his wide-brimmed hat, and

cleared his throat. 'Is that all?' he asked. 'Is that the sum total of your suggestion? Is that why I got myself dressed this afternoon, and came out to the Smithsonian, instead of taking my usual rest?'

'Nikolai Nekrasov,' said Kama, more sharply now, 'you have no hope of staying in control of the Supervisory Committee once Moscow becomes aware that RINC II has utterly failed. Even the moderates will ask for faster results; and your failure will feed added fuel to those in the Kremlin who have always opposed your chairmanship and who have always opposed gradualism.'

'And that is your offer? That I should let you take over complete control of the Autonomous Capitalist Oblast of America, and become nothing more than a national grandparent? A kind of Socialist Father Christmas?'

Kama grimaced. He had little sense of humour, and no time at all for the trappings of Christianity and other such superstitions. In his youth, he had worked doggedly against the continuing presence in Russia of Roman Catholicism and the Russian Orthodox Church in the conviction that any worship of so-called spiritual beings was a direct denial of the reality of the State.

'Well,' said Ikon, 'I am not sure that I want such a job. I am not sure that I am adequately benign.'

'*Somebody* has to explain what happened, ' Kama insisted. '*Somebody* has to explain how President Kennedy saw that America was defenceless against the missiles on Cuba. *Somebody* has to tell the American people that he had no choice at all but surrender.'

'You are talking of destroying some powerful national myths,' warned Ikon.

'There isn't any *alternative*,' said Kama. 'And besides, I believe that the American people will almost be relieved when they understand how many of their national myths were not myths or mysteries at all; but explicable fact. How long have they fretted over Kennedy's assassination? For twenty years! And after twenty years you will simply be able to tell them the truth: that he tried to go back on his promise of surrender, that he tried to organize a national resistance movement, and that he had to be eliminated to preserve a Socialist peace. The same for his brother, and all those witnesses and other malcontents who knew what had actually happened. Nikolai Nekrasov, you can tell them why they had to go to war in Viet Nam: that it was essential for China's belief in the hostility between America and the Soviet Union. And you can tell them why they lost, and had to withdraw, because it was always intended that they should. You can explain about Nixon . . . how Nixon was the only President ever to try to rebel against the Supervisory Committee, and how Watergate was engineered by the KGB to have him disgraced and ousted. The American people will see you as a great leader, as a great demystifier of everything that has confused and worried them in the past twenty years. Why did President Carter cancel the B-1 bomber? Why did President Reagan run for office as a hawk, and then become such a somnolent dove? Why did Marshall Roberts fight so hard for the RINC talks?'

Ikon listened to Kama with studied politeness. Then he pointed towards a public bench, and said, 'I think I'd like to sit down. Your offer has almost overwhelmed me.'

Kama hesitated, and looked around him. It was a nervousness born of years of political brinkmanship. He sat down, though, and Ikon sat beside him, two men on a seat in the stippled sunlight of a Washington lunchtime; two men who could have been anybody at all; a lawyer and his clerk; a father and his wayward son; an advertising executive and his brightest young copywriter.

The truth was, though, that they were the two most powerful men in the entire Western hemisphere. Between them, they could control the lives and the destinies of nearly a thousand million people.

Ikon took out a Dristan nasal spray and squirted it vigorously up each nostril. 'I have to be careful, ever since they started poisoning Tylenol and God knows what else. It might give somebody on the Supervisory Committee a bright idea.'

'You know that's not the way I want this to be,' said

Kama. 'The old techniques, the killings, that's not the way to run an Oblast like America.'

'We found Marilyn Monroe, you know,' said Ikon, with some satisfaction. 'Twenty years we've been looking for her. Twenty years! And all the time she was living in Arizona.'

'Kolpasev told me. Impressive. That was Henry Friend, wasn't it?'

'Henry Friend, yes. Well, you know it was. You called him back straight away to blow up that unfortunate police chief for you. I sent you a critical memorandum about that. Did you read it?'

'I only used him because he was the best available.'

'Still, it wasn't wise. I considered recommending to Moscow that you shouldn't be permitted to sanction any kind of termination at all.'

'He was the best; and it was essential that her body was taken away as quickly as possible. Friend should have had instructions to remove it before.'

'You really think so?' asked Ikon. His tone was altogether too bland for Kama's liking. He sounded as if he were discussing a rather dull dinner party, instead of violent assassinations and power struggles, and the fate of the entire Oblast of America.

'Of course I think so,' said Kama. 'Supposing the autopsy had revealed that she was Marilyn Monroe?'

'It wouldn't have done. Well, the chances that it would were very slim. It was necessary to remove the head, of course. Dental identification; and the risk that somebody might have recognized her picture if it were published in the newspapers. But all of this cowboys-and-Indians business to snatch her body from the Phoenix morgue. . .'

'I have the authority,' said Kama, coldly.

'Of course. But you also have the *responsibility*. And in my view you deliberately and irresponsibly instructed your agents to run amok in Phoenix in order to stir up trouble. It's a pity for you that the American media are so resolutely dense. Not one single newspaper asked the questions you wanted them to ask: was this police chief's death a conspiracy? If so, who were the conspirators? That was your aim, wasn't it, as it's always been? To have the conquest of America discovered by the media, so that you don't have to explain to Moscow why you personally decided to announce it?'

Ikon adjusted his horn-rimmed spectacles, and looked upwards. An American Airlines jet was turning noisily over the city, its silver body sparkling in the sunlight.

'You have consistently over-reached yourself, Comrade Kama,' said Ikon. 'You have tried again and again to usurp my authority; and again and again to trigger a revelation in the Press that America may not be the democratic country that its inhabitants believe it to be. I have to say that I don't like you at all and that I like your henchmen on the Supervisory Committee almost as little. As for the human rodents your agencies employ to carry out your verminous missions . . . I think the less I say about them, the better. I was given a full report on that bombing in Phoenix, and also on what happened afterwards, when a girl reporter was kidnapped. Those were your men, weren't they? Rats, from the National Security Agency. More fuss, more trouble; more cowboys-and-Indians. Well, Comrade Kama, that is not the way in which a great Oblast can be run. An Oblast is a province of the Union of Soviet Socialist Republics; and in time this Oblast will take its place as one of those Republics. Not as a conglomeration of greedy and misguided capitalists, run by brutal and criminal socialist gangsters; no, not even with me as a figurehead. But as a proud and productive member of a worldwide socialist community; a community which at last can drop all vestiges of war and antagonism, real and pretended, and live in genuine global peace.'

Kama said, 'You're not addressing the Central Committee, Comrade Nekrasov.'

'No,' said Ikon, with some dignity, 'I'm not. I'm addressing *you*.'

Kama stood up, and buttoned his coat. 'A fine speech. You could save some of it for your valedictory address.'

'I'm not resigning,' said Ikon, hoarsely – so hoarsely that Kama scarcely caught what he said.

Kama said, 'What?'

'I said, I'm not resigning. Only death will force me to give up the chairmanship. Certainly not you.'

'Nikolai Nekrasov, RINC II is dead; and that means that *you're* dead.'

Ikon shook his head, so that his jowls wobbled. 'The only person who is dead, Comrade Kama, is Colleen Petley.'

Kama stared at him. A woman walking her poodle caught sight of his grotesque expression, and actually stopped to gawp. 'Are you all right, sir?' she asked Kama, and when he failed to answer, she touched Ikon on the shoulder and said, 'Is your friend all right?'

Ikon smiled out of one side of his mouth. 'He's very well, thank you. Better than most. He's just . . . meditating.'

The woman stared at Kama for a few moments more, and then said, 'If that's meditating, Jesus.'

Kama said, 'You'd better be joking, Nikolai Nekrasov.'

Ikon shook his head again. 'No jokes, Comrade Kama. Colleen Petley is dead.'

'There are tapes. Videotapes.'

'I have all of them.'

'Nadiana Voroshilova,' said Kama.

'Well, you could be right,' agreed Ikon.

'Nadiana Voroshilova,' Kama repeated, with such hysterical annoyance that he was almost laughing.'Nadiana Voroshilova!'

'It was your gamble, Comrade Kama. You wanted to twist Nadiana into your little blackmail too, I suppose? Well, you took the gamble, and you lost. Nadiana is no amateur. Neither am I. I'm sorry for you. Sorrow is a good Russian emotion. Here, take my hand if you want to. Sob on my shoulder. But whatever you do, believe me, RINC II will go ahead. And after RINC II is completed, there will be trade agreements, and increasing détente, and in the fullness of time, a great socialist amalgamation.'

'Nadiana Voroshilova,' whispered Kama.

Ikon coughed, and coughed again. 'I have to get back to Pennsylvania Avenue,' he said. 'I like a little fresh air . . . but not too much.'

Kama ignored him, and pressed his hand to his forehead. He was doing his best to keep himself under control, to suppress his anger. Tonight, he would go back to his apartment in Arlington and drink himself into a blind stupor with Polish Pure Spirit. Then he would probably break something; a vase, a table, a set of glasses. Not hysterically, but with all the frigid calculated fury of a man who cannot bear to be bested. His maid would sweep up.

He closed his eyes; and when he opened them again, Ikon had gone.

Twenty-Seven

Lieutenant Lindblad said, 'Somebody called me on August 1, 1962, that was the Wednesday previous to the Sunday that Marilyn was supposed to have died. They said they represented the White House and they required some local assistance in a difficult situation.'

'Did you believe them?' asked Kathy.

'I don't know. I guess I *half*-believed them. The Kennedys had been buzzing in and out of Los Angeles quite a lot in those days, so it wasn't a total surprise.'

'Why did they call *you*, in particular? Surely there were plenty of superior officers who could have helped them better.'

'I never really found out. I was young then, newly promoted; and I'd had my picture in the papers a couple of times. I guess the Kennedys just thought that I was their style. They were anxious they didn't make too many waves, too, and I guess that a superior officer would have felt himself obliged to report the matter higher on up, to the Commissioner, or the Mayor. That was the last thing they wanted.'

Daniel stayed by the window while Lieutenant Lindblad talked. The smog that had blurred Los Angeles for most of the day had thickened again, without clearing, and the sun was hovering over the Santa Monica Mountains like the dying crimson fireball of an exploded nuclear bomb. There was a strange sense of doom about the landscape: tacky Spanish-style houses, forested with TV antennae, under a sky like something by William Blake. Children played in the surrounding yards, and their cries of laughter could just as easily have been cries of desperation.

Lieutenant Lindblad drank more beer and gave himself a white foam moustache. 'They told me that it was essential that I should meet their representative at The Brown Derby on Thursday night. I said that wasn't a particularly clever place to meet, because by 1962 The Brown Derby wasn't a fashionable place to eat any more, and the chances were that me and this representative would be the only people there. So in the end they agreed on Dino's, on Sunset. At least it was dark.'

He caught sight of his wife in the doorway, and gave her another little wave, and cooed, 'It's okay, sugar, I won't be long.' Then he turned back to Kathy and said, 'You can imagine what I felt when this representative turned out to be Bobby Kennedy himself. There was one other guy there, but he didn't look too smart, and I guessed he was just a bodyguard. He didn't say anything, anyway.'

'What did Bobby Kennedy say to you? Did he seem worried?'

'Worried? The guy was jumping all over the place. He couldn't sit still for a second. He said that *a certain lady*

300

movie star, who was a friend of his, was having some trouble. Her life was in danger, he said, and it was vital that she disappear.

'I said, well, that wouldn't be too hard to arrange, but then Bobby Kennedy said that one of his aides had noticed in one of the movie magazines a girl who looked exactly like this certain lady movie star, and asked if it wouldn't be possible for the two of them to switch rôles. He said the idea was that the certain lady movie star would be spirited away and settled someplace out of town; while the look-alike girl would be spirited into the certain lady movie star's house, given a slight overdose of barbiturate drugs, and then rescued in a blaze of publicity which would establish that the certain lady movie star was still around, and still in town, but which would also give her an excuse to go into a clinic, maybe the Payne-Whitney, where she would be guarded well enough, you understand, but where she would keep any hostile attention away from the certain lady movie star herself.

'All the time, I knew he was talking about Monroe. Well, that wasn't no secret. But, I let him say "certain lady movie star" all through the conversation and I didn't argue. Well, for Christ's sake, he *was* the Attorney General. But I did ask what kind of justification he might have for exposing an innocent young girl to the sort of danger he was so anxious that his certain lady movie star shouldn't be exposed to. And he said, it was a difficult decision, but in the end it all came down to a question of national security. In the larger view, that's what he said, the whole of America was at risk.'

Daniel asked, 'Did he say any more? Did he explain what he meant by that?'

'No, sir,' said Lieutenant Lindblad. 'He took one more drink and then he left.'

'How much did he agree to pay you?'

'I didn't ask for money.'

'What did you ask for?'

'This house, that's all. A nice house in Brentwood. And

301

I asked him to fix it so that people would believe I was willed it. An old uncle of mine, that was the story.'

'You found the girl?' asked Kathy.

'Sure. Vera Rutledge. I'd seen her myself, in *Fotoplay*, something like that. Very pretty girl. Prettier than Monroe, if you ask me. Fresher. Didn't look like she'd been living on Nembutals.'

Kathy took off her spectacles and folded them up. 'Did you have any inkling at all that Vera Rutledge might be killed? There had to be a risk, after all, if they were going to give her an overdose.'

Lieutenant Lindblad gave a non-committal shrug of his shoulders. 'I wasn't particularly *impressed* by what they were trying to do. It seemed kind of amateurish, to tell you the truth. But, like I said, he *was* the Attorney General, and I did believe that he knew what he was doing. If you want my opinion, I still think he knew what he was doing, even when Vera Rutledge died. They told me that girl would be ready for rescuing round about four o'clock in the morning, without any danger at all. But they made sure that plenty of other people got around there first; people who would be independent witnesses. Mrs Murray was round there at three in the morning; then Dr Greenson; then Dr Engelberg. By the time the police arrived it was all over. She was long dead.'

Kathy said carefully, 'Marilyn Monroe made some telephone calls on her last night alive . . . I mean on Vera Rutledge's last night alive. But not many people ever admitted receiving them, and the FBI removed the taped record of calls from the Santa Monica telephone company. Have you any explanation for that?'

Lieutenant Lindblad said, 'I know for sure that the arrangement was for the real Marilyn Monroe to telephone a few people she knew, and act like she was fuzzy and sick, and going over the line from too many pills. But of course she wasn't actually calling from Brentwood, she was calling long-distance from San Diego, which is the first place they sent her to; and the telephone company's tape would have shown that no calls came from the Brentwood number to coincide with any of these San Diego calls. That's why the FBI had to collar the tape as quickly as they could, before some smartass reporter got to it.'

'Didn't anybody – ambulancemen, or doctors, anybody like that – didn't anybody recognize that this girl *wasn't* Monroe? She was quite a few years younger, after all.'

'The whole thing was rushed, on purpose, so that nobody got more than a glimpse. As far as the autopsy was concerned . . . I really don't know. My guess is that the medical examiners were looking for cause of death, in the belief that the body had already been satisfactorily identified. I really don't know for sure. Once it was out of my hands, it was out of my hands.'

They left Lieutenant Lindblad's house twenty minutes later, and drove westwards, looping around by the Will Rogers State Historical Park, and at last reaching the ocean. Daniel parked the Monaco by the side of the highway, and they took off their shoes and walked along the grey sandy beach for a while, with the Pacific seething beside them, and the unearthly twilight of a smoggy Los Angeles summer all around.

'What do you think?' asked Daniel.

'I don't know,' said Kathy. 'I guess it reinforces my Cuban theory in one way. I mean, I think it's obvious now that Bobby Kennedy really did have Marilyn Monroe smuggled out of Hollywood to save her life; and if she was prepared to agree to give up her whole career and everything, just for the sake of survival, then whoever was threatening her must have been pretty damned threatening. Well – they ended up cutting her head off, didn't they? But there still aren't any facts about Cuba or the Kennedys to get my teeth into.'

'I would have thought Skellett's behaviour was enough.'

'Skellett might be nothing more than a lone crackpot. I don't think that he actually *is*, but he could be; and we don't have any way of proving that he isn't.'

'Did you have any more luck with the National Security Agency?' asked Daniel.

303

'Unh-hunh. Wall of silence time. ''We regret that in the interests of national security we are unable to respond to your enquiries at this moment in time.'' '

Daniel stood by the shoreline, his bare toes dimpling the sand, his hands thrust into the pockets of his khaki slacks. 'What do we do now? Who else do we talk to? Or do we just give up, and throw in the towel, and go back home?'

'Is that what you want to do?'

He turned and looked at her, and then shook his head. 'Home isn't home without Susie.'

'How about Cara?'

'Cara came like all the rest of them. Pretty, footloose, sweet and kind. She went the same way. I called the hospital this morning and they said she'd discharged herself. No forwarding address.'

'I'm sorry,' said Kathy. 'You didn't tell me.'

'There wasn't any need, was there, really? They come and they go. Susie's mother was just like that. It doesn't stop you liking them; it doesn't stop you loving them sometimes. But it stops you crying over them, when they're gone.'

They walked back to the car. A few yards further along the Pacific Coast Highway, sitting on a large backpack, was a suntanned young man of about 27, good-looking in a way that Daniel could only think of as prematurely battered, drinking a can of Tab. He wore *lederhosen*, with a halter front, and a green check short-sleeved shirt, and large grubby sneakers.

'Hey, sir!' he called, as Daniel opened the door of the car. 'Pardon me, sir!'

Daniel paused, and looked at him over the roof of the car. The young man hopped to his feet, disentangling his sneakers from the strap of his backpack, and said, 'You don't happen to be heading towards Hollywood? Well, I know you're pointing south, but the way you walked on the beach, I wondered if you were heading back east.'

'You're on a north-south highway and you want a ride *east*?'

The young man sheepishly rubbed at the back of his neck. 'Actually, I was trying to thumb a ride north, to Santa Barbara. I had a row with my girl this afternoon, and she sort of threw me out. I was going back home to see my parents. Now I've been sitting here for two hours without getting a ride and I've kind of cooled towards it, you know? I was thinking of going back to Hollywood and looking up this other girl I know.'

'Indecisive, huh?' asked Kathy.

The young man nodded. 'I guess you could say that. Mind you, it doesn't take a lot to change my mind about going home to see my folks. They're very heavily into Roche-Bobois furniture and Cy Twombly graphics.'

Daniel reached into the car and pressed the trunk-release button. 'Get in,' he told the young man. 'We can take you as far as Doheny.'

On the way back along Sunset, the young man leaned forward and folded his arms on the front seats and told them all about his girlfriend. 'She's from weird, you know? I guess most Hollywood ladies are. Very beautiful. Excellent. But really from weird. Ever since she found out that Halley's Comet was on the way back, she's started getting these *feelings*. She thinks the comet's going to fly past the Earth just to investigate *her*.'

'Maybe she's right,' said Daniel. 'You mustn't underestimate the importance of the individual.'

'Hey,' frowned the young man. '*You're* not into that stuff too, are you?'

'I'm beginning to feel that I might be.'

The young man looked towards Kathy, and said, 'Is your husband feeling okay, ma'am?'

'He's not my husband. But, sure, yes, he's feeling all right.'

The young man suddenly stuck out his hand. 'I didn't introduce myself. What an airhead. My name's Rick Terroni. You've seen me a hundred times before, on the movies. And television. Pratfaller Extraordinaire, that's how I advertise myself. That's a specialist kind of a stuntman, like I make my living falling on my ass. Somebody

305

gets pushed over, hit by a car, kicked by a horse, sits on a collapsing deckchair, slips on a squashed tomato, that's what I do. You ever see that movie where Ryan O'Neal walks up those steps and then slides on all of those marbles? That was me, doing the sliding. Let's face it, Ryan O'Neal doesn't want to walk around for the rest of the week with a multi-coloured ass.'

'Pleased to know you,' said Daniel.

They drove in silence for a while, past the gates of Bel Air, and then Rick Terroni said, 'You guys seem kind of down. Is that impolite of me to say so? Is there a bereavement in the family? You're coming back from a funeral?'

Daniel said, 'It's nothing, okay?'

'If you say so. It's just that I've got a nose for misery.'

'A nose for misery?' asked Kathy. 'What kind of a self-commendation is that?'

'Did I say it was a self-commendation?'

Daniel pulled up at Doheny, with an unnecessarily violent jerk on the brakes. 'That's it, then,' he said. 'You're back in Hollywood.'

Rick peered out of the Monaco's window. 'Hm,' he said, 'Doheny Drive.'

'That's where I told you, Doheny.'

'You can't take me any further?'

'Unh-hunh. That is it.'

Rick took a breath. 'Listen,' he said, 'the real truth is that I don't have anyplace to go.'

'You want a home, as well as a ride?' asked Daniel.

'I didn't say that,' Rick protested. 'If you want me to get out, I'll get out.'

'Daniel,' said Kathy, 'He's not a *bum*. Come on, we can give him one square meal and floorspace for tonight. The *Flag* will pay for it. Hell, the *Flag's* paying for this car, *and* for you. So you and he are just about equals, when you think about it. Two bums together.'

Daniel turned around to Rick with a smile that would have soured cream. 'You'll have to excuse my wife,' he said, as he pulled out into the traffic of Sunset Boulevard again. At the moment, he didn't particularly care, one way or the other. He didn't even know why he was here. He should be in Arizona, taking care of Cara and waiting for news of Susie. Two days ago, following Kathy Forbes to Hollywood had seemed like the only positive thing he could do. But now he was beginning to feel that it was a terrible dead end, a news story that never was, the tearful parent interviewed on the evening news bulletin, 'If I'd known what those animals were doing to my daughter. . . .'

He made a squealing left into Sunset Plaza, narrowly avoiding an oncoming truck, and pulled up beside their rented house. Kathy touched his arm, and said, 'Are you all right?'

He stared at her. He felt as if his eyelids would never close again. 'Yes, sure, I'm all right. A little tired, maybe.'

Rick Terroni said, 'Listen, if you guys are into something that's none of my business . . . I mean, I feel like I'm interfering or something like that . . . I can easily find someplace to sleep. . . .'

Kathy said, 'Do your parents really live in Santa Barbara?'

'Sure they do.'

'And do they really have Roche-Bobois furniture and prints by Cy Twombly?'

Rick looked away; at a huge billboard of Olivia Newton-John. 'Well, not precisely. But they'd like to. That's if they knew what it was. I saw it in *Architectural Digest* while I was waiting at the dentist.'

'When was the last time you worked? In movies, I mean, or in television?'

'Couple of months ago. I doubled for Keiller Pierce in *Nightmare II*. He had to fall off a balcony. He looked over that balcony, you know, down at the ground where he was supposed to fall, and he said, "If you think I'm going to jump down there, you've got to be fucking joking." And the director said, "Keiller, it's cinchy," and gave him a shove, and Keiller toppled right off that balcony and broke both of his ankles, and the picture was held up for seven months while he learned how to walk all over again.

So that's why, when it came to the balcony scene, they made *me* do it.'

'And that was the last job you had?'

'I'm shortlisted for *Son of Cannon*. That's a new TV detective series, with this young fat guy. Well, plump.'

Kathy shook her head, and smiled at him. 'Come on,' she said, 'Daniel will fix you some of his special fried shrimp. Daniel runs a restaurant, you know. He's a genius when it comes to cooking.'

'Cooking is a substitute for oral sex, didn't you know that?' said Daniel.

'I thought it was the other way around,' said Rick. 'I thought oral sex was a substitute for cooking.'

They went into the house, Rick carrying his backpack slung over his shoulder. It was a typical rented Hollywood house: with a Spanish-style sitting-room with dark polished floortiles, a fitted kitchen, and off-white bedroom rugs that had probably been white when they were new.

'It's not the Wilshire House,' said Daniel.

'Who cares? As long as it's not the Y.'

Kathy said, '*Daniel*.' There was a warning in her voice which immediately made Daniel freeze.

'What is it?'

'Someone's been in here. Look. The garden door's been broken open. I left it locked.'

Daniel felt a chill sensation of sudden alarm. He moved quickly and quietly past Kathy, and checked the bedroom; then the bathroom, kicking the door open with his foot. The house was empty, but there was no question that during the afternoon someone had intruded here. Rick stayed where he was, in the hallway, his pack by his feet, looking puzzled and anxious.

'Are you sure you guys really want me around? I don't mind leaving if I'm getting in your way.'

'It's all right,' said Daniel. 'At least, I *think* it's all right.'

'There couldn't be a bomb anywhere, could there?' asked Kathy.

'A *bomb*?' asked Rick. 'You're not the men from UNCLE are you?'

'I'm not a man from anywhere,' said Kathy.

'Jesus,' said Rick. 'I think I'm beginning to wish I was back on the Pacific Coast Highway.'

'Have a beer and settle down,' said Daniel. 'They're in the icebox.'

Rick opened the icebox and took out a six-pack of Coors.

'At least the icebox isn't booby-trapped,' said Kathy.

Rick stared at her. '*Supposing it had been?*'

Daniel shrugged.

They found the letter in the sitting-room, on the table beside the sofa. It was neatly addressed to *D Korvitz*, in green fibre-tipped pen. Kathy said, 'You think you should touch it? Maybe it's got fingerprints on it.' Daniel ignored her, and tore it open.

In the same green handwriting, the letter said simply, 'Dear Mr Korvitz. We are now in Los Angeles, and we have your daughter with us. We have some serious business to discuss with you, and we would like to meet you personally. If you come to the multi-storey parking lot on Santa Monica Boulevard at Wilcox at 9.15 a.m. tomorrow morning, we will return your daughter and take you with us to a suitable locale for more extensive talks.'

Daniel's hand was shaking as he read the letter. When he had finished, he handed it to Kathy without a word.

'You know what they meant by wanting to discuss *business* with me, don't you?' he asked.

Kathy folded up the letter, and laid a hand on his arm. 'They want to kill you, Daniel, I'm sure of it. You can't possibly go.'

'And Susie?'

'I don't know. I don't know what to say. Maybe it's time we called the police.'

'They probably *are* the police, if what you're saying about Cuba has any truth in it.'

'So what are you going to do?' Kathy demanded. 'Give yourself up like a cow going to the cannery? What's the point of Susie going free if they kill you? Who's going to look after her?'

'She's got a mother.'

'Oh, stop trying to be so ridiculously heroic.'

Daniel snatched the letter away from her. 'Damn it, it's nothing to do with heroism, Kathy. She's my little girl. I've brought her up day by day from the time she was tiny. She's seven years old, and God knows what those bastards have been doing to her. Think what they did to you. Besides, they probably don't want to kill me. Just frighten me off.'

'Daniel,' Kathy retorted, 'if you were them, and you knew that somebody had discovered everything about the killings you'd been doing; and why you'd done them; what the hell would you do?'

'I'm still going,' Daniel insisted. His fear and anger about Susie were almost overwhelming. He felt like shouting at Kathy, except that none of it was Kathy's fault. By God, if those animals had so much as laid one finger on Susie . . . But all he could think of was Susie's face, bruised from repeated beatings; and Susie's body, raped by foul-smelling men.

'Daniel,' said Kathy. Then, when he turned away, 'Daniel. There has to be some other kind of answer.'

'I can't think of one, can you? What's the choice? Either Susie dies or else I take my chances. Come on, Kathy, I'm older than Susie. At least I've got the strength and the experience to protect myself. She's just a seven-year-old kid who's never known anything but friendly smiling people.'

'Daniel –'

'You can't change my mind! Don't try!'

Kathy rubbed her eyes in tension and tiredness. Daniel screwed off the cap of a bottle of Coors, and poured it out, too quickly, so that the glass was filled to the brim with foam. 'Shit,' he said, but drank it all the same.

Rick said, 'I honestly feel like I'm intruding or something.'

'You're not intruding,' said Daniel. 'Just shut up and find yourself someplace to crash down.'

'I don't mean to be presumptuous or anything,' said

Rick, 'but it seems like you've got some kind of real gnarly problem going on here. Maybe I could help.'

'Have you ever seen anybody killed?' asked Daniel.

'Only by accident. One stuntman I knew, got smashed up in a car crash when they were shooting *The Kings of Ozark.*'

Daniel finished his foamy beer, and poured himself some more. Rick watched him expectantly. 'Let me tell you something,' said Daniel. 'Tomorrow morning at a quarter after nine I'm supposed to go to a multi-level parking-lot on Santa Monica Boulevard and surrender myself to one or more known killers in exchange for my seven-year-old daughter Susie, who was kidnapped in Arizona last week. The possibility is that the killers will seek to widen their expertise by killing me, too.'

'Are you kidding?' asked Rick. 'Is this *Candid Camera* or something?'

'It doesn't matter to you whether I'm kidding or not,' Daniel told him. 'You don't have to be there. You don't have to worry about any of us. So why don't you just unpack your bag, make yourself comfortable, and keep your mouth shut. What you don't know about won't hurt you.'

Rick pushed his hands into the tight pockets of his *lederhosen.* 'Is that the parking lot at Seward, or the parking lot at Wilcox?'

'Wilcox. Why?'

'Well . . . this is only a thought . . . but a friend of mine got spaced out one day when he was driving into the Wilcox parking-lot, and he drove right through the railings between Level 3 and the roof of the building next door to the parking lot, and that's where he ended up, parked on the roof.'

'What the hell does that have to do with anything?' asked Daniel.

'Well, just hold up a minute; what my friend said was that anybody who might have had a mind to could have driven clear across the roof, and clear across the roof of the next building, as far as Cole.'

Kathy said tautly, 'I still don't understand what you're saying.'

'Well, is this real, what you're telling me, or are you making a movie?' asked Rick. He bit his lip, and his eyes flicked from Daniel to Kathy, and back to Daniel. 'I mean, is it *real*?'

'Supposing it were?' asked Kathy.

'Well, if it's real . . . if you've really got to come face-to-face with some killers in the Wilcox Avenue parking lot, then you've got to plan it like a movie stunt, you know? Plan it first. I'm always looking for good stunt locations, and this place is one of them. I mean, you could snatch your daughter back, right, and then drive up the ramp instead of out of the parking lot – which is the way they'd normally expect you to go – and right through the railings and over the next-door rooftops. Then you could leap out of the car and get away while these killers are still fooling around wondering which level you're on.'

'You're nuts,' said Kathy.

'But it's what people do in the movies. For Christ's sake. And if they can do it in the movies, why can't you do it for real?'

Daniel set down his glass, and looked at Rick thoughtfully. At last, he said, 'Let's go down to Wilcox, and see what this parking lot looks like. Maybe you're right. Maybe we do have a chance. You said, drive across the rooftops?'

'That's right. You might knock over a couple of ventilation stacks, but nothing worse than that. You see what I'm trying to say to you, don't you? You could snatch your daughter back and get away yourself, if you planned it properly. I can tell you something, all of the stunts we do for the movies are planned like clockwork. We could be in and out of that place in six seconds flat, and nobody would scarcely know we'd been there.'

'We?'

'You don't think you're going to leave me out of this, do you? Besides, I don't have anyplace else to stay.'

312

Daniel looked down at his empty glass. *'Melech Ham'lo-chim,'* he said, under his breath.

Twenty-Eight

The same afternoon, Titus left the State Department and drove in his own Porsche down to Bolling Air Force Base in Virginia, wearing dark sunglasses and a white fishing hat in the hope that nobody would recognize him. The sentry outside Bolling had already been alerted to let him through without stopping him, and he was waved by a white-gloved MP towards the outer perimeter road, past rows of giant C-141 Starlifters, and all the organized confusion of Jeeps and ammunition boxes and half-tracked vehicles that were the hallmark of a Military Airlift Command base.

General Caulfield's shiny black Lincoln was parked under the shade of a large Virginia oak, not far from the perimeter fence. General Caulfield himself was standing nearby with his hands on his hips, watching a C-5A transport taxi around to the main runway in preparation for take-off. The noise and the heat came in waves.

'How are you keeping, Pierce?' asked Titus, as he slammed the door of his car and came walking across with his white fishing hat held in his hands.

'I'm well,' said General Caulfield. He had a relentlessly short military haircut which gave him the appearance of a 55-year-old boy. 'I haven't had too much time for fishing lately; but I guess we all have our crosses to bear.'

'Fishing is the least of my worries right now,' said Titus.

'Well, I guess. It shook me, when I was first told about it. I couldn't believe my own ears. It depressed me, I can tell you. It does, when you first understand that everything you ever fought for, everything you ever believed in, your flag, your country, it's all been taken away from you and you never knew.'

'Then it's true,' said Titus. He looked at Pierce Caulfield narrowly, his head slightly angled to one side, as if he were challenging the general to deny everything; to admit that Ikon was all an impossible joke.

Pierce Caulfield watched the C-5A thundering up from the runway, one of the largest aircraft in the world, capable of carrying 125,000 lbs for 8,000 miles. Then he turned to Titus, and said, crisply, 'Yes, it's true. The United States has been administered by the Soviet Union since the summer of 1962. And one of the very first things the Soviets did was to ensure that the American forces could no longer effectively threaten the Soviet Union.'

'But why didn't they simply dismantle the US forces? Surely that would have been easier than all this elaborate pretence?'

'They weren't stupid,' said Pierce. 'They knew that in spite of the nuclear edge they had managed to win over us, it would still be touch and go if they tried to take us over by brute force. I don't know all of the details; I wasn't privy to what was going on at the time. In fact, I personally wasn't told until 1974, nearly twelve years later. But, as far as I can gather, they decided to convert us to Communism over a very long period of time; to break us down, socially and morally, politically and economically, until at last we would consider that Communism was the only option left open to us, and we would consider that amalgamating with the Soviet Union was the only sensible answer.'

'You have to be kidding,' said Titus.

Pierce shook his head. 'I think that they were far too optimistic about the time that it would take for the American people to be converted to international socialism. I believe that Ikon's been having some trouble over that with the Kremlin. But the deliberate destruction of the US economy seems to have gone according to plan; and there's no question that it's brought with it all the social disillusionment that Russia expected.'

Titus stood with his head lowered while Pierce Caulfield shaded his eyes and followed the flight-path of the C-5A as it turned around and headed west. 'That's a magnificent airplane, you know that? An amazing technical achievement. Do you know how much that airplane weighs? Over 325,000 lbs, empty. They had some difficulty with wing fatigue, but they've solved it now. That's one of the reasons the Soviets didn't want to tamper too much with America as she was. They recognized our technical expertise, they recognized our educational advancement, they saw us as leaders in almost every field of sophisticated life. It would have been absurd and wasteful of them to throw our space programme away; or take our armed forces to pieces. What was the point, when they could infiltrate enough of their own officers into US military ranks to ensure that our key defences were useless; and that none of our major weapons would ever work? All that our Distant Early Warning stations do these days is to monitor air traffic, for the express benefit of Aeroflot and the Soviet forces. There's no threat from the Soviet Union any more, there hasn't been for twenty years. It's no good fearing the coming conflict; it's all over, and all of us here in America are nothing more than prisoners of war.'

'But our missiles – ' said Titus. 'Our troops, our airplanes . . . We've just ordered a new *tank*, damn it!'

'I know,' said Pierce, with great calmness. 'I know how you must be feeling. I wondered when I first found out if I ought to kill myself; I even considered launching a one-man suicide mission against the Kremlin. But, in the end, it was strangely reassuring to know that everything that had happened in American life over the past twenty years was *planned*, that America's recent moral decay was not our fault. The sexual revolution was planned; the widespread introduction of addictive and hallucinogenic drugs was planned; so was large-scale birth control in order to keep the American population under control.

Every major national trend – from student uprisings to EST to jogging to conservative chic – was a part of a carefully-devised socio-psychological scheme to make Americans more uncertain of their future, more critical of their past. Thus, when Ikon considers that the time is right, the new golden age of socialism will be announced. A full détente between America and the Soviet Union will form the basis for a 'proletarian amalgamation'. In five or ten years' time, we'll all be drinking vodka and singing *The Red Flag*.'

'But how did they do it? How did they do it without anybody finding *out*?' demanded Titus.

'A great many people *did* find out. Some have been killed. Others have decided that it is probably safer to keep quiet. Like me. They summoned me up to the Pentagon one September morning and said that they were going to tell me something I wouldn't much like; but that if I didn't help them, my sons and daughters and wife would all be murdered. So you can see that I didn't really have very much choice, did I? I was personally to ensure that all Minutemen missiles were safe, by which they meant that not one of them was to carry a warhead that actually worked. The delivery systems are still functional; and Boeings are still carrying out research on new warheads. But they will never be used against the Soviet Union. If they are ever re-activated and used against anybody at all, it will be the Chinese. We have to be quite clear of this, Titus. Ever since Khruschev called up Kennedy and said that there were dozens of long-range nuclear missiles on Cuba, all aimed toward the American heartland, Kennedy didn't have any choice. Kennedy surrendered, and then to keep the world on an even political keel he and Khruschev decided between them to make it appear that Khruschev had stood down, and agreed to withdraw the missiles. I guess it was surprising that nobody realized what had actually happened at the time. I suppose we were all too relieved. But that was the *only* occasion on which Khruschev ever appeared to back down. Backing down just wasn't in his character. Here, come into the car, let me show you something. I expect you could use a drink, too.'

The two old friends sat in the back of the Lincoln limousine, and closed the doors. Pierce let down the walnut cocktail table, and poured them each a large glassful of Wild Turkey. Then he produced a brown envelope, with a HIGHLY SECRET label on it, and shook out two or three old but still glossy photographs.

'These are the pictures we *didn't* release to the media, the day that the Russians supposedly started shipping their missiles back to the Soviet Union.'

Titus picked them up, and frowned at them quickly. 'What am I looking at?' he wanted to know. 'They look just the same as any other picture to me. Missile tubes on the decks of Russian freighters.'

'Ah, but you look here. The airplane taking the picture has flown quite low. *Too* low, as it turns out. You can see quite clearly that the nearest missile container, on the port side of the deck, is *hollow*. The sun's shining through it. You see here, where the sun falls on the bulkhead? These missile tubes are nothing but shams. Cuba is still bristling with strategic nuclear missiles and always will be.'

Titus sipped his whiskey, and then sat back in his seat and looked at Pierce with an expression that was half-defeat, half-resentment.

'Why didn't you tell me, Pierce? All these years, and I never even guessed. Jesus, Pierce, I was in *charge* of most of those weapons. It never once occurred to me that there was anything wrong with them. Blind faith, I suppose. Blind stupidity.'

'You weren't to know, Titus. It wasn't the ordinary kind of sabotage. It was a massive and systematic programme of secret disarmament, carried out by experts who weren't afraid to use maximum force. I know for a fact that at least a hundred service-men have been killed over the years for trying to disclose secret information to the media. And quite a few of the media people have found themselves being blackmailed or threatened. One reporter who was working on a nuclear disarmament story for the

317

Reader's Digest was found in his car at the bottom of Chincoteague Bay. It's quite possible that if anyone finds out what I've been saying to you, then *I'll* be at serious risk, too. But when you called me this morning, I couldn't very well fob you off. It's time you knew. I just hope that you'll be able to face up to the implications of it.'

'It means I'm a captive,' said Titus, in a throaty voice. 'It means I'm not free any more.'

'You haven't been free for twenty years.'

'But, damn it, Pierce, now I *know* it! Last week I was the happy idiot who didn't realize that he was locked up in a cage; now I can feel the bars.'

Pierce laid a hand on his arm. 'I don't want you to rush off and do anything *rash*, Titus. You'll be putting a whole lot of people at risk, including me and my family. Just go home tonight and think about it, and then decide what you're going to do. That's if you're going to do anything at all. Meet me tomorrow if you can around the same time, on the shoreline at Windmill Point.'

Titus finished the rest of his whiskey with one grimacing swallow. Then he climbed out of the Lincoln and walked back towards his Porsche, tugging his fishing hat on to his head as he did so.

'Remember what Kennedy once said,' Pierce called after him. 'The basic problems facing the world today are not susceptible to a military solution.'

Titus stopped, and turned around. 'That was after the option of a military solution was no longer available to him,' he snapped. 'That was after he had already sold us out.'

Pierce said something in reply, but his voice was drowned by the enormous thunder of another C-5A Galaxy, coming in to land from the west. Its shadow passed over them both like the shadow of history; a history which filled them both with fear, and which neither of them would ever be able to influence again.

Twenty-Nine

Lieutenant Berridge was out jogging with his wife Stella on the banks of the Arizona Canal. It was just six o'clock in the morning; still cool; and the slowly-rippling waters of the Indian-built canal reflected the freshly-risen sun and the overhanging leaves of the willows. They crossed the canal by the bridge which leads into the Biltmore Hotel, and turned west through the groves of orange trees, their professional running-shoes slapping on the blacktop, their Lacoste jogging suits stained down the back with sweat.

'This kidnap case isn't doing anything for my running,' protested Lieutenant Berridge. 'I'm exhausted.'

'I'm not surprised,' said Stella. Her blonde hair bounced as she ran. 'That's two nights straight without any sleep. Can't you leave it to Mulligan?'

'Not yet. Not until I find out what the hell it's all about.'

'Supposing you never do? They could have taken the girl and killed her and buried her in the desert and who would ever know?'

'*I* would know. *Me*. I have an instinct for abductions like that. But I think this girl is still alive. What's more, I think that what's-his-name – what's-his-name? – Daniel Korvitz, knows something that we don't. You know? I think he's holding something back. Because why else would he fly off to LA with that Kathy Forbes girl from the *Flag*?'

'Maybe they're in love,' said Stella.

'In love? Nobody would fancy that blue-stocking.'

'Oh, no? I thought she looked quite pretty in her photograph.'

'She's average, that's all.'

Stella dug at his ribs with her elbow. 'Whenever you say that a girl is "average, that's all" that means that you fancy her like all hell. Wolfman Berridge is on the prowl again. Thank God she's gone off to the Coast.'

They had almost reached 24th Street, although they were still screened from the main road by a right-hand curve and a thicket of orange trees. Without any warning, a pale-blue Thunderbird came rolling out of a side-turning and stopped just in front of them, wallowing on its suspension. Lieutenant Berridge broke his jogging rhythm and slowed down, catching at Stella's arm to slow her down, too. The Thunderbird stayed where it was, right on the corner, its engine running and its driver silhouetted in the shadowy interior.

'Something wrong?' Stella asked Lieutenant Berridge.

'I don't think so,' said Lieutenant Berridge cautiously, but slowed right down to a walk. He circled around the front of the Thunderbird and approached the driver's window. With the whine of a tired electric motor, the window was lowered. The numbered sticker on the car's windshield informed Lieutenant Berridge at once that this was a rental car; and the first thing he saw as the window opened was the plastic Avis tag on the ignition keys.

The driver was a man in late middle-age, wearing a poisonous brown sport shirt and sunglasses. He smiled at Lieutenant Berridge, and said, 'Anything I can do?'

'I'm a police officer. You're causing a potential obstruction here. Would you mind moving on?'

'You're a *police* officer?' asked the man, looking Lieutenant Berridge up and down.

'Even police officers get time off,' Lieutenant Berridge told him. 'But I'd appreciate it if you'd move along now, please.'

The man took off his sunglasses. His eyes were as dead as stones, and surrounded by wrinkles. The eyes of a man who has spent years searching distant horizons, years peering through smoky bars, years looking for one thing and one thing only, and has found it – and is enjoying his triumph.

'You must be Lieutenant Berridge,' the man said.

Lieutenant Berridge backed off a little and then glanced behind him at Stella. Strangers who called him by name always alarmed him. He had been on the beat with a cop

320

called O'Manion once, back in his rookie days, and one night on Indian School Road, just as they were climbing into their car, someone had yelled out, 'O'Manion!' and a shotgun blast had hit O'Manion full in the back, blood and smoke and tatters of drill-coloured uniform.

'Don't be frightened, lieutenant,' the man said. 'I'm not going to cause any trouble unless I have to. But don't try to be a hero, either. I'm holding an Ingram machine-gun in my lap, and it's pointing at you through the door, and one incautious or intemperant move will result in severe damage to this automobile's bodywork, and you.'

Lieutenant Berridge reached one hand behind him, and tried to wave at Stella to back away. But Stella came a few steps closer, and said, 'Come *on*, honey. I'm losing my adrenalin.'

'Don't say a word,' the man cautioned Lieutenant Berridge. 'I've come here to warn you, not to hurt you. You're dealing with the kidnapping of Susie Korvitz, right? And that little bit of business at Mesa.'

'That's right.' Lieutenant Berridge's face was as stiff as the celluloid features on a rag doll. 'What does that have to do with you?'

'You don't need to know. All you have to do is fail to find any useful evidence, decline to follow up any cock-and-bull leads, and eventually let both cases sink with silence and dignity into the files.'

'And what if I tell you to go fuck yourself?'

'Then I'll kill you. You remember poor Chief Ruse?'

'You killed Chief Ruse?'

'That's right. And I'll kill you too, if you don't behave yourself. Well – I have to make threats like that, you understand. They're part of my orders.'

Lieutenant Berridge said to Stella, in a clear voice, 'Back away, baby, you understand me?'

Stella said, 'What? What did you say?'

'I said back away! I said – *take cover!*'

The man in the car suddenly lifted from his lap a small black-painted gun. Lieutenant Berridge recognized it at once and felt a freezing surge of fear. For one chip of one second he couldn't decide what to do: but then he ran straight towards the car, straight towards the man with the gun, jumped up and over him, and hurled himself with a clumbering bang on to the Thunderbird's roof.

His unorthodox action saved him, for as he jumped, the man opened fire, and Lieutenant Berridge heard that brisk and terrifying burp that characterized the Ingram 11's high-speed fire. One thousand, one hundred rounds per minute, one bullet every five-hundredths of a second, with a velocity of 900 feet per second. The very first burst of thirty bullets took one-and-a-half seconds, and tore into Stella's legs as she stood in front of the car in total surprise and confusion.

Both her legs were completely severed at mid-thigh, in a horrifying splatter of blood and bone. She had time to look down at her legs with an expression of baffled hurt. She even had time to look up again, her eyes wide, searching for Lieutenant Berridge. Then her body literally fell off her legs, and she hit the ground with a hideous thump, her severed limbs collapsing in different directions. She thrashed her mutilated thighs, splashing blood across the road in an arabesque of scarlet. Her scream was so high-pitched that Lieutenant Berridge could scarcely hear it. It was the kind of scream that could wake dogs at night; the kind of scream that would come to you for year after year to come, in hideous dreams.

The man in the car wrestled to change magazines. Lieutenant Berridge slithered forward across the vinyl roof, and hooked his left arm down into the open window, grappling at the man's shoulder, and then at his neck. The man struck at him with the machine-gun, chipping flesh from his knuckles, but Lieutenant Berridge hung on to his throat and swung himself down from the car's roof. Now he could seize the man with both hands; and he did so, directly, and slammed the man's head forward so that he broke his nose against the car's window-shelf. There was a vivid splash of blood, and the man gargled and tried to wrench himself away.

'Out!' shrieked Lieutenant Berridge, hysterical. 'Out of

the fucking car!' He tore open the door and dragged the man on to the road, punching him again and again in the face. The machine-gun clattered on to the blacktop and skidded underneath the car.

The man tried to stand up, but Lieutenant Berridge gave him a karate chop to the side of his throat that snapped one of the bones in Lieutenant Berridge's right-hand pinkie. Then, as the man collapsed, Lieutenant Berridge delivered a piledriving kick in the balls, and felt a testicle smash. The man dragged himself a few feet towards the side of the road, and then collapsed, whimpering and groaning.

Lieutenant Berridge knelt down beside Stella. Her face under her suntan was the colour of ashes; as if she had suddenly become a very old woman. The blood was pumping out of her severed thighs undammed, and unstoppable, and the shock of being shot had already numbed her senses so deeply that she could only stare at him, and reach out for his arm as if she were trying to grasp the arm of a ghost. She was dying very quickly. To her, perhaps Lieutenant Berridge was already a ghost, a dim reminder of her lost lifetime, and the world which she was entering was already more real.

'Stella,' whispered Lieutenant Berridge. He knew that she couldn't hear him. He was sickeningly conscious that her left leg was lying at an odd angle within his field of vision; the shoe still laced up, the sock still as white as when she had pulled it on less than two hours ago. He said again, 'Stella,' and she died in his arms, and he thanked God in a way that she had. He knelt beside her for two or three minutes, not speaking, not thinking, wishing that this was nothing more than a butcherous illusion, and knowing all the time that it was real.

He heard a metallic clicking sound behind him, and he stiffened. Slowly, he turned his head around; and there he was. Bloody-faced, eyes bulging with agony, leaning up against the front of the Thunderbird with the Ingram upraised, and a fresh magazine already inserted.

Lieutenant Berridge stood up. 'Drop the weapon,' he said. 'You're under arrest. Homicide in the first degree.'

The man fired, a half-second snatch of bullets that blew chunks off the side of Lieutenant Berridge's head, ear, skull, and splashes of brain. But with the fixed concentration of a man who no longer cares if he lives or dies, Lieutenant Berridge walked right up to the killer, and laid his hand on his shoulder.

'I said, you're under arrest,' he repeated. The man stared at him and didn't fire again. Lieutenant Berridge could see the man's face in front of him, swollen and blurred, and a dark triangle of red which must have been the man's broken nose. The morning seemed extremely cold; almost as if somebody had opened up the door of an icebox. He shivered, but kept his grip on the man's shoulder, and said, 'arrest,' and then, in a slurrier voice, 'a. . .rest.'

His mother kept saying to him, 'Don't go outside without your rubbers. Do you hear me? Don't go outside without your rubbers.' And he was sure he could hear that Sunday churchbell tolling around the corner, on the day when the leaves began to fall.

He fell in the road. He was not quite dead. He could see the road surface close to his face. A little further away was a fallen orange. The last thing he heard was a car engine coughing into life, then the sound of a door slamming.

The man backed up the Thunderbird, then slammed it into drive, and ran deliberately straight over Lieutenant Berridge, crushing his chest with a crackle like fireworks and finishing him off. The man then drove to the intersection with 24th Street and made a left against a red light, provoking an outraged chorus of horns. He shouted at the top of his voice, 'Suck off, you bastards!' even though nobody could hear him. The pain from his broken nose was more than he could actually bear: he could feel the bone grating under the skin. And his right testicle was a complete crucifixion of agony. It felt as if it were eight times its normal size, and afire.

He reached the safe house in Tempe in twenty minutes, railing all the time against the slowness of the traffic, the stop-lights, and the monumental pain in his balls. He parked outside, and hobbled up the front steps, gasping and sweating. He fumbled for the key, and at last managed to let himself in. Then, with a terrible cry, he collapsed face-first on to the rug, and lay there shuddering and shaking and feeling as if the whole world were nothing more than two cubic inches of utter pain.

It was almost noon when the telephone rang. He managed to reach out for it and drag it on to the floor. 'Yes?' he asked, in a clotted, nasal voice.

The call was long-distance. There was a faint singing of electronics, the blurping of other people's dialling. A man's voice said, 'We just heard about Berridge. Good work. Nice and messy.'

'I'm hurt.'

'We'll be staying in Los Angeles for a week or so. Why don't you come back for good? We've got two more jobs for you; then you can retire for ever.'

'You said Ruse was the last one. Then you said that Berridge was the last one. Come on, Skellett, I'm hurt. I don't want any more. I'm finished.'

'How can you be finished? You're the best.'

'I spent twenty years looking for that one woman. I'm finished. No work for twenty years and now this. Three in one week. I can't take it any more, Mr Skellett. I'm through. And, besides, I'm not sure that everybody in Washington is going to be as pleased with these jobs as you are. Some people don't like to make a fuss, that's what I've heard. Especially these days, with those nuclear talks coming up.'

'Henry,' replied Skellett, and his tone was like chilled vinegar, strained through a pot-scourer, 'Henry, nuclear talks are none of your business. You're a man for hire, that's all.'

'I'm a man for hire and right now I quit. My nose is broken. Can't you hear my nose is broken? And that goddamned Lieutenant Berridge kicked me straight between the legs. I need a doctor, goddamn it, not more work. Send me a goddamned doctor.'

There was a silence. Then Skellett said, 'Can you make the LA flight this afternoon? Western have one at 1:40.'

'I'll try. I don't know.'

'Well, try. Okay? I'll book you a room at the Welford Clinic. But I want you here. You're still the best, as far as I'm concerned, broken nose or not. You're a man after my own heart.'

'I didn't know you had one.'

Skellett laughed, jarringly. 'Make sure you catch the 1:40,' he said. 'I'll have a car waiting for you at LAX.'

'So long as you never send me back to Phoenix.'

Skellett laughed again; and then just as abruptly as he had called, hung up.

Thirty

They drew up outside the multi-storey parking-lot on Santa Monica and Wilcox, and sat staring at it like apprehensive Hobbits considering the uncertain prospects of entering some evil wizard's castle. They were driving their rented Monaco still, but Rick had spent a couple of hours last night tweaking its engine, with a flashlight clenched between his teeth and a ring spanner in each hand, and although the Monaco wasn't exactly a Shelby Cobra, it did run with a reasonably satisfying burble, and give kicky little surges of power whenever Rick put his foot down. Under the circumstances, Rick had promoted himself to driver.

'My guess is that they've arrived already,' said Daniel.

'They've probably deployed themselves around the parking-lot in case we try anything funny.'

'Funny?' said Kathy. 'What's this *funny*?'

Rick said, 'What do you want to do?'

Daniel checked his watch. 'Drive straight in, I guess, and take it as it comes. But for God's sake be careful. These guys are really dangerous. I mean, they're wild beasts.'

Rick bipped the engine, and cleared his throat. 'You ever done anything like this before?'

Daniel shook his head.

'Me neither.' Then he paused. Then he said, 'Fucking scary, isn't it?'

They turned cautiously into the parking-lot ramp, and Rick collected the ticket from the gate. Up went the barrier, and they drove into the darkness with tyres squealing loudly on the polished concrete floor.

'They didn't say what level?' asked Rick.

'They didn't even say that they'd actually be inside.'

'Well, we're just going to have to make this up as we go along.'

They reached the end of the first level, and drove through a sudden burst of sunlight up the ramp to the second level. The muffled throb of their engine echoed against the walls; and with the long-drawn-out shrieking of their tyres, the noise made the parking-lot seem more like an evil wizard's domain than ever.

Kathy whispered, 'We should have brought guns.'

'We should have brought the National Guard,' said Rick.

Daniel, thinking tensely about Susie, could say nothing at all. His fists were clenched tight and his muscles were so rigid that he felt as if they might lock.

They reached the end of the second level, and turned up the ramp to the third. Rick said, 'This is the one. Look along to the end there, where the railings are. Nothing but rows of flat rooftops. We can drive straight through the railings, right across the tops of those buildings, as far

327

as that water-tank there. Then we can get out and climb down the fire-escape.'

Daniel looked dubiously out over the tar-papered roof-tops. There seemed to be heaps of trash out there, as well as several awkwardly-protruding ventilation stacks and chimneys. 'What happens if the railings don't give way?' he wanted to know. 'And supposing we collide with one of those chimneys?'

'And supposing your killers aren't even here at all?' Rick retorted. 'We sure as hell haven't seen them yet and we're up to the third level already.'

But as they turned up the ramp to the fourth level, they heard the growl of another engine; and when they reached the top of the ramp, and turned again, the reception committee was there, waiting for them at the very end of the level, five of them, flanked by two grey Cadillac limousines, their headlights shining and their engines whistling over.

'Skellett,' said Kathy, breathlessly, recognizing at once the thin man standing in the centre of the group in his pale blue sharkskin suit and bolus tie and wide-brimmed Western hat. Next to Skellett was the man called Walsh, with the crimson strawberry-mark on his face, and a little way behind him stood three Los Angeles Hell's Angels, hard-looking men in sleeveless denim jerkins and high-heeled boots, all tattoos and earrings and studs. Presumably Skellett had paid cash for a little supportive muscle.

Daniel said to Rick, 'Stop the car. Don't get too close.'

Rick drew the car to a halt, its engine warbling, and pushed on the parking-brake. But then he leaned over to Daniel, and said in a mock-British accent, 'I think we have a slight flaw in the jolly old plan here.'

'What's that? What are you talking about?'

'Well, hate to say it, old chap; but we're up here on the fourth level, unable to turn around so that our vehicle is facing the other way because of our hostile friends here; and yet our only route of escape is *behind* us.'

Daniel said, uncomfortably, 'What does that mean?'

'That means that when we hightail it out of here, old chum, we're going to have to do it in reverse.'

Daniel peered out through the back window at the sloping concrete ramp which led down to the third level again. It was almost obscured by the Monaco's trunk. He certainly wouldn't have liked to have tried backing down there himself, even slowly.

He stared at Rick for a long time, while fifty feet away the men who had tortured Kathy and kidnapped Susie stood silent and impassive, half-obscured in front of the dazzling headlights of their parked cars, waiting like men who had all morning to kill.

'Do you think you can do it?' asked Daniel. 'If you can't, we might just as well back off now. I don't mind trading myself for Susie, if that's what the deal has to be; but I don't intend to be killed right here in front of her.'

'You don't even know that they've brought her here,' said Kathy. 'We haven't seen her yet.'

Rick lifted himself up in the driver's seat and took a good long look behind him. Then he smiled ingenuously at Daniel, and said, 'I'm a stuntman, remember. I can do these things.'

'Can you back down that ramp at high speed? And then back all the way along the third level, and across those rooftops?'

'Piece of shit,' smiled Rick. Daniel shot a look at Kathy, as if to suggest that Rick may not be as good as he boasted. But Rick caught the look, and gave Daniel a friendly punch on the upper arm, and said, 'You know what you are? A Doubting Daniel. If I came up there *forwards*, I can go down there *backwards*.'

One of the Hell's Angels came striding forward, and tapped on the Monaco's window with the tip of a baseball bat. Daniel put down the window, and said, 'What is it?'

'You're Korvitz, right?'

'That's correct.'

'Mr Skellett wants you should step out of the car.'

'Tell Mr Skellett I don't do anything until I see my daughter safe and well.'

329

The Hell's Angel thought about this for a while, and then turned around to Skellett and yelled, 'Guy says he wants to see the girl.'

Skellett didn't appear at first to have heard this raucously-broadcast message; but eventually he turned around, and beckoned to Walsh to follow him. The two men retreated to one of the grey Cadillac limousines, and opened up the back door. Dazed, her arms tied, Susie was helped out of the car, and pushed forward so that her father could see her.

'Susie?' called Daniel. His voice echoed.

'Susie?' he called again.

Susie said suddenly, 'Daddy,' in a voice of utter despair and anguish, and it took all the self control he could squeeze out of himself for Daniel not to run forward and hold her protectively in his arms. His own little girl, Candii's girl. He thought to himself: that's the first time I've ever considered Susie to be Candii's daughter. Properly, I mean. The child of Candii's fickle and transient affections. It gave him strength, somehow, a feeling that he would never really be alone.

'Skellett!' he called.

'Yes, Mr Korvitz. I hear you.'

'Skellett, I want you to let Susie go.'

'That's what we're here for, Mr Korvitz. But first, we want to hear that you're prepared to tell us what you know.'

'I don't know anything, Skellett. Nothing at all. Just let Susie go, and you won't hear anything more about anything.'

'Promises, Mr Korvitz, promises. Assurances and promises. There isn't an assurance or a promise in this whole damn world you could go out and buy yourself lunch with. Promises and assurances are so much crap. Now, get out of the car, come over here, and we'll let your daughter go.'

Daniel shifted around in his seat to look at Kathy. 'Listen,' he said, quickly, 'it strikes me that their weakest moment is going to be when they let Susie go. Susie can't

330

physically fight back at them; but *I* can, and I intend to. So the second that Susie is back at the car, tug her in, and I'll start hitting out. I may get away. I may not. But the first thing you have to do is drive directly towards me, so that I can have one good try at breaking free.'

'They're armed, for Christ's sake,' protested Rick.

'Sure they're armed. But we've got the benefit of knowing what's going to go down, and they haven't. So use the surprise.'

'You're being very masterful all of a sudden,' said Kathy.

Daniel opened the car door. 'That's my daughter out there, with one of the most sadistic people I've ever heard about. You think I care about anything else?'

'*Bonne chance*,' said Kathy.

Daniel stood beside the Monaco, using the open passenger door to shield the lower part of his body. He felt chilled, but very determined. He wanted Susie back, he wanted Susie safe. If there was anything at all that he had ever done in his entire life which was worth preserving, it was Susie. Susie had been born out of his passion for Candii, out of his pleasure and joy in those all-American girls who made the West what it was. He wanted her alive, and that was all.

'Skellett!' he called. Then, quieter, 'I'm coming across. I want you to let the girl go.'

'We'll let the girl go when you're halfway, Mr Korvitz. No point in taking risks. But I warn you – any ridiculous tricks and you're both dead meat.'

'I'm coming, Mr Skellett.'

Daniel left the car and began to walk the twenty echoing paces towards Skellett and his entourage. Susie's eyes widened as he came nearer, but she didn't cry out any more. Skellett at last gave her a gentle push and said, 'Start walking, Susie. Walk towards the blue car. Don't stop to talk to daddy. You'll be seeing him later.'

Warily, unsteadily, like a fresh-born foal, Susie began walking towards Daniel. She stared at him intently all the time, as if she was desperately hoping for some kind of

331

signal that everything was all right, that this entire pantomime of Skellett's was a bad adult joke; and that soon they would be back at the Downhome Diner, frying bacon and boiling grits and waiting for the first grumpy customers of another Apache Junction day.

As they passed each other, Daniel paused, and Susie instinctively paused, too. Skellett called, 'Come on, Korvitz. Let's move it.'

With extraordinary unpractised grace, Daniel rolled over sideways, snatching Susie as he did so, and rolled over again and again and again. For a long perceptible moment, nobody spoke, nobody reacted; but then two things happened at once. Rick gunned the Monaco's engine, and Walsh reached inside his sport coat for his gun. There was a scuffling blurt of echoes as Skellett and his three Hell's Angel bodyguards started running towards Daniel, and Daniel staggered, fell, got on to his feet, and grasped the Monaco's door-handle just as Rick skidded to a halt beside him.

Walsh fired twice: two light automatic bullets which ricocheted off the car's hood and roof, and snapped away across the parking-lot. Then Daniel had bundled Susie into the front seat of the car, and heaved himself in beside her, knocking his head against the half-open door, and Rick had thrown the Monaco into reverse and started to back up, with blue smoke screeching out from the tyres.

Walsh fired again, and the windshield turned to milk. 'Thank Christ we're going backwards!' yelled Rick, his backside half-lifted in his seat, one hand on the steering-wheel, his eyes fixed on the rear window as they skidded at 30 mph in reverse along the whole length of level four.

But at the corner his stuntman's judgement failed him: he collided heavily with a car that was parked right by the top of the ramp, and there was a smash of impacted metal. He thrust the gearshift into drive, then reverse again, and swung the Monaco wider this time, backing wildly down the concrete ramp and saying a prayer that nobody would be trying to come up the ramp in search of a parking-place.

As they swerved backwards into level three, Daniel realized with horror that Skellett had been running after them; and that he had caught up with them. Skellett thrust his gun into the open window and pointed it directly at Rick's head and screamed, 'Stop! Stop this goddamned car or I'll kill you!'

Daniel seized Skellett's wrist and twisted it around so hard that the tendons burst. The gun fired once, inside the car: a sooty hot blast of flame and smoke that tore the ceiling lining to shreds, and left them all deafened. Daniel almost let go of Skellett's arm, but Rick yelled, 'Hold on to the bastard! Daniel! Hold on to the bastard, you hear me?'

Lifting himself up in his seat again, Rick jammed his left foot against the gas pedal, and the Monaco roared backwards along the entire length of level three. Skellett, his arm twisted in Daniel's grip, was dragged along with it, his shoes bouncing and jarring on the concrete, his face contorted with surprise and pain. He shrieked. 'Go! Let me go! *Let me go!*' but Daniel held on to his arm so tightly that he succeeded only in turning himself over on to his back, and wrenching his arm muscles. He let out a long, desperate, '*Yaaaaaahhhhhh!*'

The Monaco reached the end of level three just as a small family ranch wagon appeared at the crest of the ramp. The driver of the ranch wagon jammed on his brakes and stared pop-eyed as the Monaco hurtled towards him in reverse, and then smashed through the railings at the end of level three with a noise like a derailed locomotive, and bounced out into the sunshine on to the roof of the building next door. Skellett, his legs flying in the air, was still being dragged along with them. Daniel wasn't going to release him for anything or anybody, except the Lord Himself.

'*Jesus!*' cried Skellett, in total fear. '*Jesus Christ let me go!*'

Walsh, at the far end of level three, crouched down and opened fire with his small automatic. One bullet penetrated the Monaco's radiator, and there was a sudden hiss of released pressure. Another slapped into a tyre, but didn't deflate it.

'Go!' shouted Daniel, and Rick swerved the car backwards in between the ventilation stacks and the garbage and the brick chimneys, and four buildings away they slithered to a halt beside a wide vehicle ramp, leading downwards.

'Get that bastard into the car!' said Rick. 'Quick, move!'

Daniel released Skellett's arm, then opened his door, and opened the back door, and heaved Skellett on the back seat, next to Kathy. Kathy stared at Skellett in fright and distaste, but Skellett was too bruised and concussed even to notice her. He groaned, and sank down on to the seat, and hunched there with bloody dribble hanging down on to the lapel of his powder-blue suit.

'Where does that ramp lead?' asked Kathy.

'It looks like a car showroom,' said Daniel. 'That means that we should be able to drive all the way out to the street.'

'Daddy!' shouted Susie. 'Daddy, they're coming!'

Daniel stuck his head quickly out of the Monaco's side window, and saw that Skellett's assistants must have run back to their limousines, and were speeding towards them along level three, headlights blazing. Rick wrapped his shirt-tail around his wrist and punched out the milked-over windshield; then gunned the engine again, and drove the Monaco straight down the vehicle ramp into the dark depths of the building at nearly 40 mph.

They collided against the left-hand wall as the ramp spiralled tightly downwards, losing hubcaps and door-handles and ribbons of chrome trim. They passed a bodyshop floor, where mechanics were working on cars with acetylene torches and hammers; then they passed an upper showroom floor, crowded with sparkling new cars. Then they suddenly found themselves zooming into a first-floor showroom, with bright lights and brand-new Toyotas on turntables, and customers walking between the cars, peering into the windows and browsing through brochures.

'Oh, God!' gasped Rick. He didn't have to tell them that he couldn't stop. The Monaco careened across the show-room floor at full speed, its tyres howling on the polished marble, colliding with potted palm trees, desks, cardboard displays, light fixtures, and chairs. It rear-ended a brand-new bright-red Toyota estate car, crushing the back end and sending it nose-first into a concrete pillar. Then, when Rick frantically tried to back up, the Monaco's rear bumper caught a new Toyota's bumper, and tore off half the front grille.

'Daddy, they're here!' cried Susie and with a throaty scream of engines and a scraping of metal, Skellett's two grey Cadillacs came barrelling out of the service ramp like huge hungry wolves, lights full on, horns blaring.

'Here goes!' Rick shouted, and banged his foot down on to the gas pedal.

Daniel saw what happened next as a spectacular day-dream. The Monaco burst straight through the car show-room's front window into the street, with glittering glass exploding everywhere, and tumbling in the morning sun-light. There were fragments like diamonds, fragments like swords, and all the time his ears were filled with a sound like breaking glaciers, creaking and crackling and tinkling and pattering.

The first of Skellett's Cadillac limousines skidded around sideways in a vain attempt to chase them. Its long rear-end slammed against the red Toyota station wagon which Rick had already wrecked. Its wheels spun on the polished floor. The second Cadillac collided with it, dent-ing its nearside door, and then tried to drive around the side of the showroom and chase the Monaco by heading towards another window. But it skidded, struck a concrete pillar, and came to an abrupt dead stop.

There was a huge explosion as the Cadillac's gas tank blew. A rolling mushroom of orange fire incinerated the car, and everything living or mechanical within twenty feet. Then the first Cadillac's tank blew, too, and the showroom was turned into a furnace. A woman with her hair on fire, her dress turned into flags of flame, went screaming into the street. A man who didn't even look like a man managed to crawl out on to the sidewalk, to lie there burning and shuddering and far beyond help. There was nobody else. The showroom blazed with a hungry rumbling sound, and all that anybody could do was stand and watch, and thank God that they hadn't been inside.

Thirty-One

They stripped Skellett naked, tied him with cord, and locked him into the bathroom, which was the only room without a window. Rick and Daniel and Kathy went into the sitting-room and awarded themselves a large whiskey each, and sat there staring at each other in delayed shock and overwhelming relief. It was extraordinary to Daniel that the sun was still shining through the patterned net curtains, and that it wasn't even lunchtime. They still had plenty of time to go to Butterfield's for a salad and a glass of wine, or to the Cock'n'Bull for ribs. Not that any of them had the stomach.

Susie had seemed unmarked, and unhurt, although her hair was filthy and she hadn't changed her clothes since she had been kidnapped. Daniel had gently bathed her, and given her milk to drink, and a child's sedative, and tucked her into his own bed. She had fallen asleep within minutes, a child's immediate and innocent reaction to being safe.

Rick yawned, loudly. 'I'm sorry,' he said. 'I always yawn when the tension's over.'

Daniel glanced over at Kathy, and wondered if she were thinking the same things that he was.

Rick said, 'Those guys are madmen, right? I mean, they're really crazies. Just like you said.'

Daniel nodded, and sipped his whiskey.

Kathy said, 'I couldn't believe the way we went right through that showroom. I'm going to have nightmares about that tonight.'

'Pretty fancy piece of driving,' said Daniel.

'Why, thank you,' Rick acknowledged.

'Pretty fancy piece of lying, too,' said Daniel.

Rick swallowed whiskey, and then sat up straight in his chair, pointing at his own chest. 'You mean me? Is that *me* you're talking about?'

'That's right. Rick Terroni, the happy-go-lucky stunt-man and fortunate hitch-hiker. Let's say rather *too* fortunate hitch-hiker. The hitch-hiker who doesn't quite know where he's going, and doesn't quite know where he's been. The hitch-hiker who's got friends all over town and no place to stay. The hitch-hiker who will happily spend half the night tuning a car for a dangerous and crazy expedition with total strangers, and never complain once.'

'I think you've got me wrong, Daniel,' frowned Rick. 'I think you've got me completely mixed-up.'

Daniel shook his head. 'One thing gave you away more than anything else. Why did you insist that I held on to Skellett, and why did you make sure that I dragged him into the car? If you were nothing more than a hitch-hiker, you wouldn't care what happened to Skellett; in fact you'd probably be delighted to see the back of him. You certainly wouldn't insist that we took him along with us, or take such obvious relish in tying him up and locking him into the john. You're not what you say you are, Rick. I don't quite understand what you really might be, or what interest you could possibly have in any of this. But you *do* have an interest, and I'd like for you to explain it to me.'

Rick grinned, and finished his whiskey, and gave both of them a cheerful smile. 'You're not satisfied you got the little girl back?'

'I'm more than satisfied. I'll never be able to repay you

for what you did today. I mean that. But I still believe that you're lying.'

'Well, there are lies and lies.'

'Which particular kind of lies do you tell?'

'I tell the patriotic kind of lies.'

'Can there *be* such a thing?' asked Kathy, caustically.

'Of course. Any lie that you have to lie in defence of the American people and their right to be free, that's a patriotic lie, you get me? And therefore forgivable at all times.'

'Rick,' said Daniel, gently, 'I want to thank you with everything I possibly can for saving Susie today. For saving all of us. That was a wild and risky plan, but as it turned out, it worked. *You* made it work, with that *Dukes of Hazzard* driving of yours. But there's something you have to know. We're not just dealing with hoodlums and kidnappers here. We're dealing with political conspiracy; something far greater and far more frightening than anything this nation had to face before. Leastways, that's what we believe it to be.'

'Well,' said Rick, 'that's what I *know* it to be.'

'You *know* about this?' asked Kathy, in disbelief. 'You know about Cuba and Kennedy, and Marilyn Monroe?'

'I don't know about Marilyn Monroe – what about Marilyn Monroe?'

'She was killed because she was involved in all this, whatever it is. But not in 1962 . . . this month, only a week ago.'

Rick said, 'Listen, I'll have to come clean with you people. I intended to a little later anyway. But our meeting out there on the Pacific Coast Highway wasn't an accident. I'd been following your car for two days, seeing what you were up to. When you stopped by the beach, my friend left me by the side of the highway there, and I asked you for a ride. If you'd turned me down, well, my friend would have picked me up straight away and we would have followed you again. But we reckoned that you looked like the kind of people who might give a guy a ride in their car – and that hitching a ride would be one of the best ways of getting to know you.'

'Who are you?' Kathy asked him. 'Are you some kind of detective, or what? You're obviously not in cahoots with *those* people.' She nodded towards the bathroom where Skellett was locked up.

'No, I'm not,' said Rick. He tugged his fingers through his hair, and stretched himself out, relaxing. 'I'm the chapter chief of Free Columbia. You've heard of Free Columbia?'

Daniel shook his head, but Kathy said, 'I've heard some rumours about it. It's supposed to be an amalgamation of all the subversive groups of the 1960s, isn't it? The Panthers, the Weathermen, the Yippies. Some people even say ex-Mansonites, the Dune Buggy Attack Battalion.'

'Whatever you've read about it, or heard about it, is bullshit,' said Rick. 'Free Columbia was a get-together of all these groups to liberate America from one thing and one thing only: the Soviets. Of course, the propaganda you get in the media makes us out to be a bunch of irresponsible terrorists. And anybody who attempts to stand up and tell the truth gets wasted pretty quickly. But it's true. Ever since 1962 the United States has been controlled by a Soviet committee, chaired by an old-time Bolshevik politician they call Ikon.'

'Are you high or something?' Daniel demanded.

'I wish I was,' Rick told him. 'But I'm not, and it's true. Kennedy didn't succeed in facing down Khruschev over the Cuban missiles at all. By the time the "Cuban missile crisis" was supposed to be coming to a head, the Russians were already in charge, and infiltrating the government and the armed forces. As far as any of us have been able to find out the missile crisis was simply a way of concealing the shift in government and giving the American public a feeling of false security. It also made the fake "disarmament" talks of 1963 seem justified. You know, we've licked the Russians, let's be magnanimous.'

Daniel said, 'You're trying to tell me that the Soviet Union is in charge of America? That's what you're saying?'

339

'Don't worry,' Rick reassured him. 'Everybody reacts the same way when they first find out. A couple of people I know have even committed suicide. You know, suddenly they discover that the life they've been living for the past twenty years was something altogether different. The world is someplace alien and strange.'

'But how can it possibly have been kept a secret for so long? When so many people must know?'

'How did Hitler keep the concentration camps secret? How did Stalin conceal the deaths of thousands of Russians? A secret doesn't have to be too much of a secret if you can enforce its secrecy with terror. You say they killed Marilyn Monroe, recently. Well, I believe you. That's exactly the way they do things. They never let you escape. They hunt you down and hunt you down until they find you, and then they kill you and there's no mercy. I mean that. We lost eight Panthers in April. Did you hear about eight black guys dying in a blazing bus in Georgia? Not the kind of news story you'd remember, is it? But that bus was bombed by Ikon's people. Look at you – you're afraid to go to the police. You don't know who's going to be a Soviet stool-pigeon and who isn't; and believe me, if you open your mouth to the wrong person, you're dead.'

He reached over and poured himself some more whiskey. 'I don't know how many members Free Columbia has altogether. It could be as few as thirty thousand, or as many as a million. We're trying all the time to raise the public's awareness to the Soviet take-over, but do you know how *difficult* it is to get a message like that across? One of our members used to work for a print union, and he managed to run a story in *The New York Times*, foot of page one, announcing that the United States was under the control of the Soviet Union and that we should all rise up and overthrow them. That was July 17, 1964. And do you know what happened? Two people called up *The New York Times* and asked if it were true. Two people. And of course that brought the story to the attention of the subeditors, and they knocked it out and replaced it with a story about a British mail strike. A week later the guy who had sneaked the story into print was found drowned.'

Kathy said, 'I don't understand why the Soviets haven't put the country under more overt Russian rule.'

'They don't need to. They can exploit us economically and politically without having to turn us all into Communists – although we've always believed that this is their eventual aim. That's what all these disarmament talks are all about: they want gradually to educate the American public into thinking that there's no more prospect of nuclear war, and that it's time the USA and the USSR were all buddies. That's what this economic recession is all about, too. The Soviets are manipulating American banks and funds so that huge amounts of investment money simply aren't reaching American industry. The recession isn't real at all. We're simply the victims of the greatest siege in global history. Outside of our borders, in Japan and Switzerland and the Soviet Union, there's enough American money stashed away to end the recession overnight – and I mean *overnight*. But the Soviets aren't going to let us get our hands on it until we've turned to international socialism, and Leninism, and it's only *then* they're going to release their grip on the world economy, so that we believe that Communism has brought us instant prosperity.'

They sat in silence while the sunshine blew through the net curtains, and the sounds of Sunset Strip came faintly across the flowering back yard. Daniel felt as if he were dreaming, as if he would wake up in a minute or two and find that he was back in his bed in Apache Junction. Kathy finished her drink, and then said, 'I'm stunned. I don't know what to think about it. I mean, the whole of my world has turned out to be something I didn't imagine it ever could be, and I don't know how to work it out in my mind any more. There's nothing to relate to any more.'

'There *is* one thing,' said Rick, 'and if you ever thought you'd hear a one-time card-carrying member of the Weather Underground say this . . . well, I wouldn't believe you. But the one thing you *can* relate to is the Amer-

341

ican Constitution. What it says in the Constitution is what we're fighting for now. And everything you learned in school. John Paul Jones, Sam Houston, Benjamin Franklin, George Washington. The spirit lives on – and always will do. They still have their own heroes in Poland, remember. They still remember Imre Nagy in Hungary.'

Softly, Kathy said, 'What are we going to do?'

'There's nothing we *can* do, except go on fighting. If you want to join in, you're welcome.'

Daniel said, 'The risk – '

'Is very high,' Rick interrupted. 'You saw for yourself today what Ikon's hit-men can do. It was only by plain old California luck that we managed to get away.'

'Why were you so keen on capturing Skellett?'

'He's a leading agent of theirs, that's why. And he has a reputation for being one of the most vicious. We'll take him out to the Mojave Movie Ranch, that's where we usually take any Soviet infiltrators we capture. We'll interrogate him; and then I guess we'll probably kill him.'

'That's murder.'

'You think so? There are dozens of agents like Skellett, and they're all as cold-blooded as anybody can be. They've got Siberian ice-water in their veins.'

'Is he Russian?'

'Some of them are, not him. The Soviets have a programme of recruitment from most of the major American penitentiaries. They pick the real hard nuts and train them in weapons and unarmed combat to make them even harder. Some of them are kind of weird, you know, head-cases. That's why you get the occasional well-publicized mass-murder, or shoot-out. And we've believed for about a year now that there's something of a power struggle going on inside the Soviet committee, and that some of Ikon's agents have become polarized to another leader. Ikon is obviously ruthless, but there's some evidence now that one or two agents are acting even more violently and even more openly than Ikon's men usually do. It could be that one of the Soviet leaders is trying to show Ikon up, or threaten him in some way. We don't know, and that's why I want to interrogate Skellett.'

'Do you think he'll tell you anything?'

'I don't know. Some of them do. We've captured maybe six in the past three years. But some of the new agents are like kamikaze pilots, completely indoctrinated to the point where they'll shoot themselves just to annoy you.'

'I saw one like that,' said Kathy. 'A young man in Arizona, who packed his own intestines with explosives and blew himself up, simply to give Skellett time to escape.'

'Some way to go, huh?' nodded Rick.

Later, Daniel went into Susie's room and watched her sleeping. Her hair was spread on the pillow, one hand was clutching the sheet, as if to prevent herself from falling into some dark and unwanted dream. Daniel wondered how he would ever be able to explain to her that America was no longer free, that within her lifetime she may be a slave to Communism, that the land he had hoped to give her as her birthright had been forfeited before she had even been born.

'My daddy is dead, but I can't tell you how
He left me six horses to follow the plow.
I sold my six horses to buy me a cow;
And wasn't that a pretty thing to follow the plow?
I sold my cow to buy me a cat,
To sit down before the fire to warm her little back.
I sold my cat to buy me a mouse,
But she took fire in her tail and burn'd down my house.
With my whim wham waddle ho!'

Susie stirred. Daniel closed the bedroom door, although he stood outside for a long time, listening, keeping guard.

Thirty-Two

Nadine came back to the house at midnight that night to find that Titus was still up, sitting by himself in the library, drinking the bottle of 1924 brandy which had been given him by President Giscard d'Estaing of France, and which he had always sworn he would never open. He raised his head in some surprise as she came through the door, and stood there in her smart grey-flecked dress, her gloves upraised in one hand, her hat at an angle so that the brim shadowed her face.

'Well,' he said gruffly, 'you've got a goddammed nerve. I'm surprised they let you in.'

'Don't worry. They've probably called the FBI already.'

Titus said, 'You killed those people, all of them. You actually killed them.'

'You won't find any proof. Nor will you ever find your precious videos again.'

'God damn it, Nadine. I know you killed those people.'

'What you know and what you can prove are two very different things. Now, since you've opened up your precious bottle of 1924 brandy, aren't you going to offer any to me?'

A security guard arrived breathlessly in the hallway outside, and knocked on the panelling.

'Mr Secretary? Are you okay?'

'It's just as well that I am,' growled Titus. 'If she'd had any intention of killing me, I would have been well dead by now.'

'Yes, sir. I'm sorry, sir.'

'You're *sorry*? Get back to your station.'

Titus poured Nadine a small measure of brandy and held it out to her, without getting up from his chair. Nadine came forward with an arch smile and took it.

'I'm sorry it had to happen this way,' she said. 'You didn't leave me with any alternative.'

'I've been hearing a lot of people saying that lately.'

'You seem angry.'

'I am angry. I'm also sick, confused, bewildered, frightened, disoriented, upset, and tired.'

'That's quite a list.'

Titus swallowed the remaining liquor in his glass, stared at the bottle, and then poured himself another one, much larger this time. 'What the hell, it's only brandy.'

Nadine sniffed it. 'It's very fine.'

Titus said, 'Yesterday afternoon I went down to Bolling Air Force Base and spoke to my old friend Pierce Caulfield.'

'General Caulfield? I know him.'

'You should. He's one of your stooges. He's known about Ikon since 1974, and do you know something, he's never once breathed a word about it. Never once! God damn it all, I've been to dinner with that man, gone fishing with him, attended his stupid daughter's wedding, and all the time he knew about Ikon and he never told me!'

Nadine sat down on the floor, and rested one hand on Titus' knee. 'I'm sorry,' she said. 'You've been a remarkable husband, even if we have argued all the time. An unparalleled lover. And you're the best Secretary of State that America ever had.'

'America?' asked Titus, bitterly. 'The Autonomous Capitalist Oblast of Sod-all.'

Nadine said, 'Joe was one of ours too, you know.'

Titus stared at her; and then said, 'Really?' and then 'Mmh', as if he didn't care at all. He had already suffered the greatest disenchantment, a few minor betrayals didn't seem to make very much difference.

'I wasn't going to leave you, you know,' said Nadine.

'I think I'd prefer it if you did.'

'I want you to come and meet Ikon.'

'You want what?'

'Tomorrow morning, I want you to come and meet Ikon. I want you to see what he's like, talk to him, and understand his problems. Ikon needs all the help he can get right now, and whatever you think about the Capi-

345

talist Oblast of America, Ikon is the lesser of two evils. I think you have a duty to help him survive.'

'I'll tear his goddammed Commie head off.'

'Titus, please. I'm trying to help.'

'How can you help?' Titus shouted at her. 'How can you possibly help? My entire life was flushed down some sneaky historical toilet when I wasn't looking, and for twenty years I've been marching forward with my head in the air and my pants round my goddammed ankles. How the hell can you *help*?'

'Titus – '

'Leave me alone, Nadine, for the love of God. I've got a bottle of brandy to finish.'

'Titus, please.'

Titus shook his head, again and again and again, until his jowls wobbled. Then he stamped both feet on the floor and roared, 'No! No! No! No! No!'

Nadine put down her drink, stood up quietly, and left him. On the way out, the security guard said, 'Everything all right, Mrs Alexander?'

'Everything's fine, thank you. Oh – and could you do something for me? Could you arrange for Mr Alexander's car to be waiting outside for us at ten o'clock tomorrow morning? We have an appointment on Pennsylvania Avenue.'

The security guard glanced into the library where Titus was glowering at the floor as if he could make the rug catch fire by the heat of his vision alone. 'Sure thing, Mrs Alexander,' he said, in a cautious voice. 'Ten o'clock sharp.'

Thirty-Three

Two other incidents occurred at midnight that night, although in Las Vegas, Nevada, in the Pacific Time Zone, midnight came three hours later. A chambermaid from the Las Vegas Futura Hotel left the hotel's service entrance and walked north-eastwards along the alleyway which led out on to Bonanza Road, where she intended to catch a cab to take her home. Her cleaning shift had finished at 11:15 p.m., but she had spent three-quarters of an hour in the hotel kitchen, talking to a friend who had recently divorced her husband and eating a supper of cold ham, cheese, and salad.

She was halfway along the alleyway when a voice called out, 'Anna!' She turned around to say, 'I'm not Anna,' when there was a deafening shotgun blast, then another. The shots were fired at such close range that she was completely eviscerated, and she died before she fell to the ground. The Chinese night-chef, who had heard the shots, came running out to the alleyway to find it plastered spectacularly in blood. But there was no sign of the chambermaid's killer; only an inquisitive cat which had jumped away when the gun first went off, and had now returned to sniff the warm scent of death.

At home, on the scrubby edge of the Nevada desert, the chambermaid's husband lay awake, waiting for the familiar sound of the cab bringing his wife back from town. The radio beside his bed was turned down low, so that it wouldn't wake up the children. It played *Stand By Your Man*, by Tammy Wynette, and he whistled along with it, under his breath.

He had never known that two years ago his wife had caught a glimpse of Senator Marshall Roberts leaving Room 1198 of the Futura Hotel with a high-class hooker known as Rheta Haze. He never would know. But, in about twenty minutes' time, he would hear the warble-scribble-warble of a police siren as a patrol-car sped out

347

along the desert road to bring him the news that his wife was dead. He would see the red light flashing across his bedroom ceiling and know, before they told him, that something had gone terribly wrong.

Also at midnight, the President of the United States Marshall Roberts was undressing for bed when there was a ring on his private telephone. He called to his wife, 'It's all right, dear, I'll get it,' and walked across the white-carpeted bedroom, unbuttoning his cuffs as he went. He picked up the Louis Quinze-style telephone, and said, 'Marshall Roberts.'

'Good evening, Mr President,' said a thick voice. 'This is Nikolai. Please forgive me for calling you so late.'

'Not at all,' said Marshall, although without much patience. 'What can I do for you, Nikolai?'

'I couldn't sleep, Mr President.'

'Is that unusual?'

'Well, I have my tablets. But it is not the pain . . . I have a feeling of fear, Mr President. I feel like Caesar before the Ides of March.'

'Is it Kama you're worried about?'

'I'm not sure. I've never felt like this before, not in my entire career. Mr President, do you think perhaps that tonight is the night when I am going to die?'

'Don't talk nonsense. You're probably over-tired.'

'Perhaps.' There was a breathy pause. Then Ikon said, 'You know that the RINC talks may now proceed. All opposition has been completely eliminated.'

'The chambermaid?'

'Later tonight. But there won't be any slip-ups.'

'I see. Well, I'll start drafting the announcement tomorrow.'

There was another, longer pause. Marshall Roberts said, 'Is that all, Nikolai? I'm quite tired. I'd like to get some sleep now.'

'I'm afraid, Mr President. Don't you think that's strange?'

'Not in your position, not at your time of life.'

'But I'm afraid.'

348

'Have a drink. Some of that cherry vodka of yours. Then count sheep. Or blessings.'

'What blessings do I have, Mr President?'

'You're still alive, Nikolai. That's a blessing. And the world hasn't yet been incinerated by nuclear weapons. That's another blessing. And, if you like, I'll stop by at Pennsylvania Avenue tomorrow afternoon and share a drink with you.'

'Very well,' said Ikon, with audible uncertainty. Then, 'Very well, I will try to sleep. But this feeling I have . . . of death. It makes me cold!'

'Try an electric blanket,' suggested Marshall Roberts, and hung up.

Thirty-Four

That night, as Daniel lay in bed, he heard the door creak open. He froze, and reached across for the three-foot long section of angle-iron which he had left beside his bed-head. The room was utterly dark, except for a single yellow wedge of light, the size of a piece of cheese, on the opposite side of the ceiling.

'Who's there?' Daniel whispered. His nose had been feeling slightly blocked up, which was one reason he had been finding it difficult to sleep; but now his sinuses emptied instantly. His balls tightened, and there was a flicker of nerves in his stomach.

'It's *me*,' came the whispered reply. 'Kathy. Can I come in?'

Daniel let out a breath, and relaxed. 'For God's sake, I could have killed you. What do you want?'

She tiptoed across the room and leaned over him. He

saw dimly the shape of her breasts, and realized that she was naked. She smelled of Cie. 'I can't get to sleep in that room, right next to the bathroom. Skellett keeps banging his head against the wall and making terrible groaning noises.'

'Well, jump in here, then.'

She lifted the cover and bounced in beside him, taking him immediately into her arms. She was warm and rounded and soft, but her nipples were as stiff and sweet and wrinkled as California dried plums. She thrust one leg in between Daniel's legs, so that she was straddling his thigh; and the message of that move was obvious when he felt the night-cooled stickiness of her pubic hair against his bare skin. He said, 'Kathy?' But questions were unnecessary. His cock rose against her stomach until it was pushing against her navel; and he took her face in her hands and kissed her, deeply and urgently.

'Don't let's wait,' she gasped. 'Please don't let's wait.'

He twisted around in the bedsheets, and climbed on top of her. She reached down and held his erection in her hand, and guided it up between her legs. He hesitated for a second, and then pushed slowly forward so that he slid deep into her slippery warmth, until it was impossible for him to push any deeper.

'Fuck me,' she demanded, digging her fingernails into the muscles at the small of his back. 'I don't want to *think*, I don't want to do *anything*. I just want to fuck.'

They made love for nearly an hour, strenuously and sometimes furiously. She cursed him and cooed at him, stroked him and bit him. She forced her hips up against him whenever he began to falter, and coaxed him into one erection after another. Then the moment came when she was straddling him, pushing herself up and down on him so quickly that with each upward stroke she almost lost the tip of his penis. And in that moment she seemed to collapse like a convolvulus flower, like a dark warm wind drawing in on itself, and she trembled and shook and cried out to him, 'Daniel, save me! Daniel!'

They lay for a long time side by side in silence. It had

all happened so quickly that they had to turn it over in their minds, from the moment when Kathy had first opened the door, and Daniel had reached for his home-made billy-club. Kathy said, after a while, 'You're thinking what a whore I am.'

'A whore? No? Exactly the opposite. Whores do it for money. You did it because you wanted to.'

'And you?'

'I did it because I like you, and because I think you're very pretty, and very attractive, and because you're exactly my type.'

'I thought country-and-western heroines were your type.'

'Isn't a man allowed to change his type?'

'A man's allowed to do anything he wants to. But then so is a woman.'

Daniel reached across her and switched on the bedside lamp. 'Do you want a drink or anything? I don't think I'm going to be able to sleep tonight. I keep thinking about Ikon.'

She kissed his shoulder. 'You know something . . . when I went out to report on Margot Schneider's murder . . . I never dreamed it would lead to anything like this.'

'Neither did Willy Monahan. God, if only he'd known.'

'Poor Willy.'

'Yes,' said Daniel. 'Poor Willy.'

Kathy stroked the inside of his upraised arm. 'You know something?' she said, 'I liked the look of you the moment I first met you. Did anyone tell you how attractive you are, as a man? You have this beautiful face. You look sensitive, but you look strong, too.'

He leaned forward and kissed her. 'I'm not always strong. I haven't been particularly strong over the past few years.'

'But why not? You have a charm about you, did you know that? A real sexual grace. And yet you don't have the confidence that ought to go with it.'

'Well, I guess it's partly because Candii walked out on

me. She was kind of my dream girl. That was before I changed my type, I hasten to add.'

Kathy laughed. 'You don't have to change your type, just for me.'

'The way you raped me just then, I think it's the least I can do.'

'I raped you? I didn't notice you protesting.'

'I was afraid you might hurt me if I did.'

Kathy held herself close to him, her breasts pressed against his chest, her hand proprietorially cupping his soft penis. She said, very quietly, 'I can hear your heart beating. That frightens me, sometimes, to hear somebody's heart beating. I keep thinking that it's going to stop.'

Daniel said nothing, but stroked her hair. In spite of Kathy's company, in spite of her closeness, he felt peculiarly lonesome. Perhaps it was the cold knowledge that America was no longer free, and that the future was no longer certain. How long before the Soviets would openly reveal their ownership of the United States, and begin to suppress free speech? How long before nobody would be allowed to say or write anything against the State and even the everyday grumbles at the Downhome Diner would be censored by fear? How long before the late-night television news would report nothing more than official party information, and all the silliness and eccentricity and childish greed of American television was lost forever? He thought of the Joni Mitchell song which had warned 'you don't miss what you've got 'till it's gone,' and already, in Kathy's arms, he began to miss America.

Kathy said, 'I don't know what to think about Kennedy any more. I used to adore him. He was my hero, when I was fourteen years old. And Jackie!'

'It probably wasn't his fault,' said Daniel. 'God Almighty – what would *you* have done, if somebody had told you that fifty 10-megaton missiles were aimed at New York, and St Louis, and Chicago, and Denver, and that they were so close that you had no possible chance of stopping them? Do you know how long it would take a missile to get from Cuba to Houston? Well, I don't know either, but it can't be more than a couple of minutes. Willy would have known.'

Kathy didn't answer. She was completely at a loss to judge what Kennedy had done; how right or wrong it might have been that he had sold America short to the Soviet Union. She didn't know what threats he had faced, or what military and historical pressures had weighed against him. What was more, everything she had learned about the United States in the past twenty years had been part of an elaborate worldwide confidence trick, a global sham; and so every single political point-of-view which she had formed over the past twenty years – every single opinion on which she might have been able to base an assessment of Kennedy – was distorted, simply a conditioned reaction to a bogus situation. She felt duped and confused and stateless, and that was part of the reason she had made her way into Daniel's bedroom and made love to him. Daniel at least was Daniel. He had a daughter and a diner and a place to go. He was a Jew, too, and that meant he had Israel, as well as America. He had some roots, some sureness, something to tell him what he was and what opinions he ought to hold. She felt herself as if someone had suddenly told her that she was an orphan, and that the people she had thought were her parents had been only actors, paid to convince her that she was a normal child.

'I'll have that drink now,' she told Daniel, gently. 'A vodka, if there's any left. I guess I might as well get used to drinking the stuff.'

Daniel climbed over her, and out of bed. He bent over and kissed her, and said, 'You don't want a midnight hamburger, do you? I'm beginning to feel like cooking again. There's plenty of ground beef in the icebox, and onions.'

'What are you trying to do, turn me into a San Francisco sideshow? The Fattest Female Reporter in the West?'

'I'm beginning to miss cooking, that's all.'

353

'Well, don't start taking your culinary obsessions out on me.'

Daniel raised both of his hands in surrender. 'Okay, I promise I won't cook you a hamburger. But don't start complaining when you see mine.'

'Daniel,' she said, as he put his hand on the doorhandle.

He looked at her, his smile only just beginning to fade. Sitting up in bed, she looked pretty and short-sighted, vulnerable and almost childish. One breast was bare, soft and curved and pink-nippled.

'What we did tonight, don't read any special meanings into it,' she said. 'It was just that I was tired, and frightened, and I wanted you. But don't expect anything out of it tomorrow.

'Tomorrow?' asked Daniel. 'I never look that far ahead. Tell me about tomorrow when it's tomorrow.'

He opened the door, and there was Skellett. Not only Skellett, but Walsh, and both of them were armed.

'Back into the room,' said Skellett. Daniel hesitated, and Skellett shrieked at him, *'Back into the room, dummy!'*

Daniel backed away, holding up his hands. Both Skellett and Walsh were carrying .45 automatics, powerful enough to blow off the average human head and leave nothing but red string. Daniel stepped back as far as the bedroom wall, and stood there stock still, his hands still held high, saying nothing.

Skellett said, tartly, 'Mr Walsh and the Los Angeles Police Department wish to thank you for your consideration in leaving your car parked right outside the house where you happen to be staying, and for checking in with the house-rental agency under your real, undisguised names. You couldn't have made it easier for them to locate you if you'd fired signal rockets off from the roof.'

'How did you get away?' Kathy asked Skellett. 'I thought you were tied up naked in the bathroom.'

'I was, lady, I was, and believe me I won't forget it. But Mr Walsh here has an incomparable way with locked doors, don't you, Mr Walsh? He tears them off their hinges. And damned lucky for you that you didn't throw away my clothes, that sharkskin suit cost $450, and that was without the vest.'

'Where's Rick?' asked Daniel. 'Rick Terroni, the other guy who was here?'

'Oh, Rick *Terroni*. That's it! Rick Terroni, Pratfaller Extraordinaire. Well, he's comfortably tied up in his room right now, courtesy of Mr Walsh, and there isn't much chance that he's going to be able to get away. The simple reason is, we've nailed his hands to the floor.'

'God, you're a savage bastard,' said Kathy.

Skellett stalked across to the bed, raised his hand, and slapped Kathy right across the cheek, a cracking slap that broke the skin, and left the clear imprint of a man's hand on her face.

'You got away from me once, lady. You should have *kept* away.'

Daniel lowered his hands, his blood thundering through his veins like boiling mercury; but Skellett did nothing more than swing his .45 around to point directly at Daniel's face. 'As for you, *schmuck*, you should have stayed out of it, too. You and your nosy Air Force friend.'

'You hit her again – ' warned Daniel.

Skellett stalked up to him, and pointed the automatic right between his eyes. 'Yes?' he demanded. 'I hit her again, and *what*? What are you going to do about it?'

Daniel lowered his head. 'Just do what you've got to do,' he said, in a humiliated mutter. 'Just do it, all right?'

Skellett stared at Daniel with eyes like pebbles. 'If it was up to me, friend, I'd kill you here and now. Four of our people, dead, because of what you did yesterday morning, at the Wilcox Street parking-lot. Four trained agents, three of them spent years infiltrating the California Hell's Angels. You know what you threw away yesterday, with those stunts of yours? Years of patient work. *Years*.'

Daniel said, 'Don't touch Ms Forbes again, you hear?'

'I'll do what I'm going to do, and I'll do what I have to do.'

'Skellett – '

'Don't annoy me, do you understand? Just don't annoy me. I'm taking all of you to Washington. I don't want to, I'd rather blow your fucking heads off, personally. Right here, kill the whole damn lot of you, Susie included. But it seems like you know much more than you ought to, and the *boyars* in Washington want to know exactly *how* much. They want to put you through the mill, you get me?'

Skellett said to Kathy, 'Get dressed. We have a plane leaving from Burbank at three o'clock.'

Kathy hesitantly held the sheets up against her naked body.

'Get dressed!' snapped Skellett. 'We've seen it all before!'

But both he and Walsh watched her pruriently as she wrapped the sheet around herself and trailed through the door to her own bedroom.

'Keep an eye on her, Walsh,' said Skellett. 'Korvitz – you get dressed, too. Come on, let's get going. I've had it up to here with this dump of a house.'

Daniel quickly pulled on his jeans and his Arizona sweatshirt, and then went into Susie's room to get her dressed, too. When she saw Skellett standing in the doorway, her face went rigid with fright, but Daniel sat down beside her and said, 'It's okay. You understand? We're all together this time. Nothing's going to happen.'

Skellett cleared his throat loudly and nastily, but didn't make any comments.

They came across Rick in the hallway, stretched out on his stomach like a man crucified, with a dishcloth forced into his mouth. He was very white, and he was trembling with unstoppable quakes like an epileptic. His hands had been pierced by kitchen knives, the points of which had been stuck deeply into the polished wooden floor. Skellett stood over him for a while, watching him with distant satisfaction, and then said, 'All right, Walsh. Release him. He's coming with us.'

Walsh plucked out the knives, one after the other, and tossed them across the hallway. Rick stayed where he was, shaking, white as death. Walsh kicked him in the ribs; and then turned him over with his foot.

'Get up, okay?' he demanded. 'You want me to jump on your guts?'

Shivering, wild-eyed, Rick managed to sit up. Walsh cuffed him, hard enough to send him sprawling, and then kicked him again. 'I told you to get up, didn't I? What's the matter with you? Get up!'

Rick at last managed to pull himself up on to his feet. He stared at Daniel as if he didn't recognize him. Daniel said nothing, but kept his arm around Susie, and prayed again and again that Skellett wasn't going to kill them. Not now, oh Lord. Please not now.

Thirty-Five

Ikon was still asleep at ten o'clock the following morning; even though two important parties were arriving almost simultaneously at the large grey-stone building on Pennsylvania Avenue. At the front entrance, with its six semi-circular steps, and its uniformed doorman, a long dark-grey Cadillac Fleetwood containing Titus and Nadine Alexander was drawing up.

At the back entrance, in a plain brown panel-van, Skellett was arriving with Daniel, Kathy, Rick, and Susie. They had been flown in a Gulfstream III from Burbank to College Park Airport, just north-east of Washington, and then been driven into the city along Highway 1. Skellett had ordered them not to speak to each other, and so for hours they had remained in anxious silence. Susie had only just recovered from her first kidnap by Skellett and Walsh; now she was being abducted again, and her face was as drawn and tense as the face of an old woman. Daniel kept his arm tightly around her, but that was all he could do.

'Okay, *out*,' said Skellett, as the doors of the panel-van were opened up. 'And don't try anything stupid. There's nothing that you can possibly do here that's worth dying for. You understand me? Just do what you're told, keep quiet, and you may survive.'

'You're a *gem*,' said Kathy, as she stepped out of the van, and followed Rick towards the building's back entrance.

'Well, so I'm told,' grinned Skellett.

They were ushered quickly along a peeling green-painted corridor until they reached a service elevator. Skellett pushed the call-button, and while they waited, he stood there smiling at them as if they were school-children, and he was taking them to see the head teacher. There was that particularly wolfish look on his face all the time: You wait until you see what we've got in store for *you*.

The service elevator rose with a jarring shudder to the 10th floor, and then Skellett drew back the gates and said, 'Out. Walk straight ahead of you. Keep on going until you reach the end of the corridor. Then make a left.'

They walked along the fluorescent-lit corridor in silence. The only sound was the squeak and clatter of their shoes. At the end of the corridor, they were met by two men who looked like security guards, dressed in grey uniforms with badges on their shoulders that Daniel had never seen before, but whose meaning he immediately grasped. They showed an eagle, perched on a sickle. The motif of the Autonomous Capitalist Oblast of America. Kathy glanced across at Daniel for the first time since they had been herded into the building, and he knew what she was thinking. There wouldn't be guards with special badges if Ikon wasn't true; if everything that Rick had said about a Soviet takeover of the United States hadn't been a reality.

Skellett said, 'This way. You can wait in here.' Then he

said something in Russian to the two security guards, who briskly answered him back, and saluted.

The four of them were pushed into a plain, green-painted room with a morning-misted view of the Internal Revenue Service building. There was no furniture, no drapes, no carpet. The door was slammed shut behind them and locked.

They went to the window and looked down the ten dizzying storeys at Pennsylvania Avenue. Rick tentatively tried the window-catch, and said, 'It's not locked. We could all just about squeeze out of here.' The window was hinged at the top, so that when it was open they could peer straight down at Pennsylvania Avenue.

'Three hundred feet in the air?' said Daniel. 'You have to be joking.'

Rick opened the window wider. 'There's a ledge below us, as a matter of fact. We could climb out on to the ledge.'

'Forget it, Rick. We're not stuntmen, like you. We're just ordinary people who don't feel like climbing all over high-rise buildings. Besides if we got out on that ledge, where could we possibly go?'

Kathy said seriously, 'Do you think they're going to – well, do you think they're going to torture us? I'm not sure I could take any more of what Skellett did to me in Phoenix.'

Daniel reached out and held her arm, but there was nothing he could do to reassure her. The chances were high that they would all be tortured, all of them except Susie, who didn't know anything at all; and she would be tortured enough by the pain that her father would have to bear. Susie would be tortured beyond endurance if Daniel were to die.

Rick said, 'Listen, will you listen? We could climb out on to the ledge, and then we could climb upwards.'

'What are you talking about?' Daniel demanded. 'We're ten storeys up in the air. We're supposed to climb out of a window and then climb *higher*?'

'We can do it, God damn it,' said Rick. 'The ledges only

start on the ninth floor, but then there's all this decorative moulding that goes right up to the roof. If we climb out on to the ledge below this window, and make our way along to the corner of the building, there's a whole lot of concrete acanthus leaves; and we could climb up on those to the roof.'

'Rick, I've got a seven-year-old girl here.'

'What's wrong with that? A seven-year-old girl could climb up there easy. Better than you can, probably.'

'But Jesus, Rick, *it's three hundred feet to the ground.*'

Rick stood up straight, and spread his arms. 'Daniel, we're not *going* to the ground. We're going to the roof.'

Daniel stared at Rick with an expression that could have bored holes in solid concrete; but when Rick refused to flinch, he knew that Rick was sure that they could make it; or at least that their chances of surviving outside on the ledge were higher than their chances of surviving at the hands of Skellett and Walsh, and whatever other torturers Ikon could call upon. He turned away, and looked at Kathy, and Susie, and all he could feel was fear. Fear for them, because he knew that they were weaker, and that if anybody was going to fall from the ledge, it was going to be one of them. Fear for himself, too: for what he was going to have to do, and for the responsibility of looking after all these beloved lives.

There was a sharp rapping at the door. A voice said, 'Ten minutes, then you see Ikon! Make smart!'

'You hear that?' asked Rick. 'We've got ten minutes to make our minds up. Less than that. We've got two minutes to make up our minds, and eight minutes to climb out of that Goddamned window.'

Daniel closed his eyes for a moment.

'You praying again?' asked Rick.

Daniel opened his eyes again.

'I was just trying to work out what I would say to God on the way down to the sidewalk. "Forgive me, Lord, for I lost my footing?" Did you ever see that girl who threw herself off the Empire State Building in the 1930s? Perfectly intact, except that she'd dented the roof of a car two feet deep. Good thing it wasn't a ragtop.'

Kathy took Daniel's arm. 'Come on, Daniel. Calm down. We don't have to do it, any of us, if we really don't want to.'

'Are you going to do it?'

'I'm going to try.'

'Are you wearing any underwear?'

'What the hell does that have to do with it?'

'I don't know. Jealousy? You're going to be ten storeys up in the air, three hundred feet, out on a ledge with no panties?'

'There are worse ways of getting attention.'

Rick opened the window as far as it would go. Although it was such a still, misty morning, the wind blew in through the foot-wide aperture with a sound like howling demons. 'I think I'd better go first, then I can show you the best way to climb. The rule is, don't hurry, don't make a step unless you're sure where your foot's going to land, and stay confident. We're all going to make it. Nobody's going to fall; and that's all there is to it.'

He lifted himself up on to the window-sill, and then lowered himself feet-first down through the open casement until his feet had reached the ledge. 'It's okay,' he said. 'The ledge is pretty wide. Three inches at least. Let's have Susie next, then Kathy. Daniel, you can bring up the rear. Catch anybody if they look like they're dropping off.'

'Are you kidding?' asked Daniel.

'Who's kidding?'

Daniel leaned over beside Susie, and said quietly, 'We're going to try to get away by climbing out of this window and up on to the roof. It's going to be scary, okay? But Kathy and me are going to be right behind you all the time, and all I want you to do is hold on tight and do everything that Rick tells you to do.'

Susie nodded. There was a glistening in her eyes that looked suspiciously like the glistening of tears. Daniel hugged her close, and kissed her. Then he lifted her up, and helped her to scramble over the window-sill, down through the open window, and on to the narrow ledge. Rick held her close to him, and showed her how to hold on.

'You don't have to look down if you don't want to,' said Rick. 'But if you do, just think of it as Toytown. Nothing to get alarmed about.'

Kathy climbed out next, then Daniel. Now they were standing in a line, their heads, with the exception of Susie's, still up inside the open window. They would have to edge their way sideways to the left, ducking their heads under the metal supporting arm which kept the window open, and then cross three feet of open space before they reached the decorative concrete mouldings on the corner.

The wind gusted and moaned, and Daniel felt as if it were going to suck him off the side of the building. He had only glanced down once, at the beetling traffic and the crowds of tiny pedestrians, and in that one downward glance, he had felt as if his entire psyche had dropped three hundred feet to the sidewalk and vanished through the concrete into some strange Purgatory of sewers and conduits and cables, to be fed away into some utility system somewhere. A light flickers at Bloom's the tailors, three blocks away. 'What's that, Moishe?' 'That's young Daniel's soul, that's all. God bless him.'

Rick shouted at them, 'Take one sideways step at a time. Move one foot and then slide the other foot along to join it. Don't try to move both feet at once. You get me? Okay, let's go.'

Rick ducked under the window-bar, and started making his way to the corner. Susie looked back at Daniel, her eyes wide, but Daniel managed to grin at her and say, 'Go on. You're going to be fine.'

Kathy, under her breath, said something that sounded like a private prayer. But then she turned around to Daniel, and kissed him quickly, and said, 'Let's go. Who's afraid of a little height?'

It took them almost five minutes to edge their way to the acanthus leaves on the corner. It was windier here:

unexpected blasts of chilly air kept soughing and moaning around the building from the north-west front, and they all had to grip the concrete tight.

Rick arched his head back and looked up towards the building's roof. 'It's only two storeys. If you had to climb this moulding from ground-level upwards, you'd be able to go running up there like a monkey up a coconut tree. Come on, let's get going before they find out where we've gone.'

Inch by inch, gingerly clutching at each concrete leaf, Rick climbed up the corner of the building to the level of the next storey. Susie came carefully up behind him. Kathy was more hesitant, but occasionally Rick would look down and tell her, 'Put your hand there, on that leaf there. That's right. Now your foot there. And up. That's terrific.'

Another ten minutes went by before Rick finally managed to reach the curled-over leaves of the top parapet. He edged himself up, and at last managed to swing himself over the parapet on to the building's roof. 'Be careful of that corner moulding. I felt it shift a little. It's probably safe, but don't risk putting your full weight on it.'

He reached down and helped Susie to climb up the last two feet, then held out his hand for Kathy. As Kathy was climbing up, she suddenly lost her foothold, and her feet scrabbled desperately at the building's concrete face. She gasped, and then drew her breath in with a sound like a bellows. She was too frightened to scream. Daniel reached up and managed to hold her left foot. 'Stop kicking!' he shouted. 'Kathy, *stop kicking*! There's a foothold here!'

She jabbed her foot towards the top of one of the concrete leaves, and at last found somewhere to lodge her toe. Then she managed to climb up the last three feet to the roof, although she was shaking as she did so.

Daniel glanced down again. The sidewalk seemed even further away than twelve storeys. He felt as if he were on top of a dizzying mountain, and that the world had shrunk so far away that it had completely lost any reality. He grasped the last corner moulding, and pulled himself up; but as he did so, there was a grating noise, and a shower of mortar, and suddenly the moulding toppled off the side of the building and fell towards the ground.

Daniel almost went with it. But Rick had snatched his sleeve to steady him; and with a last panting scramble, Daniel swung himself up and over the parapet. He looked down and saw the concrete moulding dwindle and dwindle and dwindle, and at last hit the sidewalk below like a bomb. Pedestrians scattered in all directions, and several cars swerved, but nobody was hit.

'We'd better move,' said Rick. 'It won't be long before somebody starts asking where that lump of stone came from.'

'But how are we going to get out of here?' asked Kathy. 'They're bound to search the building when they find out we're gone; and all the entrances are guarded.'

'We *don't* get out,' said Daniel.

'You got an idea?' asked Rick.

'We don't get out. It's the only way. The first thing they'll be expecting us to do is make a run for it; and of course they'll be waiting for us. So what we have to do is stay inside the building. The best place is probably the basement. There'll be plenty of places to hide down there, and we won't be too far from the exits when we feel we're ready to make our break.'

'Sounds like some sort of sense to me,' said Kathy.

'It doesn't sound very *heroic*,' said Rick.

'You want heroic, you make a dash for the entrance and see how far you get,' said Daniel.

'Okay,' said Rick, dubiously. 'We'd better find ourselves an elevator. Let's just hope the door to the roof isn't locked.'

They heard sirens in the street below. The Washington Fire Department, investigating the falling moulding. Kathy said, 'Let's move it. *Anywhere's* got to be safer than here.'

Thirty-Six

Kama had intended that morning to fly to New York to talk to Serge Gaponenko at the United Nations. But Gaponenko had been called back to Moscow for an important briefing, and so Kama had decided instead to call on Nikolai Nekrasov at Pennsylvania Avenue; to see if it wasn't time for him to beard the mangy old lion in his den.

Kama was still furious at the way in which Ikon had outwitted him; and at the way in which he had so badly underestimated the old man's ruthlessness. His ears still went hot when he thought about how he had offered Ikon the job of a harmless 'figurehead' when all the time Ikon had already destroyed all the evidence that would have halted the RINC talks. How Ikon must have been laughing at him!

Now, to cap everything, his limousine was stuck in a gridlock traffic-jam on E Street, and the car's air-conditioning was faltering. He sweated and ground his teeth, and every now and then he punched one hand into the palm of the other as if he could scarcely wait to hit that complacent Nikolai Nekrasov right where it would hurt him the most.

In his darkened room on Pennsylvania Avenue, however, Nikolai Nekrasov was enjoying his breakfast. Swathed in a silk smoking-robe patterned with dragons which had been given to him by Chai Zemin, the Chinese Ambassador to the Autonomous Capitalist Oblast of America, he was spreading Mexican honey on to thick slices of wholemeal bread, and drinking lemon tea out of a Russian glass.

Titus sat on the opposite side of the room, stiff as a tailor's dummy. Nadine sat a little way away from him, as chic as ever, her hair drawn back, watching this first encounter between the two most important men in her life with a mixture of pride and deep apprehension. They were both fierce-willed, both uncompromising; and while Nikolai Nekrasov felt that his administration of America was both rightful and historic, Titus saw him as a usurper, and a bitter enemy. More so because Nikolai Nekrasov had secretly controlled Titus' life and his destiny for more than twenty years, and Titus had only just found out about it.

'This honey is very good,' said Ikon. 'Are you sure you won't join me for breakfast?'

Titus didn't answer.

'I have always believed in eating a slow and satisfying breakfast,' Ikon went on, unperturbed. 'After that, there is nothing that the day can bring that cannot be dealt with calmly and effectively.'

'You know that I wasn't particularly anxious to come to meet you,' said Titus. His voice sounded like a steel spring being bent back.

'Well, that is only natural,' said Ikon. 'It must have been greatly disturbing for you to discover that so much of what you have been doing was for other ends entirely.'

'I don't know how the hell you managed to get away with this for so long.'

Ikon raised his shaggy eyebrows, and smiled. 'It was a question of preserving that valuable ideal known as "the American Way". In the Kremlin, very few of my colleagues actually understand what "the American Way" means, and how strongly it motivates the American people. But, I took pains to understand it, and to keep it as the central core of my administration. Slowly, over the years, I have tried to alter your national conception of "the American Way", so that in a comparatively short time from today, international socialism and "the American Way" will be seen in the American mind to be almost indistinguishable from each other.'

Titus was silent for a very long moment. Then he said, 'I see it as nothing more than treachery, subversion, betrayal, and criminal activity.'

Ikon nodded. 'I thought you would.'

Thirty-Seven

At that second, Daniel and Susie and Rick and Kathy had reached the basement. The door to the roof had been locked from inside with a single bolt, but between them Daniel and Rick had been able to kick it free; then they had quickly run down two flights of stairs to the eleventh-floor elevator. They had been obliged to wait while it climbed slowly up to them from 5, stopping at almost every floor, but at last it had arrived and it had been empty. They had pressed the button for LG, and prayed that nobody would stop them on the way down.

Down on basement level, there was a corridor of white-washed brick with three doors in it. The first door led to the boiler-room; the second to the broom cupboard. The third door was fastened with a padlock.

'What do we do now?' asked Kathy.

Rick smiled. 'It's very easy. All padlocks are susceptible to being picked, and if there is *one* small talent I have, apart from acrobatics, and sex, it's picking locks. I used to work for a locksmith on Pico Boulevard: keys cut, cars broken into, ladies rescued from lavatories. All part of a day's toil.'

In the broom cupboard, Rick found a cardboard box of rubbish, which included paper-clips from the upstairs offices. He twisted one of the paper-clips around, and inserted it into the padlock. They watched and waited in tense silence while he attempted to release the levers.

'I don't think this particular padlock is going to prove susceptible,' said Kathy.

'Patience,' Rick told her.

They waited five more minutes. Rick's forehead was crowned in sweat, and his tongue was jammed between his teeth in concentration. Still the padlock refused to open.

'The elevator's coming down again,' said Susie. 'Look, the light's gone green.'

'I think you'd better get that damn door open,' said Kathy.

'*Patience*, for Christ's sake,' said Rick.

Daniel said, 'Here, let me try it.'

'What do *you* know about picking locks?'

'Will you let me try it? I couldn't do any worse than you.'

Rick stood up straight, and then handed the paper-clip to Daniel. 'A paper-clip isn't strong enough. I need a sharp metal lock-pick, or something like it.'

Daniel took the padlock in his hand. It was warm and sweaty from Rick's attempts to open it. He thrust the paper-clip straight into the keyhole, jiggled it violently, and said, 'Open up, will you. Just for God's sake, open up.'

Rick said, 'He's *talking* to it, would you believe?'

There was a sharp springing noise and the padlock opened. Daniel unhooked it from the hasp, and threw it at Rick with an expression of mock-professional nonchalance, and then laughed.

'You did it, you bastard!'

Daniel put his hand over his mouth, and then let out a breath. 'I never did that before in my life, do you know that?'

They could hear the elevator descending towards the basement. The cables were rattling inside the shaft. Quickly, they opened the basement door, stepped inside, and found themselves in a huge darkened storage-room.

'The light, for God's sake,' said Daniel.

Rick found the switch and turned it on. Kathy quietly closed the door behind them, and then ushered Susie off to the side.

The storage-room smelled very dry and cool, as if it was being kept at a regulated temperature. There was another smell, too: a faintly nutty odour which reminded Daniel of something, but which he couldn't quite place. One wall of the room was stacked high with small wooden crates, each bearing a stencil of the eagle-and-sickle symbol, and a legend in Russian, including the code RPG7V. Rick immediately walked across to the crates, and sniffed at them. Then he scouted around the basement until he found a screwdriver.

'If these boxes contain what I think they do . . .' he said, and started prizing off one of the lids. There was a splintering sound, and a pop of nails, and the lid came up, and dropped to the floor. There was sawdust packing inside, and nestling in the sawdust packing were six four-inch high-explosive rockets.

'Are those *bombs*?' asked Kathy.

Rick picked one up and turned it over. 'Rocket bombs. Presumably they keep them here as siege supplies, in case anything goes wrong, and the building gets attacked. Most of the major embassies have arsenals of one kind or another, even if it's only a couple of machine-guns.'

'Well, for God's sake be careful with it,' said Kathy.

'It won't go off until it's triggered,' Rick told her, putting it back in the crate. 'It has an electric fuse which detonates it automatically after it's been fired. It's usually launched from an RPG7, that's a kind of one-man rocket gun. The Russians used to dish them out to guerrilla organizations, like the PLO, and the IRA. They even sent some to the Weathermen, but I think they were seized by US Coastguard.'

'There must be at least a couple of *thousand* of them here,' said Daniel. 'There isn't any way to trigger them without a launcher, is there?'

'Well, sure, you could – ' Rick started to say, but then he raised his hands warningly, and said, 'Oh, no. You're not thinking what I *think* you're thinking, are you? You mean you want to – '

'Why not? We could bring down the whole headquarters of the Autonomous Capitalist Oblast of America, all at once. And presumably Ikon's here, too.'

Rick looked at Kathy. 'You understand what this man's saying?'

'Sure, I understand.'

Rick looked back at Daniel. 'You know something,' he said. 'You're crazier than I thought. If we set this little

369

stack of goodies off, what are *we* going to do? How the hell are *we* going to get out of here?'

'You fix a way of setting it all off; I'll think about how we escape,' said Daniel.

Rick wiped his hands on his jeans. The blood from his two knife-wounds had dried into black stigmata. 'All right,' he said, resignedly. 'I'll do my best.'

It took Rick nearly an hour to set up a timing-device. He used Daniel's wrist-watch, and connected it to a second light-switch at the far end of the store-room, so that when the hands of the watch reached a pre-selected time, the full 120-volt mains current would run into the electric timing device of one of the RPG7 rocket bombs. He was proud of his handiwork when he was finished, although he was sweating from concentration and starry-eyed from connecting tiny pieces of wire from the watch to the light-switch.

'I hope you've thought of a way to get out of here,' he said, wiping his forehead on his sleeve. 'I don't intend to stay around here for one minute when this lot goes up in the air.'

Daniel said, 'I think the riskiest way is going to be the best. I think we should set the timing-device for no more than three minutes, then simply take the elevator to the lobby, and attempt to walk straight out of the front door. When these bombs go off, nobody will worry what we're doing.'

'You hope,' said Rick.

'I can *hope*, can't I?' retorted Daniel.

They discussed the plan for ten minutes more. Then Kathy said, 'If we're going to do it, we might as well do it. Rick – you set the timing device. We'll call the elevator and make sure we keep it here until it's time to leave.'

Cautiously, they opened the storage-room door again, and emerged into the whitewashed corridor. Susie pressed the button for the elevator, and they heard it clank and whine and start on its journey downwards.

'Are you ready yet?' Daniel called to Rick. 'The elevator's almost here.'

'I'm coming! We've got three minutes dead!'

Rick came running out of the storage-room just as the elevator doors opened. To their mutual surprise, there was a Soviet security guard standing inside.

'I want your hands up!' he demanded, unbuttoning his holster. But Rick was too quick for him. With a flying drop-kick that he had learned for his stunt parts in *Kung-Fu*, he belted the guard under the chin with his sneakers, and both of them crashed to the floor of the elevator in a tangled heap.

Daniel dragged the stunned security guard out into the corridor, and then all of them crowded into the elevator and pressed the button for G. The elevator doors closed, hesitated, opened again, and then eventually closed again. They stood staring at each other in total silence as the elevator rose to the first floor, and then opened.

The lobby was busy with security-guards and diplomats and messengers. It was a high-vaulted room, clad in mottled grey marble, with a huge chandelier suspended from the centre of the ceiling in the grandiose style of the Hotel Moscow. Telephones rang, feet clattered, and there was a busy buzz of conversation.

'Come on,' said Daniel. 'All we have to do is look natural.'

'*Natural*?' queried Rick, looking around at all the Soviet diplomats and office-workers in their tight dark suits and their polished black shoes.

They crossed the lobby without being challenged, and pushed their way through the revolving-doors. Now they were out on the steps that led down to the sidewalk, and sunshine, and freedom. Susie gave a little childish whimper of tension.

'We've made it,' said Rick. 'Would you believe it – we've made it.'

At that moment, two uniformed security guards stepped out in front of them. Out here on the street, they wore no badges, and carried their guns under their coats; but from the Cossack stolidity of their faces, and the way in which their hands were held in their pockets, it was obvious that they would have no compunction about shooting to kill.

'You will please return to the building,' said one of the guards.

They stopped where they were. Rick started to raise his hands.

'You will not put up your hands. You will do nothing more than turn around and re-enter the building.'

Daniel reached out and held Susie's hand. 'Mister,' he said, 'I've got a little girl here. She's only seven. Have a heart, will you, let her go? She's not going to do *you* any harm.'

Rick glanced at Daniel and all over his face was written the muscle-tightening message: *Supposing the timing-device hasn't worked. Supposing the rockets don't explode.*

One of the guards said to the other, 'Call Comrade Skellett. These are the prisoners who escaped from the 10th floor. Tell him to come down here urgently.'

Then the guard turned to Daniel, and said, 'The girl must remain here until your business with Comrade Skellett is completely settled. Those are my instructions.'

'What did you say?' asked Daniel.

The guard came up one step nearer, his coat held out threateningly. 'I said – '

But his words were totally obliterated in the most colossal explosion that Daniel had ever heard. The marble-clad steps beneath their feet jumped into the air two or three feet, and threw all of them out across the sidewalk like skittles, scratched and bruised and breathless and tumbling over and over as if it would be impossible for them ever to stop.

There was a second explosion, then a third. Daniel, dazed, picked himself out of the roadway, and looked around for Susie. To his relief, she was only a few yards away, being helped out of the gutter by an elderly man. Kathy too was safe, and so was Rick, although Rick's face was badly gashed.

A fourth explosion shook Pennsylvania Avenue, and huge chunks of masonry began to tumble from the Ikon building as if it was an erupting volcano. Showers of glass and twisted aluminium window-frames clattered and sparkled down on all sides. Daniel picked up Susie in his arms and ran across the street, through the halted traffic, and as far away from the building as he could.

What happened next was spectacular: the public fall of a secret empire.

The first floor of the building collapsed into the basement, in a rolling billow of dust and smoke. Then, floor by floor, the entire building dropped in on itself, with a rending, thundering, tearing noise that made any kind of conversation inaudible, any kind of sensible thought impossible. Massive steel girders clanged down like the bells of doom, one on top of the other, and all the time there was a steady drumroll of breaking concrete, collapsing floors, tearing pipework, falling staircases. Soon it was impossible to see where the building had been: there was nothing but a cloud of dust, rising hundreds and hundreds of feet into the misty morning sky, and a persistent drizzle of grit.

It took the building more than ten minutes to fall, although most of its collapse was obscured from sight by dust. By the time the roof had fallen in, and the last showers of glass had come down, the emergency services had already arrived, and Pennsylvania Avenue was crowded with fire-trucks, ambulances, and police cars. Most of them were parked on the grass opposite the Post Office Department, some were parked on the sidewalks by the Internal Revenue Service building.

Skellett had died on his way down to the lobby in the elevator. He had reached the fifth floor when the rockets exploded, and the building started to collapse. The elevator shaft had gradually been compressed between two main structural beams, squashing the elevator sideways, and squashing Skellett with it. He had felt a hideous pressure on his ribcage, and on his skull, an intolerable compression that had made him want to scream out loud, if there had been any way of drawing breath to scream.

His last conscious feeling had been of his eyeballs being

squeezed one by one out of their sockets, and of suddenly looking down at his own chest through blurry, dangling, unfocused lenses.

Ikon had died even before the ceiling came down, of a massive coronary. He had cried out, *'No!'* just as Titus had cried out the very same words the previous night and then he had fallen across his breakfast table, his hand resting on a thickly-honeyed piece of bread.

Titus and Nadine, in fright, had got up from their seats. Nadine had said, 'My God, it's an earthquake! The building's coming down!'

But Titus had turned back to her almost gleefully and shouted, 'Earthquake, nothing! Some son-of-a-bitch has blown the whole damn thing up!'

Then the ceiling came down, tons of masonry and steel and concrete, and both Titus and Nadine had been swallowed. They were found later by firemen, bruised, crushed, but still holding hands.

Kama was saved by the traffic-jam on E Street. His limousine reached the intersection of E Street and 14th Street just as the Ikon building blew up, and he immediately ordered his driver to turn around. Through the tinted rear window, he saw dust and debris rising into the air, and knew that it had to be the headquarters of the Autonomous Capitalist Oblast of America.

If Ikon had been there when the building blew up, then the strong possibility was that ACOA would soon be his.

'Where to, sir?' his driver asked him.

'Nowhere in particular. Don't worry. Tomorrow, we'll decide where to go next.'

Thirty-Eight

Daniel opened his eyes and looked up at the ceiling. It was six-thirty in the morning, and the Arizona sun was already shining in bright bands through the drapes. He yawned, and rubbed his face, and then sat up.

Cara was still dreaming. He looked at her russet curls, at her pale bare back, at the flared curve of her bottom. He knew she was dreaming because she was murmuring to herself. He couldn't guess what she was dreaming about, though. She was one of those ladies with secrets.

He climbed out of bed. It was four days since he and Susie had returned to Apache Junction; and they were settled now. Daniel was cooking up bacon and eggs as usual, Susie was back at school.

The pleasantest surprise had been to find that Cara was waiting for him when he returned; that she had hitch-hiked west as far as Havasu City, and then decided to turn around and come back. 'Don't call it love,' she had told him. 'But I do want to stay.'

Kathy Forbes had gone back to the *Flag* to begin work on a multi-part exposé of what she had learned and experienced; a feature which her editor would eventually spike. 'Nobody's going to believe this,' he would tell her, kindly. 'If it's true, and Ikon's dead, then it doesn't matter. If it *isn't* true, it doesn't matter, either. People don't want to hear about this kind of thing. I'm in the business of selling newspapers, not scaring people half to death.'

Rick Terroni had returned to Hollywood, and to the half-world of Free Columbia. He would die a year later in a traffic accident on the Ventura Freeway. The death would be reported in *Variety*, two lines.

Daniel picked his jeans up off the floor and wrestled his way into them. He thought of Willy Monahan, and what Willy would have said if he had ever found out what had happened. Perhaps Willy knew anyway, somewhere in Nirvana. Daniel had tried calling Williams AFB for news of Willy's funeral, but he had repeatedly been met with a courteous 'Sorry, that's family information. We're not permitted to release it.'

He looked out of the window as he buttoned up his plaid Western shirt. He thought: at least America's free again. A country that never even knew it was conquered. He tucked in his shirt, turned around, and went down to the kitchen to start breakfast.

What he had failed to see when he looked out across Apache Junction was the dark-blue rented Pontiac with the Texas plates parked next to Feeley's Drugs. Inside it, listening to the radio with the patience of a man who has waited for hours, for days, for whole years for what he is after, sat Henry Friend.

The announcer said, 'Good morning, folks. It's going to be another hot one today.'

STAR BOOKS BESTSELLERS

THRILLERS

SHATTERED	John Farris	£1.50*	☐
BLOODSPORT	Henry Denker	£1.75*	☐
THE AIRLINE PIRATES	John Gardner	£1.25	☐
THE INFILTRATOR	Michael Hughes	£1.60	☐
IKON	Graham Masterton	£2.50*	☐
TERROR OF THE TRIADS	Sean O'Callaghan	£1.50	☐
HUNTED	Jeremy Scott	£1.50	☐
DIRTY HARRY	Philip Rock	£1.25*	☐
MAGNUM FORCE	Mel Valley	£1.50*	☐

WAR

BLAZE OF GLORY	Michael Carreck	£1.80	☐
CONVOY OF STEEL	Wolf Kruger	£1.80	☐
BLOOD AND HONOUR	Wolf Kruger	£1.80	☐
PANZER GRENADIERS	Heinrich Conrad Muller	£1.95*	☐
THE RAID	Julian Romanes	£1.80*	☐
GUNSHIPS: NEEDLEPOINT	Jack Hamilton Teed	£1.95	☐
THE SKY IS BURNING	D. Mark Carter	£1.60	☐
TASK FORCE BATTALION	Tom Lambert	£1.60	☐

STAR BOOKS BESTSELLERS

CHILLERS

CHAINSAW TERROR	*Nick Blake*	£1.80 ☐
SLUGS	*Shawn Hutson*	£1.60 ☐
SPAWN	*Shawn Hutson*	£1.80 ☐
CARNOSAUR	*Harry Adam Knight*	£1.95 ☐
SLIMER	*Harry Adam Knight*	£1.95 ☐
BLOWFLY	*David Lowman*	£1.95 ☐
THE PARIAH	*Graham Masterton*	£1.95* ☐
THE PLAGUE	*Graham Masterton*	£1.80* ☐
THE MANITOU	*Graham Masterton*	£1.50* ☐
SATAN'S LOVE CHILD	*Brian McNaughton*	£1.35* ☐
SATAN'S SEDUCTRESS	*Brian McNaughton*	£1.25* ☐

STAR Books are obtainable from many booksellers and newsagents. If you have any difficulty tick the titles you want and fill in the form below.

Name _____

Address _____

_____

Send to: Star Books Cash Sales, P.O. Box 11, Falmouth, Cornwall. TR10 9EN.

Please send a cheque or postal order to the value of the cover price plus:
UK: 45p for the first book, 20p for the second book and 14p for each additional book ordered to the maximum charge of £1.63.

BFPO and EIRE: 45p for the first book, 20p for the second book, 14p per copy for the next 7 books, thereafter 8p per book.

OVERSEAS: 75p for the first book and 21p per copy for each additional book.

While every effort is made to keep prices low, it is sometimes necessary to increase prices at short notice. Star Books reserve the right to show new retail prices on covers which may differ from those advertised in the text or elsewhere.

*NOT FOR SALE IN CANADA

STAR BOOKS BESTSELLERS

FICTION

THE PROTOCOL	*Sarah Allan Borish*	£2.25*	☐
SEASON OF CHANGE	*Lois Battle*	£2.25*	☐
LET'S KEEP IN TOUCH	*Elaine Bissel*	£2.50*	☐
DANCEHALL	*Bernard F. Conners*	£1.95*	☐
DREAMS OF GLORY	*Thomas Fleming*	£2.50*	☐
DEAR STRANGER	*Catherine Kidwell*	£1.95*	☐
PHANTOMS	*Dean R. Koontz*	£2.25*	☐
THE PAINTED LADY	*Françoise Sagan*	£2.25*	☐
LAMIA	*Tristan Travis*	£2.75*	☐

FILM TIE-INS

EDUCATING RITA	*Peter Chepstow*	£1.60	☐
TERMS OF ENDEARMENT	*Larry McMurtry*	£1.95*	☐
PARTY PARTY	*Jane Coleman*	£1.35	☐
THE WICKED LADY	*Magdalen King-Hall*	£1.60	☐
SCRUBBERS	*Alexis Lykiard*	£1.60	☐
BULL SHOT	*Martin Noble*	£1.80	☐
BLOODBATH AT THE HOUSE OF DEATH	*Martin Noble*	£1.80	☐

STAR BOOKS BESTSELLERS

NON-FICTION

BODYGUARD OF LIES	*Antony Cave Brown*	£2.50* ☐
OIL SHEIKHS	*Linda Blandford*	£1.95 ☐
WHY MEN RAPE	*S. Levine & J. Koenig*	£1.95* ☐
THE COMPLETE JACK THE RIPPER	*Donald Rumberlow*	£1.60 ☐
CRIME SCIENTIST	*John Thompson*	£1.60 ☐
THE ELEPHANT MAN	*Sir Frederick Treves*	95p ☐

BIOGRAPHIES

RICHARD BURTON	*Fergus Cashin*	£1.95 ☐
CLINT EASTWOOD: MOVIN' ON	*Peter Douglas*	£1.00* ☐
CHARLES BRONSON	*David Downing*	£1.95 ☐
IT'S A FUNNY GAME	*Brian Johnston*	£1.95 ☐
IT'S BEEN A LOT OF FUN	*Brian Johnston*	£1.80 ☐
ORDEAL	*Linda Lovelace with Mike McGrady*	£1.50* ☐
BETTE DAVIS: MOTHER GODDAM	*Whitney Stine with Bette Davis*	£2.25* ☐

STAR Books are obtainable from many booksellers and newsagents. If you have any difficulty tick the titles you want and fill in the form below.

Name _____

Address _____

_____

Send to: Star Books Cash Sales, P.O. Box 11, Falmouth, Cornwall. TR10 9EN.

Please send a cheque or postal order to the value of the cover price plus: UK: 45p for the first book, 20p for the second book and 14p for each additional book ordered to the maximum charge of £1.63.

BFPO and EIRE: 45p for the first book, 20p for the second book, 14p per copy for the next 7 books, thereafter 8p per book.

OVERSEAS: 75p for the first book and 21p per copy for each additional book.

While every effort is made to keep prices low, it is sometimes necessary to increase prices at short notice. Star Books reserve the right to show new retail prices on covers which may differ from those advertised in the text or elsewhere.

NOT FOR SALE IN CANADA